Until the Tide

For the one who named me.

Until the Tide

Christopher Kent

PROLOGUE

THE LITTLE GIRL, who had recently turned seven, has hair the color of dull copper and wears a pair of overalls that has seen better days, cut off just below her knees. Strings of denim turn dark in the soil as she squats next to her father.

"Daddy?" she asks, pursing her lips as she flicks at an ant crawling across her leg.

"Yes?" he replies, pulling up to his knees, which rest upon a small square of red foam, an old stadium seat cushion that had long been used for this purpose instead. His tall stature casts a long shadow across a large patch of recently planted petunias.

"Why do you call me Cora?" she asks as she looks up at him sideways, shielding her eyes from the sunlight that is just peeking out the side of a fluffy white cloud, in stark contrast to the cobalt blue sky.

"Well, that's a good question," he replies. "Why do you ask?"

"I dunno," she answers. "I figure it is my name, so I ought to know why I have it."

"Good answer," he says as he reaches forward and pulls up a clump of dead flowers. He shakes his head, temporarily distracted, "I don't understand why these things are dead."

"All of yours, you mean," Cora corrects him with pride.

The man turns back towards her and feigns insult.

"Well, it's true," she insists.

He sighs, nods, and then throws the clump onto the ground to join a pile of other dead flowers. "What were we talking about?" he asks playfully.

"You were telling me about my name."

"Oh, that's right," he says, brushing his hands across his dirty jeans. "Do you know what coral is?"

Cora shrugs then wipes at her nose. "Nope."

"Well, coral is a living animal."

"You named me after an animal?" Cora suddenly looks disgusted, and it earns a soft laugh from her dad.

"Well, yeah," he says, nodding. "I guess I did."

"But why, Daddy?"

"Well, coral is one of God's most beautiful creations. It is a community of tiny animals that build underwater castles that are the colors of the rainbow. And these little castles are important to the ocean and all the fish."

"Like seahorses and stuff?"

"Sure."

"What about an octopus?"

"I guess so."

She thinks for a moment then nods. "Well, that is neat, I guess. I like castles, especially rainbow ones."

"They are pretty cool," he agrees.

Cora nods slowly as her mind wanders, visualizing what coral looks like. After a moment, she blinks then looks back towards her father, who has pulled another dead plant from the ground.

"How come all the ones I planted died and all the ones you planted look perfect?"

Cora throws up her hands in surrender, "I guess they just like me."

"I think you are right, babydoll."

Cora leans forward and looks at the plant in her father's hand. "What will happen to me when you die?" she asks abruptly.

He lays the plant on the ground then reaches over and pats her head. "Don't you worry, little girl. Daddy isn't going anywhere anytime soon. Plus, you have your Mama who loves you very much." The answer doesn't seem to satisfy her.

"But what if you do?"

"I won't. Not for a long time."

Cora looks at him as if not sure she can trust his answer. "But what if?" she asks again.

He reaches over and rubs her messy blonde curls. "You have friends, don't you?"

"Duh," Cora says without hesitation, rolling her eyes.

"Well, Daddy does too."

"How many?"

He shrugs. "Not many, but it is quality over quantity, babydoll."

"What do you mean?"

He chuckles. "Daddy's friends will look after you if something happens to me. Good friends are always there when you need them most."

"And your friends are good friends?"

"The very best."

She contemplates his words, and starts to ask another question, but pauses suddenly as he stands and in one swift motion, lifts her high above his head and spins.

Cora giggles, "Stop, Daddy!"

He slows his pace after a moment then holds her softly to his chest. "You remember this, babydoll. I will always be there, even when I'm not."

Cora buries her face into his blue plaid shirt. "I love you, Daddy."

"I love you, too, Cora," he says then abruptly spins again, causing her to burst out in a fit of giggles. "My glorious little green thumb!"

PART ONE
GLORY'S KEY

CHAPTER 1

THE FLUORESCENT LIGHTS hum like angry wasps overhead, matching the buzzing of my phone. Nick, again. Twelve missed calls. Each vibration sends lightning bolts of pain through my bruised ribs, a reminder of when he pushed me down the concrete stairs of our building.

I shift in the plastic chair, trying to find a position that does not hurt. The elderly woman across from me peers over her Kindle. I touch my cheek self-consciously, though I know the bruises there are well-hidden. The ones beneath my University of Tennessee Medical sweater are another story—a constellation of purple and yellow that makes even breathing painful.

A forced cough breaks through my racing thoughts. The receptionist waves me over, impatience etched across her face. I approach the desk with measured steps, each movement calculated to minimize pain. The withdrawal forms in my backpack feel like lead weights. I printed them a few buildings over at the library and filled them out the best that I could.

"May I help you?" She tilts her head down, silver bushy eyebrows expanding over tortoiseshell glasses.

"I—" My voice catches. I clear my throat and try again. "I need to see an academic counselor."

She rolls her eyes, and the gesture makes me shrink further

into myself. "You'll need to sign in." Her manicured fingernail taps sharply against the clipboard.

My hands tremble as I grab the pen attached to a metal beaded chain. After signing my name, I pause at the "appointment time" field. "Excuse me? Do I need an appointment?"

"Yes," she says flatly, already looking back at her computer screen.

"But I thought students could visit a counselor any time." My voice comes out smaller than intended, just like it does with Nick when he is in one of his moods.

Her eyes dart upward with practiced annoyance. "Appointments are required and must be booked at least a week in advance." She taps the edge of a large acrylic display sign: Appointment Required.

The room spins as I stumble back. Fresh tears spring to my eyes—not from physical pain this time, but from the overwhelming realization that I have nowhere else to go. My phone buzzes again in my pocket. Nick's rage radiates through the screen.

I need help now. Not in a week. Not when Nick finally makes good on his threats to "shut me up permanently."

"I didn't know I needed an appointment," I whisper, more to myself than anyone else. The woman doesn't glance up this time but ignores me instead, her face remaining fixed to her screen.

I rush out through the double doors into a small alcove beside the building. Outside, I instinctively scan the area. Nick could be anywhere—behind a bush, around that corner, watching from his black BMW. Despite the warm spring air, the feeling of being hunted sends shivers down my spine.

A vacant bench, partially hidden by a massive magnolia tree, catches my eye. I duck under the glossy leaves and settle on the far end, trying to make myself as small as possible. Just like I used to do during Dad's sales trips, curling up in the backseat with my worn copy of "The Little Mermaid," dreaming of diving into a different world while he navigated unfamiliar highways.

What do I do now?

I close my eyes, but that only brings flashes of traumatic memories—bright, fractured scenes that make me flinch. Nick's face contorted with rage. The sickening sensation of falling. The concrete stairs rushing up to meet me. My chest tightens and head begins to pound as my breathing becomes more erratic. This must be what a panic attack feels like.

I have to get out of town before he finds me—before he finishes what he started on those stairs.

My phone chimes.

Shit.

I reach into my pocket and grasp the old iPhone. My thumb traces the crack in the screen.

"Just look at the phone, Glory," I whisper to myself.

But I can't. I am afraid. I know it is him. It has to be him.

Look at it! Look at it! Nick's voice invades my mind.

"Fine," I say meekly into the soft breeze, cringing as I swipe up.

Nick: Where the fuck are you?

Nick: Tell me where you are!

I stare at his texts, reading them over and over, my hands trembling too much to even consider replying.

"What have I done?" I say softly to myself. "Maybe I can just go back to him. If I can just get through this one last—"

He will kill you, Glory.

The monotone voice in my head is my own, but stronger, more confident. It's the voice of someone I used to be, someone with hopes and dreams that after all this time, can't seem to remember.

"But if I leave, I'll fail my classes and throw it all away," I say into the breeze. "I need permission to withdraw from classes, right?" I try to recall what my teachers had said, but I'm too distracted to know for sure.

He will kill you, Glory.

The voice grows firmer, more insistent. For strength, I reach for the necklace Dad gave me when I was thirteen—a gold infinity symbol surrounded by a silver heart. The voice falls silent, replaced by the soft echo of Dad's singing—some tune I can't recognize.

I'll love you through the ebb and flow.

If he were still alive, he'd help me get away. I squeeze the pendant harder, letting the edges dig into my palm. As I do, I squeeze my eyes impossibly tight, bright lights flash, and I reach my hand to my head as it throbs uncontrollably. Then suddenly, it stops.

"Glory Dawson?"

I squeeze the pendant harder, letting the edges dig into my palm. My head begins to throb harder. I reach up and press my hand to my temples and squeeze my eyes so tight, blue lights flash behind closed lids. Just as tears begin to stream down my face, I hear my name.

"Glory?"

I startle at the rich Southern drawl, my eyes opening as my body jolts. I cautiously lean out from behind the leaves and find myself staring into the brightest cobalt-blue eyes I have ever seen. Their owner radiates the kind of confidence that I'd lost years ago. She's wearing a teal sundress that moves like water when she rises to her tiptoes. Her yellow sandals seem to catch and hold the sunlight.

"Are you Glory?"

I study her for a moment, struck by how different she is from me—stunning, with short, blonde hair and summer-red lips that perfectly complement her tanned skin. Something comforting about her presence draws me from my hiding place.

She furrows her brows when she sees me fully, and I suddenly realize how I must look—disheveled, tear-stained, broken. I turn away quickly to wipe my eyes and run my fingers through my tangled hair.

"I'm Cora," she says when I finally face her again. She raises a petite hand in greeting.

My eyes find her bright orange UT nametag: Cora, Academic Counselor.

"I-I'm Glory," I stammer, my voice barely above a whisper.

"Oh good! I thought I might not catch you." Her smile brightens, but there is something careful in her eyes like she's trying not to spook a wounded animal. "I'm so sorry about the misunderstanding."

I take a few cautious steps closer. "Misunderstanding?"

"With the receptionist." She waves toward the building. "She said you couldn't be helped without an appointment, right?"

I nod, wrapping my arms around my midsection.

"Well, actually, I can help. We usually have one or two openings each day from cancellations," she says, shrugging like it's no big deal. "I'm sorry she didn't mention it."

"I don't need an appointment?" My voice cracks with hope.

"No appointment needed. Just follow me, and we will take care of you."

Relief floods through me, washing away some of the despair. As I step toward the door, Cora's hand finds my back, gently guiding me back into the Counseling Center.

Thank God.

We pass by the receptionist, who is still buried in her screen. Beyond reception, we turn down a long corridor lined with closed doors; the fluorescent panels overhead flicker ominously. Our footsteps echo in the silence.

"Just over here," Cora says as she motions me through a door that's cracked slightly open.

I step in front of her and push it open, my eyes widening as I take in the beautiful office. It's painted a soft seafoam green, a stark contrast to the sterile white bedroom that I'm used to. The walls remind me of the ocean.

"Please have a seat," Cora says, extending an arm with a smile.

"Your office is beautiful," I say.

The focal point of Cora's space is an antique maple desk with a subtle shine that speaks to its age. Two worn but inviting leather chairs sit before it, one occupied by an old teddy bear with large blue button eyes. Floor-to-ceiling bookcases filled with books line the walls behind the chairs, their shelves also holding photos and various knickknacks, including a small owl statue made from pristine white shells.

Cora settles behind her desk and gestures to the chairs. "Please make yourself comfortable."

I choose the seat closest to the door and glance over at the bear, who seems to be smiling knowingly at me. Despite its matted, discolored fur, it has a certain familiar charm. "Nice bear."

"His name is Grumbles," she says as she turns and looks at it affectionately. "He goes everywhere with me."

I nod and hug my bag closer to my chest.

Cora cocks her head slightly to the side. "So, what has brought you in today?"

I exhale as I reach into my bag for the withdrawal slip that I filled out this morning. "I need permission to withdraw from classes this semester." I swallow hard. "I decided to take a break because…" I pause, weighing my words carefully. I can't tell her about Nick. She might make me file a police report, which isn't an option. "I just need a break," I blurt out instead.

She leans forward, resting her head on one hand as if waiting for me to continue. Her eyes dart to the edge of a bruise that peeks out from my sleeve. "I see," she says simply.

"I can take my final classes online. I explained that in the notes section on the withdrawal forms. I have them here somewhere." I continue to fumble through my bag and then finally produce the completed forms. I hand them to her, watching anxiously as she scans them. After a moment, she shrugs, then looks up and winks. "Okay."

My heart drops. "Okay?"

She smiles. "Okay. I will clear you."

"I can withdraw?" I confirm yet again, dumbfounded. I hadn't expected it to be that easy. I was convinced I would have had missing information on the forms or made some mistake. The bureaucracy of academia can be staggering.

"Yep," she says. The cobalt flecks in her eyes seem to sparkle. "I'll approve you to withdraw."

"Not a Withdrawal Fail?"

"Nope. Just a Withdrawal. Approved and without a negative impact on your GPA." Another wink.

I stand excitedly and nearly topple my chair.

Cora pulls back slightly, eyebrows raised in surprise. "Well, I'm glad you're happy."

"I am. Thank you so much. You don't know what this means to me. I was nearly having a panic attack on the bench back there. I didn't want him to take my—" I catch myself before I let any more details slip.

Cora bites her lip as if she senses there is more to my story, but she doesn't pry. After a moment, she shakes her head as if emerging from a daydream, then looks down and signs the slip. She then stands and extends her hand forward as if to conclude our business. "All done. You are withdrawn."

"Thanks," I say, then reach forward to shake her hand.

"There's just one thing, Glory."

My hand falls to my side, my smile fading into a nervous frown. "Is there something else that I need to do?"

Cora waves dismissively. "No, no. Nothing like that. It's just I noticed you didn't put a return address on your forms." Her brows furrow. "Do you have a place to go?"

It is a good question. Where would I go? I'd considered

Mom's, but it would never work. Mom had always adored Nick, and I couldn't risk her playing peacekeeper and Nick suddenly showing up at her house. She would do that, thinking that she was helping. "Nick's so helpful," she always says. "He is a real catch."

Cora stands, walks to the bookshelf behind me, and then leans forward to study a large photo. "Check this out," she says, motioning for me to join her.

I walk to her side and lean in to examine a colorful photo of eight people in scuba gear floating underwater before a massive arc of multicolored coral. Everyone is giving the camera a thumbs-up.

"My friends and I love the ocean," Cora says, a smile dancing across her face. "We used to get together during the summer and do a group dive in the Florida Keys. It's beautiful down there, and you can't beat the laid-back atmosphere."

"That sounds amazing," I say, still studying the picture. The divers look so free, suspended in the endless blue.

"Have you ever been?"

"To the beach?"

"No, no." She waves playfully. "Not *any* beach. The grand, the incredible," she throws her arms wide theatrically, "Florida Keys!"

When I was younger, Dad and I traveled throughout Florida on sales trips. I was with him most summers growing up. Mom loved the opportunity it gave her to enjoy time with her boyfriends, of which there were many. Most of our trips were around Tampa and Orlando, I think, never that far south. I shake my head. "I don't think so."

"It's amazing and so, so beautiful." Cora returns to her desk and opens a file drawer, digging around before pulling out a bright green flyer and a small postcard. She pushes both toward me.

"Check this place out."

"Okay," I say, uncertain.

"It's incredible, and I have a feeling it may be perfect for you."

"For me?" I point to myself as I unfold what appears to be an advertisement for a scuba diving resort: *Dave's Outdoor Water Sports*. The ad is attractive enough, filled with photos of colorful fish, tropical flowers, and smiling faces. "What is this place?"

"Well…" She points back to the group photo. "That is Dave's. It's incredible, Glory. *Really* incredible."

I tilt my head skeptically. "You want me to go scuba diving?"

She shrugs. "Maybe?"

I instinctively tilt my head. "But I don't know how to scuba dive."

She ignores me as she continues. "I was thinking you could get a job there for the summer, or longer."

I stare at her, lifting both hands in confusion. "But I don't scuba dive," I repeat.

"Oh, never mind that. A minor detail."

"A minor detail?"

"Yep. It's like riding a bike."

I rub my face, then bite my lip. "I can't just get up and move to Florida and work for some dive resort." The words come out sharper than intended.

She reaches out and takes my hands in hers. "Glory, listen. It's not just about diving. The resort is a full operation, with a restaurant, bar, rental condos, a dock…everything. And like you said, it is beautiful." She looks up as if reminiscing. "It is so colorful during the sunrise, like rainbow Jell-O."

"Jell-O?"

Her enthusiasm dims slightly, replaced by something more serious. "Glory, can I be straight with you?"

I tense at first, but after a moment, I nod.

"You need to get away from here. I don't know exactly what's going on, but you need to get away. You need to heal."

The comments hang in the air between us. She is right. I do

need to take myself as far away from here, from Nick, as I can. My phone buzzes again in my pocket, causing me to shift nervously.

"I do," I admit as I stick my hand in my pocket and fumble with my phone.

"Then why not consider paradise?" she says, smiling again.

She does have a point. Why not? Nick would check Mom's place first, but the Florida Keys? He'd never expect it.

"Not everyone dives," Cora continues softly. "But you could learn if you wanted to. When you're ready. I have a feeling that you would be a natural."

"What?" My voice rises. "Dive?"

"Yeah. It's fun. I learned there, and it just took one weekend. There's something freeing about being underwater. The world gets quiet, peaceful. Sometimes that's exactly what we need."

I take note of how she emphasized the word peaceful. I look back at the photo of those divers suspended so calmly. There is something so freeing about it—the opposite of how I've felt these past two years. After a moment, I turn back towards her as intrusive doubt overcomes my curiosity. "I don't think they're looking for my type down there."

"What do you mean?" she says, genuinely surprised. "It's a great scene for people our age. I have several friends who have worked there. You would fit right in. I just know it."

Her conviction stirs something in me—maybe hope, maybe desperation. "You think?"

She puts her hands on her hips and frowns. "Do you have any idea where you're going when you leave my office?"

I hesitate before shaking my head. "No."

"And I'm assuming you need a job, right?"

I nod. I don't have family sending me checks every month, and I have less than five hundred dollars to my name.

"You could also benefit from a vacation, Glory. You *need* this."

The gentleness in her voice nearly breaks me. When was the last time someone cared about what I needed?

"Well, that's true, I guess."

"So, why not have a vacation and peace?"

"I don't know, Cora. I think—"

"If it helps, I heard the pay is great," she interrupts, her voice laced with confidence. "You would get hourly and tips. They even provide health insurance free of charge."

"Really?" I desperately need health insurance, especially given the state of my ribs.

"Since it's technically considered a hazardous position," she adds.

"What?"

"Yep."

"You're serious?"

"Hazardous-smazardous." Cora waves dismissively and purses her lips. "It's just insurance talk. But Glory…" She leans forward, her voice dropping. "I wouldn't suggest this if I thought you'd be in danger. The owner is amazing. They look out for their staff."

I lift the flyer again, suddenly more curious. I cannot believe that I am considering it.

I look back at Cora, who smiles softly. "So?"

"I don't remember the last time I was at the ocean, but I do remember loving the water and the sand on my feet, and the sunshine…"

"You're definitely a beach person," she says gently. "I can tell."

I glance down at my frumpy sweatshirt and jogging pants.

"You're stronger than you think, Glory," she says, and something in her voice makes me look up. "And I know you'll love it there."

"But what if there isn't a job opening?"

"There are always openings this time of year. From what I've heard, they've been short-staffed for a couple of years."

"You think?" I close my eyes and let myself imagine it: warm sun on my skin, fresh ocean air filling my lungs, steady pay, health insurance, and most importantly, hundreds of miles away from Nick.

Be brave.

I open my eyes, and the words tumble out as if not my own. "I'll do it."

"You'll do it?" Her voice is quiet, serious.

I nod, confirming, even though I am taken aback by my sudden bravery. It's not me. It's someone else.

"If you are planning to leave today, you should get on the road now, so you make it to Florida by the end of the day. The sooner you're out of Tennessee, the better."

I am not sure if she understands the gravity of her words, but I could not agree more. "I guess I'll go then," I say, picking up my bag and following her as she exits her office with small, quick steps and motions me with both hands to follow. I speed up to match her pace and follow her down the hall toward a side exit. At the door, I pause. "Shouldn't I call Dave's first to let them know I'm coming?"

"Tell you what. You focus on driving, and I'll email them now for you. I know some of those guys, and they're always looking for good people. Just ask for Dave when you get there. He will be around."

"That would be great," I say, relieved by her offer.

As I step outside, I'm met by a crisp spring air that feels somehow different now, full of possibility instead of fear. I walk a few steps past the magnolia, then turn back toward Cora. "I really appreciate everything you've done for me."

"Of course!" she says, filtered sunlight dancing across her face. "We have to help each other from time to time…to find peace, to heal."

I nod and then reach up to pull my hood over my head. I give her one last small wave, then turn and dart toward the parking deck. Just before crossing the quad, I glance back one final time. Cora is still standing in the same spot, watching, her bright dress billowing behind her in the lingering breeze. The light dances around her, radiating hope.

Chapter 2

The twelve-hour drive passes in a blur of gas stations and rest stops. The sun melts into the horizon by the time I turn onto Route 1, a narrow strip of roadway winding south toward the Keys. Water stretches endlessly on both sides, making it feel like a tightrope strung between sky and sea. Though darkness has begun to settle in, there's still a hint of orange light bleeding into the western sky, painting the water in shades of blue and purple.

Did I really do this?

The thought overwhelms me, so to push it away, I roll down the window, letting the sea air rush over my outstretched hand. It's a contradiction of sensations—warm one moment, cool the next, as mercurial as my emotions. For the first time since leaving Tennessee, I let myself breathe deeply, even though it makes my ribs ache.

After another hour or so, Waze navigation leads me to a large, brightly lit billboard on my left: *DAVE'S: Turn Here for Florida's Top Dive Resort.*

My leg starts bobbing nervously as I follow the arrow down a narrow road lined with small homes and sprinkled with a few neighborhood stores. After nearly a mile, I spot it—a large, yellow sign painted with bright blue letters: Dave's.

The entrance is an oversized driveway flanked by palm trees and planters overflowing with crimson hibiscus. Past the entrance, the drive winds for about fifty yards before opening into a large roundabout. At its center, three flags snap in the ocean breeze—American, dive, and Florida state flags, their shadows dancing in the moonlight.

As I circle the roundabout, the resort comes into view, and my breath catches. Dave's spreads out before me like something from a travel magazine: freshly cut grass dotted with tropical flowers extends in both directions. Swaying palms and manicured hedges glow under a soft gold and blue lights. Stone walkways lead to a large wooden welcome sign ringed by directional arrows: dive shop, rentals, pier, harbor, condos, and something called the Hut.

I follow a sign to the parking area and ease into an empty spot. My old truck lets out a tired groan as I cut the engine. "Easy there, old boy," I say, patting the dashboard affectionately. This truck has never failed me—Dad's high school graduation gift that means more than just reliable transportation. Even with its advanced age and six-digit mileage, it is still my most precious possession.

Grabbing my bag, I slide out onto the pavement and at once regret the quick movement. I clench my eyes as my body protests with sharp jolts of pain.

After the pain subsides, I look out across the landscape, then walk to where the wooden sign stands. I choose to head to the right, toward the dive shop where I hope Dave's office might be. I have no idea what I will do if I can't find Dave.

Following the path towards the dive shop leads me deeper into Dave's wonderland. The ambiance is surreal, almost like something I had seen in a dream. Real gas lanterns tower overhead, reminiscent of New Orleans' French Quarter, casting warm light through the palm fronds. Beautiful wooden benches made of twisted vines and slabs of natural edge wood give everything a subtle rustic feel.

Even the air smells different, almost as if I'm inhaling the combined scents of an extravagant fruit bowl all at once. And it feels oddly safe, like home, even though I still catalog escape routes out of habit: three paths leading to different parts of the property, easy access to the main road, and plenty of places to hide if needed.

Around a curve in the path, a building appears, highlighted by soft blue spotlights. The sign reads "Dive Shop," topped by a carved wooden fish painted in festive green and red. "Welcome," curves across its center in cheerful yellow script. A display of bathing suits blocks the view through a large front window.

I start toward the entrance but stop short when a flicker of moonlight glinting off water catches my eye through a line of palms to the left. I turn my head towards the distraction and twist my neck to get a better view.

"That must be the ocean," I say to myself, and like a siren's call, it draws me off my course.

I back up and turn down a path that winds behind the shop through the vegetation, and after a minute or so, I emerge onto a stretch of manicured lawn that extends fifty feet to what appears to be a massive stone seawall. My breath catches as I walk forward; the nighttime ocean spreads out before me. I pull my hands from my pocket and lift them to my mouth in amazement. I can't remember seeing something so beautiful before.

Waves glow silver under the full moon while distant boats scatter orange and red reflections across the water. My gaze follows the seawall in both directions as it stretches hundreds of yards.

As I take in the full scope of Dave's, my eyes widen in wonder. This resort is enormous, much larger than I'd imagined. I look to the south where a row of pastel-colored condos, like the ones from *Full House*, are lined up like solders facing the water. To the north, I can see the back of the dive shop, where there are large docks lined with boats of varying sizes. Between them stretches a pristine white sand beach dotted with chairs and umbrellas, and I can just make out the silhouette of what appears to be a thatched-roof tiki bar, just off of a dimly lit pier that reaches out towards the ebony horizon.

"Is this place for real?"

I approach the seawall, stopping just short of a salty mist that rises from the light crash of the night tide. I feel a yawn building as I look up to a bright, full moon. I haven't really slept well for what feels like years, and the oddly comforting nature of the resort is lulling me to sleep.

"Don't yawn," a deep voice says from behind me.

I spin around, arms instinctively crossing my torso, protecting my bruised ribs, and my head angled down so my dark brown hair hangs over my face. As I make out slightly more than a silhouette in the moonlight, relief floods through me—it's not Nick. This man is taller, leaner. Nick is stockier, more compact, like a coiled spring ready to snap.

"You're going to make me yawn," the voice continues.

"Excuse me?" I ask before taking two careful steps back, keeping my distance and keeping my face out of the lunar light.

"Your yawn," he says, his tone carrying an edge of sarcasm. "Yawns are contagious, you know."

"Really?" I watch as the shadow steps forward, my body tensing instinctively.

The stubborn yawn finally escapes, but I continue speaking through it. "I've been driving a while and haven't had the best sleep lately." His body catches the moonlight. "My God," I add as I emerge from the yawn, keeping my face down and hiding in the welcome shadows of the summer night.

He raises a sly eyebrow, clearly used to this type of reaction. And he should be. He is a gorgeous man with sandy blonde hair, longer on top, framing a face that belongs on a magazine cover.

And of course he's shirtless, his tan body sculpted to perfection, with blue board shorts hanging low on his hips. Everything about him screams confidence.

My body betrays me as I instinctively look up. As I do, my eyes lock with his deep blue eyes, which immediately narrow.

"Can I help you with something?" His tone shifts suddenly, becoming flat, irritated. His head cocks suspiciously to the side. His body twitches as if reacting to an enemy.

I gesture toward the water, suddenly, trying to say anything to counter his shift in mood. "It's beautiful."

His eyes flick to the ocean, then back, assessing me with an intense curiosity. "Yeah," he says dismissively. "It is." After an awkward pause, he glances over his shoulder impatiently. "I just saw you here and wanted to make sure you weren't lost. I didn't know who you were. When did you get here?"

"Yeah, I just got here." My voice comes out smaller than intended. "I just need to find Dave." I point towards the dive shop and force a smile. "*The* Dave."

"You need to find Dave," he repeats slowly, each word dripping with something that reminds me too much of Nick's pre-explosion tone.

"Yes, I need—"

"Why?" His interruption is sharp, hostile.

"Well, I just got here from Tennessee, and he was supposed to be getting an email about a job."

"What job?"

I shrug. "I'm actually not sure."

"Are you here for a job?" Annoyance darkens his tone.

I nod. "Maybe?" I fight the urge to step back again. "I don't really know."

His chin drops in disbelief, and his earlier playfulness completely vanishes, replaced by a rigid posture.

We face each other in tense silence. I try to look anywhere

but his eyes, but when I chance a glance up, he visibly cringes as if my gaze causes physical pain. I quickly look away, wondering how this man transformed from charming to antagonistic in mere seconds.

"The Dave who owns this place?" I prompt, my voice artificially bright, the same tone I used to use when trying to defuse Nick's moods.

His eyes scan me like he's assessing a threat, looking me up and down in detail as if trying to remember if he has seen me before. After a moment, he pinches his nose, clearly disappointed.

"You've never been here before, have you?"

"No," I say as I extend my hand cautiously, "I'm Glory."

He looks down then steps forward and grabs my hand, holding it for an awkward moment before letting it fall to my side. "I'm Ellis. I work here."

"You work here?"

"What do you think?"

I know when to stay quiet and when to make myself small, but now, as I stare at this stranger, I feel oddly comfortable to push back at his sarcastic tone. I straighten my spine despite my protesting ribs. "Actually," I say, keeping my voice level. "I think someone's being unnecessarily rude."

His eyebrows shoot up suddenly in surprise, replacing some of his uncalled-for hostility. He sighs again, then looks away. "We're not hiring," he says abruptly.

"I was told you were," I counter, still unexpectedly confrontational.

He shakes his head and forces a faux laugh, a surrender of sorts. "Says who?"

"Can you just take me to Dave?"

He narrows his eyes and cocks his head as if searching for whether to push back, but then his shoulders rise and fall in defeat. "Come with me."

I follow him as he turns and walks down a path leading to the docks. As I do, I touch the necklace for courage, tracing the rise and fall of the infinity symbol.

Chapter 3

"Look," I say as I trail Ellis along the water toward the docks, "I'm sorry if I've upset you in some way." The words come automatically and are the same ones I use with Nick when he shows up to my place in a bad mood.

He glances over his shoulder, eyes narrowed. "Whatever."

I fall silent, swallowing my frustration and the urge to apologize again. Walking on eggshells around Nick has taught me that sometimes silence is safer.

We reach the end of a long wooden walkway leading to the main dock. In the moonlight, shadows dance across three large boats that bob gently in the waves. Ellis hops over a small wooden gate and leaves me. "Dave!"

Silence answers. The darkness reveals nothing but the gentle lap of water against moonlit wood.

"Dave!" Ellis says again, his voice rising sharply. I follow his gaze down the center of the dock, fighting the urge to wrap my arms around my aching ribs. He opens his mouth to shout again but stops as an older man emerges from the shadows. The man climbs up a ramp from the lower deck of the largest boat docked—a bright blue vessel with "Seahorse I" emblazoned on its side.

Dave.

"What's up Ellis, my man?" Dave's voice is kind, and his

appearance is startlingly reminiscent of Jerry Garcia—the kind of man Dad used to hang out with at Grateful Dead concerts. My Dad might have been friends with someone like Dave.

"Look who just showed up," Ellis says as he jabs a thumb in my direction. "What am I supposed to do now?" Dave looks confused at first then his eyes find me. My stomach clenches, preparing for rejection. One more door closing, one less escape route.

But it's not rejection in Dave's eyes. Instead, confusion flickers across his face before he finally smiles and raises a hand as if seeing an old friend.

I smile back then look to Ellis, who watches me in disgust, rolling his eyes dramatically. Before I can speak, movement draws my attention back to the boat as the largest man I've ever seen steps onto the dock, positioning himself at Dave's right. My eyes widen involuntarily, and I take an instinctive step back. He must be close to seven feet tall and as wide as anyone on Tennessee's defensive line. His chestnut brown hair, nearly black, is cut short on the sides and longer on top. When he notices me, a warm smile spreads across his face. The contrast between his intimidating size and gentle demeanor throws me off balance. Nick was always the opposite—average size but radiating menace.

"Not you, too, Noah," Ellis snaps.

"What?" Noah's voice is surprisingly gentle, his smile lingering. "Look at—"

"Shh," Ellis says, interrupting him.

Dave looks back towards me and nods, holding up one finger as if asking me to wait. He then beckons Ellis closer with both hands. After a hesitant glance back at me, Ellis walks the twenty feet or so to where Dave and Noah stand.

I wait awkwardly, trying not to eavesdrop on their hushed, heated discussion. Though I can't make out Ellis's words, his sharp tone carries clearly across the dock. He is so upset.

Minutes later, Ellis turns, grunts in frustration, and storms back toward me. As he does, I study my shoes until his presence forces me to look up. Our eyes lock for an instant, and in that moment, I glimpse something unexpected—confusion, torment, pain. It's an expression that I've seen in my own mirror too many times.

"Fine. Let her stay," he shouts over his shoulder, breaking our connection. "It doesn't matter anyway. It doesn't change anything." Then, with one final glare, he turns, then bolts to my right along a path to a staircase and through a door into the back of what must be the dive shop.

I stand there, mouth agape, wishing I understood why Ellis seems so troubled by my presence. Part of me wants to run, but where would I go? *Give this a chance*, I tell myself. At least Ellis's anger seems directed at Dave, not me. That's different. That's something I might be able to handle.

I turn back to find Dave and Noah have closed the distance between us. I manage what must be an unconvincing smile while my hand automatically finds Dad's necklace again.

Dave flashes a peace sign with one hand while tilting down his tinted glasses with the other. "Welcome to Dave's."

"Not the best welcome," Noah adds in his deep voice, staring after Ellis.

"I'm Dave." He pauses a moment before adding, "I'm the owner of this fine establishment." He then extends his hand slowly as if sensing my hesitation.

"I'm Glory. From the email." I reach forward and grasp his hand briefly. As I do, I get a closer look at Dave. He has a gentle face, deeply tanned and lined with wrinkles. His Hawaiian shirt, scraggly beard, and worn visor match his laid-back demeanor.

"Sure…from the email."

"Yes, sir. I mean, I just got here from Tennessee." The words tumble out. I'm always chatty when I'm tired, which is exactly the opposite of how it should work. Nick hated that about me.

Every time he would visit me, he said I talked too much. He always preferred that I stay silent.

Dave's eyes sparkle playfully. "Sir?" He turns to Noah, who's leaning against the dock's entrance railing. "Did you hear that, Noah? She called me *sir*. She must be a keeper."

Noah nods once. "Yep." Clearly, he's a man of few words.

Dave holds up his hands in surrender. "I'm sure most here would agree that I'm not worthy of the title of *sir*. I've been way too…let's say *adventurous* with my life."

"Yep," Noah agrees.

"So, just call me Dave, or Davey, or the Dude. I've been called many things."

Noah rolls his eyes. "Just call him Dave."

"Okay," I say, glancing between them, amused despite my exhaustion. There's something comforting about their easy banter. It is so different from the tense silence that I'm used to.

Dave leans up against a nearby wood post with enviable casualness, as if talking to an old friend. I glance back toward where Ellis disappeared. "I'm really sorry for all that. I think I upset him."

Dave shakes his head. "Nah. You didn't upset him. Ellis hasn't been dealt the best hand. He's just trying to navigate a diffi-cult…situation." He emphasizes the last word of the sentence, but I can't quite figure out what he means by it. Noah nods in silent agreement.

"Look, I really need this job and would be happy to apologize to Ellis if it means I can stay. It's really no big—"

Dave's raised hand stops me mid-sentence, but unlike Nick's sharp gestures, there's nothing threatening about it. "Glory, the job is yours. Of course, it is yours." He uses my name as if we have been friends for years.

"Really?" I tilt my head, hardly daring to believe it could be this easy. Nothing in my life has been easy recently.

Dave spreads his arms wide. "Welcome to Dave's."

I clasp my hands together, hiding their trembling as unexpected joy courses through me. It's been so long since I've felt anything joyful, and I have to turn away briefly to blink back tears.

"I think you will see, Glory," Dave says, "that this is exactly where you need to be." He jumps down and moves to my side, keeping a respectful distance, as if he can sense my need for space.

I force a smile, but words fail me; I can only nod appreciatively.

He walks over to join Noah. "This place is great, very serene, peaceful." Looking toward the dive shop, he adds, "Generally."

"Yep," Noah says, turning back toward the docks. He pauses to casually hoist two massive air tanks onto his shoulder.

"How much do those weigh?" I ask, thinking of the medical equipment at the clinic where I used to volunteer.

"Close to a hundred pounds each," Dave says.

"It's nothing," Noah calls over his shoulder as he walks back towards the boats.

"Noah is the strongest man I've ever known."

"He's like one of those Icelandic guys from the TV competitions," I observe.

"Totally," Dave says, "and he's a whiz with tools and electronics. He can fix anything with a motor."

"Is he a dive instructor?"

Dave laughs, shaking his head. "Not a chance. He's not a water person. Won't go in it. Took me years to get him on the boats."

"Seriously?"

"Absolutely."

Dave starts down the wooden walkway toward the dive shop's back entrance. I hitch my backpack higher and follow, noting how he naturally walks slightly ahead, giving me clear sight lines and plenty of space as if he knows that I need it.

"Ellis is harmless, you know," he says, shoving his hands into his baggy cargo shorts. "He's just going through a rocky patch."

I nod slightly, but before I can respond, a shout breaks the night's calm.

"Dave!"

We look over to see a young man, eighteen or nineteen, racing down the dive shop's back steps. My muscles tense automatically at the sudden movement, but I force myself to breathe steadily.

"What, JJ?" Dave's annoyed exhale is accompanied by an eye roll in my direction.

JJ is short and thin. His appearance is almost comical, his bright orange skin contrasting with a sky-blue Gold's Gym shirt and neon yellow board shorts. A backward Atlanta Braves cap barely contains his blonde curls.

He stops at the bottom of the stairs, throwing his hands up in frustration, seemingly oblivious to my presence. "That guy is nuts, Dave. Ellis just came into the back office—where I was minding my business gaming with a lady friend—and he nearly threw me out of the room, physically."

"Really?" Dave's feigned concern flies right over JJ's head.

"He really did, Dave. Then, he slammed the office door and told me to 'go play World of Warcraft somewhere else.' My toe just cleared the door. He could have broken it."

"Really?" Dave asks flatly.

"Yes, Dave. He almost broke my toe."

Dave glances at JJ's foot and shrugs.

"Well, you know what they say about almost," I chime in, surprising myself with my boldness.

JJ turns, cocking his head curiously.

I raise my hand and speak the words that pop up in my mind. "It only counts in hand grenades."

JJ's eyes dart towards me. "Is that—" JJ says, jabbing a thumb my way.

"A real girl," Dave interrupts.

"My girl is real, Dave. She's got long blonde hair, bright blue eyes, and huge—"

"Whoa!" Dave's hands shoot up. "Watch the content, son."

JJ rolls his eyes. "She's real. She just plays an elf."

I bite back a laugh, trying to nod seriously. There's something endearing about his earnestness though he is acting a bit off as if uncomfortable in the presence of a new person.

"Seriously. What the?"

"Did you say your girlfriend's an elf?" Dave asks, ignoring the question. "Did he say elf, Glory?"

"I think so."

"She's an elf princess, Dave—pretty powerful."

"Okay," Dave says flatly. "I'm completely lost, but whatever."

"Not whatever! He was out of line this time. Is it because—"

Dave raises his hand. "Just give him some grace today, JJ."

"But he just—"

"Just today. I'll find you in a bit and we will discuss it. Promise."

JJ grimaces, exhaling harshly. "Fine." He looks in my direction and gestures dramatically toward me with one hand.

Dave pats my back lightly. "This is Glory. She's a new hire. She'll be working here from now on."

"Nice," JJ says after an awkward pause. He then turns back towards Dave. "But you know Ellis is going to kill you, right?"

Dave's eyes dart between us. "He's not, JJ. Ellis is fine with it. I'm more concerned that you've reviewed the employee handbook on sexual harassment, little man."

JJ frowns. "Whatever. You act like I'm some sexual deviant. I have a girlfriend, remember? He nods in my direction and then forces an eye roll. "I'm out anyway. I need some sleep so I can hit the gym in the morning." He shoots me one last pointed, arrogant glance and stalks off towards the condos as if we're beneath his notice.

"JJ is full of hormones," Dave says. "If he bothers you, tell me or Noah." He pauses for a minute, then throws his hands in the air. "I have an idea. What about a late-night tour?"

"Sure," say forcing back a yawn.

"Let's do it," Dave says as he turns and motions me forward.

I follow Dave as he leads me back towards the resort entrance, near the roundabout. From there, Dave begins a cursory tour. He takes me by the condos, the storage buildings, an outdoor playground and grilling area, and a large dry dock housing various boats and jet skis.

I learn that most of Dave's acreage is undeveloped. He tells me that he has received numerous offers to develop the land, but he refuses to sell or develop it, seeing himself as a guardian of the Keys' natural environment.

"If thousands of tourists came here, I might make a small fortune, but all the reefs around here would be destroyed, eventually."

Dave's passion for the environment becomes even more evident as he describes various plant species here and there, his eyes lighting up especially at the fruit-bearing ones, like the banana trees. They're smaller than I'd imagined, with a rich scent reminiscent of fruit-flavored cereal.

"The plants are amazing," I say as I reach out and brush my hand along the edge of a small yellow flowering bush.

"We've been blessed with some employees who really know their stuff when it comes to plants."

The tour concludes at the condos. "The rental condos are new to the resort and are already fully booked for the next twelve months," Dave says, pride evident in his voice.

They deserve the praise—each connected unit features unique

design elements and different pastel colors—nothing like the all-white, sterile cookie-cutter apartment complex where I lived.

"They're so beautiful," I say. "I love the colors."

"My girlfriend, Amber, manages the rentals and picked out the colors. She has an eye for design." He points to the end unit. "Amber and I live down there."

"I know it must be a lot of work."

Dave nods. "It is, and I regret all the work she does—I barely get to see her during the day." His lips purse in frustration. "I told her I would hire someone to do the job, but she's her own spirit, and I respect her decision to manage the rentals herself."

The way he talks about Amber—with respect and pride instead of possessiveness, makes my chest ache longingly.

As we end the tour, he stops abruptly, pawing at his beard and turning towards me. "I have to ask you a question, Glory."

"Okay, I say hesitantly, not sure what he will ask.

"I am so glad you are here. In fact, we needed you. But why? What brought you here?"

The half-truth sits uncomfortably in my stomach. I want to be honest, but the whole truth isn't an option.

"I guess I just needed a change," I blurt out instead. "This is not normal for me. I don't usually do stuff on my own. But this feels oddly right. I'm not that brave."

Dave laughs deeply, patting my back again. "Really? I would say the complete opposite."

"What do you mean?"

"Maybe you're talking about the old you."

"The old me?"

"Yeah. The old you. The one you left back in Tennessee." His expression softens as he points at me. "The real you has guts. I know she does. The real you is brave."

I nod slowly as his words sink in. He has a point. The old me would never have left Nick or fled Tennessee alone. She would never have moved to a strange place without having first secured housing or at least employment. Maybe I have changed. Maybe the old me, the scared me, died when Nick pushed me down those stairs.

I look over at Dave as he moves forward, motioning for me to follow. I do.

CHAPTER 4

RATHER THAN ENTER through the back of the dive shop, Dave and I circle to the front, where a large gas lantern casts a pale orange glow over a weathered wooden bench.

"Everything started here," Dave says softly. "After Mama died, everything came to me. Until then, I didn't really know how much land she owned. She never told me she had been buying up the surrounding lots for years. She was quiet but had an incredible mind for business."

Dave bends down and picks up a plastic straw, which he proceeds to toss in a nearby recycling can.

"I was a mama's boy, so it rattled me good when she passed." His voice carries the weight of old grief. It tugs on something in me that I push aside, listening to his every word. "But I learned to live without her, and it is through all this that I did." He looks around as if reminiscing. "After a year or so of mourning, feeling bad for myself, I started taking divers out in my boat. It started with a few friends here and there, then tourists. Everything happened so fast, and thinking back, it is all kind of a blur. But, before I knew it, I had opened a dive shop, and this place was born."

"That is incredible," I say. "It is like it was meant to be."

Dave nods. "There is a plan for all of us, Glory."

I slip into a moment of thought as I consider what that

plan might be for me. Though I believe in God, I am not sure that I believe there is something written in the stars for me. I just can't imagine the divine having its hand in the life that I've recently lived.

Dave turns and points through the tree line beyond the shop as I shake free from the thought. "You can't see Mama's house from here because of all the palms, but it's just over there."

He's right. The foliage is too thick to make out anything. "It's so amazing, Dave," I say. "Your mom would be very proud."

Dave is the type who wears his emotions openly, and I can see his mother's memory playing across his face as he stares into the distance. After two years of trying to read Nick's mercurial moods, it's refreshing.

"It's like a tropical paradise," I say, breaking the silence. "I can't imagine what it's like to live here. It must be so wonderful."

Dave's grin returns, his eyes brightening. "Well, now you can, Glory. This place is your home."

"My home," I repeat in a monotone, the words feeling surreal on my tongue. Earlier today, I was crushed—my will was broken, and my body was in pain. Now, I'm standing in paradise with a stranger who seems to care more about my well-being than Nick ever did.

I study Dave, from his worn sandals to his half-buttoned Hawaiian shirt billowing in the breeze. It's hard to reconcile this laid-back hippie with such an accomplished businessman, but I can tell he shares his mother's generous spirit and business acumen.

Dave waggles his eyebrows. "Before we check out the shop, what do you say we visit the tiki bar, which is what locals call *the Hut*, and see if Charlie and Aki are around? I'd love for you to meet them tonight before the late-night rush."

"Sounds great," I say, following him along the lighted path.

"Most people like to bring sack lunches on the boats during

dives, so our day divers don't generally hang out at the Hut. But at night, this place is the chilliest spot in a ten-mile radius, and that's a big radius in the Florida Keys. Aki makes a mean Kalua pork."

My stomach rumbles. I can't remember the last time I ate, but it was probably that gas station sandwich somewhere in Georgia. "Sounds amazing."

"Totally. Occasionally, you get the college joker who drank too much or maybe the occasional dirty old man, but if you ever get nervous down here, or if anyone gives you a tough time, tell me or one of the team. We got your back."

The casual way he offers protection, without expectation or demand, makes my throat tighten. He reminds me so much of my dad. "Thanks."

"And if we can't handle it, we'll call Noah. He *will* be able to handle it." Dave winks, and I manage a genuine smile.

When we arrive at the Hut, Dave hops onto a bar stool, drumming his hands on the counter before patting the empty seat beside him. I climb up carefully, mindful of my bruised ribs.

"Aki runs the kitchen, and Charlie is the main bartender. Charlie is JJ's grandfather, but he doesn't like people to know." Dave raises an eyebrow meaningfully. "Wonder why, right? Aki! Charlie! You two around?"

The door behind the bar swings open slowly, revealing a huge man with short dark hair and warm brown skin. His name tag confirms my guess about his Hawaiian heritage, listing his hometown as Kahului, Maui.

"And this is Aki," Dave says.

I hesitate only briefly before extending my hand forward. "Nice to meet you. I'm Glory."

He tilts his head slightly then steps forward with his hand extended. "So nice to meet you, Glory." He grins as he takes my hand in both of his and squeezes gently before letting go. His voice surprises me. It is both soft and soothing, nothing like what you'd expect from his imposing presence.

"Glory is joining the team, my man."

Aki looks pleasantly surprised at the news as he looks between Dave and me. "Well, that's great news on this fine evening," he says as he laughs deeply. "Welcome, Glory."

"Thanks," I say.

Dave nods toward the room behind the bar. "The kitchen's back there." He looks at Aki. "I told Glory that you make the best food around."

Aki waves dismissively. "Well, I try, but I don't know if it's the *best*."

"Please, brother," Dave says with mock annoyance, reaching forward and squeezing Aki's shoulder. "You're the best chef this part of the Keys has ever seen." He points to me urgently. "When you have time, stop by and try something."

Aki tries to wave away the compliment, but his wide grin and reddening cheeks betray his pleasure.

"I will," I say, warming to his gentle nature. "My dad used to say that Hawaii has the best macaroni salad." The memory of my Dad praising Hawaiian food leaps forward as if having been lost for a time.

Aki's eyes light up. "He was correct. Have you been to the islands?"

I shake my head. "No, but one day I hope to. One of my dad's best friends was Hawaiian."

"Really?"

"He used to tell me about how amazing he was. And he loved the food."

Aki takes a steadying breath. "Well, I hope you get to go one day. Maybe you will get to meet his friend, too."

"Maybe!"

"Hawaii is a wonderful place," Dave says, "a paradise really. Second only to here. Right, Aki?"

Aki rolls his eyes. "Whatever you say."

"Hey!" Dave shouts playfully.

Aki shrugs. "What can I say? Home is where the heart is."

Dave steps back, pointing upward, and I notice a series of colorful medals lining the top of the bar. "And he can do more than cook! He was a world-class Sumo wrestler. Won numerous titles, didn't you, my man?"

Aki's face radiates pride as he nods.

I examine the medals—nearly twenty, mostly gold, from the nineties.

"These are incredible," I say.

"It was a special time in my life," Aki adds as he turns to Dave, thumbing in my direction. "Knows about Hawaiian macaroni salad, loves my medals…I think this one's a keeper."

Dave grins and says, "My thoughts exactly.

"What the hell is all the noise out here?" a shaky voice demands suddenly from behind Aki, and I turn nervously just in time to see an older man approach from behind the bar, his name tag reading simply "Charlie, hometown, not your business."

I offer a nervous smile, fighting the urge to shrink into myself. His eyes narrow suspiciously as I look at Dave, who maintains his easy grin.

Although they both have white hair, the similarities between Dave and Charlie stop there. I would say Charlie is the exact opposite of a Jerry Garcia lookalike with his flat-top and navy blue T-shirt tucked tightly into old camo pants.

"Hi, Charlie, my man." Dave turns to me, eyebrows lifted. "This is our new Dive Lead."

Am I the new Dive Lead? The title catches me off guard.

Charlie exhales dramatically, waving a dismissive hand. "A Dive Lead, huh? Just what we need around here." I can't tell if he is being sarcastic. He leans closer, head tilted. "What's your name, girl?" He looks towards Dave who winks in his direction. He then looks back towards me and bites his lower lip as if contemplating what to think about my sudden appearance.

"It's Glory, sir." The 'sir' comes automatically.

He studies me for a moment before nodding sternly. "Suits you."

"Thanks," I manage softly after an awkward pause.

Charlie turns to Dave. "It's a very patriotic name."

"It is," Dave agrees as Aki nods enthusiastically.

"I dated a girl named America once," Charlie says. "That was maybe more so, but probably not."

Dave and Aki exchange puzzled looks.

"I didn't know you knew a girl named America," Dave says, smiling.

Charlie's face scrunches in irritation. "Well, you don't know everything about me, Dave. I *am* a private person, you know."

Dave raises his hands in mock surrender.

Charlie turns back towards me. "My bar just has two rules, Glory," Charlie says, holding up his hand like a gun with thumb and finger extended.

"Okay," I reply anxiously, bracing for restrictions.

"The first rule is that you don't drink unless you're twenty-one." He squints, clearly trying to gauge my age.

"I'm twenty-two," I say, and he nods.

"All y'all look like babies to me." After a cough, he continues. "The second rule is don't pester the ladies."

My eyebrows rise involuntarily. I like this rule. It's the opposite of Nick's world, where women are meant to be controlled.

"He's serious, too," Aki says with a wink.

"Yep," Dave agrees.

Charlie nods emphatically. "Damn right, I am." He turns to me. "This is a place where women will be respected. If anyone ever bothers you—*ever*—at this bar, or anywhere for that matter, you tell me, and I'll take care of it. I may be old, but I'll open a can of whoop ass, if need be, for you." He snaps his fingers, leaning closer. "You can count on it."

I nod, tears threatening to fall as his protective stance hits home. I'm not used to having male protectors, not since Dad. It feels like rediscovering something I'd lost, something I hadn't fully appreciated when I had it.

Charlie smiles approvingly, tosses his rag into the sink, and heads back through the door. "Carry on," he calls over his shoulder.

I look at Aki and Dave with wide eyes. "He seems—"

"Surly?" Aki suggests.

"Difficult?" Dave adds.

"For sure," Aki says, "but harmless."

"Generally," Dave qualifies.

"Generally," Aki agrees with a light chuckle.

Aki turns back toward me. "From all of us here, including Charlie, *kipa hou mai*. It means 'you are home.'"

"Beautiful words," I say.

"Indeed, they are," Aki agrees. "I do hope you visit Charlie and me often. I can already tell you're going to be a great addition to the family."

Family. His sincerity warms my heart.

"If you ever get hungry or need something, come find me or Charlie. Dive Leads get free meals, you know."

"Really?" I glance at Dave.

"Yep," he says, waggling his eyebrows. "Got to keep you kids fed."

"That's amazing."

"Well, it's not like you eat that much," Aki chuckles, rubbing his huge belly.

"Not as much as you, Aki, my man," Dave jokes.

"It takes work keeping up this six-pack of kegs."

"I eat more than you think," I say, surprising myself with the defiance in my voice. "I love food."

Aki pats my shoulder. "Love it!"

Dave throws an arm around each of us. "I knew she would fit in."

"Aki!" Charlie shouts from the kitchen.

Aki rolls his eyes. "Well, I better get back and help the old guy cut those potatoes. The sooner we're done, and he's out of my kitchen, the better for all of us."

Dave laughs. "Better get back to it then, my man."

"Nice seeing you, Glory."

"You too," I say as he disappears through the kitchen door with a final wave.

I wipe sweat from my forehead. "Is it normally this humid at night? My clothes feel sticky." I tug at my shirt, careful not to reveal any bruises.

Dave grins. "I have a feeling that you'll get used to it in no time."

I take in the surrounding beauty. "I definitely will. It's a small price to pay to live in paradise."

"Agreed," Dave says before turning and leading me back to the dive shop.

As we walk through the front door of the store, my eyes widen as I take it all in, from colorful fins and masks to mannequins adorned by everything from skimpy bathing suits to T-shirts printed with goofy, sometimes borderline risqué slogans: 'Dive with attitude, drink like a fish.'

Dave leads me to the back of the store, where a long glass case is filled with sunglasses and digital diving instruments. Behind it, I spot a girl in her twenties with bright red hair. She is focused intently on her computer screen. The other, a tall blonde in shorts and a frilly aqua bathing suit top perches on a stool to the right, reading what appears to be a trashy romance novel. Her tongue moves across glossy red lips as her eyes narrow in concentration.

"Ladies," Dave announces, clapping his hands, "allow me to *introduce* you to Glory, our new Dive Lead."

The blonde cocks her head suspiciously then nods in my direction, acknowledging me politely, then turns towards Dave. "Ellis is going to kill you, Dave. You know that, right?" Her matter-of-fact tone is flat and unconcerned.

Dave winks then steps toward the redhead, who has bounced up and is already around the counter. Her smile is infectious, and her classic beauty complements her pale complexion and small red curls.

"Hello, I'm—"

"Glory!" she shouts then grabs my hand, shaking it quickly before looking up at Dave with wide eyes. "Is this happening, Dave?"

"It's happening," the blonde says as Dave nods silently.

"Yes!" Red jumps up and down, still holding my hands.

"Nice to meet you," I say, my body shifting up and down with Red's excited movements. These people are clearly over the moon that they've hired what appears to be much needed extra support.

Red releases my hand then grabs my shoulders and pulls me into a tight hug. I squint to hide my discomfort. Red's enthusiasm, while sweet, is murder on my bruised ribs. When she steps back, she's beaming.

"I can't believe that this is happening!" she says, flashing a wide smile towards Dave that would rival Julia Roberts.

"Well, we need the help, and Glory is just too good to pass up."

Red gestures toward me. "She's perfect!" She looks at me and repeats herself. "You are perfect."

"Thanks," I say after a brief hesitation. She probably doesn't know how inexperienced I am, so I wonder if her sentiment will change.

"You'll have to excuse Red," Dave says. "She's normally excitable, but she's super excited about *you* being here."

"I know, you must really need help."

Red sticks her tongue out at Dave.

"Ellis is seriously going to kill you," the blonde says again without looking up.

"*This* is Blair," Red explains, nodding toward the blonde who looks back up, her smile warm but suspicious. "Just ignore her. She's my best friend, believe it or not."

"And your polar opposite," Blair adds, pursing her lips. She reminds me of the popular girls in high school who always seemed to know everyone's secrets.

"Yes, my complete, absolute polar opposite," Red agrees with a quick closed-eye grin. "But you love me."

Blair rolls her eyes. "Seriously, Dave, does Ellis know?" Blair marks her place in her book with a bright orange bookmark and stands. Her concern seems genuine, so I find myself thinking back to Dave's comment that Ellis had "not been dealt the best hand."

Dave waves dismissively. "He's totally cool with it—knows already."

"She's already seen Ellis?" Blair asks incredulously.

"Yep," Dave confirms. "It's all good, Blair. No worries."

Blair rolls her eyes. "Yeah, sure, Dave."

Dave ignores her. "I have to run and drop off some cleaning supplies to Amber. Do me a favor and take Glory to the house. She's just got here from Tennessee, and I'm sure she could use some rest."

As he speaks, a yawn escapes. The events of the past few days are catching up with me. The option to crash at their place tonight sounds heavenly. I can look for weekly motels or an Airbnb tomorrow, someplace safe and anonymous.

"Put her on the third floor. Here's the key." Dave hands Red a key that she tucks into her jean cutoffs.

"My God, Dave. Are you nuts?" Blair mutters, leaning on the display case and shaking her head. Her reaction makes me suspicious.

Red pinches Blair's shoulder.

"Ouch," Blair snaps. Red leans in to whisper something, and then they have one of those silent conversations that only best friends can manage. After a moment, Blair shrugs and returns to her book, but not before giving me one last appraising look.

Red turns to Dave. "I've got it handled. I'll make sure she's all set."

Taking my hand gently, she begins leading me away. "Blair, could you shut down the computer when you head out?" she calls over her shoulder.

"You know I will, Red," Blair replies with a crooked smile that doesn't quite reach her eyes.

"Bye, Davey Dave!" Red calls as she pulls me through the front door. I glance back to see Dave offering another peace sign.

As we step into the humid night air, I can't help but wonder what I'm walking into. But for the first time since leaving Tennessee, the uncertainty doesn't feel threatening. Oddly enough, I feel comfortable in the unknown.

Chapter 5

Red's energy reminds me of my dad's sister, Eleanor, who moved and thought faster than everyone around her. Aunt Eleanor was not religious but spiritual. She claimed being hyper was a sign of a highly evolved soul. "We are just finishing the rest of our lessons," she would say, "and we are running out of time."

"So, you met Charlie and Aki?" Red asks as I match her quick stride.

"I did," I say, glancing towards the area where the bar is just visible through the tree line. The full moon had climbed higher, making the place even more inviting.

Red stops suddenly and turns my way. "Did Dave tell you about Charlie's… history?" Red nervously picks at her thumbnail.

I shake my head. "Nothing much. I did learn about his rules."

"He is totally serious about the rules, especially if it is JJ breaking them. He's JJ's granddad, actually."

"Dave mentioned that," I say.

"If you look, you can sort of tell."

"I can see that."

"Charlie's actually famous around here. He has the record for the deepest free dive."

"Free dive?"

"Like when you dive without any tank or regulator, just your fins, mask, and snorkel."

"How deep did he dive?" I ask with newfound curiosity. He seems fit enough for someone in their seventies, but I never would have guessed he held a diving record.

"Two-hundred thirty-two feet."

My jaw drops. "What!"

"I know. It's hard to imagine. But he did it in his fifties, so he was much younger."

"His fifties? That's incredible."

"Yeah," she says, her voice suddenly heavy with sadness.

"What?"

Red cringes as if what she is saying hurts. "Charlie's son Jack, JJ's dad, actually died freediving."

"That's horrible," I whisper, as my heart sinks.

"And ever since, Charlie won't get back into the water. He blames himself, I think."

"I can't imagine losing a child," I say as I clutch my hand to my chest.

"Dave had a really close group of friends. Some of them were in the military together. Dave was actually best friends with JJ's dad, Jack, and Ellis's dad, Cole. Aki was also a part of the group, though he didn't serve in the military. They all met while they were stationed overseas.

"Oh," I say simply as I contemplate the complexity of the relationships at Dave's. This *is* like a family.

"Did you seriously just drive from Tennessee?" Red asks, bouncing to another topic as if trying to dispel the somber mood.

"Yeah," I say, another yawn escaping at the thought.

"Is that where you're from?"

I ponder my answer momentarily before responding. "I've lived in so many places, I don't really know exactly where I am from, but my mom lives in Texas and most of her family is from there. I'm from Texas. I lived in Tennessee for about four years, for school."

"University of Tennessee? A volunteer?"

"Yep."

"Fantastic!" Red claps her hands together excitedly and jumps back a bit. "We're all big SEC fans here, especially Ellis and Clinton, so I know you'll fit right in." She waves dismissively. "Even though you're a Tennessee fan."

I force a laugh then yawn again.

"You must be exhausted, Glory," Red says then gently rubs my back. "Let's find you a bed."

We pass the docks about twenty feet beyond the dive shop, then turn right onto a thin trail that leads through palm trees and large mounds of palmettos.

"This is a shortcut," Red explains. "It's a little overgrown, but it beats going back through the main gate and down the road, which is the only other way to the main house. Besides, the driveway has a gate, and it can be finicky if its sensors don't detect a car or something similar in size. It's annoying. Noah is big enough to use it, though," she laughs. "You met him, right?"

"Yeah. He is—"

"Enormous, I know," Red interrupts playfully, winking. "You should see Blair in her Mercedes convertible sitting there trying to get that gate to 'sense' her car, and then Noah walks up, and the gate lifts immediately." Red shakes her head. "Blair gets *so* pissed. It's freaking hilarious. You may think redheads are fiery, and we can be, but Blair...whew!"

I force a nervous laugh.

We turn a final corner, and I find myself standing on a red brick patio behind one of the tallest and most ornate homes I've ever seen. My gaze bounces between Red and the house, mouth agape. It's like an old Victorian mansion from Savannah or Charleston but hidden within a tropical paradise.

The house, a mansion actually, is pale green with bright white trim that pops, providing stunning detail as it catches the moonlight. Carefully placed lampposts illuminate the patio and flowers…there are so many flowers. Everywhere I look, perfectly placed blooms provide bursts of color that bring the home to life.

I tilt my head back to study the roofline. "Wow. It's so tall. How many floors does it have?"

Red shrugs casually. "Five, if you count the top level, but no one goes up there anymore except Ellis, not since—"

Red stops abruptly as if catching herself. I pretend not to notice, looking up at three beautiful spires, but I'm curious about what she was going to say. "Those are incredible," I say, forcing through the brief moment of awkwardness.

"Yeah," Red agrees, following my gaze. "This is one of the oldest homes in the Keys, so it has some unique features, like spires."

"I love the unique character of older homes like these. They feel so comfortable, like home should be."

"I agree completely. Dave said it was a mess when he got it from Mama Ruby, but she liked it as it was, and he did not argue with Mama Ruby. It had been in her family for generations. Ever since she passed, he's put a lot into it, elbow grease and money."

"I can tell."

"All of us at Dave's love this place, and each summer, on Mama Ruby's birthday, we have a little upkeep party in honor of her. Basically, everyone gets together to do a project, like landscaping or painting. And Dave gets a cake. Last year, we all pitched in and built the fire pit and brick smoker." She points to a large circle of bricks extending upward at the far side of the patio. It's surrounded by six chairs. "I even helped lay the brick," she beams. "Noah's a great teacher."

"Amazing," I say, genuinely impressed by the home and the sense of community everyone at Dave's seems to share. "Y'all love it here, don't you?"

"Absolutely," Red says, "and I guarantee that you will too."

As we approach the house, I am drawn to freshly cut grass extending to a separate ocean wall. I'd known the water was somewhere to our left as we walked through the palmettos, but I had no idea how close. The house actually sits directly on it. I narrow my eyes, watching faint white waves break under the moonlight.

"What a view," I breathe. "It must be so nice to wake up to this."

"It is," Red says softly. "You are going to love the view from your apartment up top."

My brows pull together in confusion. "I'm sorry, what?" Did she say, 'my apartment'? There's no way I can afford a beachfront room. I look at Red and begin to protest, but she ignores me, spinning with outstretched arms.

"Welcome home, Glory." After a few seconds, she stops spinning, still not registering my confusion.

I shake my head. Am I missing something? "I thought I was just staying here tonight. I was planning on finding a new place tomorrow then—"

"What! No, no, no. *This* is your place." She scrunches her nose and laughs, her face glowing under a nearby gas lantern.

"What are you talking about?"

"Your place," she repeats.

I stare at her, dumbfounded, before responding. "But I can't afford this."

Realization finally flashes across her face. "You did know that you get housing with this job, right?"

I'm sorry, what?

"I had no idea."

"Seriously?" Red cocks her head playfully. "Dave didn't mention it to you?"

"No," I say. "I didn't really know where I would be staying."

Red snorts. "Well, there's not much affordable housing in

the Keys, so most resorts, like Dave's, have live-in housing for employees. It's a benefit to the resorts too. Otherwise, they would have to pay their employees a lot more to cover housing."

"Oh, wow" is all I can manage to say.

She crosses the patio onto a long wrap-around porch lined with white rocking chairs. "The house is divided into apartments."

Am I in a dream?

She turns and motions me forward, so I follow her up the wide steps towards a wooden door that seems as tall as it is wide; its rich maple finish gleams and the floor-to-ceiling-stained glass windows on its sides shine blue and green, illuminated by a soft glow from inside.

Red inserts a key and pushes the ornate door open, leading me into a foyer that matches the door's grandeur with a maple-stained staircase stretching upward.

The walls are filled with what appear to be old family photos, interspersed with larger oil paintings of lighthouses and ocean scenes. I approach a painting of a dune, gently touching its frame. "This is beautiful."

"It is. Mama Ruby was a painter—famous in the Keys."

Before I can reply, Red continues, "Me, Blair, Noah, Clinton, and Ellis live here, and now you."

"It's amazing."

Wait. Ellis?

My eyes widen, and I clench my fists. "So, do we all share rooms—with guys?" The thought of sharing space with five strangers, including three men—one of whom hates me, makes me shudder.

Red's mouth stays open a moment, laced with confusion, before she registers my concern and responds. "No, no, no. I wouldn't work here if we had to share a home with dirty boys. I like good smells and clean floors, and Noah and Clinton's place is gross." Red scrunches her nose, and relief washes over me. "Girls stay in separate spaces, but we all hang out—guys and girls. Most of the time, it's just on the screened-in porch off the water since it has such a great view."

Thank God.

"Sounds nice," I say, pushing a wayward strand of hair from my face.

"You will love it," Red says, winking as she bites at a thumbnail. "I hope."

"So, where do you stay?"

"Well, the house is divided into four apartments. On the first floor is apartment A—Noah and Clinton's place."

I hold up my hand. "Wait. Who's Clinton?"

"Oh yeah. You didn't meet him. He was out trying to get some shopping done at the twenty-four-hour Kroger. He is Noah and Ellis's best friend from the University of Florida, and he's a Dive Lead here." She steps back and points upward. "Above them is Apartment B, the second-floor apartment where Blair and I live. Then, above us are you and Ellis." She must sense my sudden panic because she quickly adds, "There are two private one-person units on your floor."

"Great," I say, managing an uneasy smile.

"Well, except that you and Ellis share a kitchen."

I can live with that.

"And a bathroom," she adds, "at least temporarily."

Mother of God.

"His bathroom is a disaster—needs a new sink, and the shower doesn't work. Ellis keeps telling everyone he's going to fix it. Noah has offered to do it, but Ellis is being…difficult."

"Okay," I say simply, trying to sound confident.

She moves closer, sensing my unease, and touches my shoulder. "It'll be fine. Promise. Ellis is super clean, like a woman."

"That's good," I say, forcing a smile and trying to be positive.

"And your bathroom has a door that leads to the main hall-way. Just keep both doors locked, and you will be good to go."

I nod appreciatively. I'm genuinely grateful for a place to stay. It's an unexpected blessing.

"What about Charlie, Aki, and JJ?" I ask, examining another oil painting hanging by a grandfather clock. It's of the house before some of the more recent additions.

"JJ and Charlie live towards the street in what was once the in-law suite. JJ hates it, but it's perfect for Charlie since he hates climbing stairs. JJ recently tried to get Dave to let him move into the house, into your apartment, actually, but Dave decided it was best not to let his hormones loose in a house full of girls."

"Seems like a good idea."

"Totally. JJ is harmless, but that kid's a horn-ball, even compared to other guys, and he refuses to think before he speaks."

Red opens a nearby door, revealing a small laundry room. "We all share the laundry room. We just share Tide or whatever is cheapest at Kroger."

"I knew I forgot something," a deep voice says behind me. I turn to see a preppy frat-boy-type with glasses and a handsome grin coming through the front door. He's holding two paper sacks of groceries. "Blair is going to kill me."

"Clinton!" Red squeaks. "The main reason you went tonight was so Blair could wash her clothes for work tomorrow."

Clinton shrugs. "No problem. I can hand wash the hell out of some unmentionables."

A snort of laughter bubbles out of me unexpectedly.

Red walks to his side and smacks his shoulder. "You are a complete doofus, and you better not go through her dirty clothes if you know what's good for you. You know how she likes to do her own laundry."

"I know," Clinton says, hands raised in surrender before turning to me. "Is this the new tenant I heard about?"

Red gestures my way. "Sure is."

Clinton maneuvers around Red, balancing paper sacks in his left hand while extending his right. "I'm Clinton."

I shake his hand awkwardly. "I'm Glory."

Clinton nods approvingly. "Blair texted me earlier to share the news." As he pulls back, he nearly drops a bag, catching it just in time. "Here you go, Red," he says, tossing it to her, which she catches effortlessly.

"It's your stuff," Clinton explains, "but I also went ahead and got Blair a few things, too. Even though she's ignoring me."

"Thanks, kiddo." Red ruffles his dark waves. "You are too good to me. Too good to her, too."

"Never," he says.

Red winks and clicks her tongue. "Hang in there, buddy. She'll come around."

"Yep," Noah suddenly says from the doorway to Apartment A, making me jump. His size is still startling.

"And you met Noah, right?" Red points to the giant filling the door frame.

My eyes widen as I nod. As if I could miss him. "We met on the docks when I met Ellis and Dave."

They all exchange meaningful looks. "Well, I am sure that went over splendidly," Clinton jokes, and I can't help but smile.

"Noah, can you help?" Red nods to the groceries. Noah snaps to attention. "Help. Absolutely." He takes her bag. "I'll take it upstairs, my lady."

"Okay, thanks, babe," she says, patting his stomach.

Noah bends to kiss the top of Red's head. They're complete physical opposites, but their easy affection marks them as an obvious couple.

"Gross," Clinton mock-gags, tongue out and eyes squeezed shut. "Y'all need to keep that behind closed doors."

"Shut it," Noah calls over his shoulder, giving Red one more peck before heading upstairs, taking the steps two at a time. He pauses to look back. "Night, Glory."

"Night," I wave.

"Yuck," Clinton repeats.

Red pinches his cheeks. "Little Clinty…just because you and Blair don't do public affection right now doesn't mean everyone else has to hide behind closed doors."

"Hey!" Clinton sets the second bag on a long table by the door. "First off." He raises one finger. "We don't do any affection." He pauses and shakes his head left and right before adding "unless *she* is in the mood." A second finger joins the first. "Second of all, don't call me Clinty."

"What?" Red cocks her head, a mischievous smile spreading. "Clinty?"

Clinton winces.

"You don't want me to call you…Clinty?"

"No, I don't, Red," Clinton says, smiling despite his wide-eyed mock anger.

"Why?" I join in. "It's a lovely name." Red holds out her hand, and I slap it.

He pushes out his bottom lip at me. "Not you, too."

"Yeah, why, Clinty?" Red teases.

Clinton exhales, his face reddening. "It just sounds too much like…Clitty."

Doubling over, I brace myself on my knees as laughter takes control. Red is beside me, also consumed by giggles.

"What?" Clinton maintains his serious tone, though a smile threatens. "It does sound like *Clitty*."

"Why did you say it again?" Red wheezes between snorts, arms wrapped around her sides.

Red collapses into an old yellow chair. "Clitty?" she shouts, setting us off again.

"What's going on down there?" Noah's deep voice booms

from above. Through tears of laughter, I look up and see him leaning over the railing, grinning.

Red tries to speak, but Clinton shouts, "Nothing! Nothing at all!" He turns to us, whispering, "Please don't give him any ideas. I have to live with him, you know? I wouldn't live it down."

"Fine, fine," Red waves dismissively. "Nothing babe," she says as she looks back up to Noah.

Clinton's head turns towards me. "And you?"

"My lips are sealed, I promise."

He narrows his eyes playfully, clearly doubting us, then he attempts to change the subject. "So, is Glory here going to be up top with E?"

Ellis. I almost forgot.

"Yep. I was just about to tell Glory how lovely the view is."

Clinton laughs, but Red punches him. "Hey!" he says and then gestures upward. "The view is great from up there, sure." He gives me a sidelong glance. "You just have to deal with Ellis."

"Don't scare her," Red warns.

He must sense my nervousness because he shrugs. "Ellis isn't bad, for the most part. I guess it's a good trade-off. You do have the best views."

They stare at me silently, waiting for a response. I force a smile, trying to hide my apprehension, but I've never been good at masking my emotions.

"Why don't we head upstairs, Glory?" Red breaks the awkward silence. "I have to head to work in twenty minutes, and I know you need some sleep." She nods toward Clinton, who's checking his phone with sudden concern.

Red coughs, and he looks up. "Clinton will be around tonight, and so will Noah. If you need anything, they can help. That's their door." She points to a dark brown door marked Apartment A. "If they aren't home, you can generally find some, or all of us, down at the Hut. Several of us work there, and that's where I'll be tonight. Come grab some food if you get hungry."

"Thanks," I say, following her up the stairs. Halfway up, I pause and look back at Clinton, who is still fumbling with the groceries. "Night, Clinton. Nice to meet you."

He points my way. "I'm glad you're here, Glory."

Red and I climb the central staircase to the top floor, passing her and Blair's second-floor apartment—Apartment B—and storage areas along the way. The top staircase opens into a long hallway running the length of the house. Two doors face each other: Apartment C and Apartment D.

"You're just through here," Red says, opening the door to Apartment C, revealing a small but cozy living room. She heads straight to the far wall and pulls a chain, opening floor-to-ceiling blinds.

"Incredible," I breathe as a stunning ocean view unfolds. Even at night, it's breathtaking. I shake my head, rubbing my face with both hands. I still can't believe I'm standing in my own waterfront apartment in the Florida Keys, that costs absolutely nothing.

"Am I dreaming?" I murmur, glancing sideways at Red. "Everything feels off, like a fuzzy memory, but I know it's not. I am actually here and for once, maybe I just got lucky."

"It does seem like a dream sometimes," she says. "I get it. We all must have done something right for God to have blessed us like this."

We stand together, staring into the liquid darkness. A tear of joy slides down my cheek. I turn quickly to wipe it away before Red notices, and as I do, my ankle twists, and I tumble backward over an old light brown loveseat. A sharp pain radiates from my lower back into my arm. My joints and muscles feel stiffer than ever, and the extra-strength Advil has long worn off. I wince as Red leans over, concern etched on her face.

"You okay, Glory?"

I manage a few inches forward before pain forces me back. My shirt rides up against the fabric, and I quickly tug it down.

Please don't let her see the bruises.

I catch Red staring, her face lined with worry, but I don't think she saw anything. I force a smile. "I'm fine. Just been a long ride. I'm a little stiff."

"Thank goodness," Red says. "We can't have you hurt on your first day."

I take a deep breath and stand slowly, using the armrest for leverage. Somehow, standing hurts less than sitting.

"See?" I say. "All better."

Red smiles. "Good." She steps around me, pointing to a short, darkened hallway. "Let me show you the bedroom."

She flips on the light, revealing two entryways, then leads me through the door to my left. "This is the bedroom, fully furnished. The bottom drawer has extra sheets and pillowcases."

I walk in, smiling at the light green walls adorned with hand-drawn fish illustrations. "It's perfect. I love this color, and the art is great." I sit on the bed, another yawn escaping.

Red smiles silently then gestures to the second door behind her. "The bathroom is in here."

Our bathroom.

I lean forward, glimpsing the long space with its double vanities.

"The water pressure is fantastic," Red winks.

"A shower sounds so nice," I say before a yawn interrupts my train of thought.

Red watches from the doorway. "I know you're exhausted, so why don't I head out, and you take it easy? Do you want me to bring you something to eat, a sandwich or maybe some fries?"

I rub my stomach, but the comfort of a soft bed calls louder.

"No thanks. I'll come down if I get hungry. I think I just need to rest."

"Sounds like a plan. The kitchen closes at eleven, but the bar is open until 1 am. I'm behind the bar tonight, so I can get you some cold stuff, like sandwiches, if you wake up hungry and we're still open."

"That sounds amazing."

We walk back to the front door. "You are going to love it here," Red says. "I promise."

"I am. I mean, I already do. It just feels so comfortable."

Red nods then starts to leave but stops. "Almost forgot to mention. The kitchen is at the end of the hall," she says, pointing. "But I guarantee there is absolutely no food in there, knowing Ellis."

I peek out, spotting the door. "I might wait to check it out until tomorrow."

"Sounds like a plan." Red hugs me quickly. "Let's plan to meet at the dive shop at 7 AM. We generally get an early start around here, but we do get off early, too, which makes up for it. Sleep can get a bit scarce at times, but all in all, it's not bad, especially if you like to nap, like I do."

"Sounds good."

Red nods and turns toward the stairs. "See you then, Glory." She waves as she descends, leaving me alone outside my new apartment.

I take a deep breath, rub my face, and exhale slowly. Closing my eyes, I whisper a prayer of gratitude: "Thank you, God. Earlier this morning, I was standing in the counseling center lobby. I was broken and hurt, and I had lost all hope. Now look at me." I think back to what Red said. I do feel blessed to be here at Dave's, but do I deserve it? I also can't help but consider whether I deserved Nick.

Back in the bedroom, I practically collapse onto the bed.

Turning on my side, I pull my arm under my head as a pillow. Through the window, I watch hints of palm fronds swaying in the breeze and listen to a symphony of crickets that seem to be singing me to sleep.

Chapter 6

I wake up gasping for air.

My eyes dart around the dark, unfamiliar room as I struggle to remember where I am. My hair is a tangled mess; my shirt is drenched in sweat.

A nightmare.

I still feel myself falling, rolling down the steps as Nick laughs from above. I can feel my head slam into the concrete.

Sitting up, I reach for the throbbing bruise hidden within my hairline. The room is pitch black except for a hint of moonlight. I fumble for the bedside lamp, relief flooding through me as soft yellow light chases away the shadows.

Nick's intrusive voice invades my thoughts: "Get up bitch! Quit fucking around! Quit pretending! You just want attention!"

"Calm down, Glory," I whisper, squeezing my eyes shut to stifle them.

After a moment, my breathing steadies. I fall back onto the bed, staring at the ceiling as the window air conditioner clicks on, pushing cool air across my sweat-dampened skin. I reach for my phone, lying half off the far side of the bed, probably kicked there during the nightmare.

10:45 PM.

Rising unsteadily, I make my way to the living room. Everything is eerily quiet as moonlight streams in through the large windows. After a lingering yawn, I study the dark ocean for a moment before moving to the front door. I press my ear against its cold surface. I'm uneasy in these new surroundings, which has exacerbated my habitual need to be on guard.

Nothing.

I peer through the peephole.

Nothing.

Slowly, I unlatch the deadbolt and open the door, looking left and right.

Nothing.

My stomach rumbles as my gaze fixes on the door at the end of the hall…the shared kitchen.

I slip into the hallway and approach the kitchen door, easing it open. My hand finds the light switch in the darkness, and an industrial fluorescent fixture flickers reluctantly to life, revealing a small galley kitchen. I step inside quietly.

The space is surprisingly clean and even pleasant-smelling. A bowl of fresh fruit, filled with apples, oranges, and one very ripe banana, sits beside the fridge and small oven.

To the other side, a sink and dishwasher are flanked by counter space. Wooden blinds cover the window above the sink, blocking any view outside. At the far end stands a small two-seat table along the wall and two doorless cabinets serving as a pantry, virtually empty except for what looks like some basic spices and a half bag of sugar.

Beyond the table, a closed door with a deadbolt catches my attention. I study it briefly before stepping forward and opening the fridge carefully, mindful of noise in case Ellis is in his apartment. I expect to find snacks, some drinks maybe, but I only find an out-of-date box of baking powder and a half-empty jar of pickles. I'll need to stock up on essentials if I plan to cook, which I do. Eating out isn't a luxury I can afford, and I can't entirely rely on free meals from Dave's.

I walk back to the kitchen entry, but before switching off the light, I glance again at the mystery door once more. Maybe it leads to Ellis's place.

Back in my bedroom, I grab my old blue Jansport from beside the bed, its surface still covered in ink doodles from high school. Everything I own is in this bag. In my rush to escape Nick, I'd only grabbed the essentials. I didn't have much to begin with though.

After pulling on the sweatshirt and jeans, I return to the window. Tiny lights bob on the horizon where boats rest at anchor. Further out, large shrimping vessels move slowly out to sea.

I shut off the air conditioner and listen. Faint music and laughter drift from the direction of the Hut. My stomach growls again at the thought of food. "Hold on," I murmur, rubbing it.

Remembering Charlie and Red's invitation, and given the empty kitchen and the late hour that rules out grocery shopping, I decide the tiki bar—I mean the Hut—is my best option.

I ease into the hallway, pausing to listen for movement in the house. I only hear a muffled television from below, probably the guys.

Descending past Red and Blair's floor to the empty foyer, I slip out to the patio and follow the sandy path toward the main resort. As I approach, music and laughter grow louder. I round the final corner, then walk behind the shop and towards the condos. Stepping on the well-manicured lawn of the resort, I stop as I spot the Hut in the distance, multicolored lights standing out in the dimly lit landscape.

As I approach, I notice how the Hut has transformed. Instead of scattered customers sipping frozen drinks over quiet conversation, the bar is packed with college-aged revelers smiling, laughing, and even dancing. A live musician sings a Jimmy Buffet song, his gear set up along the perimeter of what appears to be a beach volleyball court that I had not noticed before. It's a completely different scene, and I absolutely love it.

I move forward cautiously, unable to hide my intrigue. At the bar, Red is putting on a show, tossing liquor bottles high in the air with graceful precision, drawing cheers from the crowd. I slip into a small gap at the bar where there are a pair of empty bar stools. I also see Blair sitting ten or so seats away, head buried in a book. I turn outward and rest my elbows on the bar behind me. The grassy expanse leading to the sea wall stretches before me, and to one side, opposite the band and volleyball court, groups cluster around a sandy horseshoe pit, beers in hand. Everyone radiates joy.

Red's voice sounds behind me, so I turn to catch her attention. As I do, my smile falters—Ellis rises from behind the bar, two cartons of Piña Colada in his hands. His own smile vanishes as our eyes meet.

Shit.

His dark stare holds my attention momentarily before he turns away and resumes his earlier laughter as if I'm invisible. I watch him approach a group of girls with matching platinum blonde hair and identical silver sorority necklaces.

As I turn away, one of the Greeks catches me looking and squeals, pointing. "Oh my God, Ellis, look at that girl."

Ellis turns in my direction, frowning once more.

"You are so cute," another girl says to me before turning to whisper into the first girl's ear. They're mocking me, but I ignore them. Maybe if I don't engage, they'll lose interest.

"Do you have a crush on him or something?" someone says, but I am not sure who.

"Nope," I say flatly to no one specifically, eyes darting now for escape routes.

"Right," Ellis interjects, and I shoot him a glare. A smirk

flashes across his beautiful face before he whispers something to the girls that makes them giggle.

"Oh, man!" the tallest girl looks directly at me and crows, disrupting the group's laughter. "I am so sorry, but he doesn't date girls who don't know how to dress." Her Southern accent drips like honey. This must be the Regina George of the crew. "You do realize this is the Florida Keys, right?" She feigns genuine concern before picking up her Moscow Mule for another sip.

"Oh, leave her alone, Trish, she doesn't seem right…you know, in the head," an accomplice adds.

The evil one has a name. *Trish.*

I glance down at my clothes briefly, then between Trish and Ellis. The ridiculousness of my outfit in this climate hits me, and I flush with embarrassment. Though they have a point, embarrassed or not, I can't wear shorts and a tee—not with the bruising.

"Trust me when I tell you that something is definitely not right," Ellis says, wearing a slight smile as he watches their attack. He's enjoying this.

I shake my head. I'm too exhausted to fight back; besides, I'm not a fighter. I start to turn but feel a soft hand on my arm that stops me.

Red.

She surveys the scene, eyes moving between Ellis, the girls, and my expression. She holds up one finger. "Just a minute, babe." Looking over her shoulder, she tilts her chin toward Blair, still reading. "Blair, hun? Can we get a little BB over here?"

"BB?" I whisper.

"Bitch back-up," Red explains, adding a small cough.

I raise my hands frantically. "No, don't. Really. It's no big deal."

Blair looks up from her book as if she heard a plea for help. Her eyes dart to Red and me, and Red motions toward Ellis and the Greeks. Her mouth pulls into something fierce, so I know things have escalated beyond my control.

Red squeezes my arm, sensing my unease. "It's okay. This kind of thing happens a lot. It comes with the territory."

"But I don't want to start anything."

"Oh, honey. You didn't do anything. This family sticks together, or we'll get a bad reputation, and the next thing you know, all the crazies will be visiting this resort. We have to make sure people respect us, respect you."

I watch wide-eyed as Blair marks her place, sets down her book, and approaches Red's side like a shark that's caught the scent of blood. She positions herself between Ellis and me, and Ellis's expression darkens, jaw tightening as he frowns and shakes his head. "Everything's okay, Blair. You don't need to come over and—"

"Shh," Blair says as she reaches out and presses a finger to his lips, instantly quieting him. Ellis rolls his eyes but doesn't move. They stand like that for a couple of moments before Ellis shrugs, and Blair's finger rises in the air and becomes one palm of two that come together with a loud *POP!*

The bar falls silent. Even the music scratches to a halt. She spins once, then stops to face Ellis and Trish. "Listen up, Ellis and his sorority entourage." She leans towards Trish, eyes locked. "You all better shut the hell up and watch how you speak to people who work here, or I am going to go crazy redneck bitch on all of you."

She points at the girls and Ellis then turns to address the whole bar. She's downright terrifying. I see an older gentleman, quite large, slowly back away from the bar. I hear someone else mutter "*day-um*" in a hushed tone to my left.

Ellis starts to speak, but Blair cuts him off. "And you just be quiet." Her finger darts down and connects with his nose, making him flinch. It would be funny if Blair weren't so serious.

"You ought to be ashamed of yourself for letting these college ho-bags bully her around. You might be mad, Ellis, but it's not her fault." Blair points towards me and then continues. "And she works here; she's family, whether you like it or not."

"You don't—" Ellis starts to object but is cut off immediately.

"Nope, Ellis." Blair closes her eyes, breathing deeply through her nose. "Just nope. This can't happen. You know better."

Trish snorts. "Who are you calling—"

"These are the same types that visit here every year," Blair talks over Trish dismissively. "Now *you know* that you have the opportunity to do better than this." She points palm up to Trish.

"Excuse me?" Trish cocks her head, leaning forward on the bar, pushing her enhanced cleavage together between her arms. Ellis's eyes predictably drop.

"Shut up, bitch," Blair says flatly without sparing her a glance. She smacks Ellis's shoulder, pointing at me again. "We stick together."

"Who are you calling a bitch, bitch?" Trish rolls her eyes, forcing a nervous laugh. Her friends remain quiet, not as brazen.

My jaw drops as Blair steps around Ellis and slams her hands on the bar so hard everyone jumps, including Ellis.

"Could you please get your ugly fake tits off my bar, *bitch*?" Blair asks Trish, who recoils in shock.

"Come on, Blair," Ellis mutters, barely concealing a laugh.

"Just be quiet," Blair snaps.

The sorority girls freeze, uncertain. When Trish opens her mouth again, Blair cuts her off: "Just give me one more fucking reason to bust your crooked nose." Trish's hand flies to her nose as she looks at her friends in confusion. When no one comes to her aid, Trish looks genuinely shocked.

Score another one for Blair.

Trish turns towards Blair and puffs up her chest as if to respond, but her courage falters when she meets Blair's eyes. I understand why—Blair's eyes hold a dangerous gleam as if she's hoping for an excuse to smack Trish.

"I told you she's a good person to have in your corner," Red whispers to me, and I nod slowly, bringing my hand up to cover a slight smile that has crept up.

"Why is she defending me?" I whisper back. "She doesn't even know me."

"You're one of us, Glory, and Dave's girls stick together. It's an unbreakable rule."

"Unbreakable?"

"Unbreakable."

I catch Ellis watching our exchange. He grits his teeth, scowling. He's clearly unhappy that Red and Blair are in my corner.

Blair continues with the last word as she leans on the bar, fists clenched. "If you hang at this bar, Dave's bar, including you," she points at Ellis, who rolls his eyes but gives a slight nod, "you best keep your Mean Girls shit in check. There's enough dick to go around for all you whores."

The bar bursts out in laughter and holding back from joining in physically hurts. Red seems equally strained, lips pressed tight, eyes watering. I bury my face in my hands, and though I feel Ellis staring, I force myself not to speak.

After a moment, the sorority girls stand silent, exchanging uncertain glances. Even Trish doesn't dare speak.

Satisfied by their silence, Blair nods and returns to her seat, where she resumes her romance novel and sips on a blue martini as if nothing happened. The music starts back up, screeching to life a moment later, followed by the resumption of normal bar chatter and activity.

"That a girl," comes a wobbly male voice from nearby. I lean forward to see Clinton grinning at Blair from a few seats over. He must have arrived at the bar just in time to see the exchange.

"Shut it, Clinton Crosby," Blair shouts, pointing while sipping her drink.

Ellis flips Clinton off and turns back to the blondes, apparently smoothing things over because he soon has them all laughing again and leaning into his presence.

Note to self: Ellis is a first-class charmer.

"Blair's the unofficial bouncer around here," Red says, mixing an orange drink in front of me.

"And she's hotter than brimstone when she's angry," Clinton adds, moving to squeeze onto the stool beside me. "So sexy."

"I appreciate her help," I say softly. "I had a nap but woke up starving. I was hoping to grab something to eat."

Red bites her lip thoughtfully. "Let me go and see what Aki has in the back."

"Thanks," I say as she bounces away. I turn to Clinton just as he downs a bright green shot, grimacing.

"Good God, that's nasty," he says, shaking his head and pursing lips back and forth.

"What is it?" I ask.

"The Green Octopus."

"Sounds interesting."

"The name's the hook, Glory. It tastes terrible. But then again, all of Ellis's drink specials suck."

I glance over as Ellis tosses a bottle, catching it smoothly before his adoring audience. Though he's a complete ass, the way he moves does something to my stomach.

"It's not you," Clinton says, catching me staring. "It's the situation."

"I hope not," I murmur, though I'm not sure what he means by *situation.*

"Nope," Clinton slurs without hesitation. "It's not you at all. It's definitely the situation." Clinton grabs an empty shot glass and sets it before me, raising his hand. "Have a drink."

I stare at the empty glass, confused, as Clinton calls out, "Ellis! Shots for Glory and me!"

Ellis turns abruptly and shakes his head.

"See," I say. "He hates me."

"Nope. He just doesn't want me to drink anymore." Clinton inverts his glass. "It's been a bad night, so I'm drinking away my troubles. He's right."

"Is everything okay?"

Clinton doesn't answer, but sadness flashes across his face as he stares towards Blair.

Red returns with a to-go bag and interrupts the exchange. "Does a turkey sandwich and fries work?"

My eyes light up. "Perfect!" I haven't eaten all day, so I couldn't be more grateful. A yawn escapes. "I better get back, or I might fall asleep on this bar."

"Go relax and enjoy the sandwich," Red says. "We'll see you in the morning."

"Good idea," I say as I start away from the bar before stopping and looking back. "Tell Blair thanks. I'm not used to people sticking up for me."

"Will do," Clinton says as he lifts his empty glass. Red only nods, her head tilted slightly as if pondering the story behind my comment.

When I reach the front porch, the sandwich and most of the fries are gone, and as soon as I am upstairs, I toss out the food and then collapse on the couch. I take a steadying breath and marvel inwardly at how the Keys—at least Dave's—smells of citrus.

I close my eyes just as thunder sounds in the distance. By the time the rain starts, I'm sound asleep.

CHAPTER 7

THUMP.

"What's that sound?" I mutter, squinting into the darkness from the couch.

Thump.

I fumble for my phone. 12:42 AM.

Thump. Thump.

I rub my eyes and sit up, listening as the sounds grow more frequent and insistent. Nick's image flashes unbidden in my mind, and my heart thunders in response.

Thump.

The sound is coming from outside my apartment door.

I approach slowly, pausing to press my ear against its surface. A whisper drifts through the wood, too faint to make out.

I peer through the peephole.

Nothing.

"Just open the door," I say softly to myself.

With trembling fingers, I engage the security chain before turning the deadbolt. The door opens a couple of inches before catching on the chain.

I lean forward to scan the hallway. Large, masculine legs extend from someone seated to my left. Even through the narrow gap, I can tell it's not Nick—these legs are tan and athletic, nothing like his stocky limbs. Relief floods through me as my heartbeat steadies. After a moment, I watch as a foot lifts, hovers in the air for a moment, then drops.

Thump.

"Hello?" I call softly. No response.

I unlatch the chain and ease the door wider, but it catches on something. Bracing myself, I push harder.

"Ouch!" a deep voice protests.

Shit.

With the door halfway open, I step into the hall and see Ellis sprawled against the wall, rubbing his forehead with one hand while clutching a half-empty bottle of Jack with the other. His hair is wet, and his shirt is stained with grass and sand as if he's face-planted down a hill.

"Are you okay?"

"What?" he growls without looking up.

"Are you okay? You look like you fell." The reek of alcohol hits me, and I cringe. "Are you drunk?" The question slips out needlessly—he's clearly beyond drunk. I brace for hostility, but he just sighs as he runs a hand over his face and the back of his head. I pray I haven't given him a concussion.

"Why did you go and do that?" Ellis whines, looking up with one eye squeezed shut.

I step into the hallway and crouch to his level. "Sorry. Are you okay?"

"It hurts," he says, glancing between me and his leg.

Following his gaze, I see that his shorts are pulled high, revealing a series of deep scrapes along his thigh.

"Shit," I say as I reach instinctively to examine the wound, turning his leg without his consent. Big mistake. His eyes darken as he jerks his leg forward and out of my hand, causing me to stumble.

"Don't touch me," he snarls.

"Sorry. I just—"

"I...I don't need anybody's help—I don't need *your* help."

I raise my hands in surrender. "Okay, fine. Sorry." But as I start to stand, his fingers encircle my wrist. His eyes hold conflict.

"It hurts," he repeats.

I look back at his leg. "Well, let me help you clean it at least, and—"

He slaps his thigh sharply, making me flinch.

"Not my leg." He says softly through what must be a hideous sting. "Not my leg, Glory." Taking my hand, he presses it to his chest, just above his heart.

"I hurt here."

I stare at our joined hands. His grip is gentle, his chest radiating heat beneath my palm. I can feel his heartbeat—slow, dull, mournful. Biting my lip, I wonder what could cause such pain in someone so seemingly untouchable.

"Why do you have to torture me?" he blurts out. I blink in confusion as he releases my hand, letting it fall into his lap near his crotch.

I jerk my hand back and look away, fighting the blush spreading across my cheeks.

"Why do *you* have to torture me?" he demands, his voice louder and gravelly. His eyes bore into my profile, waiting for an answer.

"I don't know what you're talking about, Ellis," I say. "I'm not trying to hurt you," I add after a moment.

I've known you for less than a day. Why do you hate me so much?

Glancing over, I watch him exhale in annoyance and let his head fall back against the wall. His mouth hangs open as if catching flies. And again, he lifts his leg and lets it drop.

Thump.

After a minute of stillness, I lean in to check his breathing. His rank exhale hits me full force, making me recoil.

Drunk breath...yuck.

His head wobbles as he starts sliding down the wall, catching himself with one arm to push himself upright. His eyes flutter open as his shirt rides up, revealing an impossibly perfect abdomen. How can someone this drunk look this good? Bad breath aside, Ellis is infuriatingly attractive.

"What are you looking at?" he slurs.

I ignore him, gesturing toward his apartment. "Ellis, you should get up and go to bed. Please."

He rolls his head, mumbling something unintelligible before toppling sideways across my feet.

"No, no," I say, and then poke him with my index finger. "You need to sit up, Ellis."

I grab his hand and use my body weight to haul him upright. Ellis is built like an NFL quarterback, lean but solid, so it takes considerable effort to sit him upright.

His head lolls back as his eyes open. "I'm going to forget everything. I'm going to forget you," he murmurs.

"Forget who?" I reach down instinctively and brush the hair from his eyes. This time, he doesn't flinch at my touch.

I notice a glint of metal as his keys peek out from his pocket. An opportunity…

"Can't have you driving," I mutter, carefully gripping his key ring. As I tug it free, I lose my balance and land hard. "Damn," I scramble up, cheeks burning.

Ellis reaches vaguely in my direction before his arm drops. "Give me back my keys. I need to get out of here. It hurts too bad to be here, to be here with you."

"No," I whisper, finding a tiny sliver of courage as I stand.

He grunts, attempting to push up before sliding back down, and then he jabs an unsteady finger at me. "You don't belong here. We don't need another Dive Lead. He's just doing this to push her away." He frowns and shifts until he is more upright.

I don't respond, and we stare at each other in silence until

Ellis abruptly erupts in laughter. The genuine laughter echoes through the hall, and through the commotion, he manages to stand by clinging to my door frame.

As he does, I retreat, ready to bolt if he lunges. I don't care if he insults me, but I won't let him have his keys.

He takes a step forward, and I flinch as my hands dart up in front of my face. After a moment, I lower them and open my eyes. Ellis has taken a step back and cocked his head sideways in confusion.

"I'm not going to hurt you," he says condescendingly, raising his hands. "Calm down, drama queen."

Drama queen. Is that what people will call me?

I flush with embarrassment. Though I truly believe Ellis won't hurt me, it doesn't matter. I can't control how my body reacts. I'm broken—like an animal beaten into submission. I wipe away a tear before it can fall. I want to explain my reaction, but instead, I ask, "Why do you hate me?"

Ellis opens his mouth but stops, focusing on something behind me. I turn to find Red and Noah in the hallway.

"Damn it, Ellis," Noah says as he steps forward and helps prop up his friend, disappointment etched across his face.

Red follows. "You okay up here, Glory?"

I nod as Ellis's chin drops to his chest.

Noah shakes him. "Wake up, dude."

Ellis mumbles and then leans into Noah's side.

"What's wrong with him?" I can't help asking. "He just seems so...sad."

Red nods solemnly. "He's had a rough couple of years."

"That's not an excuse for this," Noah stands, frowning at Red.

"It's not, Hun. You're right."

Noah exhales deeply. "Thanks for putting up with this jackass, Glory." He looks down at Ellis, who seems to have fallen asleep standing against Noah's side.

"Yeah, thank you," Red echoes.

"He can't keep doing this shit," Noah says. "Clinton and I are going to talk to him tomorrow."

"Whatever," Ellis mumbles, rolling his head up for a moment before letting it fall back into Noah's side.

I remember that I have the keys, so I hand them to Red. "We appreciate you checking on him, Glory," she says. "It makes us feel better knowing you're up top with him. We wouldn't have even known he was up here if we hadn't heard you talking to him."

"We all try to keep an eye on him," Noah says. "Appreciate your stepping up tonight to help us out."

"Had you not been here, no telling what would have happened," Red adds. "The possibilities are endless."

Noah nods in agreement. "Danger tends to follow Ellis these days."

I pinch the bridge of my nose as questions swirl through my mind: What happened to make Ellis this way? What was he like before this, and most importantly, what caused him to take this dark turn?

Noah hauls Ellis forward with one arm supporting him. Red and I watch in silence as Noah opens Ellis's door, and they march into the darkness of his apartment.

I turn back towards Red just as she steps to the side and peers into my apartment. "How are you liking it?"

"It's great," I say as I walk past her and pick up the blanket that had fallen on the floor. "I guess I will try to go back to bed."

"Sounds good," she says. "Night, Glory." She starts to pull the door closed but stops and turns back towards me. "I know we were going to meet after seven, but would you be interested in joining us for breakfast beforehand?"

My eyebrows rise as I yawn. "When?"

Red smiles as she checks her watch. "In about five hours, at six-thirty? We all meet on the screened porch every morning to watch the sunrise, eat breakfast, and nurse several cups of coffee. It's hard to get used to, but it's a wonderful way to start the day. We generally bring our own breakfast, but sometimes one of us will splurge and bring something to share."

"That sounds amazing," I say, bewildered by how closeknit everyone seems to be.

"We have good coffee, too. Every now and then, one of us will grab coffee for everyone from Big Jaws Joe down the road."

"Love me some Big Jaws," Noah confirms, appearing beside Red.

"Everyone comes, except when it is raining, or someone is sick." She turns to Noah. "Will he be okay?"

"Yeah." Noah grins. "He is fast asleep."

She nods and then faces me. "No worries if you would rather catch up on sleep. Just know that you are always invited."

I've always been an early riser, and it would be a great chance to get to know everyone. I love breakfast food, just like Dad.

"Okay," I agree before I can change my mind.

"Great!" Red beams as Noah nods approvingly.

"I'm going to stay up here," Noah tells Red, kissing her temple.

"Okay," she says, standing on her tiptoes to kiss Noah's cheek.

"Night, y'all." He offers a wave then disappears back into Ellis's apartment.

Red steps back with a small wave in response. "Thanks again, Glory. See you in…" she checks her watch, "four hours and fifty-two minutes."

"Sounds good," I manage through another yawn.

Chapter 8

I open my eyes and reach for the phone—5 AM. Nick's been busy—two more missed calls and three texts. I fight the urge to check them. Part of me desperately wants to know what he's saying, but I can't bring myself to look. He's either threatening me and calling me every name in the book or turning on the charm with flowing apologies.

In the bathroom, I search for signs of Ellis. The space is small but remarkably clean for a shared bathroom, especially one a guy uses. I open cabinet doors and the small, mirrored medicine cabinet, but find nothing. No manly deodorant, old blue toothbrush, or Irish Spring soap. The bathroom is empty.

I lock the door leading to the main hallway—Ellis's entrance. The last thing I need is someone walking in on me, especially him.

Running a comb through my tangled mess of hair, I apply lotion and brush my teeth. The mirror reflects back dark circles under my eyes, and I hardly recognize myself.

"Jesus, Glory," I whisper. "You look like death."

And I do—like someone beaten down, both literally and figuratively.

After dabbing on lip gloss, I pull my hair into a ponytail and head back to change into navy sweats and a simple white long-sleeved shirt.

My stomach rumbles as I lace up my old sneakers. I need coffee, lots of coffee, and…pancakes.

The clock reads 5:15 AM, just over an hour before I meet everyone on the porch. An idea forms and I grab the keys from the dresser. I quietly leave the house and make my way across the resort towards my truck. The morning air is chilly and fresh. I can still hear the soft buzz of the evening insects, but they are joined sporadically by a bird's song, calling out in cheerful anticipation of the morning sun.

Thirty minutes later, I'm back in the kitchen with two bags from the twenty-four-hour Kroger. Though money is tight, the act is worth it to show everyone that I'm a team player, and with Ellis nursing his hangover, I should have the kitchen to myself.

Dad's world-class pancake recipe comes together quickly, and soon, I have a cookie sheet covered in stacks of crispy, thin pancakes. After heating syrup in the microwave and gathering some paper plates and forks, which I find in the cabinets, I have five minutes to spare.

I descend two flights of stairs, carefully balancing everything on the pan. I walk down the central hallway, which stretches toward the water, then push forward through the door at the end of the hall, which I correctly assume is the porch.

Noah and Red are already there, tangled together on a long wicker couch, Noah's legs dangling off the sides as Red snores into his chest.

Noah raises his hand in silent greeting, eyebrows dancing at the sight of the pancakes. I set everything on the small glass table in the center of the porch.

"Are those pancakes?" Clinton says as he appears behind me.

"Duh," comes a dry voice from my right that startles me. I hadn't noticed Blair huddled nearly invisible under a blanket in a brown chair, clutching what appears to be another romance novel. She shakes her head side to side curtly and then looks towards me. "Master of the obvious."

"What?" Clinton says as he walks over to Blair, reaches into his pocket, and opens his hand. "Breath mints. Just for you."

"Dumbass," Blair mutters without looking up.

Clinton laughs and then raises an excited finger in her direction. "Guess what else I brought?" he says as he spins and rushes back inside. The others ignore his antics, and I'm learning that Clinton is a bit of a goofball.

Moments later, he struts back out with two large cup holders of drinks. Big Jaws Joe is written along the cups' sides. "You love me now?"

Blair sniffs the air, confusion melting into a radiant smile. "I do!" She jumps up, diving for a coffee.

Clinton lifts the trays high out of reach—his six-foot-three frame giving him quite the advantage.

"Wait one minute there, B. Don't you owe me something? A kiss, perhaps?"

Blair's smile vanishes into a scowl. She raises a threatening fist. "Don't mess with me, buddy." Her other hand extends. "Coffee. Now."

Clinton laughs, lowering the drinks. "Guess which one is yours?"

Blair inspects the writing on each cup, including one marked 'Glory.' She pulls out a drink with 'My one true love' written in pink bubble letters.

"Yes! Correct!" Clinton celebrates as if winning a secret victory.

"You wish," Blair mumbles, turning her attention to the pancakes.

"Get a room already!" JJ calls as he pushes through the door. He nods suspiciously towards me before the food captures his attention. "What the hell is this?" he says as he reaches forward and grabs a stack with one hand, cramming it into his mouth.

He pauses mid-chew and winks at me in thanks after he realizes I made them.

"Manners," Blair says dryly before standing and placing a short stack on a plate with a modest drizzle of syrup. "You definitely scored some cool points today, Glory. Thank you."

"What am I smelling?" Red sits up suddenly, rubbing sleep from her eyes. "Pancakes and Big Jaws? Am I in heaven?"

"And I see an angel," Clinton says as he teasingly grins at Blair, waggling his eyebrows. She peers at him over her coffee cup, eyes rolling.

"You have to quit saying shit like that," Noah rumbles, interrupting.

"Cheese, Clinton," Blair says between sips.

"You love it, Blair. Just admit it, and your life will be complete."

Blair waves dismissively, ignoring him.

Red, Clinton, and Noah fix their plates before Clinton and JJ settle on a couch in front of an old box TV. Clinton flips a switch while JJ powers up an old model PlayStation.

"Boys and their video games," Red sighs at my watching.

I angle my wooden chair for an ocean view. The sun rises in the east, making cobalt waters sparkle across the horizon. "Thanks for the coffee," I tell Clinton.

He looks up, smiling. "No problem at all. Especially since you made those incredible pancakes for us."

"Seriously, G," Noah mumbles around a mouthful. "These are incredible. I haven't had any this good in a long time."

Red nods enthusiastically. "Delicious!"

"Thanks, y'all. It's my dad's recipe."

"Of course, waking up is so much easier when you have something beautiful waiting for you," Clinton says. I look up and catch him staring at Blair over his coffee.

"Cheese," Red singsongs while Blair steadfastly ignores him, focused on her book between bites.

Clinton is clearly a flirt and has a special interest in Blair. It is also clear that Blair isn't interested in him, or at least she's pretending not to be.

"Too much PDA this early in the morning," a voice behind me nearly makes me drop my plate. Ellis stands in the doorway, watching Noah and Red whisper and giggle.

He strolls in wearing bright blue board shorts and a thin yellow tee and completely ignores me. Despite being drunk hours ago, he looks remarkably composed.

He loads a plate and sits directly across from me, his leg brushing mine. Though he must know I'm here, he keeps his face down, focused entirely on his food.

"So, Glory, where are you from?" Clinton asks. I flush as Ellis's eyes dart up, seemingly interested. Our gazes lock briefly before he returns to his plate, stabbing pancakes and soaking up excess syrup. He shares my fondness for syrup.

"I'm from Texas," I say then smile tightlipped.

"They must have good pancakes in Texas," Clinton jokes.

"They did until Glory left," Noah adds with a thumbs up.

Ellis stops chewing, staring at his plate as if lost in thought. He cocks his head toward Red. "I thought you made these."

"Nope," Red says, "Glory made 'em. Her dad's recipe. Great, aren't they?"

Blair looks up, winking at me. "Pancakes are Ellis's favorite food."

I offer Ellis a small smile. "Glad you like them."

Ellis stands abruptly, stretching an arm high to reveal a strip of skin above his waistband.

Do. Not. Look.

"Who said I like them?" he says as he walks to the trash, knocking his food in with one sharp smack. Our eyes meet, and I hold his cold stare momentarily before standing and moving to the back of the porch, where I sit on a long porch swing that overlooks the water.

He is not worth it.

"You're an asshole, Ellis," Red whispers to him, but I pretend not to notice and stay focused on the view.

As a hushed conversation continues behind me, I'm lost in the water, watching sunlight paint the surface in shades of green, orange, red, purple, and blue between whitecaps. I smile at a sudden thought. "You know, it does kind of look like a big bowl of rainbow Jell-O."

Turning back after a moment, I find everyone staring. Ellis has gone pale.

"What did you say?" he asks softly.

I glance around at their faces. "What? It does."

Ellis doesn't respond but instead walks abruptly back into the house.

"Well, that was interesting," Red says before looking in my direction. "Sorry, Glory. He will come around." The others take turns nodding in agreement, though I can't tell if they really believe he will.

I hold up my hand. "No worries," I lie.

After ten or so minutes of silence, except for the clicks of the game controllers, Red stands. "Do you want to meet at the dive shop in like thirty minutes?" she asks.

"Sure," I say simply as my mind races to analyze the highs and lows of my first morning at Dave's.

Chapter 9

Ten minutes later, I'm in the bathroom studying my reflection. Bruises map my body. I touch my left side gently—they've faded some but seeing them still makes me cringe.

I turn the shower on as hot as I can stand before stepping into the pounding stream. The warm steam fills the room, and I moan softly as the hot water makes my scrapes tingle with pain. It's a temporary discomfort that I'm willing to bear for the long-term benefit of my injured muscles.

Through the pain, my mind drifts back to the porch, to Ellis. I hope I made a good impression on everyone, at least everyone not named Ellis and—

"Are you going to get out of there this year?" a deep male voice suddenly calls from beyond the curtain.

Nick.

I jump with a high-pitched squeal. Frantically backing away from the curtain, I slip on the slick tub. My hands catch the shower curtain as I fall forward and land hard against something solid—someone. I scream again as Nick's face flashes through my mind.

He found me.

"What the hell?!" comes a voice—not Nick's. A large body rolls out from under me causing my butt to hit the hard tile floor with a thud.

"Ouch!" I say as I look up to find a frustrated, shirtless Ellis. *I forgot the deadbolt.*

"What the hell was that?" Ellis throws his arms up, moaning as he rubs his lower back. "You about broke my back, you know?"

I stare at him, speechless. Ellis just walked in on me! Why is he angry? But my anger fades as fast as it comes, overwhelmed by relief that it's not Nick. For a moment, I even forget that I'm naked on the floor, wrapped in nothing but thin, opaque plastic and—

Shit! I'm naked!

In a chaotic haze, I pull the curtain tighter, ignoring the tender spot I hit under my left breast.

"What the hell happened there?" Ellis says abruptly, his head cocking sideways as he studies my right shoulder.

I flush, realizing what he's seen. After the fall down the stairs, my arms had taken the worst of the bruising. I'd wrapped them around my head protectively as I tumbled, which saved my face but left my arms a mottled mess. The lemon-sized brown mark on my shoulder is just one of many, but thankfully, he cannot see the others.

I tuck my arm under the curtain. "I'm a klutz." I force a giggle, a stupid sound, then ready myself to counter his response with another excuse. Excuses are the twisted cry of a battered woman.

Concern flickers across his face then gives way to acceptance as he shakes his head, exhaling sharply. "Whatever," he mutters as he stands slowly and walks to the sink. He pulls on a white undershirt and removes his toothbrush from a small black bag.

I gape at him. Is he just going to brush his teeth? He hasn't even offered to help me up. Sensing my annoyance, he smirks at me through the mirror. He's deliberately being irritating.

"You could have waited until I got out or knocked," I say sharply. "You scared me to death. And now look at me." I gesture with one hand. "But you know what the worst part is, Ellis?"

He rolls his eyes dramatically in the mirror before turning to wipe his mouth with his shirt. "What?" he asks, clearly disinterested.

"You haven't even bothered to help me up."

"Maybe I'm not a gentleman," he says without missing a beat.

"Ha!" I nearly snort. "Maybe?"

Ellis's smile falters as he points a finger, twirling it. "This is actually a shared bathroom, princess."

"Don't call me that," I say, closing my eyes. I'm losing my temper—it reminds me too much of Nick. I can't let myself become him. I take a steadying breath. "When is your bathroom supposed to be fixed?"

Ellis shrugs. "How would I know? Ask Dave."

"Fine."

"I'm not in a hurry to get it fixed, especially now." He winks before turning back to floss, humming an infuriating little tune.

This guy is so irritating.

I grit my teeth and pull myself up, getting to one knee. Ellis watches through the mirror, floss dangling from his mouth.

"Could you stop gawking at me?" I snap. "A little privacy would be nice so I can get up off the floor."

His eyes drop in something akin to shame before looking away silently. I use the moment to push up on my other knee, keeping the curtain tight around my chest. As I start to stand, my eyes catch on Ellis's shapely backside in his terry cloth shorts. It's infuriating how attractive he is. Why would God give this dickhead the long, lean body of an Olympic swimmer?

A forced cough draws my guilty gaze upward. Caught. Ellis stares down at me, brooding.

"Could you stop gawking at me," he mimics in a shrill voice.

"I do not sound like that."

"Yep, you do," he says curtly, checking his watch.

"No I—"

"Whatever," he interrupts, hand raised. "Could you just hurry?"

He exhales in frustration before turning and extending his hand. I stare at it momentarily before reaching out. He grasps my hand and helps me to my feet. I quickly pull the curtain around me, and by the time I look up, he's gone.

I stare into the empty doorway before pushing the door closed and engaging the deadbolt. I don't think he'll return, but I've learned my lesson. From now on, all doors stay locked.

Swapping the curtain for a towel, I brush my hair while studying my reflection. Each breath brings a wince. Though I seem to be healing more each day, the shower tumble has awakened old pains.

Back in my room, I pull on jeans and a long-sleeved tee and check my watch. Ten minutes until I meet Red. Turning to leave, I catch sight of an angry red mark blooming on my neck. "Just another bruise," I mutter sarcastically.

The path to the resort takes less than a minute to traverse. As I pass by the Hut, I wave to Charlie, but he doesn't see me, absorbed in wiping off bar stools and muttering what suspiciously sounds like "damn kids."

At the dive shop, I find Noah emptying a large trash can. "Hi, Noah."

He looks up with a smile. "Thanks again for those pancakes." He pats his stomach.

"Glad you liked 'em."

"Good stuff." He steps forward to hold open the door. Ellis could learn something about manners from this guy.

"Thanks."

Inside, only a few lights illuminate the back counter.

"Over here," Red calls from beyond three mannequins that seem to be watching me with their blank faces and bright red lips. I've never liked mannequins, especially these eyeless ones.

Creepy.

Past the mannequins, I find Red at her computer while Blair leans against Dave's office door, ear pressed to the wood.

They both look over as I approach. Red waves while Blair signals for silence.

"It's Ellis and Dave," Red whispers, pointing to the office. I lean against the counter, confused by their concern.

A sudden shout from inside makes us jump.

"Was that Ellis or Dave?" I ask Red.

"Blair?"

"I don't know," Blair responds, "but we all know that Dave isn't the type to shout."

"Good point," Red says before motioning to Blair urgently with both hands. "Get away from there before they come out."

Blair rolls her eyes but retreats to her reading stool, where she pulls out her book. I can't help but smile at the cover—a muscled, shirtless man with fangs clutching a busty blonde. It's some kind of paranormal romance, no doubt full of "supernatural, burning loins" and "long, ghastly, rock-hard members."

I giggle and Blair narrows her eyes. "Any good?" I ask.

"Oh, it's really good," Red interjects.

Blair studies the cover as if she's forgotten the title. "*Desires in Demon Valley.*"

"Desires in Demon Valley," Red echoes in an exaggerated sultry voice.

"Nice." I waggle my eyebrows. Though I've never read much risqué romance, I'm not opposed. Escapism, even the erotic kind, has always appealed to me.

Red giggles. "Literary porn."

"Hey!" Blair protests. "Don't knock it 'till you've tried it." She flutters her eyelashes, fanning herself. "Actually, this is better than any coffee, ladies. My blood is pumping, and I'm totally on the verge of having an—"

"Stop!" Red holds up both hands. "Can we not talk about your sex drive this early in the morning? Please?"

"Oh, can we please?" Clinton says as he appears in the back doorway, wearing a dull gray T-shirt and tight black sweats that showcase his athletic frame. He joins me at the counter, resting his unshaven chin in his hand.

She pointedly ignores him and returns to her book. Clinton purses his lips, watches her longingly. When he notices the book she's reading, his face breaks into a wolfish grin.

"That stuff is gross, Blair." He reaches out and tugs playfully at her book, earning a glare. "I mean, that guy looks so creepy with his ten—no, twelve-pack and hairy ass half-wolf arms." He leans closer, grimacing. "And what the hell is up with his nipples?"

Red nearly spits out her water, and I struggle to contain my laughter. Blair looks at him over the top of her book, eyes narrowed.

"Gross," he continues, mock-gagging. "They're like bright red pepperonis."

Blair furrows her brow then flips the book around to examine the cover. "They are not."

"Yep." Clinton nods toward Red and me. "Totally gross. His name is probably Wolfsbane or Kane—some shit like that."

Blair's lips press into a tight scowl.

"Better back off, Clinty," Red winks at me. "You know how protective she is of her stories."

Ignoring the warning, Clinton rounds the counter and softly rests his hand on Blair's leg. Her eyes fix on the contact.

He's playing with fire.

"Well, all I'm saying is that it's real gross." He exaggerates the word 'gross.'

Blair reaches down and smacks his hand away before leaning

forward with a seductive smile. "Well, Wolfsbane keeps me company at night."

"Ooo," Red's eyes widen as she watches the exchange. I bite my thumbnail nervously.

Clinton sighs, and I see a flicker of irritation flash across his face.

"You're probably just jealous that my date with Wolfsbane went so well," Blair adds. "Next time I need some company, I might just reach out to him again." She leans forward and adds, "Or someone else."

"Oh, Lord," Red mutters as Clinton's face reddens visibly. Blair knows exactly which buttons to push.

"Jealous?"

Clinton shakes his head, exhaling sharply. "Please, Blair."

"You are," she sings.

Clinton paces away before whirling back, finger raised. "Wait! I have an idea. Why don't we get Wolfsbane to change those lightbulbs for you or get your groceries?"

Red whispers in my ear, "Now he's done it." My eyes widen in anticipation. Clinton is so screwed.

Blair slides off her stool, placing her book face-down. She tugs her red shorts higher on her hips and flashes a sensuous smile. Clinton rolls his eyes but can't look away.

Like a predator stalking prey, she sways toward him. Clinton tries but fails to maintain his composure, an undeniable attraction to the gorgeous blonde easily overwhelming his defenses.

Blair reaches forward and runs her hand across his face. Clinton leans into the touch, eyes closed like a hypnotized cat. She brushes her lips against his, cocking her head to study his brown eyes from the side. He swallows hard, gaze tracing her features.

"Well, if he is going to be the one to change my little bitty lightbulbs—" She grabs a fistful of his hair, making him wince.

"Then maybe I'll call him next time I've had too much to drink and need someone to lick my p——"

"Whoa!" Red jumps up, waving frantically. "Let's not go there, you two. For God's sake."

Clinton laughs, slowly extracting himself from Blair's grip before trying to pull her into a hug. She swats him away, fighting a smile. "Go on."

He pats her backside as she turns, barely dodging her retaliating swipe. As he heads for the back room, Red grabs his shirt.

"Wouldn't go in there, Clinton."

"Huh?" he says, just as a fresh round of shouting comes from the office. "What's going on?" He points to the door, clearly confused.

"What's going on where?" JJ enters through the side door, dropping a mesh bag of dive masks on the floor carelessly, and then walks towards the closed door.

"Stay out, JJ," Red warns, but that doesn't stop him from cracking open the office door.

"Out!" Ellis shouts, sending JJ backward, wide-eyed.

"Doofus," Clinton says, half-mocking Blair.

JJ starts to say something but stops as he sees a small white-board beside Red. His face reddens with frustration. "I thought I was going to Captain the boat this morning! What the hell?"

Red spins in her chair, rolling her eyes. "Not today, buddy."

"You mean to tell me that Red won't let an unlicensed high school student drive a two-hundred-thousand-dollar boat loaded with passengers into the Atlantic Ocean?" Clinton feigns shock. "You ought to be ashamed, Red."

"Oh, shut it, Clinton," JJ snaps. "Y'all know I can drive that thing better than any of you."

"Nope," Red says flatly, exchanging amused looks with Blair.

"This is bullshit," JJ mutters.

"Language, little man," Clinton winks, making JJ clench his teeth.

JJ grabs a bag of snorkels from under the counter and storms out the back door with a dramatic huff.

"Was it something I said?" Clinton calls after him.

"Oh, leave him alone, Clinton," Blair swats his shoulder with her book. He grabs her sides, tickling her until she collapses under the desk, laughing uncontrollably.

"Stop!" she squeals.

They are so in love.

Red and I exchange knowing looks just as the office door swings open. Ellis emerges first, followed by Dave. Ellis's fury is palpable as he lowers his Maui Jim aviators and leans against the desk. His anger manifests in every line of his body—lowered brows, clenched fists, rigid posture. He stares straight ahead, almost statue-like. I can't help noticing how his neon green shorts contrast with his yellow tank top—a combination that should look ridiculous but somehow works on him.

"Can I help you with something?" His dark tone startles me from my stare. I quickly turn to Dave, pretending I don't hear the question. Dave's empathetic smile suggests their argument was about me. It's an uncomfortable realization but it's what I had expected.

Dave whistles softly and turns to retrieve a clipboard. "Okay, team. I am happy to report that, officially, our family has once again expanded. I know you all have met Ms. Glory by now and agree that she will be a rockin' addition to the team." He looks at me and winks.

His gaze shifts meaningfully to Ellis. "Help her learn all she can. She'll need training on the boat, with the equipment, and in the water. I've asked Ellis to give her basic open water lessons in between trips during the week, but if everyone can pitch in, she'll have her sea legs in no time. I have a feeling that she'll be a natural."

I'll have to take lessons from Ellis?

Blood rushes from my head, leaving me lightheaded. I glance at Ellis, still motionless, then squeeze my hands across my stomach, suddenly vulnerable. Trying to focus on anything else, I watch JJ peek back in, still vexed about his thwarted captaining dreams.

"We'll have two trips in the morning and one in the afternoon," Dave continues. "Red, Blair, and JJ will be on Seahorse I, and Ellis, Clinton, and Glory will go out on Seahorse 2. The afternoon dive is a private two-person dive with Amber and I."

"You better take me," a soft voice calls from my left, and I turn to see a slender woman in her mid-forties approach from the front of the shop. Noah trails behind her. She has long brown hair in a cloth-tied bun and is wearing blue yoga pants and a fitted Aerosmith tee.

"Dave's girl, Amber," Clinton whispers in my ear.

"Wouldn't leave you, babe." Dave smiles as she and Noah join JJ against the wall.

"We have a group of college kids, sorority girls, I think, coming in first thing."

"Yes!" JJ raises his hand for a high-five that Noah pointedly ignores.

"Jesus," Blair mutters to Clinton. "When do boys grow out of this phase?"

"Hey!" JJ protests. "I'm no boy. I can show you if you—"

Smack.

Noah's hand returns to his side. "Manners, kid." JJ falls silent.

Dave rubs his eyes, clearly frustrated. "They should be here in twenty minutes. And JJ, Noah's right—be mindful of your manners. These girls are coming here because we're the best diving around. They're not interested in making out. I don't want a repeat of last summer."

Red leans close to whisper, "I'll tell you later, but for now, just know that it involved two college girls, JJ, and peanut butter."

I disguise my laugh as a cough. Ellis's head snaps toward me, but no one else notices.

"That's so funny, Dave," JJ huffs, returning to his phone.

"Amber, this is Glory," Dave gestures to me.

Amber takes my hands, squeezing gently. "Hi Glory. Glad you are here." Though she is a person of few words, she communicates her welcome enough through her gentle spirit and soft smile.

"Thanks," I say simply, aware that Ellis is watching the exchange.

"Well, that's it, y'all," Dave says as he claps. "Let's have a great day."

"Everyone turn on your handhelds," Clinton says as he pointedly looks at JJ.

Red tosses me a small red walkie-talkie. "Click it on at the top, then push the side to talk."

I turn the knob until it clicks and beeps.

"We use these to stay connected throughout the day. They come in handy."

"But they can also be annoying in the wrong hands," Blair says, eyeing Clinton.

"I know you aren't talking about me," he narrows his gaze playfully. Clinton scurries to the back door, watching Blair like she might pounce. "Come on, Glory. Let's blow this joint before I get into trouble."

"Good idea," Blair says and then returns to her book.

CHAPTER 10

I FOLLOW CLINTON and Ellis down the ramp leading out from the back of the dive shop down a few stairs to the dock area. The morning air carries a slight chill under overcast skies, and a round white seagull watches me with beady black eyes.

As I look out, I see six boats of various sizes tied along the resort's main docks. There are also ten Jet Skis raised in pairs out of the water on small lifts. I move past Ellis as he fiddles with a large wooden storage chest to my right and watch Clinton jog down the dock, twirling a key. He stops halfway down beside the largest boat, "Seahorse I," written in fancy green lettering along its side. The vessel appears to be three stories: below deck, the main deck, and a small area at the top.

A bright orange canvas bag lands at my feet, catching me by surprise. I look up towards a smirking Ellis. He hoists two similar bags easily over his shoulders while I glare at him.

"Come on," he barks without looking at me. "We need to move. We greet everyone in ten, and guests won't be happy if they have to wait on you."

I squat to examine my bag; it's heavy with neon orange life vests. Gritting my teeth against the lingering soreness from my fall, I heave the straps across my shoulders, maintaining a neutral expression. I need to pull my weight, especially around Ellis.

He strides toward Seahorse I as I struggle to keep pace, my

bag swaying with the dock's gentle rise and fall. At the boat, he tosses his bags onto the main deck before extending his hand in my direction. "Bag," he snaps. I pull it off my shoulder and then hold it out. He impatiently jerks it from my grasp and tosses it by the others. Then, with one fluid motion, he leaps onto the boat, turning to offer his hand.

"Come on," he barks.

I take his firm hand, and he pulls—practically yanks—me over the rail before dropping my hand as if it burns to his touch.

"Thanks," I say to his back as he walks away without acknowledgment.

Clinton looks over from where he is examining a clipboard, then walks over and folds down one of the boat's side walls, pushing it forward until it connects with the dock. He steps on it, jumping slightly until it's totally flat. "It makes it easier," he grins.

"Hey," Ellis snaps his fingers at me, pointing to a series of long metal benches outlining the boat's perimeter. "The small red dots mark each seat. Put a pair of fins and a snorkel mask set at each seat." He indicates a corner where a bright green mesh bag bulges with rubber fins. "The fins are there."

"Okay," I nod with fake enthusiasm as he slides out a plastic bin and opens the lid.

"The masks and snorkels are here."

He stares at me, face rigid. "Do you understand? Do you even know what a snorkel is?"

"Okay," is all I manage before he rolls his eyes and hops back to the dock, disappearing toward the dive shop.

Ten minutes later, halfway through sorting masks and fins, Ellis returns with Trish, the evil blonde from the bar, at his side.

"Damn," I mutter.

Behind them trails a line of college girls in tiny blue shorts and bright orange sorority tanks, Greek letters stamped above 'Gator Girls Senior Weekend.'

Within minutes, Trish and her sisters settle in—ten guests in total. I position myself beside Clinton as he begins basic open-water instructions. Several girls watch him too intently, and I'm suddenly grateful Blair isn't here. Though I've known her less than a day, there's clearly something between her and Clinton, and I'd bet money she wouldn't appreciate these girls ogling him.

But Clinton stays professional, unfazed even as they strip to orange and blue bikinis, bending unnecessarily low in his line of sight.

Ellis, however, shows no such restraint. He sprawls between Trish and another girl, manspreading with arms stretched behind them both. Though sunglasses hide his eyes, I know he's drinking in the sorority display around him.

As if sensing my thoughts, his head twitches my way. I quickly return my attention to Clinton.

Clinton takes everyone through essential safety training about staying together, water currents, and clearing the snorkel of water. I listen intently, needing to learn for both my benefit and the need to keep guests safe. It will also help me avoid looking incompetent in the future.

Clinton also demonstrates proper equipment handling, both in and out of water. One crucial skill is clearing water from a mask while submerged or at the surface.

"It's easier to put the mask on underwater and clear it there," Clinton explains. "But if you can't get the water out, don't freak out. Just surface, clear it, and go back under. We're not very deep here."

"How *deep* are we?" asks one of the girls, her tone dripping with innuendo.

Clinton maintains his professionalism. "Twenty to twenty-five feet," he answers plainly, focused on his clipboard.

"I thought it would be deeper this far out," I say unintendedly.

"That's because you don't know what you're doing," Ellis mutters.

Clinton frowns at Ellis before pulling out brochures showing underwater hand signals. "Could you pass these out, Glory?"

"Sure."

"I'm going to take us out. After you pass those around, you can stay down here or come up top. The view's really nice up top, though."

"Okay, thanks."

I straighten the stack and start with the only non-sorority guests—two older couples seated together. Making my way around the deck, I finally reach Trish and Ellis, who appear deep in whispered conversation.

"Here you go," I offer the brochures.

They continue talking, either ignoring me or too absorbed in their flirting to notice.

I clear my throat softly. "Here you go."

Nothing.

I try once more, a bit louder this time. "Here you go."

It works. Ellis turns with a frown, extending his hand. "Thank you so much, Glory. What would we do without your help with these?"

My eyes narrow. *Asshole.*

Trish laughs—a sharp, snorting sound—before scanning me head to toe. "What are you wearing this time?" Her face scrunches in disgust.

"What?" I glance down at my blue windbreaker and jeans, chosen tactfully to hide my still-dark bruises. "What's wrong with jeans?"

"You are in the Florida Keys, honey. Are you really on a boat in jeans?"

"Yeah," I say simply.

"Bless her heart," another girl chimes in.

"Oh my God, Trish!" one girl stage-whispers. "Look at her. You're embarrassing her."

"Her face is turning red," another piranha adds.

"I'm not embarrassed," I manage weakly, hating how meek I sound. I try to stand taller but find myself shrinking instead. I suddenly wish that I had Blair's confidence.

Trish doesn't miss a beat. "It's okay if you are," she says, feigning concern before her face splits into a cruel smile.

I freeze like prey, unsure of what to do. Instinctively, I look to Ellis for support, but he's laughing behind his fist.

I need to escape.

Feeling tears gather, I turn quickly toward the upper deck stairs. One escapes down my cheek, but I don't give them the satisfaction of wiping it away.

"I didn't mean to hurt your feelings or anything," Trish calls to my back as I climb.

Clinton cranks the engine just as I reach the top deck. He doesn't notice me slip into a seat behind him, giving me time to compose myself.

I watch him navigate away from the dock towards the open ocean. He's right—the view *is* incredible. Orange sunlight glows on emerald water while bright white clouds drift peacefully through the cobalt sky. I look back towards the land as the boat glides further towards the horizon.

After about ten minutes, Clinton retrieves a clipboard from under his seat, noticing me. "Hey, G."

"Hi," I smile, turning toward the water to hide my flushed cheeks. "It's just so beautiful," I add in an artificially bright tone.

"Yeah, it is," he says, his voice raised over the engine. He tilts his head toward his clipboard, peering over his sunglasses. "You wouldn't want to learn how to read a nautical map, would you? If you're the First Mate one day, you need to have a general idea about these things."

I smile and nod enthusiastically, grateful for his willingness to teach me, when my *assigned* instructor is probably downstairs trying to get into some girl's swimsuit.

"You really think I could be a First Mate one day?" I ask.

"Absolutely. The person who had the position is a bit preoccupied, so I'm demoting him."

"Sounds just and fair to me," I say.

"Definitely." He unfolds the top page to twice the clipboard's length. "Check this out."

I furrow my brows at the strange image filled with squiggly lines and numbers. I've never been any good at reading maps, but this is beyond any road map. I bite my thumbnail nervously.

"Do you always bite your nails?" Clinton asks, smiling.

I drop my hand. "Only when I'm nervous."

He waves dismissively. "Nothing to it. I promise."

Scooting closer, he traces several lines. "These lines here and around here represent the natural height of the seabed. The numbers are the depths, and for this particular map, the darker the area, the deeper the water."

After a minute of studying the lines and numbers, it starts making sense, except— "How do you know your location?"

"Great question, G." He indicates barely visible baby blue horizontal and vertical lines, each marked with small numbers. "These tell you your longitude and latitude, which tell you your—"

"Coordinates," I interrupt unintentionally as the answer pops forward from some hidden source of knowledge.

"Exactly. And there," he points to the boat's control display, "are your coordinates. Match the map's coordinates with the boats', and you're set."

"And these numbers represent water depths, right?"

Clinton throws his hands up triumphantly. "Exactly! You're a natural." He playfully strokes his chin. "You know, Glory. You just might be Captain material."

We laugh and the stress from before washes away as Clinton delves deeper into navigation—explaining seabed features, coastline details, hazards, and human-made structures. He also goes over some of the main controls, where I learn that nautical maps are not necessarily needed anymore. Everything is literally digital. We're both surprised by how quickly I grasp all he shows me. It's so engaging that when I finally look up, the land has completely vanished, leaving only the merging blues of sea and sky.

"That's it for now," Clinton says. "You'll be captaining dive trips in no time."

I raise my hands in protest. "I think I'm fine just being a second mate or whatever, but thanks for showing me everything. You're a good teacher."

Clinton smiles crookedly. "It's good stuff to know in emergencies or if you plan on getting a boating license one day." He winks. "You never know where life will take you."

"That's very true," I say.

"What's very true?" comes a gruff voice. We turn to find Ellis leading Trish onto the upper deck. She flashes Clinton a smile but ignores me completely.

"This is where the Captain hangs out," Ellis announces, giving Clinton a pointed wink. Trish giggles, pressing against Ellis and stroking his bare abs with one hand. My stomach turns.

"You mean me," says Clinton, "since today I'm the—"

"First mate," Ellis interrupts, finishing the sentence for him. His eyes widen, silently pleading with Clinton, who eventually sighs and nods in agreement.

Ellis perks up. "I can take it from here, Clinty. I'm going to show Trish a few things, and then we'll join you down below."

"Like the wheel?" Trish squeals.

"That's right," Ellis says in mock enthusiasm that Trish doesn't pick up.

"Jesus," Clinton mutters, stepping back from the helm with a sarcastic bow. "By all means, Captain."

Ellis guides Trish to the control panel, positioning himself unnecessarily close behind her.

"Just make sure we stay on course, Ellis." Clinton shakes his head as Ellis nods silently, pushing the throttle forward.

"Wow, that's fast!" Trish shrieks over the wind.

Clinton taps my shoulder. "Let's get out of here and let him do his thing. I need to make a few announcements to our guests anyway, and I can tell them what kind of fish they may see and stuff like that. May try to scare them too," he deadpans. "Perhaps I'll mention the various shark species they may encounter?"

"Sharks?" I ask nervously, following him down.

He responds with exaggerated spooky sounds, earning a playful smack.

On the main deck, Clinton is captivating as he seamlessly blends safety information with storytelling. His natural style, coupled with his playful spirit, keeps everyone engaged.

He finishes just as the boat slows to a stop. The water is calm, so the boat only lifts and falls slightly as it rides the gentle water currents. Clinton walks to the boat's side and unfolds a large silver ladder into the water.

"Can I help with anything?"

He nods toward a small black nylon bag. "Could you get the flag out?"

"Sure," I say, grabbing the dive flag on a long white pole, its base stuck in a bright blue float like a giant bobber. "What's this for?"

"It signals to other boats that divers are in the water and helps keep everyone together. Ellis will tie it to his vest, and it'll float around, following us along the reef."

"Snorkel time!" calls Clinton, and I shift my attention to Ellis and Trish, who have decided to join us. Trish skips back to her friends while Ellis and Clinton move to help everyone suit up.

I stand close to Clinton, watching him as he helps guests with everything from adjusting mask straps to answering any lingering questions. Within minutes, all guests are ready for the dive.

I turn towards Ellis just as he peels off his shirt in one fluid motion.

Wow.

"Holy shit," several girls whisper. I understand their reaction. Though his personality is severely lacking, Ellis's physique is perfect—every female eye fixes on that tantalizing "V" of his lower abs, naturally drawing our attention south.

"Okay, kiddos!" Clinton's call breaks our collective trance. He reviews his clipboard. "As I call your name, hop in. Stay near the boat until everyone's in the water. We'll be circling toward the starboard side. And remember, always follow the flag."

I hand the flag to Ellis, who ties it to his bicep before gripping the float and jumping in. I watch him surface yards away, tossing wet hair from his face.

Clinton calls names until only we remain on deck. Ellis shouts up from the water. "Looks like that's everyone, so I'll see you soon."

"Sounds good, bro," Clinton responds. "Stay safe."

"Don't let her wreck the boat," Ellis calls out just before disappearing underwater. We stand for a moment and watch the amoeba of fins and snorkels drift away.

"How long will they stay out?" I ask, ignoring Ellis.

"About thirty minutes, but it's really up to Ellis. He could stay longer or bring them in early."

"What determines how long they're out for?"

"His mood," Clinton forces a laugh, squinting against the bright sunlight peeking through the clouds. "Well, his mood and the currents. It's possible for a diver to drift too far if the current's strong enough."

"Seriously?"

He nods, biting his lip. "Ellis will track the currents and keep things smooth. He may be acting like a complete jackass right now, but he's one of the best divers in this area." He turns and surveys the horizon. "Weather's nice this morning, so it shouldn't be a problem."

I watch the dive flag bob along the waves, drifting further out. "That would be so scary, just drifting away, lost at sea." The thought makes a shiver of fear race up my spine.

"Yes, it would. Almost happened to Ellis's girlfriend Jane once." Clinton freezes as if catching himself then looks at me, pursing his lips.

Jane.

"Ellis has a girlfriend and acts like that?" I swallow hard, frowning at the distant flag attached to Ellis.

Clinton shakes his head. "No. I misspoke. Ellis doesn't have a girlfriend."

I cock my head, confused.

"Well, he did, but she… she died two years ago."

I cringe as I bite my lip, wishing I had not pried.

"It's really messed him up," Clinton adds as we stare across the water.

"That's so sad," I whisper into a sudden breeze.

"He's not himself with anyone anymore—not me, not Dave. He's just—"

"Angry?"

Clinton nods. "Exactly. He hates himself, and I don't know why. He's not getting better. He refused counseling even though Dave offered to pay. He's moody as hell, drinks too much, and he's reckless."

"That's so sad, Clinton."

"It's a mess, and I don't know what to do. He's taking too many risks, and there have been too many close calls. I can't see him lasting much—" Clinton catches himself, pauses, then forces a smile. "We're all praying for healing."

"I'm sorry." The words feel inadequate.

"Jane and Ellis are soulmates, so it's hard."

"Do you believe in soulmates, Clinton?" I whisper.

A faint smile touches his mouth. "Yeah, I think I do. What about you?"

"Maybe. I am not sure." It's as honest an answer as I can give. "I just hate that she died," I say softly.

Clinton rubs his cheek. "Look, Glory. You're the first person Dave has hired since Jane."

"Oh," I cross my arms over my stomach; the confirmation of what I think deep down I already knew is unsettling.

"She actually had your job when she passed."

"She did?"

"Yeah."

My eyes widen. "So, I'm Jane's replacement?"

Clinton nods solemnly. "Yeah, I guess you are. I think that's why he is being an ass. It's a lot for him to handle, so he's lashing out at you."

I cringe. I hate that my presence causes Ellis pain and is playing such a pointed role in his grief. Just my being here is forcing him to recover from Jane's death, and that doesn't seem natural or fair…to either of us.

I rub my temples as thoughts of quitting Dave's race through my mind. Clinton frowns at my pained expression.

"It's not you, Glory."

"I just hate that I'm hurting him. My being here doesn't seem right."

Clinton reaches over and pats my shoulder. "It's not you, Glory," he repeats. "It's not. Dave would have hired someone else if you hadn't taken this job. He doesn't have a choice. Dave's has nearly doubled in size in five years. It's grown by leaps and bounds, and Dave's invested a lot in renovations and new equipment. The resort can't afford to be short-staffed. We must make the most of the season to cover our off-season expenses. Competition between dive resorts down here is brutal."

His logic makes sense. They do seem extremely busy.

"There's another silver lining to you being here, too," he adds.

"What?"

"Ellis has been in a bad spot for some time now since Jane." Clinton chooses his words carefully. "Rough around the edges. He's doing some dangerous stuff."

"Like what?"

"Nothing illegal, but stuff that could get him hurt or even killed."

I wait for him to continue.

"Cliff diving when he's trashed, snorkeling in strong currents, and having lots of casual…relations." He gauges my reaction.

Sex. Lots of sex.

Brief flashes of tan muscles invade my mind. I bite my lip, blurting the first distraction that comes to mind. "He's a good-looking guy, I guess. It would be normal for him to want to…you know."

Clinton shakes his head. "Not Ellis. He's always been the romantic type. Jane was his first—" He stops abruptly, glancing at the distant divers as if Ellis might hear.

"Oh," I say simply. A flutter races through my stomach, and I brush stray hair from my eyes. "Dangerous stuff, huh?"

Clinton nods. "Yep. So, you can see why this might be help-ful, even if it's…forcing him to…address his anger, his pain. I like to think of it as a gentle nudge."

"That makes sense, I guess," I say. "I just wish he would talk to someone."

"Me too. But he refuses. He won't even talk to me about it."

Pain flashes in Clinton's eyes. He obviously wants to help his best friend and feels obligated—but can't.

"Your being here will help Ellis find closure," Clinton explains. "I believe with all my heart that you are meant to be here."

Though I nod in agreement, I am not so sure I see it that way.

For several minutes, we watch silently as the dive flag circles the boat. Eventually, Clinton retrieves an academic book of some sorts and heads to the cozier top deck seats, inviting me to join. I decide to stay below and take time to process what I have learned.

Lying back on a metal bench, I let the crisp wind and gentle rocking of waves wash over me. Though I try to clear my mind, my thoughts race uncontrolled—Nick, Mom, Dad, Dave's, Ellis. I imagine Ellis before Jane, what their relationship was like, and darker, how it ended. Clinton hadn't detailed Jane's death, leaving me susceptible to morbid curiosity.

CHAPTER 11

I SIT UP at the sound of snorkelers emerging one by one from the water. It doesn't feel like thirty minutes has passed.

"They're back," I call over my shoulder, which prompts Clinton to descend to the main deck.

"Right on schedule." He checks his watch, waggling his eyebrows. "With Ellis, that's a good thing. Let's help them back onto the deck—the steps can be tricky."

We assist guests aboard, and I force smiles at the sneering blondes. Clinton has me collect snorkels and masks while he runs through his checklist, ensuring no one is left in the water.

Five minutes later, most guests are aboard except Ellis and Trish, who seem to be dawdling. Clinton's irritation grows visible as the dive flag and snorkel tips inch slowly toward the boat.

"Damn it, Ellis," he mutters under his breath.

Most guests radiate post-dive joy, all smiles and laughter—except for two sorority girls, one of whom looks particularly green.

"Are you all right?" I ask as I walk up to her and collect her gear.

"She's fine," her friend snaps, roughly shoving the equipment into my hands.

Minutes later, loud laughter announces Ellis and Trish's return. Clinton glares as he leans past Ellis and secures the ladder, clearly annoyed by their delay.

"Ellis," he says firmly. "Get the anchor up. We're behind schedule and need to head out in—"

"I think I'm gonna be sick!" someone shouts from behind me. I turn to see the green-faced girl running for the rail. She doesn't make it.

Please, God, no.

Time slows until someone—Ellis—shouts, "Oh, shit!"

"Vomit!" a girl shrieks.

I open my eyes to survey the damage. I'm coated in what appears to be a partially digested breakfast smoothie, warm and reeking of fermented fruit.

"That's nasty," Trish snickers behind her hand.

I freeze, aware of Ellis's pointed stare.

Clinton snaps into action, though clearly flustered. "Okay, Glory. Hang on. Let's see." He grabs resort towels, frantically tossing them my way. I catch one while the others fall into the mess.

"Jesus Christ," I manage as I wipe the splatter from my face first.

"Sorry," squeaks the sick girl, in between dry heaving into a mop bucket to my side.

"Does this ship have a shower, a hose, anything?" I fight rising panic.

"No hose, but there's a bathroom downstairs," Clinton offers.

"Why don't you just jump in the water?" Trish suggests, her entourage agreeing. I involuntarily meet her gaze. She's hanging on Ellis, chomping gum. "Are you shy or something?"

I'm not shy, but I can't risk exposing my bruises. I turn toward the lower deck bathroom.

"Wait," Ellis calls. I look back as he detaches from Trish. "The water pressure sucks—if it's working at all." He approaches, carefully avoiding the mess, and takes my hand. "Come on."

"Where are we going?" I snap as he pulls me along a walkway

extending the length of the boat. Just as we round the corner out of sight, I yank my hand free and stop.

He turns back, rolling his eyes. "We're going to the bow of the boat."

I say nothing.

"The front of the boat," he explains slowly, as if to a child.

"I know what a bow is," I snap again. My typical temperament isn't hostile, but Ellis has worn my patience thin.

He tugs at his pointed blonde hair, rolling his eyes. "Would you just come on? You're getting little bits of vomit chunk everywhere."

Looking down, I cringe and throw up my hands in defeat before following him forward.

After another ten feet, the alley opens onto a large flat area at the bow. Ellis moves to the far side, flipping a small ladder into the water.

"Get in." He points down. "You need to clean off—and you stink."

"What?"

He gags theatrically. "God, you smell so bad."

"And this is my fault?" I snap. "My God, did she have to aim her projectile splash directly into my chest?"

Ellis bursts into genuine laughter. "She didn't do it on purpose."

I step forward, fists clenched. "She did." An angry tear escapes.

He stops laughing, hands raised in mock surrender. "Okay, maybe she did."

"She did."

"But does it matter? Just get in." He pats the ladder, nodding toward the water.

With the anchor down, the water looks calm enough for an easy climb.

"I really do stink," I mutter, catching another whiff of my shirt.

"You do, and baking in the sun isn't helping."

I cover my face as embarrassment settles in. "This sucks."

"Look." Ellis's voice softens, losing its edge. "Please get in the water." He extends his hand. "I will help you down."

I exhale loudly. "Okay."

"But first, you need to take off those clothes." A slight smile plays at his mouth.

I narrow my eyes. "Oh no, sir. You are not going to watch me strip down and get in that water." Even perfectly healed, I wouldn't give him the satisfaction of seeing my body.

Hell.

No.

He shrugs. "I will close my eyes."

"Oh, right. I believe that." My snort makes him cock his head curiously, one brow raised. "Just leave," I plead. "I will be fine."

He shakes his head. "Nope. I have to be here. You can't get into the water without a buddy. Resort rules, not mine."

I roll my eyes. "Right. How convenient for you, huh?" Sarcasm drips from my every word.

"Do you even know how to swim?" His signature smirk returns.

"What?" I pause before flipping him off.

He laughs.

"Yes, thank you very much. I know how to swim. What kind of question is that?"

"Well, how would I know?"

I grit my teeth. "Do you really think I could make it into my twenties not knowing how to swim?"

Ellis checks his watch, sighing. "Just get in. We're running late as it is."

Anxiety builds as I acknowledge he's right. I can't bake in vomit for the ride home, and I can't stand here forever.

"Okay," I blurt. I twirl my finger sharply. "Turn around."

Ellis throws up his hands in defeat. "Whatever. Just get in." He steps away, turning as he mutters something unintelligible.

"Okay, I'm getting undressed. Don't peek."

"Never," he replies flatly.

Once confident he won't look, I strip to my bright red bikini with spaghetti straps and low-cut bottoms. I'd put it on this morning, never intending to be seen in it until fully healed.

I approach the edge, checking over my shoulder that Ellis isn't peeking, and then dive in.

The cool sea instantly refreshes me. I close my eyes as bubbles rush past, pausing to float weightlessly while scrubbing with both hands. I can instantly feel the grime lifting from my skin.

After a moment, I kick to the surface, continuing to clean my hair and body. For a moment, I lose myself in the sensation of cool water—until I notice Ellis has moved to the edge, crouching to watch me intently. Too intently.

Does he see the bruises?

"What?" I demand.

Ellis shakes his head as if waking from a dream, rubbing his eyes. "Nothing. Just watching for sharks."

I freeze, eyes darting side to side. "Excuse me?"

"You do realize you're basically chum in the water right now—with all that vomit."

"What?"

"I can see little bits floating all around you."

"What do you mean?"

"Haven't you seen Jaws?"

"Yes, I've seen Jaws. What the hell?" Blood drains from my face as I frantically swim back. Scrub down officially over.

"By all means, swim back like you're an injured seal, flapping this way and that."

"Shut up!" I shout, reaching the ladder.

"A loud seal," he adds.

I glare, gritting my teeth. As I grasp the first step, I point at him sharply, still scanning for giant shark faces. "Turn around! Hurry!"

Ellis leans down smugly, hands on hips. "What's the magic word?"

I check over my shoulder again. "Now!"

"Nope."

"You're an ass."

"Nope."

"Please!"

"Fine, fine." He throws up an eyebrow instead of his hands, turning away on a low laugh.

I bolt from the water, shivering in the cool breeze. Looking at my dirty clothes, I realize—no towel, no clean clothes. "Shit," I mutter.

"What?" Ellis starts to turn.

I jump forward, stepping in close so my body blocks his turn. "Don't move!"

"Man, you are shy." He laughs, but the comment freezes my blood.

"Do you have a shirt or something I could borrow?" I bite my lip in frustration.

Ellis turns his head slightly, eyeing the way I'm half-braced at his side.

"Sorry," I pull back a pace, forcing my arms to drop to my sides.

He faces forward again. "Be right back."

Ellis walks away without turning. Moments later, a loud

squeak and splash makes me jump, and I turn just as a large grey nose emerges from the water.

Dolphin!

I rush to the side and extend an arm forward. "Hey, cutie!" The dolphin's sleek body breaks the surface.

I reach out as it bobs up and down. "Hey, little guy. Sorry, I dirtied up your area. Some skank vomited all over me."

It squeaks and whistles as if understanding.

"I know! Do you believe it? No manners at all."

The dolphin dips under, reappearing twenty yards out in a graceful leap. I smile as it vanishes, tilting my face to the warming sun. For the first time in ages, my body feels relaxed.

Wait…my body.

"What happened to you?" comes a soft voice.

I spin, wrapping my arms around my waist. But it's useless—Ellis has seen the bruises. I don't have enough hands to cover them all, especially the ones on my back.

His posture stiffens, and his eyebrows lower, showing signs of concern and confusion. After a moment, he steps forward, his arm extended as he clenches a bright green T-shirt and small garbage bag, his knuckles white under the pressure.

I cautiously take them, then quickly pull on the shirt. Though it hangs to my knees, I tug it down further, crossing my arms. I feel my cheeks burn with shame.

He moves closer. I can see him processing, trying to understand my battered state. "You're covered in bruises, scrapes. What happened? Did you fall or something?"

I meet his gaze, fighting the urge to flee. But where to?

"Or something," I manage before looking away. I don't know why I don't lie or make up something.

I grab my clothes, stuffing them in the bag without looking up. Ellis takes another careful step forward as if approaching an injured animal. "Did someone do this to you?"

I pretend not to hear his question, stepping around him toward the main deck. "We probably should get back." I force a small smile. "I'm fine. No big deal."

"Wait," his voice wavers.

I turn, raising both hands. "Please don't pity me." I shake my head and hold back tears with all my might. I don't want his pity. I don't want anyone to pity me.

"I don't pity you," he says gently, tone stripped of its usual edge.

"Thank you," I manage, forcing back anger—not at Ellis, but at my situation, at my abuser.

"Who did this to you?"

"Just some guy."

"Just some guy?" He shakes his head in disbelief. "Somebody—hit you?"

"My boyfriend pushed me," I mutter. "My ex-boyfriend."

"Pushed you?"

"He got mad and pushed me down some stairs."

My voice cracks as I speak, and my shoulders slump as an enormous weight lifts. Ellis, this stranger, is the first person I've told about the abuse. But in this moment, I need to know what he's thinking. Our eyes lock—his gaze magnetic, impossible to break. His bright blue eyes hold sadness, exhaustion, concern. I brace for his questions, his critique. I wait for him to ask why I stayed and how I let this happen.

But to my surprise, the questions never come.

"I'm sorry," he says instead, squeezing his eyes shut.

"Don't apologize," I say. "I'm used to it." I feign brightness. "It's behind me now."

"You are used to it?"

"He always said I was a burden, and I think it made him mad."

Ellis opens and closes his eyes slowly, repeatedly, taking long, deep breaths as if trying to calm himself. When he finally focuses on me again, he's biting his lip, seemingly at a loss for words.

He moves to the rail, gripping it as he leans forward to stare into the crystal water.

"I just don't get it," he says, face scrunching. "How could someone hurt you—*beat* you."

I inhale sharply at the word "beat." I'd never openly used that term to describe Nick's actions, and hearing someone else apply it to my abuse makes my stomach drop.

"I don't get guys like that, *criminals* like that." He turns, staring with such intensity my heart flutters.

His anger is visible now, his nostrils flaring, and his face is red. "He should rot in jail. You're so small and so damn—" He stops abruptly, eyes scanning my body. "It's just bullshit. You should have been protected." He bites his lip, turning to lean wholly against the rail.

"I broke up with him though and left Tennessee, so he can't find me, and—"

"Let's go, Ellis!" Clinton interrupts. We both turn toward the back of the boat.

Ellis shakes his head then stands straight. He takes a few calming breaths, his chest visibly shaking as it rises up and down slowly. "We better get going," Ellis says, extending his hand. "Let's get back to the group."

I freeze, staring at his outstretched hand. The reality hits me like a freight train—I've told someone about Nick, told *Ellis* about Nick. This man who hates me might tell everyone. I want to jump overboard.

"I won't say anything," he assures me, as if reading my mind.

I nod slowly. "Thank you. You're the only person I've told."

"You can trust me."

"What choice do I have?" I say. The words are harsher than I intended, and I see Ellis subtly recoil.

As he does, I reach out and take his outstretched hand. He guides me forward but stops just before we enter the side alley. "I'm sorry for how I've acted, Glory. For how I've treated you. You of all people."

I'm shocked by his unexpected apology, so words fail me.

"It's not you," he continues. "I'm just…" He squeezes his eyes shut, opening them heavy and dark. "I'm just fucked up, Glory."

I watch him breathe in and out, clearly in pain. I feel sorry for this man, and in this moment, I decide to offer my forgiveness. "Let's just start over," I blurt out, squeezing his hand gently. I genuinely want to, but I also just need to escape this charged moment.

He rubs his face, exhaling deeply in relief. "That would be great."

As we make our way back, Ellis gently steadies me with a hand at my side—a small gesture that speaks volumes. I can't help but notice how the energy between us has shifted.

When we reach the main deck, Clinton is splashing away the last traces of vomit. The guests seem oblivious to our return, except Trish, who springs up and rushes to Ellis, claiming him with a possessive squeeze.

"Took you long enough," she jokes, tossing her hair in my direction with a glare.

Ellis doesn't acknowledge her.

"What?" Trish huffs, frowning.

Ellis shrugs casually, bending to retrieve Clinton's cleaning bucket. "Seeing your friend's early morning smoothie splattered across this boat and my coworker has ruined the mood." He tosses the bucket's contents overboard before turning back to her.

Trish starts to speak but redirects to me instead. "No offense, but you still kinda stink." She pinches her nose with an exaggerated grimace.

I sniff my shoulder self-consciously.

"Ignore her," Clinton says. "You're fine. Come up top with me and let Ellis handle all this." He waves dismissively at Trish.

"If you can't play nice, you'll be asked to check out early," Ellis warns, defending me in a way that causes Clinton and I to turn in surprise.

"Whatever, E. Quit overreacting." She shoots me another glare before rejoining her friends.

"Let's get out of here," Clinton says as he takes my hand, leading me upstairs. At the helm, he turns abruptly. "What was that about?"

I shrug.

"Did Ellis just stick up for you?"

"I think so."

"What happened?"

Clinton doesn't know about Ellis's apology or our fresh start. "When we were washing off, he apologized."

"Really?"

"Yeah." I smile uneasily. "I think Ellis and I may have come to an understanding." I choose my words deliberately, not wanting to overstate things. For all I know, Ellis will hate me again tomorrow.

Clinton flashes a wide grin. "Well, that's good to hear—great to hear, actually."

"Seahorse II to Seahorse I," a feminine voice crackles through the radio. Clinton grabs it. *"This is the great Captain Clinton speaking, and who, pray tell, is this? Over."*

"Shut it. You know who this is. Over."

Clinton winks at me.

"Tell Blair hi," I say, pushing hair from my face.

"Glory says hi. Over."

"Hi Glory! Over."

"Wait until you hear about this trip. It's for the record books. Over."

"What happened!" Blair squeals. "Over."

"Nope," Clinton teases. "Not until I get back. Over."

"You better tell me what you know, you A—"

A loud BEEP cuts her off as Clinton hits a button to turn off the radio.

"Oops. I guess she got disconnected."

I shake my head. "She's going to kill you, you know."

He sighs dreamily. "Probably try. But that's okay. I like her when she's fiery."

"Who's fiery?" Ellis asks, appearing at the stairs.

"Blair," Clinton answers.

"Yep," Ellis agrees. "Like the devil."

"All set downstairs?" Clinton asks.

"All set."

"Good deal." Clinton starts the engine, its rumble shaking the boat. The anchor winch groans as its cable rolls forward.

When the cranking stops, Ellis turns to where I'm seated, acknowledging me with a slight head tilt before doing something completely unexpected—he drops down beside me.

My body tenses instantly and Clinton's eyebrows shoot up.

"You mind if I join ya?" Ellis says as he offers a tight-lipped smile.

I hesitate before saying, "Sure."

He stretches out, extending his long tan legs over the rail and resting his head back on the seat just inches from mine.

His body radiates heat against my side, and the scent of salt and suntan lotion rises from his skin. It's intoxicating. As he stares into the distance, I allow myself an uninterrupted admiration of his physique.

Sensing my attention, he glances over his shoulder with a sly smile. Though he can't see my eyes, I instinctively look away.

"Let me know if I'm crowding you."

I shake my head. "I'm good. Even though you take up

more than half this bench yourself. What are you like, six-two or something?"

"Six-four," he waggles his eyebrows, stretching his legs further.

I catch Clinton watching our interaction curiously. Gradually, my body relaxes, and I lean back, turning my face into the afternoon sun.

The boat picks up speed, and the steady rhythm of wind and motor carries me away. I dream of dolphins.

CHAPTER 12

What's that chanting?

"Glory. Glory. Glory."

Is that Clinton?

"Wake up, Glory."

I blink awake, covering a yawn with my hand.

Shit. I fell asleep.

I sit up quickly and then look around as I blink awake. Several smiling faces greet me—Noah, Blair, Clinton, and even JJ. "Sorry. I must have fallen asleep."

I realize we're docked back at Dave's. I rub my eyes and glance back at their continuing stares. "Am I drooling or something?" I wipe my mouth.

"Not you," Noah says, eyebrows raised as he exchanges looks with the others.

"What? What do you—" A loud snore from my lap cuts me off. I look down, nearly jumping at the sight of Ellis deeply asleep across my thighs. I look up, eyes wide with confusion.

"Awe," Red says as she appears from behind Noah.

I start to inch away carefully.

"Where ya going?" Ellis mumbles, barely audible, wrapping an arm around my thighs.

I freeze, looking at everyone desperately. "What do I do?" I whisper-panic.

"Just get up," JJ suggests. "He'll move or bump his head." Noah starts to nod but stops at Red's chastising look for agreeing with JJ.

Another snore draws my attention back to Ellis. He looks so peaceful. "What about everyone else, the sorority girls?" I ask, looking up.

"They left an hour ago," Clinton laughs.

"Thank you, Jesus," Blair adds, earning Red's agreeing snort.

"Sorry, I fell asleep on the job." It's probably not great to pass out on day one, but no one seems to care. My predicament just amuses them.

"No worries," Clinton says. "Dave told us to let y'all sleep."

"And we did for a while," Blair adds, "but damn, this is just too freaking funny." The others nod in agreement.

"You don't want to know how many pics they've taken of the two of you," JJ quips.

"Some," Noah rumbles.

"It's just adorable," Red says, "and Ellis hasn't looked this peaceful in a long time."

"True," Blair nods.

He hasn't looked this peaceful since Jane died, they mean.

"Should I wake him up?" I ask softly.

"Nah!" JJ shouts. "Don't wake Ellis up!"

"JJ!" Blair hisses, but it's too late. Ellis stirs in my lap.

"Shut up, JJ," Ellis mumbles groggily, wiping drool from his face without opening his eyes. His grip on my thighs loosens. "What are you yelling about?" He rolls onto his back, rubbing his eyes, head still warm against my leg. When he finally blinks awake and sees me, he launches himself up so fast I barely dodge a broken nose.

"What the hell!" His wide eyes dart around the boat, confused and suspicious.

"You needed rest," Noah says, shrugging and turning to head

down to the main deck. Ellis's face deepens to crimson as the realization hits.

"All right, guys, the show's over," Red announces, giving me a small wave and wink before following Noah.

"That was the funniest crap I've seen all year," Blair says as she tugs Clinton's hand. "Later." At the stairs, she turns back. "JJ! Move! You got wash duty."

"It's not my turn," JJ whines.

"Don't argue with the boss lady," Clinton says, fingers laced tightly with Blair's as they disappear behind Red and Noah. JJ follows, muttering expletives.

Ellis and I sit silently, listening to their laughter and chatter fade toward the resort.

"Sorry about that," he says finally, breaking the tension. His eyes meet mine briefly before returning to his drawstring, where he's fidgeting nervously.

"No big deal," I say, feigning relaxed, standing to smooth his shirt where it hits my knees. "You were tired—me too."

"Yeah."

"I mean, I fell asleep too." I retrieve my bag and the trash bag of ruined clothes from the captain's seat. Turning back to Ellis, still staring at the ocean, I start, "Ellis?"

He looks up and our eyes lock. I lose my train of thought, captivated by the bright white rings around his pupils. They must be what makes his eyes so...electric.

When I recover, it's too late—whatever I meant to say is gone. Instead, I blurt, "Do you have the time?"

He stares blankly for a moment before checking his watch. "4:30."

"Thanks," I say lamely.

The day's events feel suddenly surreal and awkward. Not just that Ellis and I slept together on the ride home—*you know what I mean*—but that he knows about Nick. It makes me feel anxious and vulnerable. You'd think someone vomiting on you would be the day's defining moment, good or bad, but it's dwarfed by what's transpired between Ellis and me. Though the vomit *is* horrifying.

I glance down at his shirt, then up to find him stretching overhead with that distinctly male grunt. He cracks his knuckles above his head, steps forward, and then notices me fidgeting with his shirt.

"Let me wash this tonight," I say. "I'll get it back to you tomorrow."

He looks up with a hint of a playful smile that softens his face. "I think I'll take it now."

My eyes widen. "What? Well. If I can just get a towel." I start to lift the hem, but his hand stops mine.

"I'm just kidding." He releases my hand.

"Oh." I tug the shirt back down.

"Just keep it." He waves dismissively. "I've got another just like it." He grabs his sunglasses from the bench, then steps behind me, touching the small of my back. "After you."

Shivers run down my spine at his light touch. "Okay," I say, starting down the stairs.

He helps me off the boat at the main deck but catches my shoulder before I can walk away. I turn back to look at him.

"Look, Glory. I'm sorry about that."

"About what?"

"About making fun of your clothes." He rubs his face, exhaling shakily.

"It's fine."

He bites his lip, shaking his head. "No. It's not."

"It's okay, Ellis," I try again.

"No," he insists. "I know it's hard to believe, but that person who did that is not me. I mean, it's me, but I normally don't act like—"

"An ass?" I bite my lip at my harsh tone, but he smiles.

"Exactly."

"I believe you."

He smiles. "Good."

"New start, remember?"

"Right. A new start."

"Good," I echo.

He runs a hand through his messy, nearly dry hair, making the surfer look even more appealing. "But I'm gonna make it up to you."

I hesitate before nodding. I'm unsure exactly how, but I appreciate his sincerity.

"Bet you want to take a shower," he says after a minute.

I pull at a strand of hair, sniffing it with a scrunched nose. "Probably a good idea. That was so gross."

"Yeah."

"Maybe a good idea for you too? Since you kinda got all up on me for an hour or so."

"All up on you?" He feigns offense, then cocks his head to sniff suspiciously. "Probably wouldn't hurt."

"Shall we then?" He gestures toward the dive shop's rear, slinging a bright orange bag marked 'ELLIS' in block letters over his shoulder.

"Sounds good," I say sheepishly, forcing a smile before starting down the dock at a brisk pace. I don't look back, though I can hear him following and feel his gaze on me.

I bypass the dive shop, heading straight for the house.

In the bathroom, I turn the deadbolt multiple times until I am absolutely certain it is locked.

Half a bar of soap and an empty shampoo bottle later, I'm finally satisfied that all traces of my first diving trip are gone forever. After toweling off and dressing, I battle my tangled hair, wind-whipped from the boat ride. As I secure it in a loose bun, my phone buzzes.

Mom.

Nick has called her—it would've been his first move after discovering I'd left. He would have played the distressed boyfriend, exaggerating my departure. Nick's a good actor, and Mom would buy his bullshit hook, line and sinker. She adores Nick because he comes from old money, not because of his personality. Mom says, "A real man must be able to provide a comfortable living for his family."

I struggle to understand how my parents fell in love. Dad understood what mattered—love and family—while Mom is materialistic, even at the expense of family.

I debate letting the call go to voicemail. I don't want to talk, but Nick might have convinced her I'm missing—that something's happened to me. That could mean police involvement or worse, Nick finding me. Mom may not win parenting awards, but she wouldn't hesitate to call the authorities if she thought I was in danger.

I hit answer. "Hi, Mom," I force brightness into my voice.

"Nice of you to answer your phone, Glory."

"Sorry, I've been swamped."

"Well, not with school, I hear."

I sigh.

"And you didn't tell me you planned to break up with Nick."

Straight to the point.

"He's devastated, Glory."

"Trust me, Mom, he's not."

She ignores me. "He told me that he came to help get you, and you had just left on your own, gone to God knows where."

"It's no big deal, Mom. The relationship just ran its course."

"No big deal? Nick has done so much to help you. He's always been there for you, for us."

"I don't want to be with him, Mom."

She ignores me. "I'm worried about you. Nick is worried."

Cliff's voice mumbles something intelligible in the background. My wealthy, alcoholic stepfather and I have a mutual understanding: he stays out of my life, and I keep calls infrequent.

"Cliff wants to know if you have a drug problem." What he really wants to know is if I'll cost him rehab money.

"I am pretty sure that Cliff thinks all people under thirty have drug problems—well, drugs and prostitution."

"Don't be dramatic, Glory. He is just concerned."

"Fine."

"Well, what is it then? Are you in trouble?"

"No, Mom," I say flatly, my voice sharper than intended.

"Nick seems to think you ran off with—"

"I didn't, Mom," I interrupt, patience wearing thin. She needs to accept it's over. "I'm fine. Nick and I just aren't working out. We grew apart. That's all there is to it." I consider telling her more, but Mom's best kept at arm's length.

"Don't you just want to try once more, Glory, to make it work? He's smart, handsome, and one of Tennessee's most well-connected young men. What's not working out? Because—"

I finally snap. "We aren't getting back together, Mom!" I cringe.

"I'm only trying to help, Glory." *She's playing the victim now.*

"Look, Mom. I moved to Florida. I took a job in—"

"Florida?" she interrupts. "What in God's name are you doing in that mosquito-infested swamp? Well, unless you're in Palm Beach, which is ultra-luxurious. Please tell me you're in Palm Beach."

"I'm not."

"Of course, you aren't." Disappointment drips from every word. "You are just like your father."

"Florida's all right," Cliff mutters in the background. Obviously—it's further from him than Tennessee was.

"I think I will like it here."

She breathes out a long, exaggerated sigh. "Well, it sounds like you're making a huge mistake, but don't take my word for it. What would I know? No one ever listens to me."

"Look, Mom. I'm going to be here awhile. A friend told me about a job down here. I didn't want to miss out on the opportunity."

"What about school, Glory? We paid an arm and a leg to send you to that out-of-state school."

"I can finish online. No big deal."

"Online, Glory? Dear God. I can't believe you would work that hard and finish online—like some kind of community college flunky."

She is so judgmental it turns my stomach. "I will still get the degree from the University of Tennessee. I just wanted to get a jump start on the summer and take this job to make a little extra money. It pays well, and there was a lot of competition for the one opening." A small lie won't hurt.

"Well, you just can't leave Nick," she whines in her high-pitched Southern drawl.

"I don't want you to listen to what Nick says to you. I broke up with him, and he's pissed, and—"

"I just don't want you to throw away your relationship with him for some summer fling," she interrupts.

Summer fling? Where does she come up with this stuff?

"Glory? Are you still there?"

"Look, Mom. I know you like Nick, whatever, but it's over between us. Please just quit speaking to him and let it go. And whatever you do, do not tell him where I am."

More talking and laughter in the background. "Mom?"

"Yes, Glory. I'm here, but unfortunately, I need to skedaddle.

Your father is taking me out tonight. We are going with a few of his colleagues ballroom dancing. It is *so* much fun."

She's no longer listening. Having decided I'm not in immediate danger, she's moved on.

I seize the opportunity to escape the conversation. "Okay, Mom," I say brightly. "Have fun."

"I will, honey!" she shrieks over background laughter. "Let's talk again very soon."

"Okay," I say to dead air. She's already hung up.

CHAPTER 13

HAVING USED THE kitchen briefly for pancakes, I know there's nothing in the cabinets or fridge except for an old jar of pickles and some baking soda. The pancake supplies in the refrigerator won't do me much good when I need to make lunch or dinner, and if I'm staying at Dave's, I need groceries.

I count what's left in my lime green wallet—not much. Stuffing a fifty-dollar bill in my front pocket, I head to my truck. The nearest Kroger is only a few miles away.

Thirty minutes later, I'm moving up and down aisles at the Kroger, and I've gathered many key essentials: canned meals, staples like salt and pepper, basic spices, butter, milk, hummus, chips, coffee, apples, and carrots.

Near the wine section, I discover a tourist clothing display. Among the racks, I find water sport leggings with a matching short-sleeve top on clearance.

Glancing around, I check my sleeve. The bruising on my right side is healing quickly. With luck, I can forgo the wind-breaker tomorrow, so the short sleeves might work.

"Perfect," I whisper cheerfully. With a job and budding friendships—even with Ellis—things feel more hopeful.

By eight, I'm sneaking around Dave's main resort area with my bags, avoiding guests. The setting sun accompanies music and chatter from the Hut. Though it sounds fun, I crave a quiet evening in my new apartment.

After unpacking, I make a plate of hummus, pita chips, and veggies.

I'm standing at the counter, mid-scarf, when a cool breeze grazes my left arm. I follow the current to its source—the door at the kitchen's far end, the one with the lock, and it's cracked open.

"Hello?" I call through my mouthful of hummus, suddenly nervous. "Is someone there?"

Silence.

I approach the door as another current of air pushes it wider. The breeze carries an intoxicating blend of sweet citrus and salt. I reach out and give the door a gentle pull, and it glides open silently.

Stepping through, I find myself in what appears to be a small mudroom. An unlit lantern-style fixture hangs overhead, and a small bookcase lines the left wall. At the far end, another door stands propped open with a paint can, feeding that steady, fragrant breeze. I walk over and bend down to remove the can but stop as curiosity gets the best of me. Instead, I push it open.

"Wow," I breathe as my eyes adjust to the fading light.

I'm standing on a small balcony that wraps around the house's top edge, just below the roofline. The view stuns me; a crystal blue ocean stretches westward, perfectly framing the setting sun. It's the kind of vista you'd expect from a million-dollar beachfront condo. I take a few more steps forward, and the balcony reveals itself as much larger than it first appeared, about the size of the kitchen, and to the far end of it, there is an open-air brick staircase that appears to lead to the roof level. This must be what Red was talking about when I first arrived.

I turn back toward the mudroom and finally notice a door opposite the balcony, one that had been hidden when I came in from the kitchen. Ellis's apartment. It, too, swings open and shut in the evening breeze.

"Get out of here," I hiss to myself.

I start to retreat but turn back for another glimpse at the view—it's just so captivating, and I can't help but wonder what's up those stairs. The overwhelming curiosity eventually pulls me forward, and though I should turn back and flee to the kitchen, I begin a cautious ascent up the mystery stairs.

Heights don't usually bother me, but climbing this older staircase into the open sky, even though there are iron rails, is unsettling.

Rounding the final turn, I gasp as my eyes clear the top level.

"Oh my God." My jaw drops in shock.

Words fail before the beauty—and fragrance—surrounding me.

I find myself standing on a tropical rooftop garden that stretches across the length of the house. Large planters hold miniature trees covered in yellow star-shaped flowers, and between and around them, containers of every shape, size, and color burst with blooms in endless hues: roses, hydrangeas, birds-of-paradise, jasmine—a rainbow of species thriving in this hidden paradise.

A freshly stained wooden pergola anchors the garden. Beneath it, a wooden swing sways in the salty breeze, shaded by climbing pink roses that twist from base to peak. Small wooden tables flank the swing, one holding a pot overflowing with fresh herbs—thyme, oregano, and basil, I think.

Setting my plate on the empty table, I turn slowly, drinking in the view. A burst of color draws me to a small tree with delicate flowers. I gently pull up its label.

Florida key lime.

"You have to be kidding me." I replace the marker and lean in to smell the blooms; their sweet scent is intoxicating.

I explore for several minutes, occasionally drawn to the ocean, though even its hypnotic waves and distant lights can't compete with this garden. Eventually, I return to the swing, where I sit and finish my hummus as I admire the beauty of it all.

Even though the rooftop is new to me, and technically I am trespassing, it's oddly comforting, like an old friend.

Eventually, my gaze extends beyond the garden as I watch moonlight paint flickering white paths across the distant water, its bright orb just above the horizon. I sit my plate back on the side table when I am done and close my eyes, kicking my legs slightly so the swing sways before pulling my legs underneath me.

I'm not sure how long I sat in silence for—eyes closed, breath steady—but eventually, sleep finds me. I dream that I am somewhere warm and sunny, a Corona in hand. It tastes like oranges. A blurry male figure approaches on my right—I can't see his face, but his body is glorious. "I know you," I say dreamily.

The figure starts chanting my name. Glory. Over and over.

"Wake up, sleepy head," a voice calls.

Who is that?

"Wake up, Glory," firmer now.

I snap from my dream into total darkness. I sit up urgently, suddenly confused. It takes a moment to remember—I'm still on the swing. I blink rapidly, noticing twinkling Christmas lights now wrapping the pergola, illuminating the flowers. "These weren't here before."

A deep chuckle to my left startles me, and I jump up with a squeak, turning towards the sound.

A tall figure emerges from the shadows, holding something.

Ellis.

I release a held breath. For a second, I'd thought Nick had found me.

Ellis steps into the moonlight, moving carefully as if not to frighten me. He takes another step, and my eyes fix on his hands.

"Are you holding a watering can?" I ask.

Ellis glances at the dented metal container, smiling. "It appears that way. Someone has to water these plants."

I watch Ellis tilt the can into a nearby planter, and it hits me—this immaculate garden is his. "You did all this?" I ask, gesturing around us.

The question immediately feels ridiculous. Of course, it's Ellis's garden. It is only accessible through his apartment.

He winks, then moves forward to the next plant in line, one with long, thin green leaves and small orange flowers. It's a variety that I've seen sprinkled here and there throughout the resort.

"Wait, are you also in charge of the landscaping around here?"

What do you think?" he says as a flicker of pride moves across his face.

"You definitely are."

He gives a gentle nod.

"Are you serious?" I ask, as he continues watering silently. "This is incredible. The landscaping here looks like it's from a magazine. It actually makes this place the paradise that it is."

He glances sideways with a soft smile. "Thanks. I have been working on it a lot more lately."

I watch him move through the garden in silence, watering can tilting here and there. He tests soil with gentle fingers and inspects leaves and blooms as if they're made of glass.

"How did you learn to do all this?"

He gazes blankly at the plants. "Someone showed me the basics, helped me get started, then I kind of…took over."

Jane? I dare not ask.

He watches me, seemingly waiting for another question. When none comes, he pulls out a small pocketknife. I flinch involuntarily.

He approaches a large bird-of-paradise in a waist-high cedar planter. With one swift movement, a flower drops into his hand. Pocketing the knife, he walks over casually and hands it to me.

I stare blankly at the offered bloom. The small kindness catches me off-guard. I take it carefully. "Thank you. I love it."

Ellis settles on the other end of the swing. Though he doesn't touch me, heat radiates from his leg like a furnace. He kicks us into a gentle sway. "So, am I forgiven?"

I pretend to consider his question, biting my lip. "I guess."

"You guess? You're not sure?"

"I guess, I'm sure."

Ellis smiles. "I'll take it."

"A new start."

"Yeah. A new start." He throws a leg over the armrest, leaning back with a shaky breath. I can't stop staring at his salt-tousled blonde hair, standing in every direction.

"Did you have a nice nap?" he asks, eyebrows raised expectantly.

"Oh, God." The memory of sneaking into his apartment floods back. I cover my face. "I'm sorry. Your door was cracked open, and I just got curious. I didn't know it was your place. Well, not at first." I peek up to find him smiling silently, clearly enjoying this.

Words tumble out nervously. "It's amazing. I mean…it just feels so…" My voice falls off as I can't find the words to describe how comforting the rooftop is. "I guess I fell asleep and—"

Ellis mercifully raises his hand. "Seriously, don't worry about it." He stretches his arms behind his head with a playful smirk. "I'm happy to share it with you."

"Really? You're not mad?"

"Nope. You can come up here anytime. I'll leave the door unlocked. "

"Thanks," I whisper. He acknowledges with a nod.

"No one else has been up here in a while. It makes me feel good to see you enjoying it."

Does he mean Jane?

After sitting in silence for some time, enjoying the peace and company, Ellis stands, motioning for me to follow. "It's going to be cold up here soon. I don't want you nodding off and turning into a popsicle."

A cold breeze rattles leaves and tosses my hair, and as if on cue, I shiver.

"Good idea." I start to stand but collapse back like a plank as pain slices through my lower back. Ellis darts towards me.

"Are you okay?" Ellis asks as he offers me an extended hand.

I wince and nod. "My legs are still sore from the…" My awkward laugh doesn't dispel the concern flashing across his face. I force an unsteady smile. "I'll be fine."

"Let me help you," he offers again after a moment. I take his hand, and his fingers wrap warmly around mine. He supports my shoulder with his other hand and pulls me up slowly.

I hold on longer than necessary, steadying myself.

"Okay. I'm fine now. Thanks so much." Releasing his hand, I move cautiously toward the stairs.

As Ellis follows, new tension fills the air.

"Glory?" He taps my shoulder softly.

"Yeah?" I say as I turn towards his voice.

"Are you okay?" His tone carries sincere concern, not judgment.

He stands a few feet away, hands in his pockets. I blame myself for his glum mood.

Just trust him. The soft voice persuades me.

"It's strange that I'm telling you this," I say. "I've not wanted to share this with anyone else. I don't want anyone to pity me."

"You can trust me," he says as he steps forward.

I bring my hands forward and fidget with a nail as I speak. "I'm sorry you had to see all of that."

"All of what?"

I gesture to my bruises. "All of the…bruises and stuff."

Ellis's lips pull tight. "Is that why you're so sore?"

I nod. "My memories are a bit mixed up right now, and it happened so fast, but he got mad. I was trying to get away, and I think that made him even angrier. He came up behind me and just pushed me hard. The steps were concrete and—"

"What?" Ellis interrupts as he steps forward. "That son-of-a-bitch pushed you down steps?" Suddenly, he's in front of me, hands gently over mine. His eyes burn with anger, but not at me, *for* me. At first, I bristle at being treated as fragile, but then I realize he's just doing what most men are programmed to do: to protect.

"I was scared, and I thought I was going to die." I cringe, pulling a hand up to wipe at a stray tear.

Ellis rubs my hand with his thumb gently before pulling me into a soft embrace. "Please, Glory. Never apologize for that criminal again." He pulls back, jaw working beneath his lips. "He deserves to be in jail."

As I look up, our eyes lock as I search for judgment or pity, but I find neither. Relief washes over me. I'm suddenly so grateful for Ellis's reaction to my secret.

After a moment, Ellis drops his hands and turns away in silence. I watch his shoulders rise and fall in measured breaths.

"Please don't be upset." I reach out and gently rub his back, feeling the hard corded muscle beneath his shirt. "It's okay. *I'm* okay."

After a moment, he shakes his head and turns back. "I'm sorry you had to go through that. And I'm sorry no one was there to prevent it from happening."

"Me too. But it's over now."

"It is," he says sternly. "He will never hurt you again. I promise you that."

I don't understand how he can make that promise, even as my friend, but I nod. I want him to believe that he can protect me from Nick.

"And don't worry, Glory. I won't say anything—to Dave or anyone."

"Thanks," I say, grateful for reinforcing his promise. His sincerity means everything. Though I've opened up to him, I'm still uneasy about sharing with others.

Just outside the balcony door, we stand staring at each other for a moment before I give him a silent nod and push through the door into his apartment. In the kitchen, I turn back, half-expecting him to have followed me in, but he hasn't.

CHAPTER 14

WHEN MY ALARM sounds, I wake in anticipation of the day. Looking forward to something when you haven't in so long is a strange feeling. It's one of several emotions that have crept back into my life in the last couple of days, tangible evidence that the power Nick has over me is slipping.

I dress quickly and head to the kitchen, grabbing the orange juice I'd bought yesterday. On the porch, I raise my hand silently as I enter. Noah nods, Red asleep in his lap. Blair doesn't notice, buried in another romance novel. Clinton and JJ barely glance up from their video game, offering simple man-nods.

I pour juice and settle on the same long bench swing as last time—perfect for watching the others while maintaining an unobstructed ocean view. Pulling my legs up, I cradle my juice in both hands and close my eyes. The swing's gentle motion and cool ocean breeze nearly lull me back to sleep.

"Mind if I sit?"

The deep voice startles me back to reality.

Ellis. I hadn't heard him approach.

"Hi," I smile, swinging my legs down and spilling juice on my new pants.

Ellis reaches down and rubs the spot until it disappears. "Sorry about that." Though friendly, his touch brings heat to my cheeks.

"No problem," I say, sitting straighter and motioning for him to join me. Looking around, I catch Blair and Noah watching us curiously. They don't know about last night on the roof or our fresh start. Ellis's sudden attitude shift must seem dramatic. Just yesterday, he looked at me like he wanted me to get hit by a bus. Now he's falling asleep in my lap and choosing to sit beside me, leg inches from mine.

Ellis leans back with a slight moan, stretching his arms overhead. A strip of skin shows above his Calvin Klein waistband, drawing my eyes briefly before I catch myself.

"So?" he asks playfully, tilting his head.

I look around, avoiding his blue gaze, but when our eyes meet, I smile, tucking a strand of hair behind my ear.

"So?"

"So, I think you're headed out with Red, Blair, and the troll today."

"Hey!" JJ looks up from his game, but Ellis ignores him.

"Should be fun."

"Cool," I say nodding.

"I was also thinking that we should get you in the water soon. What do you think about a short open water snorkeling lesson tomorrow morning at, let's say, 6 AM? We need to work on those sea legs, right?"

I nod, excitement and nerves coursing through me. "That would be great." Snorkeling seems fun, and if I'm staying at Dave's long-term, I should learn to snorkel, and eventually, scuba dive.

I still feel the others watching our interaction from the corners of my eyes. Then, a thought hits me. "But it's dark at six."

"Yeah," Ellis smirks. "It is."

"You want to train me at night?" I ask cautiously. "What about sharks?"

Ellis cocks his head, smiling. "What's wrong with sharks?"

He suddenly looks predatory, and my eyes flutter to his lips, searching for sharp teeth.

Jesus, this guy has a beautiful smile.

It's genuine and infectious, and his teeth aren't pointy at all; they're perfect. I love a guy with nice teeth.

That's enough, Glory.

He catches me staring, so I try to cover. "Sharks have a lot of teeth."

He chuckles. "They sure do. *Hundreds.*"

I narrow my eyes. "I'm serious." Looking around, I find that everyone is smiling wide.

"What?" I say seriously, though a smile tugs at my mouth. "It's a legitimate question." The laughter grows louder. Blair nearly snorts into her book.

Red shifts in Noah's lap so she's facing me. "Sharks are not going to bother you."

"You sound like my mom, Glory," Clinton adds, as he looks up and shakes his head.

"She does," Blair agrees, exchanging a look with Clinton as he winks.

"Mom hates the water, always worried about tentacles and teeth." Clinton wiggles his fingers at Blair, who rolls her eyes.

Ellis grins widely. "Glory. You'll be fine."

"What about that guy from Alabama?" JJ pipes up. Everyone goes silent, turning to him. I narrow my eyes.

"Shut up, JJ!" Blair and Clinton say simultaneously, exchanging nervous glances.

"Leave it to JJ," Noah says flatly.

"*What* guy from Alabama?" I ask softly.

JJ starts to speak, but Ellis raises a finger to his lips, silencing him. He turns from me. "There's no guy from Alabama, Glory."

"Well, there *was* a guy," JJ persists, "before he got eaten alive." He dodges Noah's thrown pillow.

I start to stand. "Oh, hell no."

Everyone bursts out laughing again, and I feel Ellis's hand on my knee, firm and comforting. The heat from his touch penetrates my pants. When I glance down, he's already withdrawn.

"Look, Glory," he says seriously. "There was this guy from Alabama several years ago. He decided that getting into a tug-of-war match with a ten-foot tiger shark over a grouper he had caught while spearfishing was a good idea. The guy was dragged underwater and ended up drowning. He didn't get eaten."

"But there were bite marks," JJ says as he stands. He bolts from the room as Noah hurls a pillow at his head.

I look to Ellis, who nods and shrugs. "You can't expect wild animals to let a good meal slip away."

I cringe at the grotesque image.

Ellis pats my leg again. "We're not getting into the ocean, so it doesn't matter."

One brow raises involuntarily. "We're not?"

"No. Not because of sharks, or scary fish, but because of currents and visibility."

"Oh, okay," I say, trying to hide the relief running through me. I don't mind fish. Actually, I love the idea of swimming with them. I used to dream about gliding through clear, coral and bright tropical fish surrounding me. It's a common kind of dream, I think—like flying.

"We'll do a basic open water crash course in the pool. It'll be fun."

"The pool?"

"Yep."

"Thank the Lord," I say suddenly, and everyone breaks out in a fit of laughs. I look up blushing.

"We're not judging," Red says. "You need to be mindful of the ocean life, but honestly, you're more likely to be struck by lightning."

"Definitely," Clinton adds. "But it's a common fear."

Ellis winks at Clinton before standing to grab his canvas bag. As he bends forward, I can't help noticing how his low-rise board shorts frame his perfect backside. I quickly avert my stare when I catch Red watching me with narrowed eyes.

Ellis stands then turns and pats my shoulder. "Stick to the girls today, and you'll learn a lot." Before anyone can respond, he walks forward then pushes through the screen door behind the swing. I turn and see him walking slowly down the path to the resort.

After a moment, I turn back and catch everyone exchanging dumbfounded looks.

"Well, that was certainly interesting," Red says suspiciously, breaking the silence.

"I'd say so," Clinton adds. "He's not being a dickhead."

I press my lips together, feigning ignorance. I don't want to explain Ellis's sudden change of heart.

Twenty minutes later, we're all on the dock as Dave assigns the day's tasks. "Okay, folks. Thank you for everyone being here on time today." He glances over his shoulder, winking at Ellis, who rolls his eyes.

"We'll have two main dives today, both this morning. Red will take out a small group on Seahorse II with JJ, Blair, and Glory assisting."

"Jesus," JJ whispers, earning a head smack from Noah. Dave ignores them.

"Ellis and Clinton will handle the group on Seahorse I. Ellis?" He turns. "If you need a third, I will join."

"Sure thing, boss," Ellis says as Clinton salutes.

"Let's see how many show up this morning. Once Glory's fully trained, Noah and I will stick to the dock, and we'll divide into two standing teams of three."

"Why do I have to go with the girls, Dave?" JJ whines.

"You are one of the girls," Blair says flatly, examining her nail. JJ falls silent.

Dave rolls his eyes. "Everybody knows the Porter family, and they've specifically requested Ellis and Clinton."

"Of course," Blair snarls. "Tramps."

"What can I say?" Clinton shrugs. "Those sisters love us." Blair scrunches her face, flipping him off. Noah whistles low.

"Well," Dave continues, "since they're some of our best customers, it's hard to turn them down. Just keep Melanie at arm's length, Clinton—"

"Like I do every year," Clinton interjects.

"Ellis has a little tougher job," Dave adds. "Maggie is particularly persistent."

"Cougar," Blair supplies.

"She's been after Ellis the past several seasons," Red whispers in my ear. "He's nice to her and maybe even flirts a bit, but it's all smoke and mirrors. It used to piss off—" She stops abruptly, waving her hand as she pulls back. "Never mind."

"Oh, okay," I say, watching Ellis focus on Dave. Red doesn't know Clinton's told me about Jane, so I play dumb.

"Why does the one who looks like a pro wrestler have to like me?" Clinton asks.

Blair chuckles. "You know you secretly like the big ones."

"You like my big—"

"Dude!" Dave says, throwing up both hands. "Please, no, my man. This old guy can't take it." Dave sighs as he hangs the clipboard back up.

For the next hour, I shadow Red and Blair, helping load dive equipment, collecting sack lunches from Aki, and wiping down Seahorse II's main deck, which is about half the size of Seahorse I.

"So, Red's the Captain of Seahorse II?" I ask.

"Generally," Blair says. "But only because I prefer to read on the way out." Red sticks her tongue out at Blair.

"And what about Seahorse I? Ellis?"

"Yep," Red says.

"When he's not trying to get into some girl's panties," Blair adds, "at which point, Clinton takes the reins."

Red ignores her. "Ellis's dad, Jim, was big into boating. That's how he and Dave became best friends. "So, Ellis is a natural boat-head."

"Does Ellis's family live nearby?"

Red frowns, shaking her head. "Dave and Jim were in Iraq together in the early nineties, and both suffered PTSD. Dave managed to overcome it and start a thriving business, but Jim turned to drugs and alcohol. Just after Ellis's Mom died of breast cancer, Jim passed away, and Ellis moved in with Dave."

"That is terrible," I say. I am curious to know more but don't pry for details. I had a friend in high school whose mother died of breast cancer. Watching her endure the ups and downs of treatment was painful. I have a special place in my heart for caregivers.

"How old was Ellis when he moved in with Dave?" Blair asks, untangling masks. "I don't think he ever told me."

"Ten, I think," Red says, joining us in sorting equipment.

"What about Clinton? How did he end up here?" I ask, and Blair visibly stiffens.

"Clinton was a friend of Ellis's at the University of Florida," Red answers. "He's worked here since his freshman year. Since graduation, he's just kind of stuck around."

Blair tosses fins onto the deck harshly. "Yeah, well the idiot needs to move on."

Red gives Blair a side hug. "He just can't resist that coot coot."

"Red!" Blair squeaks, face purpling. "Don't ever talk about my coot coot."

I can't help giggling but stop when I notice Blair tearing up. Red leans in and whispers something in her ear that she nods to. Though curious about Blair and Clinton's situation, I ignore their exchange.

Minutes later, Blair's recovered, and we're chatting again. This time, we are talking about JJ, who appears shirtless nearby, flexing while balancing an air tank on his shoulder. Blair and Red notice his exaggerated looks in our direction.

"Put a shirt on, lover boy," Blair calls as Red mimics bodybuilder poses.

As passengers arrive, Red hands me a clipboard to check names. First comes an elderly couple with their teenage grandson, beaming with excitement. The others consist of newlyweds, some college guys, and two women in their forties—fourteen passengers plus our crew. Thankfully, there are no sorority girls.

I find an empty spot near the loading ramp as Red starts the engines. Blair and JJ take center stage for rules and safety instructions. This is a scuba trip, so I listen intently. Blair's no-nonsense delivery carries a softer edge than usual, but she still commands everyone's attention. Even JJ performs professionally, following Blair's lead with equipment demonstrations.

Twenty minutes out, we drop anchor, land still visible on the horizon. I start to ask JJ about our distance but stop as I see him lean in to say something to the newly married lady.

"Hey there," he says as his head follows the elevator movement of his eyes behind lowered sunglasses.

If she notices his attention, which she must, she ignores it. But JJ persists, leaning against the rail beside her, flexing. Her eyes flick his way before rolling skyward.

"So…you like scuba diving, huh?"

She responds by flashing her wedding ring. JJ's brow furrows in confusion—he probably doesn't recognize what it means. But understanding arrives when her massive fiancé emerges from the bathroom.

"What the fuck are you doing, twerp?"

JJ throws up his hands, eyes wide. He may be a smartass, but he's not stupid. "Just trying to make sure the lady—your lady—doesn't need any other equipment." Catching his own innuendo, he quickly adds, "*Dive* equipment."

The guy steps closer, narrowing his eyes. "Why are you still here?"

Blair smacks JJ's shoulder with a loud pop. "Could you please take the anchor line down, JJ?"

Most guests, including the newlyweds, seem experienced, donning gear confidently. Only one older lady, apparently traveling with her sister, looks new to diving. They bicker as the experienced sister demonstrates proper mask technique. I smile at their exchange. Although I never had siblings, I always wanted a sister. I imagine it's like the friendship Blair and Red share.

Red then joins us on deck, helping guests adjust equipment and checking connections. When one young guy puts his tank on backwards, she quickly fixes it.

"Don't worry about it," she assures, as his face reddens in embarrassment. "Happens all the time."

"Hey, Glory," Blair calls while tightening a tank strap. "Red and I are going to suit up topside. Come with, so Red can show you the controls."

Following them up, Red motions me to the helm. "There's not much to do, but you should know the basics just in case of emergencies."

The controls mirror Seahorse I's, which Clinton had covered during my first trip. I easily grasp anchor operation, radio protocols, and basic navigation.

"How did you learn all this?" I ask, gripping the helm and experimenting with movements, pretending competence.

"Dave. He taught me everything." She smacks me playfully in the arm. "We will have to get you certified to operate this bad boy."

"Red's the teacher's pet," Blair teases, sticking out her tongue.

"Yeah, I am," Red smiles. "He is my dad and all."

"Wait," I say. "Dave's your dad?"

"Not biological, but before Mom died, he officially adopted me. Honestly, even if he hadn't, I'd still consider him my dad. Mom and Dave married when I was two, and he's the only dad I've known. The only reason he didn't adopt me sooner was because Mom wouldn't let him."

Red's smile turns sad but accepting. "It'll be five years this September."

"I'm sorry, Red," I say softly. "I know what it's like to lose someone you love."

"Who did you lose?" Red asks directly, adjusting her BC straps.

"My dad," I say after a moment of thought. "The person who loved me most in this world." My unblinking gaze shifts between them as memories flood back—watching baseball, riding I-95 on sales calls, Saturday morning pancakes. Dad made the best pancakes. That's how I learned. I raise a hand to my temple as images twist incoherently in my mind and a sharp pain jolts across the side of my head. Stress lately has made it so difficult for me to focus.

"Are we leaving or what?" JJ shouts from below, interrupting the moment. I'm grateful.

Red exhales dramatically. "JJ always manages to chime in at the most awkward times."

"Yeah," I say in agreement, as I force a smile.

CHAPTER 15

I WATCH AS Red, Blair, and JJ lead their groups into the water, leaving me alone on the boat. The dive flag, attached to JJ, floats along the surface.

Though Red assured me I don't need to stay "glued to the helm," several minutes pass before I feel comfortable stepping away. After circling the boat twice to familiarize myself with doors, closets, and the bathroom, I find myself beside the ladder leading into the bright blue water, watching out over the horizon. Everything is eerily silent except for the boat's creaks and bumps as it rocks on the calm sea.

I watch for ten minutes, letting myself get lost in the hum of the waves before me, before retreating to the top deck, where I settle on the long bench across from the controls. I nudge Blair's yellow mesh bag aside with my foot.

Leaning back, I inhale deeply, letting the sun warm my face. The cool ocean breeze starts melting away tension when a scream shatters the peace.

"Glory!"

I bolt up and run to the boat's side, scanning the water. Nothing but bubbles.

Did I imagine that?

"Glory!" Another desperate cry.

The strained voice comes from the main deck. I hurtle down

the stairs, landing hard before spotting movement by the fold-out ladder. My face drains at the sight—Blair holds the rail with one hand while supporting a semi-conscious Red with the other. Dark red tinges the water around them.

Blood.

"What happened?" I drop to my knees, reaching for Red.

Blair pushes her toward me. "That jackass JJ." I step onto the ladder and into the water, pulling Red forward. She can walk but seems completely off-balance.

"I have a cut," Red says softly, meeting my eyes. She nods to her hand, and I grimace at the large gash across her palm, blood dripping along its side.

Blair pulls herself onto the deck before helping me steady Red's ascent. As Red takes the final step, she moans and pitches forward. I grab her side, but her weight plus equipment proves too much. We tumble, and my head strikes the edge of the metal bench. I feel a warm wetness but push past it, scrambling to Red.

Need to stop Red's bleeding.

"Shit," Blair sheds her weight belt and BC, shoving them aside. "Shit, shit, shit."

I urge Red to show me her hand. She hesitates before extending it. Blood trickles down her BC, pooling on the deck and mixing with seawater.

Everything is so red.

The deep gash runs along her outer palm, wrapping around to her thumb. Blair gags at the sight.

She holds out trembling hands. "Sorry, Red. I just—"

"I know you're squeamish," Red murmurs.

"We need to stop the blood flow," I say, grabbing rope from a nearby storage bag.

"I'm sorry, Red, but I have to do this. It will hurt." She nods in acknowledgment.

I wrap the rope tightly around her forearm, securing it with a firm knot. As I do, Red gasps, her head wobbling dangerously. The tourniquet increases her pain, but it's necessary to slow blood loss.

Blair and I then remove Red's fins and carefully pull her away from the steps. Blair releases the BC buckles, gently rolling Red to free her from the blood-soaked equipment before tossing it aside. Crimson stains spread across the deck.

"What the hell do we do?" Blair panics. "We can't leave until everyone's back!"

"It will be okay," Red whispers, trying to be brave through clenched eyes.

Her increasing unsteadiness concerns me. I slip into nurse mode. Someone needs to take charge, and Blair's in shock. I steady myself with a deep breath.

"It'll be okay," I echo confidently, for both their benefit. "I saw a first-aid kit below. Hold her for a minute."

Blair nods. "Okay."

I retrieve the kit and return in under a minute to find Red slumped in Blair's lap.

"Hang on, Red," I urge. "Do your best to stay awake." Red's passing out would make everything more complicated. Moving dead weight is nearly impossible.

"Help me sit her up, Blair," I instruct, and then we both take a side and hoist her upward.

"Sit behind her, Blair, and hold her steady."

Blair nods wide-eyed, gently wrapping her arms around Red's waist. "Like this?"

"Exactly."

With Red upright, I examine her hand. The bleeding has slowed. "Hold your arm up like this," I demonstrate.

Blair kisses Red's head. "Hang in there, girl. You'll be fine." Red manages a soft smile. Blair's wide eyes ask me silently: *Is she going to be okay?*

I nod reassuringly, and Blair exhales, relief flooding her face.

"Jesus. Is she okay?" JJ appears behind me, helping guests aboard, their faces a mix of curiosity and concern.

"No thanks to you, jackass," Blair spits.

"I didn't mean to…"

JJ looks terrified, his face drained of color. I force a smile, needing him to be functional for the guests. "She'll be fine, JJ."

Blair's pinched lips and narrowed eyes promise retribution.

JJ better sleep with one eye open.

Turning back to Red: "You will be fine."

"Thanks, G," Red pats my leg.

Thankfully, the first aid kit contains everything needed for a temporary fix: strip sutures, cotton bandages, medical tape, and betadine.

I clean the wound with a fresh bottle of spring water and betadine. As I do, Red gasps audibly in pain, which causes Blair to wince. "I am sorry, Red," I say. "I have to clean it well, or you will get an infection." A closer inspection reveals only a few deep gashes. It also doesn't appear that she has cut any major tendons. I apply the temporary sutures, per the directions, then wrap the hand tightly with a bandage. "I'll stay here with Red if you can help get everyone ready to go and drive us back." As I see Blair hesitate, I add, "She is doing fine."

Blair nods, satisfied, and then joins JJ to manage the guests. Within minutes, we're darting full speed towards the resort. I hold tightly to Red, positioning us near a small storage compartment to help shield her from the wind. Red's grimacing and teeth-grinding indicate that her pain is increasing. Post-accident, the body initially blocks pain signals. Unfortunately, the adrenaline wears off, and the nerve endings eventually reactivate.

The trip back feels short—likely due to Blair's urgent piloting. As we slow near the dock, shouts erupt. "Where is she!" Noah thunders before leaping aboard, ignoring the water and landing with enough force to rock the boat visibly. JJ retreats to the far rail, watching nervously. Noah kneels beside Red, whispering softly while stroking her head. Despite his terrified expression, his presence visibly calms her. In one fluid motion, Noah lifts Red and carries her off. Blair and I follow as he heads for the office. Behind us, JJ nervously helps disgruntled guests disembark, eyes darting around anxiously.

"Poor guy," I mutter to myself.

We enter Dave's office, where Noah places Red on the large leather couch. Dave looks up from his computer, frowning. "Already called an ambulance. They'll be here any minute. What happened?" He stands then walks over to Red and inspects her now cherry-red bandage.

"That dipshit went into the ship again and got stuck," Blair seethes.

"I told him to stay out of there," Dave says as he shakes his head in disappointment.

"Showing off, like always," Blair adds. "Red had to get him out. She got cut on rusty metal, trying to dislodge his tank. They could have died."

Noah silently holds Red, his forehead reddened, and brows lowered menacingly. I'm not used to seeing this enormous man visibly angry, and I'm suddenly grateful he smiles as much as he does.

Dave strokes Red's head. "You okay, kiddo?"

"Yeah. I think," she whispers weakly.

"Next time, you leave him in the ship," Blair says.

"He is not going back in the water," Dave asserts evenly. "Not for a very long time." He examines the cut beneath the bandages. "She'll be okay. Who bandaged her up?"

When I stay quiet, Blair points. "Glory did. She was brilliant out there."

"It's no big deal. I was happy to help."

"No big deal?" Blair pulls me into a tight hug. "You're my hero, girl."

Noah's fury softens slightly. "I owe you. I owe you big." The praise feels good, though a bit uncomfortable. I'm not used to people saying good things about me.

"Let's get her out front for the ambulance," Dave says. "Blair, can you help me carry her and—don't Noah!" Dave shouts, but Noah's already storming out.

"Noah!" Red calls weakly.

"Take her out front, Blair," Dave thrusts the insurance card and cash into her hand. "She and I have the same insurance. I need to stop Noah before JJ gets hurt. Glory, handle the guests. Tell them they'll get free store credit and passes to come back. Take everyone to the shop and wait for me."

"Okay," I say as he rushes out. "Hang in there, Red," I urge as I slip out the back behind him.

Outside, Dave calls Noah, who is stalking toward a frozen JJ. I run to address the gathered guests—some amused by the unfolding drama, others angry about the shortened trip.

"Attention everyone," I project over the chatter. "Dave is giving everyone a free voucher to return to Dave's, plus a guest voucher."

"I don't live near here," an older man snaps.

"Dave will provide store credit also."

"That's more like it," he says, interrupted by a scream.

I turn to see Noah carrying JJ overhead toward the end of the dock.

"Put me down!" JJ flails uselessly.

Dave stops by Seahorse I, hands raised. "Put him down, Noah. I know you're angry but—"

Noah hurls JJ into the water.

"He's lucky," Noah thunders to Dave before turning back to JJ bobbing below. "Pray there is no scar, you little shit!"

Dave rubs his forehead and approaches Ellis and Clinton by Seahorse I, fresh from their dive and watching, confused. They huddle as Dave explains, muttering expletives at JJ.

I start toward Dave to report on the passengers but halt when I hear my name.

"Glory saved the day," Dave's saying. His eyes find me. "Speak of the devil."

Ellis turns, exhaling before pulling me into a gentle side hug that engulfs me. "Hero, huh? Are you okay?"

Surprised by his tenderness, I can only nod and smile.

"What happened?" Clinton asks tightly.

"She saved my girl's life," Noah pats my shoulders from behind.

"And JJ's," Ellis adds softly.

Noah nods in agreement, biting his lip.

"Damn," Clinton says.

"I owe you everything," Noah says, still visibly shaking.

Just then, his phone chimes. He pulls it from his pocket and looks at its bright screen. "She just got to the ER. They are going to stich her up I am going to head that way now and check on her." He nods in my direction. "Thanks, again, G."

"It's fine. I'm just happy she's okay." I wave towards his back as he stalks away.

"But what happened?" Clinton presses.

Over the next few minutes, I recount everything—Blair's scream, the blood, the rushed trip back. They listen intently as I retell each moment, their faces tightening with every detail.

"Is JJ okay?" I ask, looking towards the end of the dock.

Ellis shrugs. "He's fine...at least for now." Ellis points past the boat.

"Idiot," Clinton mutters as we watch JJ crawl onto the resort's small fishing pier by the guest condos fifty yards away.

"Look at that guy crabbing," Clinton says as JJ passes a

bewildered guest with a trap. "Probably thinks JJ's some merman." Our laughter carries to JJ, who shakes out his hair and frowns.

"Ouch," I say as I inadvertently touch the top of my head, where dried blood has clotted around a small gash.

Ellis steps forward. "What is it?"

I hold my hands up. "I'm okay. Just a small cut."

"Holy shit," Ellis says as he steps forward and looks down at my head, clearly concerned.

"I'm fine, seriously. I just hit my head on the metal bench."

Ellis reaches forward and gently shifts my hair around.

"Is it okay?" Dave asks him.

Ellis nods before pulling his hand back. "It's okay." His eyes dart to mine. "Just be sure to clean it well."

I nod. "I will."

Ellis steps back, and I see him wipe his hand on his jeans, leaving a small streak of red behind.

CHAPTER 16

ELLIS TRIES TO get me to go shower and clean my head, but I insist on helping he and Clinton.

Over the next hour or so, the three of us handle double duty—cleaning up after the dives while Dave manages the shop and disgruntled passengers. Ellis focuses on the boats, wiping decks and hauling tanks to storage while I assist Clinton.

Clinton, again as a patient teacher, methodically demonstrates proper equipment storage. "A freshwater rinse is vital to maintaining dive equipment," he explains, dunking a regulator in a large drum.

"So, it doesn't rust?"

"Exactly."

"That's why you have mesh bags," I say as he submerges his yellow bag.

Clinton winks. "You got it, G."

After storing smaller equipment, we refuel boats, wash decks, and pack life vests. Clinton heads off to help Dave, leaving Ellis and me alone on the dock.

Ellis pulls out two water bottles. "Your reward."

"Thanks." I drink deeply, suddenly craving a cool shower.

"You were amazing today. What you did for Red means a lot to me, to us."

"No problem. I was happy to help."

"Red's cut was rough."

I nod as my stomach growls audibly.

"Someone's hungry," he says, letting the conversation slide into something easier.

"Yeah. My stomach will always let me know. It's kind of embarrassing."

"Nah. It's cute."

Cute?

"Anyway, I'm hungry too," he rubs his stomach, muscles visible through his thin green shirt. "Want to grab a bite?"

Just as I start to agree, he slaps his face in frustration. "I'm sorry. I'm an idiot. I forgot that I have something. Raincheck?" His eyebrows lift, hopefully.

"Okay," I say, trying not to sound disappointed. "I probably should shower anyway." I tug my hair. "I probably smell again."

Ellis waves his hand playfully. "Yeah, you do." He sniffs. "I do, too, apparently."

I adopt my best mock-bitch voice. "You smell."

Ellis narrows his eyes. "So, the mean girl finally comes out."

"It's not the mean girl. It's the honest girl."

"*Slam.*" Ellis steps forward, eyes heated, lips pursed.

Instead of retreating, I advance, matching his playful glare. "You better watch your back, buddy."

He moves closer until we're awkwardly near. Cocking his head, he leans to my ear, sending chills down my spine. "From what I can tell, you've been watching my *back* enough for the two of us."

I step back, fighting to keep my expression neutral. "What? No, I haven't."

He smiles smugly, one eyebrow raised, clearly doubting me. Shrugging, he bends for his bag, exaggerating the motion. Though his form is undeniable, I avoid looking.

"Hey." He turns. "Eyes up here." He points to his face while still presenting his backside.

"What?" I roll my eyes, looking anywhere but forward.

"Don't be embarrassed. It's a nice specimen."

I gasp. "Whatever. Has anyone ever told you you're a bit cocky?"

"Interesting choice of words."

My face burns. "Besides, it's just…normal." My eyes betray me with a glance. I feel my cheeks blazing.

"Normal?" He feigns offense.

"I'm not looking at your butt."

"Sure." He starts walking backward.

I narrow my eyes before cracking a smile. I like playful Ellis.

"Well, since I stink so bad, I hope you don't mind that I shower first and use up all the hot water."

"Hey!" I yelp as he bolts down the palmetto-lined trail.

By the time I am back at my apartment, Ellis has come and gone.

Opening the bathroom door releases a rush of fog and masculine scent—like Irish Spring soap.

In the shower, my thoughts race—my career, Nick, the desperate drive from Tennessee to Florida, and Ellis. It's strange how life can seem hopeless in one moment and full of possibilities in the next.

After showering, I pull on loose jogging pants and my light green T-shirt. My stomach does summersaults, grumbling deeply.

Although the Hut is an option, I choose peaceful solitude. I grab popcorn from my coffee table snack basket—perfect for midnight cravings when I don't want to brave the kitchen in pajamas.

Stretching across the sofa, I devour the popcorn in record time. With my head back and eyes closed, I let the AC unit's hum lull me to sleep despite the early hour. The day has challenged me physically and mentally.

Hours later, my phone wakes me.

Rubbing sleep from my eyes, I blindly grab my phone in the dark. I'm relieved as the soft green glow reveals a text from Red, not Nick.

Back home. Thanks again for being my hero today. Sorry about all the blood. Yuck!

I smile, sitting up and tucking one leg under me as I turn toward the window. It's 9:30 PM—I've slept for three hours.

I'm happy to have helped and glad you're okay.

I'm okay, just in pain.

Did the doctor give you pain meds?

They gave me a tetanus booster and something for pain in the ER. It's starting to wear off, though. Noah ran to the pharmacy to fill my prescription. I'm hoping he'll be back before the pain returns in full force.

Sorry! That Noah is great.

I know. He's great. I'm a lucky girl.

You are. Did you eat? Do you want me to bring you something? I have some popcorn.

We ordered burgers from downstairs. What about you? Did you get something from the bar tonight?

No. Just took a nap.

You ought to take advantage of the free meal thing you know! ;) It's a perk, and Aki's food is incredible. Bar menu now, but it's loaded with good eats. Try the fish sandwich!

My stomach rumbles at the mention of food.

I think I will.

Good! Noah just got back. Got to run and get numb. Night, Glory. Thanks again, hero!!

Night!

Standing, I exhale deeply, relieved Red's home and healing. Maybe I should take advantage of the free food.

After stretching, I throw on my flip-flops and venture out, mouth watering at the thought of a hot meal.

At the Hut, I find Blair and Ellis. Blair nods me over, clearing a spot and placing a menu down.

"The onion rings rock," she winks.

"Sounds good. A fish sandwich and onion rings."

"I'll put the order in. Did you hear Red's back?"

"Yeah. She texted me. I'm glad she's okay."

"Me too." She smiles slightly before shouting, "JJ! Get your ass over here."

I cover my face, embarrassed for him.

JJ approaches silently, solemn-faced. Blair punches his arm, earning an angry look. "Damn, girl. Don't damage the guns."

Blair nods toward JJ. "You have something to say, Jackass?"

JJ snarls at Blair before exhaling. "Sorry."

Blair narrows her eyes expectantly.

"And thank you," he adds. "You know, for helping Red." He nervously twists his hair.

"You're welcome."

"It takes a big man to own up to your mistakes, JJ," Dave says, appearing with Amber. They take seats and Blair puts a couple waters in front of them.

"Yeah, yeah, yeah." JJ rolls his eyes, glancing sheepishly at Amber.

"Dishes," Blair barks after a moment, and JJ scowls and heads to the sink full of dirty glasses.

"Has he even apologized to Red?" Blair asks Dave.

Dave sighs. "He did, and Red has forgiven him."

"Not me," Blair says flatly.

"I get it, Blair. I do. Red is my daughter. I wanted to kill that kid a couple of hours ago." Dave smiles at Amber. "But I have to remember, he's still a kid."

"People make mistakes," Amber adds, "kids more often."

"No excuse," Blair turns up her nose defiantly.

Amber winks at me before continuing. "If you can't forgive someone for the wrongs they've committed, you won't be able to move forward. It'll poison your soul. Forgiveness isn't about the person who committed the wrong but about yourself. It's your acceptance that something bad happened, and you've chosen to move on rather than be burdened by memories of pain or anger. It's your choice to be free."

Free.

"Well said," Dave adds softly.

Though not their intended target, Amber's words resonate deeply with me. Can I forgive Nick? If I can't, will I be burdened by his abuse forever?

"I get it," Blair concedes, clearly done with the topic. "I can probably forgive him, eventually. But I don't have to like him."

"No, you don't," Dave smiles. "But one day, he may just grow into someone special."

"Whatever," Blair rolls her eyes. "I promise you one thing, though." She waggles her eyebrows at me. "He's going to have one shitty shift tonight. He can count on it."

"Fair enough," Dave raises his hands. "If that's all the punishment he gets from you, he's getting off easy."

Over the next fifteen minutes, I chat with Dave and Amber. They're genuine people, relaxed and loving. Dave shares more about his connection to Ellis and his Gulf War service. Although he mentions Ellis's father's PTSD, he avoids details, which I respect.

I learn that Amber was a competitive swimmer until injury struck. She met Dave through Aki, who was one of her college friends.

As Blair brings my food, giggles erupt behind me, and I turn to see Ellis leading Trish and two of her friends to the bar area on the opposite end. My face heats up, and I'm surprised by the sudden anger I feel towards him. Like he's doing something wrong by socializing with the girls who treated me so poorly. It's an awkward feeling since Ellis owes me nothing. I'm not sure why my body is responding like a jealous ex-girlfriend.

"They're staying in one of the condos," Amber nods toward them. "I can't believe pretty girls like that are so disgusting. They leave trash everywhere." Her exaggerated disgust makes us laugh, catching Ellis's attention, who hadn't noticed me.

His eyes widen as I force a smile and wave. He returns it quickly then navigates the girls further away from me.

Dave raises a hand towards Ellis. "Be safe!"

"Who needs to be safe?" Clinton appears, resting his hands on mine and Amber's chairs.

Dave nods toward Ellis, now at the far end of the bar with the girls.

"Yep. That one does. Although…" Clinton gives me a pointed look, leaving the thought unfinished.

"Here, Clinton," Dave stands. "Take my seat. We've got to head out. I promised Amber we'd watch *Survivor* tonight, and you know how she gets if she misses it."

"Yes, I do," Clinton feigns terror. "You better head out."

Amber smacks his shoulder. "I will vote you off."

After goodbyes, Clinton takes Dave's seat, tossing a faded copy of *The Firm* on the bar.

"Good book?" I tap the cover.

Clinton's jaw drops theatrically. "Glory. It is not a good book. It's a great book. In fact, it's the best book of all time."

Blair interrupts, leaning across the bar at Clinton. "What are you doing here?"

Clinton keeps talking to me. "You would love it if you ever

read it. I just love how—" He stops as Blair snatches the book, holding it just out of reach.

"Give it back, Blair," Clinton demands.

"Are you listening to me?" Blair taps him with the book before dropping it. "What are you doing here?"

Clinton shrugs, looking around. "Just talking to Glory. That's all. I promise."

"You know what I mean. You promised."

Clinton exhales heavily, suddenly serious. "I just want to make sure none of these jackasses bother you."

"Clinton. I know you're protective, but you can't always be around. Summer will be over before you know it, and you'll be… well, you won't be here. You have to give me space. Besides, I don't need protection."

Clinton rubs his eyes, mumbling. "I'm not going anywhere, Blair," he says as if to a child. "I told you that."

Blair raises her hand. "Don't go there."

Clinton sighs in frustration. "Fine, Blair. If that's what you want."

"Hey, bartender! How 'bout a beer over here?" a balding man calls rudely from down the bar.

Clinton starts to rise, his Italian blood flaring, but Blair touches his shoulder. "I'm okay, Clinton. It's the nature of the job. I'll text you when I get off. Ellis is here if I need anything."

"He's supposed to be working," Clinton says. "But it looks like he has other priorities."

Blair waves irritably toward Ellis. "Hey Ellis! A little help here!" Their eyes meet as she gestures to waiting customers.

Ellis raises his eyebrows and one finger, clearly prioritizing the blonde—Trish.

"Really, Ellis? I have to wait for you to charm the panties off of some girl?" Blair says, sighing audibly and growing more annoyed by the minute.

"Panties?" Clinton smirks. "That's like the worst word."

"Would you shut it, Clitty," Blair says.

"Don't start," Clinton warns.

"Miss? A beer," the man calls sarcastically. Blair rolls her eyes before walking away.

I watch Clinton's usually playful eyes grow tired and drawn. "I just don't know what to do with her," he says. "I guess I got to go," he adds as he stands abruptly, visibly angry at Blair. His eyes shift empathetically to me. "See you, G."

"Okay, bye," I say as I hold a hand up.

"What was that all about?" I turn and see Ellis propped on his elbows across the bar. It's endearing.

"I don't know," I glance at the blondes—two admiring his backside while Trish looks towards me as if biting back an insult. I turn back to Ellis. "I don't think your new friends like me very much," I pop a fry in my mouth as I roll my eyes.

Ellis looks over his shoulder before turning back, releasing a sigh. "They're not friends. They're just…" He stops, pressing his lips together as if catching himself.

"Amber said they're staying in the condos."

"Yeah," he says flatly.

He reaches up and rubs a hand across his face, then looks down biting his lip as if contemplating what to say next. He seems…ashamed.

"I just wanted to hang out with them and have a little fun. I wasn't going to—"

"It's fine, Ellis," I say, cutting him off. "You don't owe me any explanation. It is none of my business."

"I know, but—"

"Have fun, or whatever." I force a smile. "If I wanted to hook up with some hot asshole tonight, it would be none of *your* business."

The harsh words don't seem to be my own. Why did I say that?

"Right," he says softly, nodding as if we agree.

I check my phone, faking a yawn. "I guess I should head out." I start to rise, but Ellis catches my shoulder, smiling hopefully. "We still on for the dive lesson in the morning?"

Excitement courses through me. I'd forgotten. "Absolutely. Thanks for the reminder."

Ellis drops his hand. "It'll be fun."

"Yeah. It will," I tuck loose hair behind my ear. "I'm looking forward to it."

"Come over here, hot boy!" A high-pitched screech pulls his attention.

He turns back, seemingly nervous. "Well, good night, Glory."

I smile in an effort to force back a giggle. "Goodnight, *hot boy*," I say.

"That's me. Hot boy."

I roll my eyes, turning away. "Tell Aki the sandwich rocked. If you see him," I shout over my shoulder.

"Will do," he calls as I push through the crowd.

Back in my apartment, I stretch out on my favorite spot—the sofa. Just as sleep approaches, my phone buzzes. I blindly fumble with it, looking forward to an update from Red.

"Hello," I mumble sleepily.

Reality hits me like a freight train. I didn't check the caller ID, and the person breathing on the other end is Nick.

CHAPTER 17

NICK DOESN'T SAY anything, but I know it's him without looking. I hear his trademark sigh, the one laced with both anger and frustration. Goosebumps ripple across my skin as my hand flies to my throat, where phantom fingers seem to squeeze.

"Why haven't you picked up your phone? I've called like a hundred times."

My heart pounds against my ribs like it's trying to escape. My right hand curls into a fist, trembling despite my effort to stay steady. A familiar paralysis creeps in. But I don't speak.

"I know you're there, Glory. For God's sake, I can hear your throaty breathing."

"What do you want?" The words burst out before I can stop them. I cringe, hating how my voice wavers. I didn't want to talk to Nick or be drawn into some conversation with him. My legs start to shake, so I stand and pace in slow circles, each step carefully measured like I'm walking on glass.

"What do you mean? You know damn well what I want. I want you. I want you back."

His voice is calm, words composed and dripping with emotion. Bullshit. He hasn't lost control yet, but he will. I know the pattern too well. This is the calm before the storm.

"Do you want me to apologize?" he says calmly, like he's

165

speaking to a child. "Because if you had picked up your phone and talked to me, I would have. I would have apologized."

"I don't want an apology."

"I love you."

The words hit me like a physical blow—insincere poison. "You don't hurt people you love." The truth of that statement surprises me, rising from some hidden source of strength, perhaps someone I used to be.

He ignores my uncontrolled response.

I stand quietly facing the front door, hands trembling as I scan every shadow, certain he's found me, preparing for him to bust into my apartment at any moment. My heart thumps frantically in my chest.

He sighs again. "I'm sorry. You know I wouldn't hurt you."

"You did hurt me."

"What do you remember?" he asks, ignoring me.

"What do you mean? I remember you pushing me down those stairs."

"Well, you were not being nice to me either, Glory."

I know he is gaslighting me, but I find myself thinking back to our argument. It's all a jumbled mess, but it has something to do with moving or driving. "I don't even know what I did."

He laughs softly into the phone. "You sure about that?" After a moment of silence, he continues, "It won't happen again. Just come back to Tennessee and we can talk it through."

"I'm not coming back, Nick." The brave words blurt out, again, not my own.

He continues as if I didn't speak. "Glory, you know how you can be."

"How can I be?" It's a serious question. What is he talking about? What is wrong with me?

"You are having a tantrum. I have done so much for you, and you repay me by just running away. You should be thanking me for all I've done. Whoever you think you are, you owe me." He's starting to lose it. His voice is getting darker.

"I'm not coming back, Nick," I say again. "And I don't owe you anything."

I feel his temper rise before he even speaks. "I'm not playing with you." His voice gets louder. "You are going to get in the piece of shit truck of yours and get your ass back here now, or by God, you will fucking regret it."

There he is. The true Nick.

"You think you hurt now? If you open your mouth, I will show you hurt."

"I'm not going to say—"

"I will fucking finish what I started, you bitch." His words are laced with venom, deadly. He's lost it.

I bring my right hand to my mouth, and a tear rolls down my cheek. His anger is just too much, even with my newfound bravery.

I don't know how to respond, so I remain speechless. I hear his breaths become more labored and agitated.

"Say something, damn it!" he yells into the receiver.

I pull the phone an inch from my ear. I should hang up, but I'm afraid. I'm secretly praying that he will tell me to "fuck off" so that he'll leave me alone. I don't want to hang up because I am hanging on to the dream that this conversation just might be our last.

But it's not going to be that easy.

"You owe me. You're mine, Glory," Nick says with a hiss, quickly shattering that hope. "That's my ass, those are my tits, and—is there another guy?"

His question is quiet but seething with anger.

"I'm not coming back," I say again, the only words I can find.

I cringe as Nick snickers into the phone. He laughs, something dark and sinister.

"So, you're a tough girl again, huh? You want to be tough?" He laughs again, and it's even more disturbing than before. It reminds me that Nick is actually insane and capable of terrible things.

I hear him take a deep, calming breath before snickering a bit.

"I want you to go to sleep tonight, Glory. Curl up in your little bed, snuggle with your sheets—some other guy—whatever. Then, I want you to dream *wonderful* dreams."

He pauses dramatically before continuing. "But just remember, Glory, I might be standing over you when you open your eyes."

My body starts to shake uncontrollably and tears stream down my face. A rush of fear radiates from my core. I quickly mute the phone, so he doesn't hear me. I can't let him hear me.

"And Glory?" he continues, his voice quiet. "I will bring you back to Tennessee."

He knows.

As if sensing my distress, he pounces. "That's right, Glory. I know you're not in Tennessee. But that's no surprise. I knew where you would end up. In the arms of some loser."

I hear Nick rustling around in the background with some paper. Something like a…a map.

"Let's see," Nick says playfully again. "Where, oh where, is Glory?"

He's actually getting off on my fear.

"Alabama?" he says. "No, not there. Texas? Nope, not there either. Florida?" His voice rises slightly as he says it.

He knows.

"Yeah, Glory," he states, his voice confident. "I'll be seeing you *real* soon."

And then there's a click, and the line goes dead.

At this moment, I realize that Nick isn't out of my life and that I may never escape him. Deep down, I knew running wouldn't be enough, but I was holding on to the hope that he would give up and move on. But it's clear now that he won't. His obsession with me is clinical, and it will push him to find me, to hurt me—kill me.

I let the phone drop to my side, then quickly walk towards the door and turn the deadbolt several times. It doesn't help. I still don't feel safe. I'm still shivering wildly at the thought of Nick being outside my door, of waking up to him hovering above me. Though I know Florida is massive, my logical brain is lost to sheer panic.

I run to my bed, pull on my sweater, and grab the small throw. I silently walk over to the front door and put my ear up to it.

Nothing.

I peer through the peephole.

Nothing.

Leaving the chain latch connected, I turn the knob, then slowly open the door as far as I can. I take my phone and snap photos in both directions, pulling it back and looking at the pictures.

Nothing.

I take a deep breath, unlatch the chain, swiftly throw open the door, and step defensively into the small hallway.

Nothing.

I close my door, lock it with my key, and then step backwards toward the kitchen. With one hand, I push open the kitchen door, my eyes still staring at the stairs, the only way to the third floor.

I step into the kitchen and close the door. I open several drawers until I find a knife. It's short and dull, but it's something. As I grasp its hilt, the fear subsides…just a bit.

I grab water from the fridge, step toward the far end of the kitchen, and slowly pull Ellis's apartment door open.

I push my face into the darkness that shrouds Ellis's apartment. "Hello?" I ask softly.

It's out of respect more than anything. I know Ellis is still at the bar.

No one answers, as expected.

The lights are off, but the moon is shining through the door leading to the patio. I walk forward, carefully stepping around Ellis's pile of shoes and a damp, bright blue wetsuit that he has hung up to dry on a metal rod extending out from the wall on a small hinge.

I open the patio door and swiftly move past the smaller landing, up the stairs, and into the main garden area. Even as my nerves and fear consume me, the beauty of the flowers and potted plants comforts me, providing me a brief, needed distraction.

I go to the pergola and sit on the bench swing, folding my legs underneath me. I throw the blanket over my body and then place the knife on a table to my right. Though I am still shaking in fear, I start to calm down, realizing that I am safe, for now. I stare out across the water, and after my breath evens out, my eyes flutter closed.

Though I expect nightmares, they never come.

Hours later, I awaken suddenly, but I'm not sure why. I reach over and grasp the knife on the table at my side, then look around, inspecting my surroundings. The wind is blowing softly, but I am alone.

Thump.

I narrow my eyes at the odd sound, looking out across the roofline, but there is still nothing. I stand and carefully step forward towards the garden stairs leading to Ellis's apartment.

Thump. Thump.

"What is that sound?" I say softly to myself.

I take a few more steps forward.

Thump.

This time, a soft, feminine moan follows.

Holy Mother of God…The source of the sounds hit me like a ton of bricks, and I'm suddenly wide awake.

Ellis and some girl, probably Trish, are having sex in his apartment. My face instantly reddens, and I feel a familiar jealous heat rise into my chest. I look around for a quick escape, but of course, I don't find one. I'm trapped. The only way out is through his apartment.

"Shit," I say softly into the crisp air.

Thump. Thump. Moan.

"I have such dumb luck," I say as I debate trying to flee the scene through Ellis's apartment. If I can be quiet and move fast, it's possible he won't see or hear me. I begin to trace the steps through my mind, but unfortunately, each time I do, the scenario ends with Ellis rushing towards me with a bat in his hand—like I'm a burglar or something. And, of course, he's completely naked each time.

Why is it suddenly so hot outside?

After a few more thumps, I decide to do my best to stick out the night. I'll set my phone alarm for five or something, then sneak out once they have finished with—whatever.

I sit back down on the swing and resume my position. I plug my ears with my pointer fingers then lean back. If I listen carefully, I can still hear thumps and moans, but I try not to focus. I pull my hood over my head and wrap the blanket tightly around my face so only my eyes are exposed to the night air.

How could he have sex with her? She's horrible.

I shake my head in frustration. I shouldn't care what he does. It's none of my business. Hell, I barely know Ellis. He could be some man-whore or something. But the thought doesn't sit well with me, especially given Jane. This must be the 'destructive' behavior Clinton was referring to.

I shake free from the intrusive thought and pull the blanket tighter against me until the dull sound of my heartbeat lulls me back to sleep.

I wake with a yawn. My eyes are closed, and the morning sun is warming my cheek. I hear birds singing, and the salty, citrus air is blowing circles around the pergola. The blanket is still wrapped around my face, so I reach up and tug it downward.

Did my alarm not go off?

I open my eyes fully after several blinks, then quickly pull myself into a seated position when I realize Ellis is sitting directly across from me in a wooden Adirondack chair. He has one leg crossed over the other, a bright green coffee mug resting naturally in his hand. His eyes are narrowly fixated on me as he takes a long, noisy sip.

I look around nervously and force a smile mid-yawn. This is so embarrassing.

"Fancy seeing you up here. Had a little campout, did you?"

I open my mouth to respond, but I'm speechless. I don't know what to say, so we sit silently for a few awkward moments.

"Are you spying on me?" he asks. "You're not one of those voyeur types, are you?"

I feel my eyes widen, and a deep feeling of dread overcomes me. He must think I'm a pervert or something. "What?"

"You know…kinky." He's smiling, but I think his question is serious.

"Kinky?" My voice goes up a shaky octave as I say the word.

"Yes?" he says, urging me to continue.

"No! I'm…" My face turns bright red. I feel it. I can actually feel the red color. I throw my hands over my face and shake my head. "I totally didn't hear anything. I just fell asleep out here."

"I doubt that," Ellis says as he stares at me playfully through suspicious eyes.

"I didn't hear anything," I say again, maybe just trying to convince myself now because he's not buying it.

Ellis lets out a soft, genuine laugh, then looks off across the morning horizon. He stretches one arm over his head. "I'm just messing with you," he says as his eyes dart back in my direction. "I just wanted to see you get flustered." He takes another sip from his coffee and turns back towards the water. "Beautiful morning."

I take a deep, steadying breath and exhale a loud sigh of relief. "Oh my God. I'm going to kill you."

He looks back towards me and then nods to my right. "Not gonna kill me with that, are ya?"

I look over to where the dull knife sits ominously and cringe. Ellis probably thinks I am crazy. I start to blurt out some excuse but stop myself. "I was…scared."

Ellis stands and walks over to sit beside me. He kicks his legs out, and the swing sways a bit. "What were you afraid of?"

I take a deep breath and quickly debate telling him the truth or making up some lie about monsters or bad dreams. But I can't bring myself to lie. What's the point? He knows about Nick, about the abuse. And it feels good. It feels really good to talk about it with someone for a change. And I trust Ellis.

"Nick."

"Nick? You mean the guy who hurt you?"

"Yeah."

"Didn't you leave him?"

"I did, but he is struggling to accept it." I think back to the cold apartment, my apartment, and images of him smacking me or pushing me into the wall flicker in my memory. But the memories are fragmented, my mind's attempt at hiding the trauma from me. "I never ran away before when he hit me. I think he believes that I am going to tell some—"

"Wait a minute," Ellis says, interrupting me as he sits forward, his eyes locked on mine. "Do you mean he's done this to you before?"

"Well, he never pushed me down stairs." I force a nervous laugh, an effort to dispel the sudden tension.

"But he hit you." It's not a question.

I furrow my eyebrows and let out a nervous laugh that sounds out of place. Ellis shakes his head as if he has been slapped and rubs one large hand across his face as he pulls himself into a higher seated position. He looks visibly distressed. It becomes apparent to me as I watch him now that he didn't realize the extent of the abuse when we spoke on the boat. He must have assumed Nick had pushed me around just the one time and that I had immediately left as a normal, sane woman would have.

I look back up and as I do, our eyes lock. Flashes of anger and sympathy alternate as we face each other, and I suddenly fear his judgment, his questions about why I didn't leave sooner. I know the stigmas associated with abused women, and I don't want Ellis to think I'm weak.

I pull my legs out from under me, positioning myself to bolt, but I stop as my feet hit the floor. Again, just like on the boat, a soft feminine voice whispers in my mind, encouraging me to trust Ellis. I want to listen to the voice. I need to listen to the voice.

Trust him.

"I'm an idiot for not leaving him sooner."

"*No*, you're not," Ellis says instantly, but I don't hear him—I ignore him.

"I'm the reason for this." I absently tug up my sleeve and move my arm around as I examine the fading bruises and scratches.

Ellis's eyes widen as he leans forward. He gently takes my hand and brings my arm up so he can inspect each mark slowly. He then sits my arm back on my lap, looks up after a moment, and shakes his head. "Don't you dare blame yourself for what that prick did to you. There is fault here, but it's the fault of others."

He looks down and wipes at his eyes with the back of his hand. It hurts me to see Ellis so upset over this. It's not his fault.

"This is my fault," I insist.

"No," he replies softly as he looks up and smiles.

"But I stayed with him," I argue. "I forgave him."

"No," he repeats. "This is not your fault."

"But I forgave him—over and over." My voice cracks as the words rush out and my voice gets louder.

"Glory," Ellis says softly as he leans forward, "you may have convinced yourself that you made this guy hurt you, but you will—*never*—convince me that this," he motions towards my arm, "or any of what he's been doing to you, is your fault. *Never.*"

Ellis's words touch me to the core. I had been so worried that he—that everyone—would judge me. I sigh deeply as my anxiety instantly lessens.

Ellis takes a deep breath and scoots to my side, so our legs are touching, just barely. He wraps his arm around me and tugs me into his chest. I don't resist. He's warm and protective, and he smells like clove. I feel safe in his arms. "Do you love him?" he asks after a moment.

"No," I say flatly. "I really don't remember ever loving him."

"Really?" His head twists in surprise.

"Is that strange?" It seems so odd to admit.

"I wonder why you were with him then, if I'm being honest."

"I honestly don't know. He just appeared in my life one day, and never really left. I thought my leaving would put an end to it all, but I'm afraid he'll never leave me alone."

"What do you mean?" Ellis asks, his face laced with concern. "Is he still bothering you?"

I shake my head in frustration. "I accidentally picked up the phone last night when Nick called—I thought it was Red. I wasn't looking at the caller ID."

"What happened?"

"He was nice at first, apologizing, but eventually the real Nick showed his face." I wrap my hands across my stomach. "He started to threaten me."

Ellis sits up higher. "What did he say?"

I blink back tears. "He told me he knew I was in Florida."

"Damn."

"He said that one day soon, I would wake up, and he would be looking down on me." I barely finish the sentence before the tears escape down my face. The fear from last night resurfaces, stronger than before.

Ellis reaches around me and slowly rubs my back. "You're safe, Glory." I look towards him, and I see his confidence fracture. He looks worried.

"I'm not sure how he would even know where I am, but he acted so confident."

"He's bluffing, Glory. Men like that are cowards, and if he were to show up here looking for trouble, he would get it. This is a tight community, and Amber's brother is the Sherrif. You are safe here, Glory. I promise."

"I hope you are right," I say.

"Have you considered talking to someone about him, like a counselor or something?"

"Maybe one day, but I'm just not ready."

"I understand," he says, "more than you know. Would you let me take you to get a restraining order?"

I take a slow, measured breath but then shake my head. "I can't get the police involved. I just can't. I don't want to get pulled into any court cases or something like that. I just want him to leave me alone."

"Okay," Ellis says nodding, "but please consider it, and let me know if you change your mind."

"Okay," I say as I stand and step towards the water. I look out over the horizon and put my hands on my hips. "I just want to forget it ever happened. I feel like the faster I can forget Nick and all of this, the faster I can move on."

I look back over my shoulder as he nods. "I get it."

"You do?"

"I do." Ellis forces a sad smile.

Ellis frowns and stares silently across the bright blue water. He rubs his hand across his jawline. I follow his gaze across the water and see that the sun has nearly cleared the horizon.

"When Dad returned from the Gulf War, I was maybe three or something. Mom loved Dad, but the war did something to him. He wasn't the same person when he returned. He became reclusive, didn't eat well, and began withdrawing from relationships he had had his entire life. He didn't spend any time with me or Mom."

I sit up and look towards Ellis.

"He and Dave were best friends in high school. They enlisted in the military together instead of going to college."

"So that's how you know Dave?"

Ellis nods. "My dad wouldn't even talk to Dave, which was completely messed up. They were generally inseparable." Ellis lets out a long breath and leans his head down. "One day, my mom and Dave confronted my dad about his behavior."

"Like an intervention?"

"Exactly," Ellis says as he leans forward and cracks his knuckles.

"When Dave returned, he dealt with similar stuff. They were both reclusive, irritable and stuff like that." Ellis pulls a leg up onto the bench and takes a deep breath. He looks towards me, but his gaze is fixed over my shoulder. "But the difference between my dad and Dave was that Dave got help. He went to a local psychologist who eventually diagnosed him with post-traumatic stress disorder."

I don't know what to say other than sounding like I'm reciting from a textbook I'd once read. "PTSD is very common among people who are in the military. Something like 38% of veterans in the United States who served on the ground."

He doesn't question how I know this.

"Yeah, it's serious shit. The killing and destruction does something to their mind."

"My dad was in the Gulf War, too."

"Oh yeah?"

"Yep. Army."

"Dad was in the Army too—Dave too."

"Your Mom and Dave were trying to convince him to see a counselor?"

"Yeah. They were both convinced that it would help him move forward."

"Did he get help?"

Ellis shakes his head. Though he's quiet, I can visibly see that the memories are causing him pain. I reach over instinctively and rub Ellis's back. He tenses at first but, after a moment, relaxes into me. "After that, Mom had some medical issues…cancer… so things got tough." He is visibly uneasy talking about all this, and I can hear his shaky breath under the weight of my resting hand. "Mom didn't live long after her diagnosis. And ultimately, Dad didn't make it either."

"I'm sorry," I say as I turn and wipe at the corner of my eye.

Ellis's face softens as he sees that his story visibly upset me. "Look, Glory. I haven't told many people that, but I just… wanted you to know."

A tear glides down my cheek. "Thank you."

Ellis nods, then takes one long gulp of coffee and forces a smile, which I return. "You want some? I'll make you a cup."

"That'd be great."

"Afterwards, we can head over to the pool." He looks down at his watch. "We're running about ten minutes late. Do you think you could get changed and meet me on the porch in ten? I'll grab the coffee." He nods down to his shorts. "I'm already in my suit."

I try to avoid looking down, but my eyes can't help but dart towards the black trunks hanging low on his hips.

I look up and see him staring at the table where the knife sits. He points towards it. "Are you going to be, okay?"

I cross my arms in front of my chest as Nick's voice plays back in my head. A little shiver races along my spine.

"I know you're scared, Glory, but you're safe here at Dave's. I promise. I won't let anything happen to you."

I take a deep breath. I want to believe Ellis—to live free of fear, but I don't know if I can.

I walk over to the knife, pick it up, and hold it sideways out to Ellis. "Here. Please don't tell anyone. They may think I'm crazy or something."

Ellis takes the knife. "After what you've been through, this," he holds up the knife, "is perfectly normal. But don't worry, I won't say a thing."

"Thanks."

I follow Ellis into his mud room, where he sets the knife on a small table inside the doorway. He starts to say something but stops just as a blonde-haired girl steps forward, rubbing her eyes. She's one of the girls from the bar—not Trish. Her mascara is smeared under one of her eyes, and she's wearing a long, bright orange shirt that says Florida Gators, probably Ellis's. It doesn't quite hang low enough to cover her ass.

She doesn't notice me at first. "I wasn't sure what happened to you. Last night was amazing, and I think we should do it again this—"

She stops as I step from behind Ellis and give her a little wave. "Hi. I'm Glory. From the bar."

No response.

She scowls at me, silently accusing me of doing who knows what with Ellis while she slept.

"I fell asleep on the porch last night." I feel the need to explain why I'm there. Ellis doesn't seem to be worried about offering any explanation.

She grits her teeth.

"Alone," I add. "Ellis found me this morning." I point towards my apartment. "I live over there, and I didn't mean to hear y'all—"

I stop speaking as Ellis suddenly looks towards me, his face a bright pink. The girl's mouth falls open.

"You were spying on us?" she says, forcing a fake laugh. "Gross."

I wave my hands in front of me. "No, no. Not at all." My voice is fast and shrill. Ellis is staring at me, his mouth agape and eyes wide.

It's time for a quick exit. I step backward silently into the kitchen, waving. "Okay. Well. See you on the porch in five," I look at the girl and then add, "or however long you need up here." My hand flies towards my mouth, and a look of embarrassment, laced with hints of amusement, spreads across Ellis's face.

"Five minutes works," Ellis says flatly, and now it's the girl's turn to stare in surprise at Ellis.

"Seriously?" she says. "It will only take you five minutes to—"

"Got to go," I interrupt as I turn and race through the kitchen, the door swinging closed behind me.

CHAPTER 18

TEN MINUTES LATER, I'm sitting on the back steps when the door opens, and a shirtless Ellis walks onto the porch. I immediately avert my eyes. He steps forward cautiously, and I stand, forcing a smile. He's staring at me from the side, eyes narrow but playful.

"Sorry, I had to, err, see my guest off. He walks forward, and I follow.

"Please don't think I'm a creeper," I say, flinching at his back. "I didn't mean to hear you have s—" I abruptly stop speaking when Ellis's head jolts around and he stops.

"Uh-huh," he says simply, forcing back a smile.

I walk towards him slowly. "If it makes you feel better, I was totally impressed by how long you—"

"Don't worry about it," Ellis interrupts as his head twists back, so he's looking away from me. He starts walking, holding his hands high in the air as if in surrender.

"Okay," I say, forcing back a giggle. "It is a complement you know. It was a real powerful sound, like a—"

"Thanks," he interjects and starts walking faster. I can tell he's not mad, but he *is* embarrassed. I don't think my comments are helping.

He stops and reaches back his hand towards me. I step forward and take it. Together, we walk down the narrow trail leading to Dave's.

When we reach the pool by the condos, Ellis asks me to go ahead and get in the water while he grabs some gear. He seems to recognize that I'm still timid about my bruises, and I appreciate the privacy.

Ellis and I spend the next hour in the pool, and time flies as he shows me basic techniques like how to perform an emergency ascent and how to remove my mask underwater and then put it back on. I pick up on everything unusually fast.

"Have you done this before?"

I cock my head to the side and my memories rush forward of me at the ocean with my dad, but I don't recall ever using a snorkel. "No, I don't think so."

As we continue the lesson, he watches me with curiosity. I guess that I'm better than most, which gives me a small sense of pride.

Ellis is a fantastic teacher. He's very thoughtful in how he instructs me, taking me through one skill at a time and doesn't move on to the next one until I'm comfortable.

"Just remember, you're never more than about fifty feet from the surface. If something goes wrong, ditch your equipment and kick like hell with both arms extended upward." He holds both arms straight up above his head. "It will increase your speed."

"Like this?" I ask as I demonstrate, pushing my arms together high over my head.

"Exactly like that."

"Also, it's important to always exhale when ascending."

I nod and then furrow my eyebrows. "Okay, but what if you don't have any air in your lungs to exhale?"

"Good question," he says as we both bob up and down in the water. "If you don't have air in your lungs, you're fine. The main reason you exhale is to prevent a pulmonary embolism."

"That doesn't sound good."

"It's not. Diving's no joke. If you have air in your lungs,

even a little, and hold your breath, the air will expand as you move towards the surface, which will force air bubbles into your bloodstream and, in some cases…pop!"

I feel my mouth open in confusion. "Why am I doing this again?"

I look over Ellis's shoulder as an elderly couple pulls together two pool chairs, watching Ellis and me curiously. They probably think we're up to no good.

No sex in the pool! I imagine them saying, which causes me to let out a little giggle.

"What?" Ellis says, looking around.

I wave at him dismissively. "Nothing. Sorry."

Ellis and I continue to go over the dangers of diving, like the bends and nitrogen narcosis. As he does, he carefully explains how to avoid each danger, which I appreciate. Though I'm nervous to learn about the most common ways to die while scuba diving, it's a relief to know that the main dangers are mostly simple to avoid. "So, it's dangerous, but if you follow the basic rules, you'll rarely have a problem. Diving is one of the most amazing experiences. It's like my third favorite thing."

"What are your other favorite things?"

He winks but doesn't answer my question. Of course, sex is on the list. I look away and pretend he didn't wink, and I'm not blushing, which I am.

When it's nearly 8:30 AM., Ellis swims to the side of the pool and lifts his body out of the water. I can't help but stare as the suit clings to his backside and other parts so perfectly.

I had avoided staring dumbstruck at his ripped body during the lesson, but it had literally taken effort. My eyes had a mind of their own and tended to wander long before my brain knew what they were up to.

Ellis turns around, and luckily, my eyes had darted away from his nether region by then.

"Let's try to meet at 6:15 every other morning for the next few weeks," he says to my back as I walk through the shallow end and start to exit the pool via the stairs, grateful that the older couple have departed. "It'll help get you up to speed on—"

Ellis stops speaking suddenly, so I turn and see that his eyes are fixated on my backside. At least I'm not the only one staring.

It takes him less than half a second to realize I'd caught him checking me out. As our eyes connect, his face goes blank, and he turns abruptly and begins drying off.

I walk over to my towel and wrap it around my body. I don't mind that he's checking me out—he's a guy—but I'm still a bit self-conscious about the bruising.

"Sound good?" Ellis says after a minute from a few seats away, his voice gruff and clipped. I turn back around and see that he's looking towards me, but not at me, as if he's afraid he won't be able to control his wondering eyes.

"Sure, great," I say as I walk forward. His gaze meets mine, and I briefly see flashes of longing and confusion before he looks away.

I force a smile. "I appreciate the help. I know you are putting in extra work."

He looks back up and seems to realize he's frowning. His eyebrows rise in an apparent effort to cover his mood. "That's fine. It's my job anyway. At least while Red is recovering."

"Okay," I say flatly, not sure how to respond.

CHAPTER 19

After my lesson, Ellis heads to the main office and I return to the house to change. A few minutes later, I'm back outside, soaking in the morning air. It's Monday, the only day Dave's is officially closed, so other than a few overnight guests scattered around enjoying the amenities, there aren't many people here. The older sisters from the trip yesterday are lounging with coffee in the grassy areas overlooking the water while I spot a younger man jogging leisurely along one of the paved paths. I walk out towards the sea wall near an older man who is moving a fishing pole up and down in the water as if he's playing with a small fish or crab. At the end of the pier, I see a young woman leaning back in one of a half-dozen lounge chairs, a book in her hands.

Blair.

I turn and make my way towards her.

"Hey," I say once I'm only a few feet away.

She doesn't respond at first but instead holds out her finger. I pause and watch silently as she gasps and then turns the page. "He didn't propose?" She looks up to me in horror and throws her empty hand in the air, clearly exasperated.

"What?" I ask.

She lets out a long sigh and taps on the cover of her book.

"This guy Zane better get his act together." She shoves a book-mark into the fold then tosses it on the deck. "What are you up to?"

"I had a lesson with Ellis this morning. I've just been wandering around since."

"Do you want to read with me?" she asks, then reaches under her chair, pulls up a book, and hands it to me.

"Sure," I say, taking the book and looking at its cover.

"Have you ever read this type of thing?" she asks.

I shrug. "I don't think so, but I will read just about anything if it is a page-turner, and I'm a sucker for romance. This," I wave the book, "may be a bit risqué for me, but who knows, I may love it."

Blair lets out a sudden snort. "You'll love it all right. Promise. I've read that like ten times."

"Thanks," I reply, suddenly excited by her infectious enthusiasm.

She begins fanning herself with her hand. "Just promise me you'll let me know what you think about Lord Cluster when you're done."

"Oh, okay," I say, nodding. "That name sounds…interesting."

"Yeah," she nods enthusiastically, smiling wide. "Like, burn your loins interesting. Trust me."

Blair and I sit for a couple of hours at the end of the pier, dangling our legs over the sides. It's warm outside, but large white clouds, which I find are very common in the Keys, block out the sun for a good chunk of time, so we don't get burnt.

Blair's right. I am immediately hooked and captivated by Lord Cluster. I don't think I look up from the book until close to eleven when I hear someone running down the pier.

"Hi, Red," I say.

"Hey, girls! Y'all hungry?" She approaches us holding out two small fabric bags, the recyclable kind like you get at the grocery store. I immediately notice the bandage wrapped around her hand and wonder how the cut is.

Blair looks up and pulls her hand up over her eyes, shielding the sun. "Does Dave have you delivering now, with that hand?" She nods towards Red's hand.

"It's fine," Red says as she shrugs. "Thanks to Glory here."

Red and Blair come over to where I am, and we sit in a small circle. Red drops the bags in the middle of us. "I couldn't decide what to get, so I just got a little of everything." Red turns to me. "I hope you're hungry, Glory, 'cause I brought you lunch too. I saw you were out here and figured you would join us."

"Thanks," I say as she pulls out various items and puts them in front of us.

I can't help but smile as Blair reaches for a tortilla chip, dips it into a large container of white cheese dip, then closes her eyes as she tosses it in her mouth. "This is freaking incredible," Blair says, shaking her head from side to side as if in disbelief that something could be that good.

"I know," Red says simply. "This place rocks."

Blair looks over to me and motions for the bag. "Try the cheese now. Seriously."

I grab a chip, dip it into cheese, and then toss it into my mouth.

Liquid heaven.

"That is incredible," I say. "How do they get those chips so thin?"

"I know, right?" Red says. "I don't understand how something like that can hold up under the weight of all the cheese."

"We do this every Monday," Blair says, her mouth nearly full. "Not always cheese…but sometimes."

"A girls' brunch," Red says. "You should join us from now on."

"It's a great way to get away from the guys." Blair nods over to Red. "And I need someone other than her to talk to sometimes."

Red scowls playfully. "Very funny."

"Love ya!" Blair says in a singsong voice.

"Love you more!" Red sings back.

I can't help but smile at their banter. It's so natural, playful. I'm suddenly envious of their closeness. Of course, I had had girlfriends in the past, before Nick, but memories of them are faint. Nick didn't like me to have company, so I had spent many nights alone in my room, the overhead lights buzzing as I stared at a white wall, hoping someone would call my apartment's land line. Nick always took my phone with him when he went back home, so I wouldn't have much connection to others. During the past couple of years, the only people I ever really saw were cleaners and delivery drivers. Other than going outside from time-to-time, Nick pretty much kept me behind closed doors. I shake my head as I think back to how I cowered to him and bent so easily to his will. Threats, spoken or unspoken, wield such great power.

Everything seems much clearer now that I am away from him, like just his presence, or my catering to his presence, created a fog miasma that clouded reality. I wonder if all of those around me could see through his manipulation. I try to shake away from the intrusive thought that's calling me 'stupid' for not realizing the extent of what was happening or ignoring it. I have left. I have taken that first step, and I need to quit playing the abuser in his absence. I need to think positively of myself and see myself as those here at Dave's see me.

I look between Red and Blair, who are now teasing each other over Red's choice of nacho toppings.

"Come on!" Red says to Blair encouragingly. "Admit that the only reason you even like jalapeños is because Clinton likes anything hot."

"Yeah, he does!" Blair says loudly, her voice full of innuendo.

"Good Lord, Blair."

"Whatever," Blair says as she shoves a nacho in her mouth. "You can't talk. I know what you and the big guy do. I've walked in on that shit."

"Shut your mouth!" Red shrieks.

"I just don't know how you fit that damn co—"

"Blair!" Red shrieks as she throws a chip at Blair, which bounces off her head. I shake my head and unsuccessfully force back short bursts of laughter. Blair is undeniably one of the funniest individuals I've ever met, and one of the toughest.

"I'm just saying," Blair adds, rolling her eyes.

Red narrows her gaze and feigns anger, and her placid face begins to fracture. In its place, a big toothy smile emerges. "I know, right?" Red says, nodding, and we all begin squealing with laughter.

Over the next hour, Red, Blair, and I discuss everything from diving to clothes to whether size matters. The conversation then focuses on Blair and Clinton's relationship.

"But you love him, right?" Red asks. Blair doesn't respond and looks away, her face rigid.

"He's got to get the hell out of here," Blair says, forcing a sad smile and looking back at us. "I can't be the reason he doesn't realize his dreams. Whether I love him or not is irrelevant."

"I don't understand," I say, looking between them both.

Red raises her eyebrows and nods pointedly towards Blair. For a moment, Blair doesn't say a word, her shoulders moving up and down as she takes long, deep breaths. But then, without warning, Blair turns towards me, her eyes glistening as she forces back tears. "Clinton is smart," Blair says. "Actually, he's fucking brilliant."

I turn to Red, who nods in agreement.

"And he got accepted into law school last spring." She pauses and dabs her eyes with her T-shirt. "He didn't go. He and I had been dating most of the spring and into the summer. He had been after me for years, but I wouldn't have anything to do with him. Not because of him or anything, but because I had been in relationships since I was seventeen and wanted to be on my own for once. Once we started dating, things moved fast. He admitted that he loved me only after a month or two, even if it took me several more months to repeat the words back to him. He had loved me for a long time, and I think the reason he hadn't said it even earlier was because—"

"He didn't want to scare you off," Red interrupts.

"Exactly," Blair agrees.

"He totally did love you back then, Blair," Red says, nodding.

"I know, I know," Blair says. "Everyone told me that. I'm just so damn stubborn sometimes."

"She is," Red chimes in, looking at me and winking.

Blair ignores Red and continues. "Well, law school is at NYU in Manhattan, and there was just no way I could leave town. Not with Mama the way she is."

My eyebrows furrow, and Blair notices.

"Mama lives at a nearby care facility. She has early-onset Alzheimer's. I'm an only child, and Dad ran off when I was little. And I can't move to New York. I just can't leave her. Even if we have money for full-time care.

"Did Clinton ask you to go to New York?" I say.

"Nope. He didn't." Her voice is trembling, laced with emotion. "He said that it wasn't even an option. New York, I mean."

"So, he's going to stay with you here?" I ask.

Blair's face suddenly becomes pale. "He can't. I won't let him."

"You love him too much to let him stay," I say softly.

She then motions to herself. "He is not risking his life—his career—for this. He's going to go to law school—to an Ivy League law school."

"He's not going anywhere, Blair," Red says softly, patting her arm.

Blair shrugs off Red's touch and then stands shaking her head, her voice elevated slightly. "I just can't be the reason he stays. He has a full ride at one of the best law schools in the nation. I can't do that to him. If he stayed, he would eventually see that he made a mistake, and then he would resent me."

"He won't," Red says.

"Maybe not this year or even in the next five years, but one day, he will, and when that day comes, he will leave me, just like Dad."

Blair sniffles and turns, dabbing her eyes again with her sleeve.

"It's his decision, Blair," Red says. "Not yours. He loves you and wants to spend the—"

"It isn't, Red," Blair interrupts, stepping back from Red's embrace, shaking her head.

"Breaking up with him isn't going to change anything, Blair. It hasn't changed anything except that both of you are miserable. Did he say anything about NYU?"

"No, but I know he's planning to go. I've seen him reading some law books lately and looking down at what appears to be a syllabus. It's his first assignment, I'm sure. And if he's moved on and leaving for NYU after the season, that's a good thing. I won't try to get back together with him and mess that up. I can't do that to him. I love him too much." She rubs both hands across her face and then looks back up. "And it's not fair because when he does leave, it will make it that much harder for me."

Blair steps forward and wraps her arms around Red. A few tears roll down her cheek, and I try not to stare. Red rubs the back of her head and whispers inaudible words softly into her ear. I feel terrible for Blair. I had realized something was happening between her and Clinton, but I wasn't exactly sure what the situation was. Now it makes sense—the way they are acting towards each other. I think back to Clinton the other day at the bar with those books. Those must be the books that Blair's referring to.

After several minutes, Blair calms down, and we all sit quietly around the food, taking a few last-minute bites.

"Thanks for lunch," I say as we all stand and start to clean up our mess.

"No problem," Red says.

"Sorry for the sappy session, girls," Blair mutters. "I'm not usually this pathetic."

"You are not pathetic," I assert, smiling. "Relationships are…" My voice fades off as flashes of memory race through my mind, pictures of hands holding and the feeling of someone rubbing the back of my head gently. As they do, three little words turn in my mind, something I have heard somewhere before, perhaps recently.

"Until the tide," I say blankly, which causes Red and Blair to turn my way, confusion etched across their face.

I wave dismissively and force a smile. "Not sure where that came from. Maybe Lord Cluster."

"Maybe," Blair says, suddenly intrigued.

I pinch my lips together and nod.

Red winks. "Do you know what the best part about having girlfriends is?"

"What?" Blair asks.

She holds her hands out. "All of this."

"Damn right," Blair agrees, stepping forward and smacking Red on her backside.

"Hey!" Red says and points towards Blair. "Noah would not like you touching my ass."

"Yeah, he would, Red."

"Yeah," Red agrees without hesitation. "He would."

We all laugh and start to walk down the pier but stop when Red shouts. "I've got it!"

Blair rolls her eyes. "What have you got, Red?"

"We all have the afternoon off, right?"

"Yeah?" Blair says flatly.

"And lunch ended on a sad note?"

Blair rolls her eyes again. "Yeah."

"Let's go shopping!" she squeals.

My eyes instantly light up. Shopping sounds like a blast, and it's something I've been meaning to do. I don't have much money, maybe a hundred dollars or so, but I need a few things. With the free food from Aki's, I should be able to buy some essentials and still make it to payday Friday.

"Okay," I say cheerfully before I can change my mind.

"I'm in," Blair says flatly as if it's not even up for consideration. "It is exactly what we need to do."

"Yes!" Red shouts. "Is the BMW at the house?"

"Yep," Blair says. "I'll grab the keys from Dave and meet y'all on the porch in ten."

"All right," Red and I say in unison as Blair jogs away toward the dive shop.

"Let's run to the house so we can get whatever we need, and then we can meet Blair on the porch."

"That works."

At our house, Red and I go our separate ways. I run to my apartment to grab my wallet, then head back down. I push onto the porch, stopping suddenly as I see three shirtless guys—beautiful and ripped guys—playing cards around the table. Red is standing behind Noah with her hands on his huge, bare shoulders. He looks like Conan the Barbarian or something, all muscle and bulk.

Clinton's frame is slim but toned, like a cyclist's. He's more tan than Noah and wears glasses with bright green frames, which play well with his quirky personality. Clinton leans down to study his cards carefully, his tongue stuck slightly outside at the corner of his mouth.

And then there's Ellis. Beautiful Ellis.

He's more muscular than Clinton, and his tan is almost as dark, contrasting sharply against his bright blond hair and crystal blue eyes. And right now, those eyes are furrowed and impatiently fixated on Clinton.

"What the hell," Ellis says. "You gonna fold?"

Clinton holds up one finger. "Patience is a virtue, young padawan."

"We agreed, *no Star Wars references*," Noah says in a deep voice before looking over to where I'm standing and flashing me a thumbs up, his trademark greeting.

Red looks up from Noah's cards and sees me. "Ready?"

"Yep," I say, waving my wallet.

Ellis looks over his shoulder and smiles when he sees me standing there. "Hey."

"Hi."

"Where y'all going?" he asks.

"Oh, just girl stuff," I say.

"Fun," Noah says in a sultry voice, causing Red to slap him on the shoulder.

"Oh, it will be," Red says, "and if you're good, I'll get you something." Red winks at Noah.

"Gross," Clinton says flatly, not looking up from his cards. "Hey, Glory," he says, nodding in my direction.

"He's a bit distracted," Ellis says, smirking. "He's only been looking at that hand for like ten minutes."

"It's driving us crazy," Noah says as he takes a deep breath.

"Maybe that's my strategy," Clinton counters.

"To bore us to death?" Noah asks.

"Yep," Clinton says. "And sci-fi references."

"Jesus," Noah says, rolling his eyes. "I think he might be serious. I don't think I can play with this nerd again."

Ellis looks back towards me. "Wanna join my team?" He

pats an empty spot to his right on the small bench he's pulled up to the table.

"Hey! No outside help!" Clinton says as he looks up and glares at Ellis before winking playfully in my direction.

"Yeah? Well, what about her?" Ellis says as he points to Red, who is bent over, studying Noah's cards with him and whispering in his ear.

"That doesn't count. You know that big doofus needs all the help he can get."

"Don't call him a doofus!" Red says, looking up through narrow eyes.

Clinton shrugs, then looks back down to his hand.

This kind of back-and-forth banter is clearly the norm for these guys.

Ellis pats the seat again, so I walk over and sit next to him. "You play cards?" he asks, looking sideways at me. The stubble on his face is adorable, highlighted by bright white teeth. I smell the soft smell of minty toothpaste.

I love a guy who has good teeth and hygiene.

"A little," I say. My Dad and I used to play when I was a kid, so I'm comfortable around traditional games like Poker, Gin, Hearts, and Spades—the usual ones that most people can play.

Ellis scoots closer to my side and my breath catches as his large leg brushes my hip. He's warm, like a soft blanket.

I look over to his cards as he holds them towards me. "Anything good?" I ask.

"Yeah," he says as he points to two pairs, one of aces and one of tens. "But we're waiting on pokey over there to put up or shut up."

Clinton quietly raises his hand and flicks off Ellis. "That's for Ellis, Glory, not you."

Just as I start to respond, the porch door swings open, and Blair steps through.

Wowzers.

I swear I hear Clinton stop breathing when he looks up over his cards towards Blair. She's wearing a loose, bright yellow sundress and matching leather gladiator sandals that lace up her ankles from some designer brand for sure. This is the first time I've noticed how large Blair's…bra size must be. Wow.

I look down at the clutch she's holding. Blair's family must have money because that clutch costs at least a month's salary at Dave's.

"Bullshit," Clinton says suddenly, eyes wide. "This is a conspiracy. Distract me and take all my money."

Blair pretends she doesn't notice Clinton or his comments. "Ready, ladies?" She tosses her golden hair over her shoulder, and I swear she pushes her chest out a little.

"Ready," Red says, briefly looking up.

"Yeah," I add.

Blair turns and starts to leave but stops as Clinton flies out of his seat and jumps in front of her. "Whoa, killer." He holds both hands out and flashes Blair a toothy smile. "Just a minute. Where ya going? You look…"

"I look what, Clinton?" Blair says as she smirks at him and twirls a long strand of blonde hair around her index finger.

"You look…amazing," Clinton manages. "Stunning, actually."

Blair narrows her eyes, but that response seems to be what she is looking for. As she stares at Clinton, a subtle smile stretches across her face. "Well, thank you." She closes her eyes and tosses her hair in gratitude. It smacks him across the face.

"I'll drive," Red offers as she scooches between Blair and Clinton, who are blocking the door. As she passes, Blair drops the keys into her hand. "I need to gas up anyway."

Ellis turns towards me as I start to rise from my seat. "Where y'all going?"

"Shopping," I say. "I need a few things."

"Lingerie shopping," Red says from the doorway, winking at Ellis.

"Not really," I say quickly to Ellis. Ellis doesn't respond but instead stares at me, his mouth slightly open.

"Can I carry the bags?" Noah asks, suddenly more interested in us than the cards.

"No thanks, big guy." Red replies, patting his shoulder. "No boys allowed."

Noah pushes out his lower lip.

"Play your cards right, Noah," Blair says, "and she might model a few purchases for you later tonight."

Noah looks over to Red, hopeful.

"We'll see," she says and winks.

I walk over to where Blair has joined Red, then look back over my shoulder to Ellis, whose eyes dart quickly upward.

Was he just looking at my ass again?

His gaze meets mine before snapping back to his cards. "Have fun," he says without looking back.

"Oh, we will," Blair says in a sultry voice as she moves by me and skips over to Ellis. Ellis looks up as she leans over and whispers something in his ear. I don't know what she says, but by the way Ellis is wiggling in his seat, I can tell it's something that's purposefully made him uncomfortable. He starts to turn back towards me, but by then, Red has pulled me into the hallway.

"I'm a big fan of lace!" I hear Clinton shout and look back to see Blair hurrying forward to catch up with us.

"He wishes," Blair says, rolling her eyes, which sends us into a frenzy of laughter.

We laugh as we make our way through a side door that leads to a driveway where a bright red BMW convertible sits parked. The top is down, and I smile as I imagine the wind in my hair. I instinctively pull a hairband from my wrist and pull it back into a ponytail.

A few minutes later, we are cruising down the road at a relaxed pace.

After a moment, Red glances over to Blair. "What'd you say to him?"

"You mean Ellis?" Blair says innocently as her head turns to the backseat where I am seated and winks.

"What did you say?" I say suddenly, also interested. I have a feeling it has something to do with me.

"Blair…" Red says, her tone suspicious. "Spill it."

"Fine. Whatever." Blair looks back at me again. "I just told him that Glory looks fantastic in red thongs."

"What?!" Red and I say simultaneously.

I'm not mad, but I'm caught off guard. I let out a little short burst of laughter, the kind you make when something is funny but unbelievable at the same time.

"Why would you say that?" Red asks. She looks at me through the rear-view mirror, probably to see if I'm upset. I'm clearly not, just amused, so she laughs.

Blair shrugs. "I dunno. I just figured he would appreciate the image. Clinton and Noah were basically salivating over us, and poor Ellis needed a visual, too." Blair turns back and scrunches up her nose. "And he totally likes you."

"What?" I ask, completely caught off-guard by her comment. Ellis hates me—well, not hates—but he certainly doesn't *like like* me.

"He does, Glory," Red adds, and my mouth drops open. What is everyone else seeing that I'm not?

"You guys must be joking. Right? I mean, there's no way. The guy hated me like only a few days ago."

"He was an ass," Blair says.

"Exactly," I concur. "That's what I mean."

"Fine, he was an ass," Red agrees. "But he has never hated you."

"Of course he does," Blair adds matter-of-factly.

"You're beautiful, Glory," Red adds, and I can see her smiling through the rear-view mirror.

"Yep," Blair says in agreement.

Their words catch me by surprise, and I inhale sharply. My face is blank, but inside, my emotions are stirring. I focus hard to hold back a tear. I haven't thought of myself as pretty, much less beautiful, in a very long time. In fact, I can't remember the last time someone referred to me as beautiful—probably my dad. I know I'm not unattractive, but Nick had told me countless times during our relationship that I had 'let myself go.' I don't even wear make-up anymore, other than some simple bubblegum pink lip gloss, because I love the taste. I haven't in years. And I can't think of the last time I have had a decent haircut. I reach up and tug at my hair.

"You, okay?" Blair asks after a moment.

I'm looking out the window when she asks, so I turn toward her and nod. "Yep. Just thinking." I cock my head to the side. "You really think he likes me? Ellis?"

Blair nods. "Does a cat like mice?"

"Did you see how he looked at you on the porch?" Blair asks.

"I did," Red says as she turns into a long parking lot next to what appears to be a small outdoor mall.

"Exactly," Blair says. "I think you remind him of someone."

Red turns into her space then looks at Blair, clearly not happy about something.

"What?" Blair says so softly, I can barely hear.

"Of Jane," I say without thinking.

Shit.

Red sits up and turns towards me, her face suddenly drained of color. "What do you know about Jane?"

"Well…" I say and then look around for an exit, even though

I know there isn't one. "Clinton told me when we were out on the boat."

I hear Red exhale then look back to Blair.

"Of course he did," Blair says, shaking her head.

I suddenly feel like I need to come to Clinton's defense or provide an explanation since it's my fault for opening my big mouth. "Clinton had noticed Ellis treating me—"

"Like shit?" Blair asks, smirking.

"Like an enemy?" Red adds.

"*Definitely* an enemy," Blair agrees.

"Well, Clinton felt bad and told me about Jane. He said that Ellis was upset because my being at Dave's was forcing Ellis to move on."

Red nods and then looks towards Blair, who's biting her lower lip. Her eyes look blank as if she's thinking back to a vivid memory.

"Well. I guess it could be good that you know about…her," Red says solemnly after a minute. She stares off into the distance, then adds, "I have missed her so much."

"We all have," Blair says as she reaches over and rubs Red's back. "She's the most wonderful person."

I clasp my hands on my lap nervously. "How did she die?"

Blair and Red exchange a nervous glance.

"What did Clinton say?" Blair asks, her eyes drawn together.

I shake my head. "Not much. Just that Ellis had lost someone very close to him. And that her name was Jane."

Red and Blair exchange a look that suggests they are silently deliberating what to say, or how much to say. A moment later, Red nods and then turns toward me. "We lost her to a car accident. Someone ran her off the road on the way to Ellis's graduation."

CHAPTER 20

I do my best to enjoy shopping with the girls, even though I am still stunned by the revelation of Jane's death. So much more makes sense now, like why Ellis blames himself for her loss. But he must know that it isn't his fault. Blame is such a vicious monster, deceptive at times, crashing around without care for the damage it does.

But I do enjoy shopping with Red and Blair. It is so comforting to find the companionship of female friends again. I feel oddly safe, too. It reminds me of the safety in numbers that lionesses have in a pride. They stick together and can overcome any challenge or foe. We give each other strength.

Though I don't buy any thongs, I do manage to grab a few items to make me a bit more comfortable in the coming days.

"Damn. I forgot to get gas," Red says as she pulls into the lot by the house and parks. "I guess I need to—"

"What's up with him?" Blair interrupts as she points to the left. Red and I turn to see Dave walking fast toward us. He seems…upset. Blair steps out of the car and folds the seat back for me. "Hey Dave, is everything—"

"Noah's bringing around the truck now," Dave interrupts. His voice is jittery, and he looks unnerved. "I need to get down to the cliffs."

"Why?" Red asks, her brows pulled low with concern.

"Ellis is up there."

"On the high one?" Blair asks.

Dave nods solemnly.

Red shakes her head in disappointment. "But we saw him a few hours ago. He seemed fine, playing cards with—"

"He was playing cards," Dave says. "Noah said that shortly after y'all left, he left too."

"Same old shit," Blair says, shaking her head in disappointment. "I thought it was over now."

"Me too," Dave agrees solemnly as he looks towards me with sympathetic eyes.

"What are the cliffs?" I ask nervously. Whatever they are, it can't be good.

Dave frowns. "They're a series of big rock formations that people love to jump from."

"Are they dangerous?" I ask.

Dave doesn't answer but instead nods, tight-lipped.

"If you stick to the smaller cliffs, they are less dangerous for experienced swimmers," Red says.

"Exactly," Dave nods.

"But Ellis doesn't do the low stuff," Blair says.

"But if it's that dangerous, why does he do it?"

"Because he has a death wish," Dave says softly. "The pain. He can't get past it."

Blair, Red, and I exchange a knowing look.

Jane.

This must be why everyone has been so worried about Ellis. I have heard of people seeking extreme thrills to mask the pain and torment of their lives, but it's just so surreal to see it in real life, actually knowing someone whose soul is suffering so much that they risk their life to find a thrill, a brief numbness to free their mind.

"And he's been drinking," Dave adds, and the girls gasp in unison, looking at each other.

"Where's Clinton?" Blair says suddenly, looking back towards Dave.

"He's with Ellis. He rode the bike down there about twenty minutes ago."

Blair's face goes white, and she starts to speak, but a loud horn interrupts as Noah pulls beside us in his truck.

"Hop in," Noah calls out the window, and we jump into the back of the truck, except for Red, who rides up front with Noah.

It takes less than ten minutes to get to the cliffs. When we pull up, I immediately see mountain-sized boulders at the end of a crystal white beach, half in and half out of the water.

"Wait, Blair!" Dave shouts as Blair jumps out of the back of the truck and darts towards the crowd.

"Come on," I hear Red say frantically as she motions us to follow. We hop out and then dart after Blair.

We arrive at the crowd, and it's smaller than I first thought. Most of the twenty or so onlookers are college-aged kids, but a few older couples have joined the crowd to see what the fuss is about.

"Get down now, Clinton!" I hear Blair shouting from somewhere in front of me. I push a chunk of hair out of my eyes, then push forward through a line of people and see everyone standing by each other, looking upward towards the boulders.

My gaze moves higher until I see, at the highest point on the highest boulder, two figures in bathing suits talking back and forth. Their voices are inaudible through the salty wind.

"Only a handful of people have gone from the top jump," I hear someone say to my right.

I look back up and see Ellis on one side, wobbling left and right. I'm not sure exactly how Ellis got in such a state in the short time since we left the house, but something must have set him off, someone must have—

Oh no. Is he up there because of me or because of what Blair said?

Without thinking, I shift back through the crowd and move silently behind everyone to where the rocks seem to be at their lowest. I glance back over my shoulder to Red and everyone, but they're too distracted to notice me.

This is my fault, and I need to make it right.

I would never do something like this on my own, but I need to be brave and do what I can to help. I move forward until I see what appear to be small rope ladders and hand-painted signs pointing toward the jump areas.

I take a deep breath and find my courage. "You can do this, Glory," I whisper into the side of the stone.

I climb the first ladder to the first level. It is only about ten feet off the ground, but it's still scary. The boulder's surface is large enough, but I can tell it's slippery. I pull myself up onto the rock and then proceed slowly toward the jumping point at the far end of the boulder. There, I find the ladder leading to the next highest boulder. I am still on the backside of the boulders, so no one can see me. I take another steadying breath and then pull myself upward.

Don't look down, Glory.

As I reach the second level of cliffs, I begin to hear loud voices from above me—from the highest jump. The surface area of this next boulder is narrower and wraps around towards what I imagine is the jumping point. I walk around the narrow passage and stop when I see JJ sitting there, playing with his fingernails. He looks up suddenly and then shakes his head in confusion as if he's seeing an illusion.

"What the hell are you doing up here?"

"Nice to see you too, JJ," I quip. I look around until I spot another ladder. This one is also made of rope but looks older and worn—like it's never been replaced.

"Don't even think about going up there. That is crazy high. I've never even done—whoa, what are you doing?"

As he asks the question, I fling my shirt to him and step out of my shorts. The bright red bathing suit doesn't cover the light remainder of my bruises, but in the moment, I do not care who sees me, all of me.

"Holy shit," I hear JJ say as I step in front of the ladder, close my eyes, and take a calming breath.

"You can do this," I say softly to myself.

I begin to pull myself upward.

"Wait!" JJ shouts, but I ignore him and climb higher.

The ladder ends abruptly at the top of a flat, rocky surface. It's wider than I had imagined—thank God—and winds around towards the ocean, like the boulder below.

I inch forward, and as I do, the voices of Clinton and Ellis become clearer.

"Just go the fuck away. I'm not a damn baby, Clitty. Haha. Clitty."

Clinton ignores his insult. "Dude, you are fucking wasted. You can't jump off the highboy like that. You could hit a rock or something. Do you think Jane would want you to—"

"Don't fucking say her name!" Ellis yells, interrupting Clinton. "She's gone forever. It doesn't matter what she would think." He laughs softly to himself and repeats more quietly, "Just like they said. Forever. And her being her is just a reminder."

"It is because of me," I say softly, my suspicious confirmed.

The path on top becomes more and more narrow as I move forward, and it's slippery as hell. A steady stream of mist drifts upward from the waves that are crashing nearly fifty feet below. After a few more steps, the mist finally clears, and I see them. Ellis is standing on the far end of the cliff, and Clinton, his back to me, is only five or six feet away. They are not speaking to each other, just standing in silence.

I look to the right, where the entire right side of the cliff has opened up to reveal a cobalt-blue sky. I look downward and can see the small crowd below. I think I hear someone shouting my name, but the wind is strong, so the various noises from below are muffled, nearly inaudible.

"But what about us?" Clinton says towards Ellis's back, breaking the silence. "Everyone else? Don't we matter? What about her? You can't just pull shit like this. Do you have a death wish or something?"

"Maybe I do!" Ellis says as he turns around and faces Clinton. His eyes are angry and red, and he doesn't notice me at first.

"Come on, Ellis. Enough of this shit."

"What is the point of liv—" He pauses suddenly as his eyes dart towards me. He instantly looks less angry as he cocks his head to the side. He shakes his head as if waking from a dream.

"What the fuck…" he says softly into the mist, pointing a finger in my direction, wobbling slightly.

Clinton starts to speak but stops and looks over his shoulder. My eyes lock with Clinton's, and though he seems extremely stressed, a hint of surprise flashes across his face.

They both stare at me in silence for a moment, and I see their concern swell as they begin to notice the extent of my bruising. Clinton's eyes meet mine, and he purses his lips before turning back towards Ellis. "Look who is here. Look."

I ignore my insecurities and instead step forward. Clinton moves to the side to make room for me. His eyes meet mine, and after a moment, he nods as if in gratitude for my help. I try to look confident and force a smile.

Both stare at me as if waiting for me to speak. I know I have to say something, do something, but what? I blurt out the first thing that comes to mind.

"I was just hoping I could jump," I say simply, pretending not to acknowledge Clinton and Ellis's argument as I move forward past Clinton. I attempt to look over the ridge, feigning curiosity. "So where do you jump from?"

Ellis holds his hands up instantly. "You're not going to jump from here," Ellis says flatly. "It's impossible."

"Why? I feel like I've done something like this before. Well, maybe not this high."

"You just can't. You could get hurt."

"Yeah, but so could you. Or anyone else that does it. What's the difference?" I focus and see my argument more clearly. Ellis is not his normal self, and I try to outwit him.

"I've done this before. Like a hundred times."

"Yeah. But you're also drunk as hell." I find inspiration from Blair in how I speak.

"Yeah, so."

Be careful. This could backfire.

"Well, that would mean we are on the same level."

"She's got a point," Clinton says as he gives me a knowing wink, playing along.

Ellis shakes his head and takes a step towards me. "No, no. Absolutely not. You can't jump. I won't let you." He closes his eyes and shakes his head. "Go back down. I should be down by the time you hit the sand."

"No way," I say defensively. "If you get to go, then so do I. It's only fair." I force myself forward again, closer to the edge, but Ellis steps forward and blocks my path. Again, I feel a source of bravery, strength, radiating from some unknown source.

"Looks like an impasse," Clinton says smugly. "And if you jump, I will let her follow right behind you."

"What!" Ellis says sharply to Clinton. "You'd let *her* jump?" He seems visibly angry at Clinton. Ellis leans to the side, steadying himself, then looks back towards me.

"Sure," Clinton says, playing his part well. "It's a free country, and she's not my best friend."

Ellis bangs a hand on the side of the rock in frustration. "That's fucking bullshit, man. You know what she—"

I start to step forward past Ellis, but he reaches out and grabs my hand. As he looks towards me, he smiles a bit. I look down at his hand and hold my head high. Just as I start to jerk free from his grasp, he lets go.

"Okay. Fine. Let's just get down from here. *Both* of us. You don't go. I don't go."

I glance back to Clinton, careful not to overplay my hand. "What do you think, Clinton?"

"It's your deal to make, Glory." He shrugs and pushes out his lips.

I stare back at Ellis, who takes my hand. I look down and squeeze it gently. "Deal. But you go down first. I will follow. I promise."

He thinks for a moment, then nods slowly, exhaling deeply. He has no choice. "Deal." He gives my hand a little squeeze then lets it drop.

Clinton doesn't give him time to change his mind. He steps towards Ellis, grabs his arm, and then gently leads him towards the ladder.

Clinton goes down first but is slow. He waits for Ellis to at least begin his descent, probably expecting him not to follow through. But after a moment, Ellis follows behind Clinton.

"Careful there, killer," Clinton says. "I don't want your big ass to fall and crush this beautiful face. Blair would eat you for dinner."

"Ugly mugly," I hear Ellis murmur.

Just before his head lowers below the rock's surface, he stops and looks at me one time for an extended moment. "Come on then, fearless," he says, slurring. "I'm gonna wait down here and make sure you follow through with your end of the bargain." He removes one hand from the ladder and points to me as he gives me a wink.

"Two hands, Ellis," I hear Clinton yell from below.

I smile. "I'm coming."

His eyes narrow and a wicked smile pulls at one end of his mouth. He starts to say something and then stops and looks down. "Damn it, Clinton. Quit pulling on my leg. I'm coming," he says, then turns back towards me and descends.

Ellis calls up to me when he reaches the bottom. "Come on, Glory."

I walk over to the ledge to see him looking up at me suspiciously. Clinton is already around to the other ledge, motioning Ellis forward. "Let's go, man."

Ellis doesn't even look at him. Instead, he remains motionless below, staring upward as if he's waiting for something. He looks smug, like he's won something. I just don't understand what—

Oh shit.

He's totally waiting for me to come down in my bathing suit so he can check out my ass. I'm suddenly glad I had the urge to shave this morning.

I shake my head and roll my eyes. He winks at me as if he knows exactly what I'm thinking.

"I just want to make sure you won't fall," Ellis says.

"Sure."

"Promise. I'm a gentleman."

I hear JJ suddenly blurt out. "I'll watch out for her if you want to go ahead down the—"

"No way!" Ellis snaps. "You go over there." Ellis points to the ladder.

JJ doesn't retort—not wanting to upset Ellis—and sheepishly walks over to the ladder.

"Turn around."

JJ lets out a sigh but doesn't object as he turns around, so his back faces me.

Knowing I can't stay up top forever waiting for Ellis to leave, I take a calming breath, turn around, and descend on the rope ladder as quickly as possible. Going down takes a lot more bravery than going up, so I clench my eyes the entire way and don't open them until my feet hit the ground below.

I turn around expecting to see Ellis, but instead, he's gone, and in his place is a smiling JJ. I narrow my eyes at his large, toothy grin.

"What?" he asks in an overly innocent tone.

I glare.

"Ellis got a good look too!"

I start to turn away towards the next ladder, but instead, with hesitation, step to my left to get a better view of the second-level jump. It's not nearly as high as the one above, but it's still scary as hell.

"You are doing this?" I ask JJ as I nod towards the edge.

"Yeah," he says, then adds, "maybe," his tone uneasy, lacking confidence. "I thought about doing it today…I dunno." He's stumbling all over his words, clearly nervous.

I inch further towards the edge and then look over to my right. Just past the tops of a few palms, I see Clinton and Ellis join Dave and the others near the crowd. I smile as Blair runs towards Clinton and gives him a long, tight hug. She then pushes off him and points towards him and Ellis. She's furious, it's clear, and I can just hear her voice, dripping with venom, as she gives them both a tongue lashing. Clinton doesn't respond, but by the way he is holding out his hands, I can tell he's trying to calm her down.

Ellis then abruptly looks back up at me, and I jump back slightly in surprise. I force a smile just as he stands a little straighter and quietly moves away from Blair and Clinton towards the crashing waves.

I try to avoid his stare. It's intense and curious. I turn back towards JJ. "Is this jump safe?"

JJ shrugs. "Yeah. I mean, not many people do it. I think Amber…and maybe one or two other girls have ever done it. Ellis and Clinton do it occasionally."

"What about Noah?"

"No way. He's scared of heights too. Big baby, that one."

I cock my head to the side, intrigued. "Really?" I still have a hard time believing Noah is afraid of anything. I look back towards the water. "How deep is it?"

"I think it's about forty feet deep—deep enough. You just have to jump ten feet or so out."

"Why?" I ask.

"So, you don't splatter your head across the rocks." He points below to a group of jagged stones. His honesty is unsettling.

"Maybe I could do it," I say softly to myself without realizing it.

"No fucking way, Glory. This is serious shit. You have to be careful."

"But you just said it's safe."

"It is. I mean, I think it is."

I roll my eyes. He just doesn't want a girl to show him up. I inch closer to the edge…

And closer…

Closer…

I look over to JJ. His eyes are wide. He's watching me intently. I look down to the beach once more. Ellis is standing in the water now, and behind him, I notice that I've captured the attention of a few others, including Dave.

"I'm going to tell everyone that you wouldn't listen to me," JJ says. "That there was nothing I could do to get you down."

I nod. "Agreed."

"Ellis is going to kill me," he says softly to the ground, shaking his head.

I inch closer…

Closer…

"Wait!" he shouts.

I stop and look over my shoulder. "Yes?"

"One more thing."

"Okay?" I say after a silent moment.

"Whatever you do, make sure you do not land flat."

"Why?"

"It would be like bellyflopping on cement. Splat!" He claps his hands together. "Get it?"

I nod. "Got it. Splat."

Be brave, Glory.

I step further towards the edge of the rock. My head starts to turn towards the crowd below, but I stop myself. Instead, I fix my gaze directly onto the horizon. It's beautiful, a deep blue that goes on and on, so familiar. I close my eyes and breathe in deeply. After a moment, I release the breath, and it carries away with it all remaining doubt. In that moment, standing on that cliff, my body visible for all to see, I feel suddenly free, truly free. I've emerged from hell, having become someone more, having become…fearless.

CHAPTER 21

As I FREE-FALL downward, I don't remember jumping. The wind is howling past my body, which seems to be positioned at a perfect ninety-degree angle to the water—thank God—and the sharp rush in my stomach is intense. Not bad, but intense. I clench my eyes tightly.

I hit the water, and my body rushes down through what feels like a cold tunnel of bubbles. I grit my teeth at the sudden chill.

After a moment I stop and open my eyes. I float silently in the deep blue water and then instinctively look upwards towards a ceiling of light twenty or so feet above. As my lungs begin to burn, I extend my hands up, and kick towards the surface, blowing out air all the way to the top.

I gasp as my face bursts into the sky. I hear shouts and whistles from behind me, so I turn towards the noise. Forcing my eyes open, I see Ellis wading out into the water towards me. He briefly looks concerned, but as soon as I smile, he mirrors me and grins from ear to ear.

"I can't believe you did that," he shouts.

I can't help but smile proudly.

I extend my arms and kick towards the beach, and within moments, my feet touch the sandy bottom. Everyone from Dave's has stepped beyond the crowd towards Ellis. Everyone is smiling and cheering loudly.

I pull my hair over my shoulders as I walk closer towards Ellis. He's happy but still clearly drunk. He blinks and his gaze quickly moves across my body.

"Are you okay?" he says softly. "Make it out without any injuries?" He wobbles a bit as the waves hit him, but he manages to stay upright.

I look down at my body curiously. "I think so."

"Good," he says before his eyes look down bashfully.

I start to walk by him, but he turns and gently takes my hand. "Wait," he says, then lets it fall back to my side. I stop and look at him as I comb my hair back with my fingers.

His head is cocked to the side, a bit playful. "You broke our deal."

"How so?"

"You said if I come down, you will too."

I smile and hold up my hand in mock defense. "Nope. I said that I wouldn't jump from the high spot—and I didn't. I said nothing about the lower jumps."

"That's a technicality." Ellis points his finger towards me and narrows his eyes.

I feign a frown and step towards him. "Maybe you shouldn't make bets after you've been drinking?" I cock my head to the side. "What do you think about that?"

"Touché."

I smile and pat his shoulder. "Come on, killer. Let's get you out of here. You need a big glass of ice water and some rest."

"You head on back. I'll be right behind you."

I let my hand drop, and then I nod. We aren't out that far, and even if he passed out, Clinton could be out there to him in five seconds flat. "Okay, but don't be too long. We need to get you home." I turn and begin wading back towards the shoreline and the crowd.

The crew from Dave's meet me as I step out of the water. I

look down briefly at my body and hope the remnants of Nick don't overshadow this small victory of mine, but if anyone seems to notice my bruising, they don't stare.

"What the hell, Glory!" Blair says. "That was awesome. I just can't believe you did it. Not many people can do that jump."

"Seriously," Red adds, handing me a towel that I wrap tightly around my torso. "You are amazing."

"Is he coming out?" Dave asks as he gently pats me on the back and stares out towards Ellis.

"Yeah," I say. "He just needs a minute. I think he's not feeling—"

"Eww!" Blair shouts suddenly over the sound of heaving.

I turn and see Ellis bent forward into the water.

"Don't stand in it!" Clinton shouts towards Ellis from Blair's side. "Aim with the current."

"That is so gross," Red says as she starts to heave. "I can't take it." Red covers her eyes, turns, and rushes to some nearby bushes, both hands over her mouth.

"She can't stand to see someone throw up," Noah says. "If she does, she'll start to gag."

"Poor thing."

Blair starts to go towards her, but Noah holds up his hand. "I've got it."

"By all means," Blair says as she stops suddenly and throws out her palm. She walks back towards me and stands between Clinton and me. I look over just as she shoots Clinton a venomous glare. "I'm still pissed at you."

Clinton looks over to her and moves behind her to rub her shoulders. "I'm sure it's nothing a back rub can't fix," he whispers in her ear, and Blair immediately closes her eyes and lets out a soft moan.

"Maybe," she says. "If it lasts more than fifteen minutes."

"Oh, I can last as long as you want, baby."

I hear a cough and look back towards a wide-eyed Dave, who steps toward us as if to remind us that he's still there.

Blair looks back at him and winks. "Making you nervous, Davey?" Blair asks playfully.

Dave rolls his eyes, then walks to my side. "Clinton told us what you did. Convincing Ellis to come down. That took a lot of guts. Thank you."

I smile. "I didn't really do anything. I just told him if he jumped, then I would jump."

"Yeah, you did," Clinton says, suddenly serious as he steps around Blair. "He was so close to jumping. He could have died, Glory. The top jump is tricky. Even when you're in the right state of mind. I couldn't have done it without you. He needed you up there."

"Would you have jumped?" Blair asks.

"I don't know," I say softly. "Maybe."

I look back out to Ellis, who has started walking back towards the shore. I can't help but feel bad for him. He looks terrible. His face is pale, and his eyes are lined with dark circles. I can't believe Ellis would risk his life just for a thrill. I can't believe he got so drunk so fast.

"Has he done this before?" I ask out of concern, knowing the answer.

"Glory, he's been here countless times," Dave says. "Looking for a quick thrill to take away the pain."

"But he's never been that close to doing it," Blair says. "He's been off the lower jumps but never the high jump."

"The lower ones can be dangerous too," Clinton says.

"True," Dave says and Blair nods in support.

"I think he would've jumped were it not for you," Clinton says. "Something set him off tonight."

I look out towards Ellis, suddenly feeling guilty. My showing up here—escaping from my nightmare—has pushed Ellis further into his. The feeling of guilt sours my stomach.

Leave.

The intrusive thought jumps to the forefront of my mind, and by the time Ellis walks up to us, it's looping through my mind. He's hurting, sick, and can hardly walk. The feeling that I need to put him out of his misery is strong—and there's only one way to do that—I need to leave.

"Okay. Let's get out of here," Ellis says, waving towards the car. "Sorry, everyone." He looks between Red and Noah, who just rejoined us, and Red wipes her mouth. "Sorry, Red."

"It's fine, E," Red says. "Just glad you're feeling better, buddy."

Ellis turns and looks towards me. He can't quite look me in the eyes. His shame is palpable.

"Hey," I say, and his eyes dart up to meet mine. I do my best to force a smile, but his eyebrows furrow in concern. I can't help but think he's looking at me right now like it's the last time we'll see each other.

"Okay, folks," Dave says, interrupting our moment. "Let's get out of here. Ellis, you're with us."

Chapter 22

When we get back to the house, I depart quickly and don't linger. I am not good with goodbyes and don't want to inadvertently reveal my plans to leave. Though they will be surprised by my departure, I don't have a choice.

Upstairs, I get changed into a tee and pajama pants, and just as I finish pulling a brush through my hair, I hear Noah and Ellis. After a few minutes, a door opens and closes, and the hallway goes silent once more. I brush my teeth, grab a glass, and head to the kitchen. As I step into the hallway, I see Noah closing the door to Ellis's apartment. He sees me and walks over.

"I got him to bed," he says, then sighs. "Made sure he's on his stomach in case he needs to puke again."

"Is he okay?"

"A little better, but he's wobbly as hell, and he's going to hurt tomorrow."

"I bet," I say.

"You all right up here?" he asks, looking casually over my shoulder.

I look behind me into the empty apartment and shrug. "Just tired," I say, avoiding eye contact. "I think I'm going to head to bed."

After a brief hesitation, Noah nods. "Well, I'll be downstairs at Red's tonight. If you need anything, come and get me."

"Okay," I say, nodding. "Night, Noah."

"Night, Glory." He starts to walk and then stops and turns. "Thanks again for what you did."

I don't respond but smile as he turns and walks down the stairs. I stand at the doorway until I hear him close the door to Red's below.

It doesn't take long to pack. Even after shopping, everything I own fits comfortably in my duffel bag and backpack. Since it's still early, and people may be up and about, I decide to rest on the couch for a few hours until I know everyone is asleep. I don't want to risk running into anyone on my way out. I look at my phone.

7:15 PM.

I set my alarm for midnight and reach for my wallet on the coffee table to count what's left of my money. My first—and last—paycheck is supposed to be automatically deposited tomorrow, so that, coupled with the $160 in my wallet, should be enough to get me wherever I'm going…I hope.

"Maybe I'll go to Texas," I whisper.

I lean back and close my eyes, hoping to get some rest before driving all night. My mind is whirling around as thoughts of Ellis, my new friends, the cliff jump, and more dance in my head. I let out a nervous sigh as I think about what it will be like when everyone figures out that I skipped town. My mind wanders from Dave and Amber, to Aki, to Charlie and even JJ. I think about the first real girlfriends that I've had in a very long time.

Then I think about the boys, Clinton and Noah. Noah is a wonderful person—kind and gentle. I'm sure that I will compare him to future love interests if I ever start dating again. Then there's Clinton. I see his silly face shift into a frown as he discovers that I've left. He will be so disappointed.

Ellis.

I feel like we could have been great friends or even more, had the circumstances been different. Had he emerged from his pain, and if I weren't damaged goods.

When the alarm goes off, I feel as though I have only slept a few minutes, but as I glance at my cell phone, I realize I have been sleeping for nearly five hours.

I pull myself up and stretch my arms to the ceiling. After I go to the bathroom, I head over to the front door and listen closely to make sure no one is awake.

Silence.

I grab both bags, place the key on the coffee table, then slowly open the door. It's dark in the hallway, but there's some light coming in from the window, just enough to prevent me from tripping. I close the door and tape a small note to it explaining in little detail that I have decided to head home to Texas.

I turn and manage only a few steps before the kitchen door opens behind me.

"What are you doing?" Ellis says softly.

I look over my shoulder and force a smile. He doesn't smile back as he looks at my bags. He stares in confusion, then his eyes widen and dart towards the note on the door. He lets out a sharp breath as he realizes what I'm doing. He then takes a cautious step forward, approaching me like an injured animal.

"Why are you leaving?"

I lower my backpack from my shoulder. It hangs limply from my hand at my side. "I...I just think it would be best."

He cocks his head as if waiting, but I don't want to explain why I'm leaving. I don't want him to know I'm leaving because of him. But then he speaks, and I realize he knows.

"It's not you, Glory. You are not the reason that I'm so messed up right now. I know it seems like it...but you're not."

I bite my lower lip and then speak softly. "I just think that it might be easier if I—"

"No," he interrupts. "It won't be easier without you. I can't explain to you why, not yet, but it won't." He takes another step towards me. "You are…helping me. I need—"

He stops talking as I hold up my hand. I'm a bit shocked by my nerve. "I just can't believe I'm helping anything, Ellis. I mean, you've been upset since I got here."

He shakes his head after an awkward silence. He looks sheepishly downward. "Look, Glory. I admit it. I wasn't happy when you arrived. But you just caught me off-guard."

"I understand."

"There is just so much you don't know. So much that I can't explain to you. Not yet."

"Okay," I say, "but even so, my being here has made things worse, Ellis."

"That's not true."

"You almost died today," I say, and as the words leave my mouth, he hangs his head in shame. "If something were to happen to you because of me…"

"I know. I'm sorry. I'm so sorry. And I'm sorry for how I've treated you."

"You don't have to apologize, Ellis, I understand."

"I do, Glory. I've been acting lack a total ass. I've been in such a bad place, and when you showed up, I couldn't manage those feelings, so I took it out on you." He takes another step forward. "But that day when we were on the boat, I realized as I saw you there playing with that damn dolphin that you weren't my demise, you were my salvation."

My hand grasps at my chest as the unexpected emotion in his words hit me like cold water. "

"I'm sorry," he says, again, shaking his head. "I'm. So. Sorry."

I step forward, the urge to comfort Ellis overwhelming me. I pull him into me and rub his back. "It's okay, Ellis," I say. "It's okay." We stand there for several minutes before I gently step away. "But why did you get so upset today? I don't understand?"

"I…I just…"

He's struggling visibly to answer my question, like he is being careful in choosing the right words. After a moment, he lets out a deep breath and rubs both hands over his face before dropping them abruptly to his sides and looking at me intensely. "Okay."

"What?"

He shrugs his shoulders and nods in defeat. "I admit it."

"Admit what?"

"Your being here terrifies me." He blinks slowly. "And the closer I get to you, the more scared I get." He closes his eyes and takes a step towards me.

"What?

He shakes his head. "I like you." He opens his eyes. "I *really* like you."

"You do?"

"I do, and it's been a long time, you know, since I've felt like this. And I'm so scared that I might lose you."

Like how he lost Jane.

My eyes widen at his honesty, and I feel myself take several short, nervous breaths. "So, I was the reason for everything this afternoon," I say softly.

He shakes his head. "No, Glory. That's not what I'm saying at all." Ellis takes both of my hands gently and pulls me forward.

I don't pull away, but instead, let him lead me closer. I haven't been touched like this in so long. And even though I'm trying to untangle my feelings for Ellis, at this moment, I feel connected to him on an intimate level. He takes a few deep breaths.

"But I don't understand," I say softly while looking down.

"What do you think about joining me in the garden?"

He steps towards the kitchen, but we stay connected by one hand. I hesitate to move forward as he urges me, looking back at the stairs.

He senses my hesitation. "If you still want to go after we have talked, I won't try to stop you, and I won't tell anyone."

After a moment, I nod and follow him forward.

We make our way up to the garden, and again, I find myself sitting on the swing underneath the pergola. The garden is as beautiful as always, and when Ellis catches me staring at a miniature lime tree, he reaches over and plucks a fresh lime.

"Here," he says. "Smell it."

I grab the lime and pull it up to my nose, inhaling. The scent is magnificent—a fresh, deep citrusy scent that's both sweet and earthy.

"This is incredible. I've smelled lime, but nothing like this."

"Nope. This is a key lime. The only lime in my book."

"Like key lime pie?"

"Exactly, but most recipes don't use real key limes. Aki makes a hell of a key lime pie." He forces a smile. "One more reason to stay."

My eyes meet his. "I admit it. I love this place. It is beautiful. The people are great, and," I hold up the lime, "the key limes are incredible. But none of this matters if I know my being here is hurting someone, hurting you."

"It's not, Glory."

I stare at him silently, and as I do, he begins to speak.

"This afternoon, when you and the girls came down to the porch, I was already upset." He pauses and furrows his brow as if it is hurting him to continue.

I put a hand on his leg. "I'm sorry. You don't have to—"

"This is just so hard to talk about, but I need to explain it to you. It would be wrong for me to let you think that this afternoon was your fault. It would be so wrong for me to let this drive you away from here."

I squeeze his leg softly and use it to pull my legs underneath me. He reaches over and hands me the throw blanket, which I place around my legs.

"Two years ago today, I was on the phone with Jane. She was my girlfriend, and everyone here knew her. She had worked at Dave's with me for several seasons. She was living in Tennessee at the time, and I was just about to graduate that weekend from Florida. We spoke nearly every day, but I knew when I picked up the phone that something was wrong."

He stands and paces back and forth before he continues. "The conversation started the usual way. She asked me how my last final went, and I asked her how her day was. I thought that perhaps she had a rough day at work. She was a server, and trying to finish her degree."

I nod slowly in agreement.

"Well, eventually, I asked her what was wrong." He pinches the bridge of his nose before walking back over and sitting on the swing at my side. I can tell that whatever he's trying to say is painful. He's hurting.

After a moment, he continues. "She didn't tell me at first, but after I kept pressing, she eventually did." Ellis stops talking and covers his face with his hands. I see a tear roll down his cheek, but I pretend not to notice.

"What did she tell you, Ellis?" I say, gently encouraging him to continue.

He looks up at me, his eyes red and squinting. "She told me that she had been with someone else. That she had cheated on me."

I cringe as the image of Jane that everyone else painted in my head—the deep connection, the once-in-a-lifetime love between Jane and Ellis—is instantly shattered.

Ellis stares blankly out to the ocean. A cool, salty breeze blows across the night sky, tossing his shaggy blonde hair across his forehead. He takes a calming breath and then looks back towards me as I wrap my arms tightly around my waist to hold in the warmth.

"You cold?" he asks.

I don't respond but nod instinctively, and Ellis immediately moves so our legs are touching. He wraps his arm around my shoulder, gently pulling me closer.

"Better?"

"Yeah. Thanks."

He nods and leans his head back, resting it on the back of the swing before continuing. "Needless to say, I was mad. So mad. Jane was supposed to come back to Florida for my graduation in a couple of weeks, then we were going to move in together and start our life. I just couldn't understand how she could have done that. It just didn't make any sense."

"I'm so sorry, Ellis," I say, and he looks at me as if he had been waiting on those words for years.

"I didn't want to see her—I couldn't see her. We talked on the phone for hours that night. She told me the guy's name, how they met, at some party, and all through the conversation, she apologized, over and over again, telling me that it was a mistake and that it would never happen again. She wanted me to immediately forgive her for everything. She wanted everything to go back to the way it was." He smiles awkwardly. "And I wanted to forgive her. I really did. I wanted to forgive her so bad—I wanted to pretend that my once perfect relationship with her had not been shattered."

I nod absently as I think back to the numerous apologies from Nick over the years, all the times he would show up to my place drunk and angry, not wanting to be there but driven by some unnamed sinister motive. It wasn't the same scenario, sure, but like Ellis, I wanted to forgive him and pretend the abuse had never happened.

I turn towards Ellis and our eyes lock. "I wanted to

forgive her, Glory. I did. But I needed time. I needed to think about everything."

"I understand."

"She kept asking me if it was over, and at first, I told her that I didn't know. But I was just so angry and hurt, and I wanted her to hurt, too. So, after a while—later in the conversation—I cracked—I just couldn't take it anymore. I lost control." He pauses and looks away from me. I can tell he's fighting back tears.

"What happened, Ellis?" I ask.

"I went off on her," he says, turning back towards me. A single tear rolls down his cheek. "I told her we were done and that I never wanted to see her again."

"You didn't mean it, Ellis."

"I did, Glory. I meant it. At least, at the time I thought I did. Now, looking back, I would trade anything in the world to be able to take back those words." He rubs his forehead. "You know what they say is true."

"What?"

"That a moment—a single word even—can change the course of your life. Or, in this case, the course of Jane's."

As he finishes the sentence, he breaks down, and I gently sit up straighter and begin to gently rub his back. "It's okay, Ellis. It's not your fault."

Ellis exhales a shaky breath. "But it is, Glory. It is. For the next several days, Jane tried to contact me. By phone, text, through mutual friends. But I didn't respond to her. I refused to talk to her."

Ellis stands up abruptly again and paces away from the swing for a moment then turns towards me. I brace myself as my heartbeat hastens.

"Then, on my graduation day, early that morning at about four o'clock, Jane got into her car and started driving to Florida. She had texted me that night telling me she was coming to support me, no matter what I said…that she wanted to be there for me. She said she would make things right and explain everything."

Ellis throws his hands in the air in painful frustration. "Of course, I didn't respond. I almost did. But in the end, I didn't."

Brace yourself, Glory.

"After about two hours into her drive," he continues, "at around six in the morning, something happened." He pauses and the tears begin to roll down his cheeks.

I stand and walk towards Ellis.

He looks blankly over my shoulder and speaks. "She ran off the road going sixty miles an hour. I lost her instantly…"

Ellis's voice trails off, and he looks at me as if waiting for my reply, my judgment. His expression is laced with anger, fear… sorrow. Reliving the trauma of Jane's death has utterly destroyed him. My heart beats loudly in my chest as I realize that Ellis has told me something he has never told anyone before. Not because he hadn't trusted anyone but because he was afraid of being judged, of being blamed, and of reliving the moment.

"So, do you understand," he asks me after taking a moment to wipe a hand across his cheek, "why I got so upset this afternoon?"

I nod and reach out, grasping his hand in mine. It's warm and clammy. "Yes, I do," I say simply.

"And do you still want to go?"

I stand there silently, considering his question.

"I really want you to stay, Glory," Ellis says. He steps forward and guides me gently into his embrace. I'm caught off-guard and gasp, and as I do, our eyes connect. Ellis's pupils dilate and his eyes narrow. I instinctively wet my lips with my tongue, which doesn't escape Ellis as his eyes suddenly dart downward. He pushes forward through those last few inches, and our lips meet.

That kiss.

At first, he's gentle and cautious, his tongue gently probing in and out of my mouth, but as I open my lips further, welcoming his touch, he crashes into me like he can't get enough. I let out a soft moan, and as I do, Ellis grips the small of my back and presses me closer to him.

That kiss.

But the pleasure doesn't last. After what seems like several minutes, he abruptly pulls away and takes a few steps backward. He squeezes his eyes shut. "I'm sorry, Glory."

I feel confusion flicker across my face. "It's okay, Ellis. I wanted to—"

"No, it's not. It's just not…I shouldn't have done that—led you on like that. I'm sorry."

Led me on?

"What do you mean?" I ask, utterly confused and frustrated at the sudden coldness I feel emanating from him.

He shakes his head. "I just can't do this right now."

"Do what?"

"It just doesn't feel right."

His words smack me with such a force I gasp. How could he not have felt what I just felt?

He points to me and then back to him. "I didn't mean to let it go this far. I just want you to stay. I want you to stay so bad."

I cross my hands over my chest, suddenly feeling embarrassed. That kiss had made me feel like he wanted something more from me, but now…I'm not sure he does. Did he kiss me because he thought it was the only way to get me to stay?

"Why do you say that you want me to stay, kiss me like that, then tell me it was all a mistake?" I ask, shocked by my sudden burst of courage. It's not like me to ask such direct questions. "I'm so confused."

Ellis cringes and steps forward. "I like you, Glory. I do. But…" He lets out a slow breath and then nods to himself. "But I can't be with you. I can't be with you like this. I just can't. It's not fair to…"

My heart shivers.

"I want you to be here—I do—but it's just…I think we should be friends."

I don't know what to say, so I say the first thing that comes to mind. "I think we should be friends too." As I say it, I look away, finding it difficult to look directly at Ellis.

"Fine," he says, and I turn to see him walking toward the stairs to his apartment. He stops, glances back at me, like he's waiting—for someone, for me.

"You want me to leave?"

He doesn't respond, so I take the hint. I'm so damn frustrated at how this guy can go from hot to cold so quickly.

I walk over to him, hoping my posture makes it clear to him that I'm pissed. "Whatever," I say simply.

I follow him down the steps towards the back door. He stops at the bottom of the stairs, but I continue past him.

"Glory, wait, I—"

I turn suddenly, my face bright red and flushed with anger. I close my eyes and take a deep breath, forcing myself to keep my cool and stay calm. "No, Ellis. I just want to go."

His eyes widen. "Wait! Are you staying? I need you to—"

"I will stay, okay?" I say as I shake my head and stare at him in silence. The anxiety in his eyes softens. "But no more risks, and no more putting yourself in danger."

Ellis looks shamefully downward. After a moment, he looks up and says, "Okay. Deal."

"I'm fine being friends, Ellis. I'm actually thankful to have a friend. I don't have many—actually, I don't have any." I ignore a tear that rolls down my cheek. "And honestly, I'm not sure if I would be ready to move to something beyond that. I'm just so…broken."

He starts to speak, but I hold up my hand and interrupt him.

"Let's just pretend this didn't happen." I quickly turn towards the door before he has a chance to speak.

"Okay," I hear him say softly towards my back.

I look back over my shoulder. He's taken a few steps towards me. "I'm sorry about Jane," I find myself saying. "I truly am. But it's not your fault, Ellis, and I know if she were here right now, she would say the same thing."

He doesn't respond but instead stares blankly across my shoulder.

I reach out with one hand to turn the knob.

It won't turn.

Chapter 23

"Shit," I say softly to myself and try again.

Nothing. It won't budge.

"What?" Ellis says from behind me, his tone suddenly curious, his voice a bit louder.

I pull at the door again, but it still doesn't move an inch. "It's stuck."

"Let me try," Ellis says as he walks to my side. He grabs the knob with one hand, then two—and pulls.

Nothing.

He then puts his foot on one side of the door and yanks again.

Nothing.

"Damn!" he says as he kicks at the door lightly. "I thought it was fixed."

"You mean it was broken?" My eyes are wide.

"Yeah," he answers, looking at me. "It recently started locking automatically. "I've been propping it open."

"Seriously?"

"Yeah." He shakes his head. "I don't know why. It's the weirdest thing."

"You've got to be kidding me." I reach into my pocket but realize my phone is in my bag, which we left in the hallway.

"My phone."

Ellis looks at me, suddenly hopeful. He clearly doesn't have his.

I point toward the door. "In my bag. Inside. Is there another way off the roof?"

He points to the door and frowns. "This is the only way. I could break the door down, I guess, but it might shatter the glass." I look back to the door, which is outlined by the same beautiful frosted blue glass that's on the front door of the house.

Ellis starts towards the door, but I hold up both hands. "No. Don't break the door. These old houses are filled with antique glass. I don't think Dave could ever replace this."

Ellis furrows his brow and looks around me at the glass. "Maybe."

"There has to be another way," I say.

"Well," Ellis says as he bites his lower lip. "I don't know any other way out, but we could wait until morning and call out to someone leaving the house. Clinton usually goes for his run at six."

I feel the worry flash across my face. Alone on the roof with Ellis—all night—not exactly the best scenario. But what else is there to do?

"Okay. That might work. But we would have to sleep out here."

"Do you have any more blankets somewhere?" It's getting late, and the cool sea wind suddenly seems more active.

"Afraid not."

"Damn," I say softly. "We are going to freeze."

I look towards Ellis just as he winks and extends a hand towards me. "I think I might have something that'll work."

Five hours later, we are sitting on the swing together, both snuggled close to each other for warmth. I scowl at Ellis as I look down at the bright orange Florida sweater I'm wearing.

"I still can't believe I'm wearing this thing," I say flatly.

"I still can't believe you're a football fan."

"And why wouldn't I be?"

"You're a girl," Ellis says, waving his hand dismissively.

I'm caught by surprise by his blatantly sexist comment, and my mouth drops open. "You did not just say that."

He looks blankly for a moment as he stares out towards the ocean, then sneaks a look at me from the corner of his eyes. "I'm kidding, G. Pulling your chain. How could you not like football? Even though you went to…" He pinches his lips together as if deep in thought, then looks at me, head cocked sideways like a big golden retriever. "What's the name of that school again?"

"Ha, ha, ha. You think you are so funny, don't you?"

"Yep," he says confidently before looking at me and waggling his eyebrows.

After several minutes of sitting in silence, I pull both legs under me and face Ellis, who is staring out towards the ocean and fidgeting with the drawstring on his pants—something I've noticed he does when his mind is running in circles.

"So, tell me something about yourself," I say, forcing my voice to be lively and upbeat, hoping to lighten the mood.

Ellis pulls out of his trance and looks at me. One corner of his mouth moves upward slightly. "There's not a whole lot to tell. What do you want to know?"

"You know, the usual. Where are you from? What are your dreams? That kind of stuff."

He lets out a light laugh. "You sure do come out swinging, don't you? Those are date questions, you know?" He looks at me, eyes suddenly narrow. "Is this a date or something?"

"You wish."

"What do you want to know first?"

"Okay. Where were you born?"

Ellis laughs. "That seems like a good place to start." He takes a short breath. "Florida. Miami, actually."

"A Florida boy, huh?"

"Yep," he says. "What about you?"

"Me?"

"The one and only."

"Oh. Um, I'm from the Texas-Louisiana border area near a place called Beaumont. My mom still lives there."

"What about your dad?" He leans in this time, as if listening more carefully.

I can't help it as the smile falls from my face. "He's from Florida, too. He met my mom in college."

"Tennessee?"

"Yeah."

"How did I guess?" Ellis says as he looks at me and his grin falters. "You okay, G?"

I force a smile. "I'm fine. It's just my dad. He died a couple of years back. I just miss him."

Ellis shakes his head and his frown mirrors mine. "I am sorry to hear that. I know how hard it can be to lose a parent. He must have been pretty amazing."

"Yeah. He was. I just wish my memories of him were clearer. I can't even remember his voice now."

"I understand. I wish I had had more time with my mom, made more memories."

"Cancer sucks," I tell him.

"Fucking sucks."

"Yes," I agree. "It *fucking* sucks."

Ellis looks at me and smiles. "Next date question."

I roll my eyes and force back a yawn before asking, "What do you want to do with your life? I mean, what do you want to be?"

Ellis bites his lower lip and shrugs. "I don't know." He starts to elaborate but then stops and exhales a long breath. Ellis looks at me as if thinking carefully about his reply. "Sorry if I'm a bit reserved. I haven't talked about this kind of stuff with someone in a very long time."

"Since Jane?" I say. I scold myself inwardly as Ellis frowns and faces away. I wish I could think before I speak. "Sorry," I say in a hushed tone.

"Don't be. You're just asking a question." He pauses and pulls his leg up onto the swing. "It's just hard for me, you know? Some things just trigger memories that I have forgotten, or just the opposite, that I can't seem to forget." He looks at me, and all I can do is nod. "But they're not all bad—most of them actually—are wonderful. They hurt too, though, sometimes more."

"You must have really loved her," I say, and Ellis's eyes dart my way.

He nods somberly. "I did…I do, I mean. So much. I just hate that I couldn't have made it better. I'm sorry I couldn't have just told her that I forgave her like she wanted."

"So, you forgive her?"

"I do. Everyone makes mistakes."

"Yeah," I agree softly.

He closes his eyes. "But now, all I can think about is how she must have felt just before she died, before the crash. How her last moments on earth were filled with suffering caused by my knee-jerk anger."

Ellis turns away from me, and I know he's trying to hide his face. I sit quietly for a moment, then gently rub his arm.

"The last time I spoke to my dad, Nick wasn't around. Nick was jealous of Dad—of how much I loved him." Ellis turns towards me, curious. He wipes at his face.

"Nick hated it when I spoke to Dad. But I always tried to sneak around and make time for him. Ten minutes here, fifteen there. Every week, I called Dad, and sometimes more than once a week. The last time we spoke, he said that he was proud of me." I pause and take a few deep breaths. "And that he would always be there for me, even if he wasn't with me. I know he sensed something was wrong, but he didn't tell me."

Ellis turns towards me, and I can tell his cheeks are wet as they glisten under the moonlight. I raise my arm and wipe a tear that rolls down my cheek. "I got a call the next day from his roommate. Dad didn't wake up that morning. He died in his sleep."

Ellis takes my hand into his. "I'm so sorry, Glory. I know he was a wonderful man and meant so much to you."

"But since his death, I keep playing back our last conversation in my head, and it helps me. Because I believe—I truly believe—that my dad is keeping his promise and that he is watching over me."

"I believe he's watching over you, too," Ellis says.

"And just as I believe that, I also believe Jane is watching out for you, and I know with all my heart that she knows you love her and have forgiven her."

Ellis drops my hand gently and his mouth opens. He looks away in thought and then smiles. "Thank you for that, Glory. It means more than you could ever truly know."

Like a divine sign from the heavens, a roar of thunder sounds from the ocean and a streak of lightning crashes across the sky in a spectacular display. Without thinking, I inch closer to Ellis. "Please don't let it rain," I say softly towards the clouds.

Ellis pats my leg. "Don't worry. We're okay. Most of the time storms float across the ocean parallel to the land. They often miss us."

"Most of the time?" I ask, eyes wide.

He shrugs. "If it gets bad, I will *gently* break down the door."

I start to object but stop as a burst of lightning streaks distantly across the sky, forming a web of brilliant cracks. "Okay," I say flatly. "If you can guarantee the glass remains intact, and only if the lightning gets close."

"Deal," he says through a yawn.

Ellis and I sit for an hour or so in silence. I'm getting sleepy very fast, and before long, I can no longer hold back a series of three yawns that escape me in sequence just like a burst of chilly wind blows across the porch. "Who knew it could get this cold in the Keys," I say as I look over at Ellis, who is also yawning. I point to him. "Contagious, aren't they? Yawns?"

"I should hear Clinton as he heads off in the morning."

"Okay," I mutter, barely audible. I can't keep my eyes open as I attempt to snuggle even closer into his side. He's just so warm. I hope I'm not making him uncomfortable, but honestly, I'm so tired I don't really care. But he doesn't object and instead pulls me closer with his arm.

I listen to the waves and feel the beat of Ellis's heart beneath my ear, which seems to be in perfect sync with the rise and fall of his chest. Without thinking, I pull my loose arm up and wrap it around his midsection. Ellis tenses for a moment before relaxing again. I can feel his abs through the thin white linen of his shirt.

I look up as the garden lights cast soft shadows across Ellis's face. He traces patterns on the top of my hand in an oddly soothing way. We've been sitting in silence for what feels like hours, the ocean breeze carrying away the last traces of tension between us.

"I keep thinking about what you said," he murmurs, and I sit up and stretch a bit before settling back in and pulling my legs onto the swing. "About Jane knowing that I forgive her."

He reaches into his pocket and pulls out something folded. From the corner of my vision, I see him staring at it closely.

"I don't want to just exist anymore, Glory…I want to live." He trails off. "But I am afraid."

"Of what?"

His thumb traces my cheekbone. "Of feeling anything intense again. Of losing someone again…" He swallows hard and then pushes the folded item into my hand. "I forgive her, Glory, but I am afraid she won't forgive me."

I unfold the thick paper and look down at an old Polaroid photo. Staring back at me is a young woman with the brightest cobalt blue eyes and brilliant blonde hair. She is wearing a beautiful teal dress and bright yellow sandals. The edges of the dress seem to be floating in the breeze. "It's Cora," I say simply.

Ellis turns towards me, his face suddenly drained of color. "How do you know Jane's first name?"

PART TWO

CORA'S KEY

CHAPTER 24

My eyes flicker open, and I instantly know something is wrong. I feel a warm hand behind my head and sense his presence before he speaks.

"Glory?"

Ellis's voice instantly comforts me. I begin to sit up assisted as he shifts to the side and wraps his free arm around my back for support.

"What happened?" I ask.

"You passed out," he says after a short pause. "I caught you before you hit the ground, but you scraped your elbow on the way down."

He gently turns my arm, and I wince at the angry scrape.

"Thanks for catching me." I start to stand, and as I do, he offers me support. I lean into him and steady myself on his shoulder.

"Be careful," he says as he shadows my movement back towards the swing. After a few steps, I reach out and take its arm then turn and sit in one gentle motion. After I sit, he stands back upright, and I notice as his gaze shifts to something at his feet, something small and folded in half.

The picture.

He looks back towards me and our eyes connect with intensity, his expression a mix of concern and fascination. He holds my gaze momentarily until he breaks the connection, leans down, and picks up the picture. He turns so his back faces me, and I notice as his head hangs lower. He is looking at it now, and I wonder what he is thinking. I have no idea how I am going to explain how I know Cora, spoke with her, and was led to this resort by her advice. She is supposed to be dead. She is dead. My head starts to spin again, so I close my eyes and breathe deeply. I need to get off this roof and back to my apartment where I can process what has happened.

I look back towards Ellis just as he shoves the photo into his pocket and turns towards me. This time, he avoids my eyes, and instead, he gazes out across a line of brilliant red flowered trees behind me to the left. I had not noticed them before. They flicker like embers under the moonlight.

"Those flame trees are beautiful," I say, which causes him to look back towards me with a subtle frown.

"They are," he says, his stare intense. "That's actually what they are called." He narrows his eyes and leans closer to me. "Are you—"

"I'm okay," I interrupt before he finishes. "Really. I am not sure what happened, but it is probably just the situation. Or, the heat," I quickly add. dare not tell him what really happened. I do not even glance down at his pocket where that picture hides. I cannot let him know that the love of his life was someone I met at the University of Tennessee only days ago when she has been dead for nearly two years.

My mind races at the possibility that I have seen something unnatural, or even worse, that something happened when Nick pushed me down those steps—something so terrible, that I am hallucinating or putting facts together that I—that's it. The idea is like a bolt of inspiration that energizes me. It is the first step to my getting out of this nightmare. Though it doesn't answer how Cora led me to this place, it will help me dispel any of this strange tension between Ellis and me. I confront it head-on.

"Sorry about the picture." I feign a frown and point to his pocket. "I must have heard the name when I was with the girls. We did talk about her a bit."

He suddenly looks disappointed. "What did you talk about?"

Damn. I don't want him to think I am talking about Jane behind his back, but this is the easiest way to explain how I know Jane's first name, even though I know the truth is impossible for me to explain. At least he seems to buy the excuse, for now.

"Nothing specific that I remember, but her name did come up a time or two."

He bites at his lip, and I can sense that he is frustrated.

"I'm sorry that I spoke about her. I didn't mean anything by it."

He shakes his head then forces a soft smile. "It's okay," he says. "I am fine if you talk about her. I didn't used to be okay with people talking about her, but well, things have changed, and I find myself wanting to remember her more than ever. Sometimes something reminds me of her so much that it disappoints me when I remember she's gone."

I stand, walk forward, and embrace him, resting my head on his chest.

"I am so sorry, Ellis." He leans his chin down and sits it gently on top of my head as he holds my hips with his hands. We stand like that for a moment until we hear a door swing open from below.

"You up here, Ellis?"

"Noah!" I say excitedly. Ellis and I shift apart and look towards the stairs just as Noah's larger footballer body appears, ascending the staircase to the top level.

"Wow, man!" I haven't been up here in a minute. This place is looking good."

Ellis nods as he steps forward. "Thanks, man. Happy you chose tonight to check it out. Glory and I have been stuck up here because of that damn door."

"Oh man. Stuck again?"

Ellis nods. "And for once, I am glad you are checking on me."

Noah waves dismissively. "Dude. I am checking on her. I am over babysitting your ass."

I force a laugh then turn and stick my tongue out at Ellis, who rolls his eyes. "He likes me more."

"Shut it," Ellis says flatly.

"It's true man," Noah concurs as he pulls up beside me, and I am again reminded how Noah dwarfs everyone around him with his massive frame.

"I am not even sure you need to be up here," Ellis says as he fake punches Noah's shoulder. "You are going to cave in this roof, and Dave is going to be pissed."

Noah doesn't respond but narrows his eyes.

I yawn and both boys turn their attention to me. "I think I am going to have to go to bed."

"Yeah, me too," Noah says, "now that I know Glory is okay."

Ellis rolls his eyes again, then he and Noah step to the side. "After you," Ellis says.

I force a smile then head past them and descend the stairs. When we reach the door, Noah fiddles with the lock. "Not sure how this got stuck," he says. "Night y'all." Noah nods as he raises a hand and steps left into the kitchen.

"Night, Noah," I call out softly as Ellis just raises his hand silently.

I follow Noah after a moment and immediately notice my luggage still sitting by the door. It doesn't appear Noah noticed it.

"Goodnight, Ellis," I say as I turn and force a smile over my shoulder. I lean over and grab the handle of my luggage and take a few steps.

"Glory?"

I stop and turn back towards Ellis. "Yeah?" My voice cracks a bit at the end. I'm trying to bury the anxiety bubbling just below the surface, but I am not sure how good of a job I am doing.

"Are you sure you are, okay?" His eyes are narrowed, and though I feel like he bought my story about Cora's name, I do feel he senses my unease.

"I am," I say as I intentionally nod a couple of times. I just need some sleep."

He stares at me a moment as if trying to find something, then his brows rise high, and he holds up a finger. "Wait one second," he says, turning behind him and pulling open a small drawer. He reaches his hand inside then holds something out to me. "A band-aid. For your scratch. You need to get that covered up,"

A small snort escapes as I reach forward after a couple steps and take it. As I do, he wraps his hand gently around mine. His warm grasp is comforting, protective, and though it catches me by surprise, the gesture is welcome. After a moment, a wisp of awkwardness is fleeting across his face, and he lets his hand open and slowly drift to his side. I see him stretch it at his side as if cramping.

Though I find myself instantly longing for his hand again, I bury that feeling and use the opportunity to part ways with a simple "thank you."

I start to turn once more but stop as he blurts out. "And thank you for staying." He hesitates before adding, "I need you here."

"You need me?" The simple phrase strikes me like a bolt to the chest, but it is also so confusing. The way he says it is as if we are much more than friends, even though you can technically 'need' a friend.

"I just…need *you*," he says, clarifying in a way that makes the exchange even more confusing.

I am not sure what exactly to say, so I say the first thing that comes to mind. "I need you too."

He's taken aback and shakes his head as if in disbelief. "You do?"

"I do," I respond without hesitation. It's true. I do need him.

"Why?" he asks, but I'm not prepared to elaborate on why I feel the way I do. And I'm not sure I can answer that question anyway. I don't know how to tell him, as a friend, that the more I am around him, the more I feel like something is growing between us. I'm not sure how to explain how the inexplicable connection scares me because I am concerned how those feelings will play out, especially given his fragile state, and mine.

I shake my head slightly. "I just do."

Ellis takes a steadying breath. "Thank you," he says.

I nod in response then turn towards my apartment, our silence an appropriate end to the emotion-laced moments we have just experienced together.

When I reach my apartment, I pull my bag inside my room and toss it on my bed. My heart continues to beat wildly, but it doesn't take long before Ellis's words are replaced by the cold slap of my reality. The calm that I portrayed as I spoke to Noah and Ellis on the rooftop fades as if a dream, and now suddenly, I am more fully aware of the complexity of the situation.

The image of Cora Jane flashes in my mind, a chilling reminder that something is very wrong.

"What is wrong with you?" I ask to myself as I rub two hands across my face then stare silently out the window towards the crashing waves. I think back to the image of Cora Jane and bite my lip in frustration.

"It is impossible," I mutter to myself. "Isn't it?" I have always believed in God and angels, but Cora was just so real. She couldn't have been a ghost.

A thought then springs forth that seems equally concerning. "Did I imagine her?"

I close my eyes and think, trying to find a solution to an impossibly complex puzzle. How is it possible? How could I have sat in Cora's office, and how could she have handed me—that's it!

"Let me see," I say as I tilt the bag on my bed and frantically dig through it, looking for that bit of evidence.

Nothing.

I spin then hurry to the living room, where my eyes dart from corner to corner.

"Where is it?"

Nothing.

I pull my hands up to my temple and start to cry but stop suddenly as I remember.

"Wait?" I say to myself then run to my side table where Blair's romance book sits, the one with Lord Cluster. I pick up the book and instantly, my heart skips a beat at the sight of a small bit of paper extending from its center pages. I flip open the book to the page I had bookmarked back at the pier, and staring back at me is a postcard for Dave's Diving Resort. It's the very one that Cora herself placed in my hands.

"Impossible," I say into the darkness as a cold chill races across my neck.

The next few hours drag. Though I am exhausted, I cannot sleep. I should sleep, because I know that this dark anxiety will only get worse if I don't rest my mind, but I long too much for an answer.

I spend the next hours lost in the darkness of web searches. I sit quietly under my covers, the soft glow of my phone illuminating a halo around me.

I start with the University of Tennessee's website. I comb through the site, including the main student counselor pages, and though they have the names and headshots of all their counselors, I cannot locate anyone that is remotely named Cora Jane. I even take time to comb through pictures and headshots to see if I can find anyone that looks like her. But there is no one there as striking as Cora.

I then shift my search to beyond the university, focusing on the name Cora Jane. It doesn't take long for me to find something that makes my eyes grow wide.

University of Tennessee Senior Critically Injured After Hit-and-Run in South Georgia

I don't immediately click on the link, afraid of the details that I might find. What if they are gory or something related to where Cora was going, or worse, who she was going to see? I take a steadying breath. I need to know everything I can about Cora. I need to find out how I sat in her office and had a conversation with her, even though I might have to rely on what my gut is screaming at me—Cora isn't real. I blink once slowly then click on the link.

> *Tifton, GA — Authorities are investigating a hit-and-run accident that left a 22-year-old woman critically injured late Tuesday night on a rural stretch of highway near Tifton, GA.*
>
> *The victim, **Cora Jane D.**, a senior at the University of Tennessee, was driving south on Highway 41 when her vehicle veered off the road and overturned. According to the Georgia State Patrol, a witness at the scene reported seeing a dark-colored sedan speeding away just moments after the incident, suggesting she may have been forced off the road.*
>
> *Emergency responders arrived at approximately 11:42*

p.m. to find her vehicle overturned in a ditch near mile marker 73. She was unconscious at the scene and sustained severe head trauma and multiple internal injuries.

Authorities have released no further information. The Tift County Sheriff's Office confirmed that the only known witness was unable to provide a license plate number or a clearer vehicle description beyond "a dark-colored sedan."

Her next of kin were unavailable for comment.

Her next of kin. She died. Cora died, but somehow, I had a conversation with her. I shake my head but bolt up from the covers as a haunting chill races along my neck. My eyes dart around the room; I suddenly feel as if I someone is there with me.

"Hello?" I say into the air. I wait for an answer that doesn't come. Of course, it isn't coming. "Calm down, Glory," I whisper to myself as I push back an intrusive thought that sends alarms racing through my body.

I plug my phone on a charger next to the bed then lay on my side facing towards the closed bedroom door. My eyes open and close heavily in exhaustion, and my breathing slows. As I drift off to sleep, one words echoes over and over in my mind.

Ghost.

CHAPTER 25

I WAKE TO the alarm from my phone and find myself in the same position. I slept like a rock, and I am thankful. No dreams, good or bad, just hard sleep that my body and mind desperately needed.

I run to the bathroom and notice Ellis has already come and gone; the smell of his deodorant and minty toothpaste lingers in the air. I quickly get ready, throw on my suit, then head softly down the stairs and out the back door. The moonlight still casts a soft glow on the tropical foliage, illuminating everything in multiple shades of deep green. I maneuver past the porch but can't tell if Red or any of the others are up yet. I love the staff tradition of meeting out back every dawn to welcome the day, enjoying breakfast and togetherness. Dave's does not have employees, not really. All those who work here are family, close family. And it has been a perfect fit for me, the perfect place to escape from Nick and the abuse I left behind in Tennessee.

Ever since arriving at Dave's, I have felt at home. Even though Ellis and I had our initial challenges to work through, we are growing closer each day, a closeness that others might see as oddly rushed. Dave's just feels right, Ellis feels right, and I need to do my best to embrace the luck of it all, or even the hand of the divine.

The thought makes me shiver as I emerge from the path that connects the house to the main resort. I walk along the sea wall past the Hut, docks, and dive shop, toward the large resort pool at the other side of Dave's. I can see it just in the distance, situated nearby the vacation rentals, a series of pastel-colored condos. Everything is so amazing at Dave's, like living in a tropical paradise, but it is the early mornings, like this, that are my favorite. They are laced with a peace unlike any I have ever known.

When I get to the pool, my eyes shift to a dark shadow moving through the pink lit water. I can tell it is Ellis even without direct light, his long narrow shadow, glides effortlessly underwater as his tussled blonde hair smooths back with his current. After a moment, Ellis emerges from the other end of the pool, facing away from me.

"Good morning," he says in a shaky voice as he looks over his shoulder and proceeds to wipe at his eyes.

"Good morning," I reply as a yawn escapes. He is still facing away, so I use the opportunity to pull off my shorts and shirt, revealing the red bikini. I start to say something just as Ellis dives back under water and shoots towards where I inch my way in. The water is crisp, but not cold. It is refreshing and brings a clarity to mind that is welcome following the evening before. Ellis eventually surfaces slowly a few feet from me, his face making an awkward goofy smile as he does. I laugh softly and splash water his way.

"What are you doing, goofball?" I say, which makes him furrow his brows in mock offense.

"Nothing. I always look like this."

I roll my eyes and nod. "That is true. You do tend to look a little…off."

He huffs in mock anger. "What did you say?" Before I can respond, he darts within inches of me so fast, I gasp a little, caught off guard.

"You better back up, mister," I say after I compose myself.

He plays smug for a moment then raises his hands as he glides back a few feet, the water parting around him.

"Okay, doofus," he says. "I will play nice." He stretches his arms high as he stands, exposing his toned abdomen that I try to avoid noticing. I dip my head into the water, a welcome distraction, then rise and smooth my hair backwards.

"What first?" I ask as I tilt my head forward. As I do, I see his eyes dart up from my chest and he spins away from me. I smirk at his back before he spins back around, smiling again. It appears that we are both having trouble with staring. He cocks his head sideways and winks pointedly. I mirror his action, which he ignores. This side of Ellis, his playful side, is something that I find myself encountering more and more, and I now realize this side of Ellis must be the side that has been lost to his grief for so long. I can see why the others spoke of missing Ellis. This Ellis, the real one not plagued by pain, regret, and self-sabotage, is oddly comforting, like a favorite sweater.

Ellis clears his throat, a sign that it is time to get to business. "You seem to be coming along with snorkeling and general dive skills, so today, I want to teach you a bit more about the *Scuba* part." He points to the side of the pool where there is a tank that I hadn't seen before, resting next to a small dive vest and some black hoses.

"Are you sure?" I say as turn towards him and force a nervous grin.

"You are going to do fine. *Promise.* Plus, once you know how to dive, and we issue you an official certification, you will be able to help around the resort in other ways.

Though I am hesitant, afraid even, I push the feelings aside. I expected that I would eventually need to learn how to Scuba dive, being employed by one of the most highly regarded dive resorts in the Keys. I just didn't expect that time to come so soon.

I hold my breath momentarily before speaking with forced pep, "Okay, let's do it."

He must sense the hesitation, because he glides forward and reaches down to take my hands underwater. His touch, even beneath the surface, is warm, reassuring. "Look, Glory. No pressure. If you want to take it slow, I get it. We can take it slow." He blinks slowly before adding, "I just find myself wanting things to move much faster with you."

His words are charged with innuendo, whether intentional or not, and for a moment, I feel that we are no longer talking about diving. And though that might have frightened me several days ago, or even last night, I can't help but feel the same way. The pull I feel towards Ellis, as we spend more and more time together, is growing stronger, and I am not sure either of us are going to be able to resist that force much longer. I cringe internally as I ponder the past, when I loathed couples who seemed to have insta-love. It has never seemed natural to me for two people to have that level of sudden attraction. It is not something that I ever remember happening to me. My hazy memories flicker back to Nick, but I will them away as I turn back towards Ellis.

"Let's do it," I say, and Ellis immediately looks down, his wet hair falling along his forehead. I can't see his eyes, but the corner of his mouth lifts to one side, so I know he is pleased by my response. He looks up after a moment and his smile falters. "You sure?" I can't help but feel he is intentionally taking things slow with me, like I am fragile. I can't help but wonder if he is like this with all others he has taught to dive.

I nod firmly to dispel his hesitation. "I am."

He cocks his head and narrows his eyes but then straightens while squeezing my hand once, as if saying amen during a meal prayer.

"Well, let's do it then," he says as he pushes off the bottom of the pool and propels himself towards the dive equipment.

Over the next thirty minutes, Ellis becomes someone different; he is serious, methodical, and instructing. He is—for this time—the lead dive instructor at Dave's, and except for a gentle caress here or a lingering gaze there, I sense I am getting the same level of instruction that he would give to any student here.

He starts with basics, like what Scuba means—self-contained underwater breathing apparatus—and he even goes through some more academic instruction, such as how to calculate NDL, or non-decompression limits, which divers learn to calculate with tables or computers to determine how long they can safely stay at a given depth before needing decompression.

"Ever heard of the Bends?" he asks as he leans forward and turns on the air to the tank, which is attached to a vest called a Buoyancy Compensator.

I feel like I know the word, but I can't remember where I learned it. I close my eyes and try to think back to what I know, but after a moment, I shake my head. "I've heard of it, but, but I just can't remember when." I comb my fingers through my hair.

He sighs heavily then rolls his neck as if pondering his next step. When his head comes back forward, it stops, and he looks down, nodding gently. "Okay, well, it's not as much of an issue now, since we are in the pool, but I am going to grab you some reading material when we get back to the shop. I want you to be safe. Promise me you will read it, and we can skip that part today and revisit it another morning."

"Promise," I say as I nod quickly, maybe a bit too fast.

He narrows his eyes, and my eyes dart downward as he wets his lips. "Maybe we should just go over it now."

I laugh and then pull my hands to my sides. "I will!"

"We have to keep you safe," he says as he wags his finger in my direction.

"I—" I start to speak but my words stumble unexpectedly. I close my eyes and take a steadying breath then start again. "I,

Glory, promise you, Ellis, that I will read all materials that you provide me." I open my eyes and Ellis has turned away.

"Okay," he says flatly before leaning down and lifting upright a vest that had fallen sideways on the ground.

Over the next several minutes, we discuss how to put on the Buoyancy Compensator vest, which does all sorts of stuff, like holding the tank and air hoses. He shows me the tank and hose hookup and goes over a small instrument panel that tracks air supply and depth. After he helps me put on the vest and fins, he teaches me how to walk like a duck, backwards.

"Very attractive," he says as I mirror his movement. I flash him a look of feigned displeasure and flick him off. He smirks as I move to the side of the pool and turn to face the water.

"Okay, just like we said."

"Um, okay," I mutter, then after a brief hesitation, I take one big step forward into the water.

Though I expect to instantly sink, I don't. Instead, I bob gently on the surface as my fins flutter beneath me. Ellis dives in after a moment then pulls up next to my side.

"Great work, Nemo," he says, patting my back before diving underwater to narrowly escape a slap to the shoulder.

The last thirty minutes of the lesson, we do some preliminary work in the water, only going under briefly. When we do, we do it together. While underwater, he teaches me how to use the octopus, a secondary air hose that others—like dive partners—can also use in emergencies. He also again makes sure I can clear my mask of water while underwater. It is a skill that I am getting better at.

At the end of the lesson, Ellis helps me to the edge of the pool. He carefully holds my side as I walk up the steps, then quietly helps me take off the equipment and unhook the tank.

"Do you want me to help you put this somewhere?" I ask as I reach down and grab a towel, wrapping it around my body.

Ellis doesn't look up at first, but when he does, he seems off. "No, I've got it." As he speaks, his body language seems tense, and it catches me by surprise. When you are around someone abusive—physically, emotionally, or mentally—it makes you hyper aware of your surroundings, like a survival instinct.

"So, how did I do?" I ask after a moment, hopeful to dispel the curious tension and honestly, eager for his assessment.

He lets the vest fall by the tank before he stands and looks up, nodding a couple times. "Fine. Fine." He forces a smile then looks back down.

"Fine," I echo, and he nods without looking back up.

The word catches me by surprise. I hadn't expected to master any skill or anything, but I had expected to have done better than *fine*.

I think back to the lesson. What was it that I might have messed up? Is it when I disconnected the octopus or managed my buoyancy? It had seemed like things were going good, great, actually. He hardly had to repeat anything and not once did he correct me. He even seemed surprised when I was able to read the dive instrument attached to my vest, gauging my air supply and depth.

After a moment, he must sense my confusion, or that I am staring at him, because he looks back up and flashes me an apologetic look. He then closes his eyes and smiles as he shakes his head as if in surrender. "Actually," he says as he opens his eyes. "You are amazing."

"Well, now you are just lying," I say then huff loudly, water flicking from my nose.

Ellis laughs genuinely as he holds up both hands and waves dismissively. "No. I'm not. You pick up on everything so easily. It just caught me off-guard."

"Really?" I am taken aback by his sudden about-face. My smile is impossible to contain.

He shrugs as he nods again. "Really," he says. "You are a natural."

I can't contain myself. I jump up then out and wrap my arms around him, burying the side of my face in his stomach. It catches us both by surprise, but he doesn't hesitate to wrap his arms around me and pull me in tighter in response. It is an amazing feeling to feel both happy and protected simultaneously. After a moment, I pull away from him and look up. His face has turned a crimson red, and from what I can feel, mine has too.

"It is so humid out here," he says after an awkward moment.

I nod in ascent as I rock back on my heels. "Okay, well," I say, stumbling over my words. "I better get cleaned up."

"Yeah," he says simply.

"Meet you in the office?"

He doesn't respond but gives me a goofy grin, the same expression he had met me with an hour earlier, but this time coupled with a thumbs up.

I don't look over my shoulder as I dart back to the house, though I sense his eyes on me the entire distance.

Once inside the apartment, I hop in the shower and rinse off as the lesson replays in my mind. I smile to myself as I enjoy reminiscing on the morning, but the escapism only lasts briefly. I step from the shower and notice the postcard laying on the bathroom counter. Instantly, the anxiety and fear that always bubbles underneath, surfaces again, and the intrusive thoughts race back to the forefront. It is in stark contrast to my time in the pool with Ellis, and it is disappointing that those brief moments of happiness don't last.

Last night, as I was researching Cora, I had made the decision to call the University of Tennessee Counseling Center to try to get answers, and that thought again was bubbling up into my stream of thoughts.

I finish getting dressed, pull my hair back, and throw on a

white ball cap I found yesterday hanging on a hook in the closet. It says Dave's, with a red-and-white dive flag on the side. I toss my still-wet suit in my bag then head to the couch, where I sit and begin dialing. I hit the speaker button just as a recording picks up. Of course, no one is in the office yet. I push the option to leave a voicemail in the general mailbox then after the beep, I speak.

"Hi, my name is Glory Dawson. I am a student. I am on leave and finishing my last few classes online. I am trying to locate a counselor by the name of Cora Jane who helped me withdraw from classes a couple of weeks ago. Could you ask that she call me back?" I quickly leave my number then pause a moment before adding, "Thank you, bye."

I slide the phone back into my pocket and stare in silence. After a moment, I close my eyes to push back the fear that is bubbling up inside. I am genuinely scared. What if I have lost my mind? What if something is very wrong with me? I shiver as I again race through scenarios and realize there is no reasonable explanation.

After a moment, my phone dings, and my eyes light up as a different, more terrifying thought crosses my mind. Nick.

I quickly pull out my phone then sigh in relief when I see it is just a spam text trying to sell me crypto currency. Nick has been eerily silent. I have not received any texts, calls, or voicemails—nothing—but silence in Nick's case is not a good thing. I wonder when he will make good on his threat.

"Stop," I say out loud as my mind again starts to race. I shake my head. There is just too much, and if I am going to make it, and survive all this, I need to be calm. I need to hang onto those moments of brief relief and happiness. Moments like my time this morning at the pool. I take a steadying breath then reach down and grab my bag.

The house is silent as I make my way down the stairs and

out the back door to the house. The crisp ocean breeze meets me as I walk softly along the winding back path towards the resort. As I emerge onto the ornate resort walkway, I am also met with the scent of tropical blooms, my gaze making its way across the orange-lit surf. The early sun is beginning to penetrate the shadows along the resort walkway, and the full colors of the resort are starting to emerge. I can't help but shake my head in disbelief at the wonder of Dave's, a place of intense beauty.

I eventually pass by the Tiki Hut, and as I do, I see Aki just heading back into the kitchen, the door swinging behind him. I smile, knowing he is probably back there dealing with JJ's granddad, Charlie, the resort's oldest, and most cantankerous, bartender. He and Aki do a great job managing the resort's only restaurant and the best Tiki bar in Florida, Keys, the Hut. I am amazed how the gentle spirit of Aki and the rough and tumble military vet, Charlie, work so well together…but they do. You might even call them close friends.

Just as I turn past the dock to the dive office and shop, I come to a stop as I see Ellis, Dave, and Amber huddled together outside the back door. They are speaking in hushed tones. I slow to a stop and shift behind a large group of palmettos. I do my best not to eavesdrop onto what appears to be a private conversation, but I can't help but hear Ellis speak.

"I just had to call her, Dave," Ellis says as he looks between Dave and Amber. He seems agitated, or maybe even pissed off.

Amber and Dave exchange looks of concern. "I know, my man," Dave says, "You did the right thing."

"It's just hard, you know?" Ellis says. His voice seems pained, and he is biting at his lip as if stifling a quiver. "She didn't even believe me. She told me it was impossible."

Who did he call that has upset him so much?

"Well, she has a right to know what's going on, whether she agrees with us or not," Dave says, his bushy white hair lifted high over concerned eyes by round gold-lined reading glasses. "We just need to be careful about that jackass."

Ellis looks up and his eyes narrow. "I hope he comes." Ellis's voice is suddenly dark, laced with venom.

"I know you do. I know. But this is not for you to manage. Getting hurt, or in trouble, doesn't help her."

Ellis shakes his head. "Maybe she's right."

Amber wipes at her face then steps forward and hugs Ellis from the side. "Ellis, I know you are scared. We all are."

Ellis accepts her affection then looks down towards his feet and nods in acceptance. "I was finally accepting that she's gone, but something is wrong. Something is very wrong." He looks up and lifts his arms as if in surrender. "I mean the call and now this. I mean, Dave, knows her full name."

Amber and Dave's eyes meet in puzzled silence.

"And her being here is not helping." Ellis points back towards the house.

I gasp slightly and hold my breath in anticipation. Is he talking about me now? Is he saying that my being here is not helping him grieve for Cora?

"I know it is hard, my man, but she is innocent. This isn't her fault."

"I know," Ellis says. "I accept that, and I will be strong, but you should have seen her, Dave." Ellis shakes his head in disbelief. "She was ridiculous this morning. I couldn't believe it."

What?

"Just be patient with her," Dave says just as the back door of the dive shop swings open and JJ steps out. Dave sighs deeply. "He is always interrupting at the wrong time."

"Red says that I can't go out on the boat, Dave. Am I still grounded from the water?"

Dave sighs and turns toward JJ. "You are grounded, my man, until Blair tells you otherwise."

"Blair?" JJ shrieks. "Are you nuts? She will never let me on that boat."

"Oh well," Dave says as he turns back towards the dive shop. He takes one step then turns back to face Ellis. "I don't have the answer for any of this right now, my man, but hang in there. We will do this together, like family. I have a friend who might be able to help. Let me get her down here and see what she thinks. She is the best of the best."

Ellis doesn't respond as Dave moves past Ellis. Amber follows Dave a moment later, rubbing Ellis's back as she passes him.

After the doors close behind Amber and Dave, Ellis runs his hands through his hair then looks out towards the water then up towards the bright blue moon off to the distance, the last remanent of the evening before still visible against the glowing morning sky. He whispers something inaudible towards the moon then turns and heads back into the dive shop. Just as he does, I sneeze, and he twists back around and stares directly in my direction. Though he can't see me, he knows I am there, so I step out from behind the palmettos.

For a moment, we stare at each other blankly, then as I sense him about to speak, I whisper, "I was ridiculous this morning?" Though my voice is soft, I know he hears me. I fold my arms across my front then take a few hesitant steps forward. I am embarrassed. I am disappointed. I thought that I had done so well, and he had told me that I had, but he had done so only after I had pressed him. I guess that was a lie.

I can't help but stumble as I take another step forward. He jolts forward as if to catch me, but I hold up my hands. "I'm fine."

He takes a hesitant step in my direction, as if approaching an injured animal, but he stops when I speak. "Don't. Just don't."

I close my eyes to fight back the sudden urge to cry then force my composure and walk forward and past him.

"That's not what I meant, Glory."

I stop and look over my shoulder. "I heard you, Ellis. What else could you have meant?"

I turn back around quickly, not wanting to hear his reply.

"Fuck," I hear Ellis mutter just as I push into the dive shop.

CHAPTER 26

ELLIS AND I are not the only ones at odds as we talk through the morning assignments. Blair and Clinton are not even looking at each other. I glance at Red, who glances between them, her brows pulled tightly together, then looks at me and shrugs.

"The Hut is boring," JJ says, throwing up his hands and huffing. "I am too good for that."

"Watch it," Noah growls.

"That's not what I meant."

Blair looks up from her book and lifts her chin. "You better get used to it, burger boy."

JJ starts to speak but is interrupted by Noah, who narrows his eyes menacingly. JJ grunts then goes back around the counter to sit on a Yeti cooler against the wall. Noah shakes his head then looks up. "Hey, Glory."

"Hi," I say and force a smile. As I do, I see Ellis from the corner of my eye dart his head in my direction. I look to Red. "So, what's the day look like?" I ask, trying to ignore Ellis and dispel some of the tension in the room.

Red looks up from the clipboard. "Well, I think this is going to be an interesting schedule to manage."

"Why's that?" Dave suddenly says from behind me, where he has emerged from his office.

She tilts her head toward Blair and Clinton, and Dave seems to catch the hint.

"Oh," he says. "Well, let me see what we got on the books."

Red holds out the clipboard and for a moment, Dave stares in contemplation through the reading glasses that hang low on his large nose. His grey hair is especially large and messy today. After a moment, he looks up.

"Got it," he says. "Girls versus guys today. Clinton, you and Ellis are going to take a group to the sand bars for some light snorkeling, and the girls are going to handle the conference group. They want to snorkel too, but not anything too deep." Dave looks at me pointedly. "You can stand on the sand bars if you want to get in the water today and try some snorkeling. Ellis said you were a natural, if you want to try it out."

My eyes dart to Ellis who forces a tight-lipped smile. Dave's comment is a contradiction to what I *thought* I heard Ellis say earlier.

As I look back towards Dave, I notice Red giving he and I the same furrowed brow look of concern she had flashed to Blair and Clinton earlier.

"Okay, thanks," is all I manage to say. Though I appreciate his confidence, I hesitate to test my skills out in the open ocean so soon.

"What conference is it?" Ellis asks after a moment and I look between he and Dave, also curious.

"It's the one they have down here every year," Dave says, "the one with the medicine."

"You mean the pharmaceutical one?" Ellis says flatly.

"The ones with the hot guys," Blair adds, before she smiles devilishly.

Ignoring Blair, Dave looks up from his phone and points in Ellis's direction. "You got it, my man."

Ellis and Clinton both look at each other with deep knowing

frowns. Even Noah looks at them, pinching his chin in consideration of something.

"Should be fun," Red says as she hops up, comes to my side, and wraps a long, freckled arm around my side. "We can handle it."

Dave looks over to Red and nods. "I know."

Blair jumps out of her seat and tosses her book under the counter. "What do you say we go get ready? They will be here in the next thirty minutes or so. Let's get ready to *play*."

Clinton holds a finger up as if to object as Blair reaches out and grabs our hands, tugging them towards the door. Red hesitates briefly to grab at her phone then follows Blair's lead out the door, her face a mix of confusion and excitement.

"These pharma sales guys are hot," Blair says as she looks back over her shoulder and grins. At the bottom of the stairs, she prances forward a few steps then turns back towards us. "I am going to wear a thong."

"Blair!" Red barks, but Blair ignores her.

"Do you think they like fish netting or sheer better?" She looks at Red then to me. I shrug, not really knowing how to respond. "I think you are, right, Glory, sheer it is."

I hold up my hands. "Please don't tell Clinton that I said that." I force a nervous smile and look to Red for back-up.

She looks towards Blair. "Clinton would probably prefer you go the simple route."

She raises her eyebrows and crosses her arms. "Yeah, I don't care what he thinks."

"What happened?" Red asks. "I thought everything was better."

"It was until last night." Red and I exchange a look of confusion. "I put out and afterwards, he wanted me to stay over. I said no, and he got mad. Can you believe that?"

Red rolls her eyes. "Oh, the audacity of him to want to cuddle," she says, her voice dripping in sarcasm. Red opens her mouth in disbelief. Clearly, she was expecting for Red to agree with her.

"Well, that's not all, Red. He also said that this was the last time. The last time he would fu—"

"Okay, Blair," Red interrupts. "We get it. But could you please think about it from his perspective? He doesn't want one-night stands. He wants commitment."

I nod in agreement with Red, for what it's worth, looking between them. I have learned over the past weeks that Blair is incredibly stubborn, especially when dealing with Clinton. The tension between them stemming from Clinton's law school plans has bubbled up repeatedly. Blair's desire to be close to Clinton is at odds with her belief that he is better off without her, and that, mixed with physical attraction, is making for a highly complex relationship challenge.

Blair ignores Red pointedly, "Definitely, the sheer one." She then waggles her eyebrows at the two of us then turns and heads off towards the house.

I look back to Red, who is staring at Blair as she walks off in the distance. After a moment, she turns my way. "What about you and Ellis? Are you all okay?"

I don't think I mask the unease I feel about Ellis. It is palpable, and my body language is a dead giveaway as I rock back on my heels. So, I lean into her inquiry, hoping that she might have some guidance about how best to deal with Ellis.

I walk her through my morning, starting with the lesson. I tell her how I thought I had done well, and how Ellis seemed to be so happy. Then I share with her how I had accidently overheard him talking to Amber and Dave, specifically telling them that my being at Dave's was not helping and that I was ridiculous.

"Really?" Red asks with sincere disbelief. "I don't understand why he would say that. And you're sure he was talking about you?"

"Definitely," I reply. "He even pointed to the house when he said it, and I don't think he was talking about you or Blair."

She shakes her head and sighs. Boys are a pain in the tail, Glory. I wish I could tell you he had had a bad night or some other excuse, but I honestly don't know what could have caused him to say that."

"That's okay," I say. "I'm sure he will get over it. I just hope he decides to like me for real next time around."

She reaches out, takes my hand, and squeezes twice. "I am not sure why he said that, but I hope he apologizes or explains why he did. If he doesn't, I will gladly mention it to Blair."

I wave dismissively with my other hand, not wanting to call in the big guns. "It's fine. I will deal with it." I finish the sentence just as Red's phone chimes. She looks down quickly then back up to me.

"Okay. It looks like the pharma-bros just arrived. Do you need to get changed?"

I pull the shorts I have on down a bit to reveal the red suit. "Nope."

Red smiles and mimics my action, revealing navy swim bottoms tied together at the side with a simple bow. "No thong here," she says, and we both laugh.

Red and I make our way to where the Seahorse II bobs on the end of the dock and as we do, we feel the docks shifts under the weight of our guests. We look back towards the shop and see five guys, all who appear to be in their mid- to late- twenties, with similar tan skin and dark hair, reminiscent of men from Italy or Greece. The man in front raises his hand as he approaches us.

"Hi, ladies," says a very attractive man with a muscular frame. His face has sharp edges and his body is heavenly. He is wearing navy swim shorts and a white linen shirt that screams wealth. "I am Nico, and these are my friends," he says in a slight accent. "This is Dimitri, Thomas, Nick, Nicolas, and Mateus."

Red steps forward and extends her hand to Nico in a business-like manner. She is setting a clear boundary by her action. "My name is Red."

Mateus leans into Nico and whispers in his ear, but Nico swats him away as he replies. "Nice to meet you, Red."

Nico then looks in my direction pointedly, and though I cannot see his eyes behind the dark tint of his sunglasses, I sense their movement across my body. For a moment, I think about the bruising, but as I look down, very little remains from my *fall* down the stairs.

"Who is this?" he asks.

I clear my throat then mimic Red as I step forward, extending my hand. "I'm Glory. Nice to meet you." He takes it gently in his for a moment, then raises it to his lips where he kisses it. I am immediately surprised by the action, but I don't pull back, recognizing that his customs might be somewhat more *European*. And though these customs are unfamiliar, they are certainly not unpleasant.

"So very nice to meet you, Glory," he says, his voice dripping in sex appeal.

He releases my hand, and my eyes shift to something back down the docks where I see Clinton, Ellis, and Noah standing, pouting in the distance. They are clearly not happy that we are taking these guys out on the water.

I ignore their glares, stepping aside and motioning them forward as Red speaks. "Right this way, and we will get going. We hear you all want to go out on some sand bars today. Maybe do a little snorkeling?"

The guys take steps onto the boat and as they do, they each take turns pulling off their shirts. Red and I exchange knowing smiles. These men are incredibly attractive, and though neither Red, nor I, are in the open market, we will certainly enjoy the day's view.

"Wait for me!" we suddenly hear just before we step onboard behind the guests. We turn our heads and see Blair jogging down the dock in a skimpy white swimsuit that is sheer along its sides, covering only the bare minimum. And though we can't see from this side of Blair, I can tell by the wide-eyed horror in Clinton's face, that she is, indeed, wearing a thong.

"Blair!" Clinton shouts, but she ignores him, coming to a stop next to the boat.

"Well, hello there," Red says as she cocks her head and looks at Blair up and down. "So nice to see you here. *All* of you"

Blair waves her away. "Oh, shut it, you." She then turns towards the guests, who are all watching her intently. "Well, isn't someone going to help me on board?" she shrieks.

As the guys all rush forward at once to assist her, Red and I quickly turn away as Blair's tan butt cheeks shine proudly towards us.

"Good lord," Red says then turns back towards Clinton and shouts, "Don't worry, buddy. We will keep an eye on her."

Except for Noah, who nods calmly, Ellis and Clinton appear to be competing for whose face is a darker shade of red. I certainly understand why Clinton is so concerned, but as Ellis's eyes catch mine, I can't help but be caught off-guard by his tight lips and intense stare.

"Are you joining us, Glory?" I suddenly hear a deep accented voice from the boat and turn to where Nico is extending a hand in my direction. I nod politely, then take his hand and step forward, not looking back.

The trip along the sand bars is more fun than I could have ever expected. Time flies as we boat around various locations and spend time at each, diving from the boat and snorkeling around the water. Red happily stays aboard during the trip, careful of her sensitive, pale skin on the cloudless day, so Blair and I spend time with the guests. Blair is tamer than usual, but she does flirt openly with Mateus in a way that I know Clinton would not be happy with. A few times, I hear Red shout her name off the boat, clearly trying to interrupt. And though I don't get into the water at every stop, I do venture in at the last stop.

While in the water, I mostly stay together with the group, except for a couple of times when Nico and I venture off to chase some underwater fish or animal. I am not sure if he is sincerely interested in the sea life, or my red bikini, but I push away any concern and try to enjoy the experience.

"This was such a good time," Nico says after we all climb back aboard and get ready for the ride back to Dave's. "I had a lot of fun with this one." He looks at his friends and points in my direction. "She knows everything about these fish and stuff."

"Thanks," I say dismissively then look to Blair, who tilts her head to the side as she wraps a towel around her lower half.

"What kind of stuff?" She asks me but then looks over to Nico.

He shrugs. "Everything. Like shells and fish and—everything."

Blair looks back towards me, eyes narrow. "Interesting. A closeted marine biologist."

We all laugh as I shrug, "I guess so." I look back to Red, who isn't laughing but nodding slowly, a hint of a smile just under the surface of her expression.

The ride back to Dave's passes in a blink, and before we know it, we are all hopping onto the dock and parting ways. This time, no one is watching us from the back of the dive shop.

"Thank you, ladies, for a wonderful afternoon," Nico says, and the others politely agree.

"We are so glad you had a nice trip," Red says, and Blair nods quickly in agreement then looks down the dock towards the dive shop, as if disappointed by something. "I will walk you to the shop, and we can settle up there."

"Perfect," he says, "but before we do, I am curious, would you ladies happen to be at the Tiki bar tonight?"

Blair's eyes dart back to the group of men. "Absolutely," she says without hesitation in a syrupy sweet tone. Red and I exchange a blank expression.

Nico claps his hands together excitedly, "Fantastico. We would love to buy you ladies a drink."

Red looks at us and holds up her hands. "Sorry, I am bartending tonight."

"We aren't!" Blair blurts out as she grabs my shoulders and pulls me to her side. I force an awkward smile as Blair stares at me from the side.

"Well then, we shall meet at this Tiki bar at let's say, seven o'clock?"

Blair doesn't give me time to object or formulate an excuse. "Perfect!"

"What's perfect?" I hear someone say, and I turn to see Ellis walking towards us.

Blair points her chin towards Ellis as if she's won a bet. "Drinks!" she says clapping. "Glory and I are just getting our evening plans in order."

Ellis stops in front of me and looks at me cautiously from the side. "Evening plans?" His voice is gruff, and I turn towards Red, so my back is to him. I'm not in the mood for Ellis's moody ass, and his being here makes me suddenly more enthusiastic about the pharma bros.

"Some drinks with Mateus, and Nico, and some of his friends," Blair says casually.

I look over my shoulder just as Ellis turns towards Nico and his smiling crew. I can't see his face, but I can imagine that it's not friendly. He turns back towards me and our eyes meet momentarily before I look down. My body instinctively turns back towards him as I do. I can't explain it, but I feel odd, ashamed.

The feeling catches me by surprise. Ellis starts to say something to me but stops when Red abruptly darts in front of him, arms raised, as if diffusing a situation.

"So apparently, *Ellis*, Glory is a bit of an expert at sea life." She then slowly turns towards me and that subtle smile of hers is back.

"She is absolutely incredible," I hear Nico say as he walks up to Ellis's side and claps him around the back. Ellis looks blankly down towards the shorter Nico then back to me.

"How is that possible?" he says flatly.

Red steps to my side, wraps one arm around my waist, and squeezes me tightly. "Interesting, isn't it?"

Ellis doesn't respond but instead looks out over the water.

We all stand there awkwardly for a moment until Nico breaks the silence. "Well, we best be off. We have some meetings we must attend this afternoon. It has been a pleasure. Until this evening." He forces another smile then he and the others make their way towards the dive shop.

"Do you happen to have a favorite?" Ellis says as he turns back towards me.

Our eyes meet, and the word "ridiculous" floods my mind.

"Nico," I say smugly, fully aware he was asking me about sea life and not Italian suitors.

CHAPTER 27

BLAIR AND I work quickly over the next hour cleaning up the boat and putting away the gear. The entire time, she is excitedly talking about the pharma bros, but not in a way that signals her romantic interest in them. Instead, she contemplates how best to use them to make Clinton jealous.

"I am totally going to wear that black dress he loves," she says.

I don't dare pry as to why she would want him to be jealous. I frankly don't get it. She is pushing him away on one hand, forcing him to consider an Ivy league law school instead of one closer to the Keys, but on the flipside, she is trying to make him jealous. I can only assume that this is her way of forcing him to move on. But how can she not see that all this effort is in vain? I've only known Clinton for a short time, but I can say for certain: Clinton is not going to leave Blair—ever.

Just as we lock the equipment shed, my stomach growls loudly and Blair looks up. "Was that me or you?"

"Me, I think."

She nods in agreement, "Yeah, but I'm right there with you. Let's hit up the Hut real fast, and we can grab three wraps. I am sure Red hasn't eaten. She always forgets to eat. I have no idea how she forgets to eat."

"Me either," I say. "I get the shakes if I don't eat. I will even pass out."

"Me too!" Blair says, raising her hand high to face me. "Food sisters!"

"Food sisters," I echo, giving her an enthusiastic high-five.

At the Hut, we grab three turkey wraps to go from JJ, who serves us with disdain and envy. Back at the office, Blair eats alone with her new romance novel as Red and I share the desk. I watch intently as she places some retail orders then pulls up an excel spreadsheet with what appears to be the accounting record for the store.

"Want to learn some of the fun stuff?" she says.

"Sure," I reply. I am of course interested in the diving and recreational aspects of Dave's but to me, the business side is just as intriguing. I think back to Dave's mom, envying how she was such an incredible businesswoman.

Over the next several hours, I learn all I can about the management of Dave's. Red answers all my questions, seemingly happy for the companionship. Blair is clearly not interested, preferring to dive deeper into the lust-filled words of what appears to be a second-chance billionaire romance of some sort. She is hyper focused as she bites at her lower lip with her feet propped up on a large stack of sealed inventory boxes.

"Are you going to put that new stuff away before next season?" Red asks as she huffs in Blair's direction.

"Just one more chapter," she says in a serious tone. "This part is getting *hot*."

"Yuck," Red replies before rolling her eyes and leading me to the front of the dive shop, where she shows me some of the inventory. She has a remarkable instinct for merchandising, and I am blown away as I watch her shift gifts, shirts, hats, and a variety of other items, this way and that, until it all looks fresh and inviting.

The day flies by, and before I know it, it is closing time. By now, the boxes that Blair was ignoring are all emptied, and even

Blair has stepped up to end the day strong, cleaning all the glass countertops and sweeping the hardwood floors.

"Okay, ladies. Let's not keep those hot Italian guys waiting," Blair says as she empties a dustpan into the trash.

Red throws her hands to her hips. "I might be behind the bar tonight, Blair, but I've got my eyes on you."

Blair ignores her and turns towards me. "Nico is pretty hot, Glory."

"Blair!" Red chastises her sharply from behind.

"What?" Blair counters over a shoulder. "A girl can look, can't she? I mean she doesn't have a ring on her finger." She looks back to me and waggles her perfectly plucked brows. "Right, Glory?"

I contemplate the question for a moment. I mean, technically, I am not cheating on anyone, on Nick. That relationship is over. That said, I still can't shake the feeling that I am doing something wrong. But to whom? I am not fully healed from Nick, physically or mentally, so maybe my subconscious is making me hesitate. But it's not like I plan on pursuing these random guys. I really just want to have fun and spend time with Blair. I exhale sharply then blurt out, "I guess since we are just having drinks, there is no harm in it." I am not sure if the words are intended for Red, Blair, or myself.

"That's right, sister!" Blair says as Red walks to my side.

Red leans over and squeezes my hand. "I am not worried about you, Glory. I know you can handle yourself. It's just this one." Red jerks her head back towards Blair and points. "She has literally been reading about hot loins for damn near two hours."

"Oh, please!" Blair says, ignoring Red again.

Red rolls her eyes playfully.

Blair then looks back to me excitedly, "I have an idea."

"What?" I say.

"Let's play dress up! You can have free reign of my closet."

I instinctively look down at my body. I guess we are similar in size.

"I have some great stuff," she continues, and I look up.

"She does," Red shrugs. "But don't look in the bottom drawer."

Blair leans over and slaps her side. "Don't reveal my secrets."

I laugh a bit at their trademark banter then shrug. "Okay," I say. "Why not?" The little clothing that I do have is not exactly something you would want to wear for a night out.

As soon as the words escape my mouth, Blair grabs my hand and tugs me away from Red towards the back door.

"Be careful, Blair," Red calls out behind us.

Back at the house, I follow Blair into her and Red's apartment. It is exactly how I pictured it: warm, comfortable, and clean. When I first arrived, Red had told me that she and Blair got along well together in part because they both value cleanliness, which is clearly the truth.

"Come through here," Blair says, and I follow her into what appears to be her room. There is a large four-post bed with a light blue linen bedspread. She has a few throw pillows on her bed in the shapes of stars. Just inside her room, to the right, she pulls open another door. "Come on in."

I follow her inside and my eyes grow wide as I take in the sight of the most organized and well-stocked closet that I have ever seen. To my left are full length dresses, pants, blouses, cardigans, and everything else under the sun, all arranged perfectly by style and color. Directly in front of me are rows and rows of various shoes, from designer heels to flip-flops.

"This is amazing, Blair," I say as I step further inside. She reaches around my back and spins the door closed, revealing a large jewelry cabinet and a floor length mirror.

"Well, go ahead. Pick out anything you like."

I look back towards her and she nods, urging me forward.

"I'm not sure where to start," I say.

"Just follow your instincts."

I look back to the closet and over the next several minutes, I walk slowly around the perimeter, examining everything in great detail, even touching the various fabrics to feel their textures. I don't remember ever being into clothing before, but seeing the variety now, I suddenly feel as though I've discovered a new-found passion.

It doesn't take long for something to stand out to me more than anything else. It's a green dress with ruffles that comes to the middle of my hips. It has a V-neck and a beautiful floral print that reminds me of the rooftop garden.

"What about this?" I say as I look back towards Blair, who is now standing just inside the closet doorway, holding up necklaces to her chest, testing them out.

She doesn't speak at first as she looks at the dress, almost as if she is reminiscing about a prior time she wore it, then looks back to me. "I couldn't have picked something better," she says as she smiles gently. She steps forward and pulls it from the hanger, holding it up to me. "Beautiful."

"You think so?"

Blair scoffs. "Seriously, Glory. You are going to really send some people over the edge tonight." She winks at me then spins to a bright yellow sundress and tugs it in my direction. "And it will go perfectly with me."

Over the next hour, we get ready. One of the best parts about having female friends is being able to share and experiment with their stuff. I take my time and use a curling iron that works with just air and suction, something that I have never seen before, and when Blair leads me to her make-up cabinet and directs me to 'use it as I see fit,' I audibly gasp. I take my time and admire all the options, hundreds of hues of eye shadow, multiple lip liners, and blush galore. I have never been one to wear much make-up, so I stick to simple shades of pink.

"Try this," she says, and she hands me a nail polish color called *sizzling shrimp*. "The name is gross, but the color is hot."

"Last but not least," she says as she reaches forward into a row of shoes, pulling back a pair of simple coral flats that match the floral pattern of the dress. "What do you think?"

"I love them," I say as I take them from her extended hands. "I didn't think we had the same size shoes, but I guess we do."

After slipping on the flats, I turn back towards the closet door and take one final look into the mirror. I nearly cry. I hardly recognize the person I'm looking at. The person staring back at me is unbruised, put-together, confident…a stark contrast to how I have seen myself, and how I have felt.

I feel so beautiful.

"Wow, Glory," Blair says as she pulls up behind me, glowing at my reaction. "You look stunning."

I look back over my shoulders. "Thanks to you."

"Nah. You have always been beautiful."

"Thanks, Blair," I say as I turn and exaggerate elevator eyes. "I would say *we* both are beautiful."

"Amen to that. Now let's go turn some heads."

Blair and I make our way along the path to the resort, taking our time to enjoy the cool ocean breeze. It is a welcomed reprieve from the early afternoon's humidity.

Aki is the first to comment as we approach the bar.

"Oh, my!" Aki says as he claps once and walks forward to the bar top. "You all are lovely tonight."

"Who is?" JJ says as he stands from the behind the bar, hair disheveled and wearing a dull green apron that appears to be stained with mustard. His head follows Aki's gaze and instantly, his eyes light up. "Wow. Okay."

I glance at Blair, who narrows her eyes towards JJ. I am beginning to believe that JJ is permanently on Blair's shit list.

Aki looks over to JJ, whose mouth is agape, his eyes a bit too obvious as they hover over our chests.

"JJ, why don't you go finish the prep, little keiki?" JJ stares unblinkingly for a moment until he hears a door slam behind him, which causes him to emerge from his boyish trance.

"Boy!" Charlie says. "Why are you here gawking at these ladies? Take your tail back there and finish what you started!"

JJ doesn't argue with Charlie but grumbles as he kicks at the ground then turns and heads back towards the kitchen.

"You better watch it," Charlie says as JJ disappears through the doors. After a moment, as if he is waiting for JJ to dare argue, he seems satisfied and turns back towards Blair and me. He smiles and walks slowly to Aki's side. "So, what have we got here?"

Blair leans forward on one elbow and winks at Charlie, "We have *dates.*"

"Dates?" Charlie says gruffly as he looks over to Aki who responds with a shrug. "I thought you were with that law nerd."

"I am *absolutely* not with the nerd anymore, Charlie," Blair's voice is laced with an exaggerated tone of finality. "We have moved on."

He looks to Aki for confirmation, who holds up his hands in surrender, daring not speak.

After a moment, Charlie's eyes dart suspiciously towards me. "And what about you, Glory?" Charlie asks.

I shrug. "I just wanted to dress up," I say truthfully. My eyes shift and I stare past Aki and Charlie for a moment, towards the water and the evening colors of amber and gold.

"I just need to get out there and enjoy all the tiny miracles," I say out of nowhere after a moment, then shake my head free from the sudden daydream. I look up towards Aki and Charlie as I pull at a wisp of curl that has caught a short burst of breeze.

"Absolutely," Aki says, nodding as he looks at each of us. "You need to enjoy life."

I look back to Charlie, who is nodding slowly, his chin rising higher than necessary in an exaggerated kind of way but fitting to his personality. "Fair enough" he agrees.

"Well, I just want to have some fun with these hot Italians," Blair says. Her direct truth causes Charlie to recoil a bit.

"Well, you make sure whoever is meeting you tonight—Italian or whatever—knows that I have my eyes peeled. And, if there is trouble, I'll be there."

Blair just rolls her eyes, so I step in front of her. "Thank you, Charlie."

Charlie cocks his head to the side and leans forward as if inspecting something.

"I feel like I've—" Charlie stops abruptly as Aki smacks his side. Charlie looks at him and barks in a hushed tone. I think Aki might be the only one that can get away with smacking Charlie.

Aki looks back towards Blair and me. "Charlie and I just want you to be safe," he says.

"Oh my, heavens," I suddenly hear from behind me, and I turn to see Red who has just walked up. She is in a pair of black shorts and a neon blue resort polo.

"I know right," Blair says as she steps to Red's side, and I realize they are both staring at me.

Red looks over to Blair, her head oddly cocked to the side. "Did you pick this out?"

Blair shakes her head. "Nope. Not at all. *She* picked it out herself."

"Huh," Red says then turns back, and after a moment of silence, begins to nod enthusiastically. "You look beautiful, Glory. I am not surprised, but this dress is just—"

"Perfect," says a gruff voice off to my side. "Just, perfect."

All of us turn towards Ellis, who is standing stiffly ten or so feet away. He is staring at me, his face a chalky white, as if stunned silent. He doesn't look pleased.

Red and Blair exchange a glance then walk towards Ellis. "She picked this out, Ellis," Red says.

"Why are you two encouraging this?" he asks coldly without responding.

Blair steps forward and chastises him in a sharp, hushed tone. "She is having a good time tonight, Ellis, so don't mess it up. She deserves this. Didn't you hear what Red said?"

After an audible grunt, Ellis rubs his hand across his face then nods in surrender. "You look—

"Glory!" a voice shouts from my other side. I turn to see Nico, Mateus, and his buddies approaching from the condos, all of them dressed in crisp linen shirts and khaki shorts.

I start to respond but Blair interrupts as she grabs my arm and tugs me towards the group. "Hey, guys. So, what do you think?" Blair spins slowly and Mateus howls playfully.

Though I don't put on a show, I smile politely, and when Nico extends his hand in my direction, I mirror his action. He nods as he gently takes my hand into his and pulls it to his lips. The action catches me off guard, so I turn away to mask a jolt of embarrassment. As I do, I see Clinton, who has joined Ellis, and both are staring daggers in our direction. A feeling of shame suddenly washes over me as my eyes connect with Ellis's. I turn quickly back to the group but feel his scrutiny still.

"What do you think, Glory?" Blair asks and I look towards her.

"Sorry, what?"

"Nico asked if we want a drink."

I look back to Nico and hold a hand up. "Oh, no thank you. I am not a big drinker." A moment of confusion flashes across his face for a moment before he forces a smile and turns towards the bar.

"I should have told him you didn't drink," Blair says into my ear.

"No problem. I'm not even sure you knew that."

Blair's head bobs, "Yeah, that's right."

Over the next hour, Blair and I get to know a bit more about the guys. We learn that they are here for an annual pharmaceutical convention in Miami and had decided to drive down to the Keys for a visit. One of the guys, the quieter one, had been to Dave's years ago and had recommended it to his buddies. He, unlike the others, lives in the U.S., Savannah, Georgia, where he manages the sales team for the Southeast.

All the guys seem to be a bit older than us, but even then, much less mature. As time goes on, and the drinks continue to flow, my patience wears thin at their increasingly loud voices and annoyingly persistent advances.

"This is a very beautiful dress you have on," Nico whispers in my ear for like the tenth time this evening, and again, I just politely nod in faux gratitude. This seems to annoy Nico, who barks something in Italian to Mateus, pulling him away from what appears to be a much more engaging conversation with Blair.

Blair looks around Mateus and furrows her brow as if asking me if something is wrong. I shake my head and roll my eyes, but in all honesty, I am not sure how much longer I can play wing woman. After a moment, and without looking back in my direction, Nico gets up abruptly and heads over to the bocce ball area. There, he joins the other guys, who are cutting up and making obscene gestures with the equipment.

"Do they ever grow up?" I mutter under my breath. I look back over to Mateus and Blair, who are reengaged in a soft-spoken conversation. Mateus's hand is now resting on Blair's leg, his thumb shifting back and forth playfully.

Poor Clinton.

I'm distracted a moment later when Nico and his friends start howling with laughter. From the corner of my eye, I notice that they are all staring in my direction. Clearly, the joke was made at my expense.

"Boys suck," I say into the wind. I then stand and walk to the bar, stopping just behind two couples that appear to be on a double date. I notice their wedding rings and slightly aged faces. I return a smile when one of the ladies looks towards me and nods.

Except for the couples and a few others, the Hut is quiet tonight. On the right side, at the far end of the bar, I notice Red and Ellis. Red is drying off some glasses and hanging them on an overhead rack while Ellis is speaking to her, one hand propping his head up. He stands back from the bar and leans forward, stretching his long torso outward toward the water. He looks stiff as if his back is hurting. Sensing someone looking at him, his neck turns and his eyes dart to Blair and Mateus. He straightens a bit and turns his body fully facing them, his brows pulling low on his face. He appears to be looking for—

"Oh," I say as his eyes shift from Blair to the bar, eventually landing on me. I see him visibly exhale before he nods slightly and turns back towards Red. His face softens just a bit as he looks away. Ellis was clearly keeping an eye on me, which I both appreciate and am also confused by.

I look away and as I do, I see Clinton on the right side of the bar. His glasses are low, balanced on his nose, and he is staring intently into a stack of papers. The stress of his and Blair's relationship is taking a toll on him. His hair is disheveled, and he has a five-o'clock shadow that makes him look older. Most of the time, Clinton's the goofball of the group, and very well put together. As he looks over his shoulder towards Blair, he sees me and waves me over.

I nod slightly then walk towards him. As I approach, he reaches over and pulls out the stool for me. He forces a soft smile that contrasts starkly with his appearance.

"You look very nice tonight, G," Clinton says as he winks.

"The color suits you." I had almost forgotten that I was wearing the dress, distracted by Nico's testosterone fueled "moves."

"Thanks. I don't remember the last time that I wore a dress."

"Well, that one is a fine choice."

I look down to the dress and pull at the fabric. It stretches forward for a moment, then springs back into place upon my release. "I love this one. I just love all the plants on it." I look back over to him. "What are you up to?"

Clinton's eyes shift towards Blair again. "You mean, besides spying?"

I follow his gaze and suddenly, I feel at fault for encouraging Blair to spend time with the guests. "I'm sorry, Clinton. I shouldn't have—"

He holds up his hand, so I stop speaking. "This is not unusual, Glory, and it is not your fault. Blair is set on ruining our relationship." He exhales and rubs his two big hands across his face. "But she can't. I won't let it happen. Even if I need to do this shit while I keep an eye on her." He nods down towards his papers.

"What are you doing with those?" I ask curiously.

He picks them up and fans his face a bit. "I have an upcoming interview with the University of Miami School of Law." He raises the papers in front of him. "This is the admissions packet and stuff."

I sit straighter on my stool. "Interview? Does that mean you are going to go there?" I knew he had been considering different schools, but I hadn't realized he had decided.

"If I don't mess it up," he says frowning. It's an odd reaction to something that is such an exciting accomplishment. I look back at Blair. It is a shame that she isn't sharing in this excitement. This is a big moment in Clinton's life. He needs someone to celebrate with. I uncross my hands and lean forward.

"This is amazing, Clinton!" I intentionally say it loudly. As

I do, I watch Clinton's eyes dart over my shoulder and lock for a moment in Blair's direction. I've clearly caught her attention. "The University of Miami is a great school, and it is so close to Dave's."

"Exactly," he says as he winks.

"Does Blair know about it?"

"She doesn't. I want to get everything set and finalized, so she doesn't have an opportunity to object. She doesn't know it, but I have already turned down the other schools. This is my only option."

I reach over and pat his leg. "You are a great guy, Clinton. She will come around."

"Yeah," he responds blankly.

"I only wish that I had someone care about me as much as you do Blair."

His head jolts suddenly towards me. "You do—I mean, you will."

"I don't know, Clinton," I say as I pull away from him and wrap my hands across my waist.

"What do you mean?"

I shake my head, trying to declutter the memories that seem to be a jumbled mess as of late. "I just can't remember anyone ever really loving me, except for my dad. He loved me, sure. But Nick couldn't have loved me."

It's Clinton's turn to lean forward. He reaches out and takes my hands into his. As he does, his eyes briefly shift across the bar to his right. I turn towards where he is looking, and just as I do, I see Ellis look from us back to Red.

"What was Nick like?" Clinton asks as he looks back towards me.

My mind flashes back to Nick for the first time today, and I shake my head slightly, willing the distorted memories of his abuse away. Though the bruises have faded, the emotional damage, I'm afraid, is far from healed.

"It was just…hard." I force the words, not wanting to elaborate. I trust Clinton completely, and though a small part of me wants to share the details of Nick's abuse with Clinton, the larger part never wants to revisit those memories again, if I even can. The more time that passes, the fuzzier all the memories get.

He squeezes my hands. "I'm sorry, G."

"Thank you."

"Hey there," I hear from behind me, and I spin in my stool, coming face to face with Nico and two of his friends. One is trying to wave down Red, who is still speaking to Ellis. "So, I am not good enough for you, but this guy is." Nico motions towards Clinton, who is quietly putting away his papers, ignoring Nico.

"Go away," I say, not wanting any drama.

"Time for you to head out," Clinton says pointedly to Nico as he flips a notebook closed and lays his glasses on the bar. He spins on his stool and stands.

Nico forces a laugh then steps forward and leans within inches of Clinton's face. "Trying to be a tough guy in front of the lady?" Nico's voice is a menacing whisper, but it has no visible impact on Clinton, who stands perfectly still, unblinking.

I watch in silence as the two men stare each other down, and suddenly, I am overcome by a sense of responsibility, and perhaps a bit of bravery. I can't let these guys get into a fight and risk someone getting hurt over me. I've already caused too much drama at Dave's just by being here. I seize the opportunity, stepping in front of Clinton and holding up my hands, forcing Nico to instinctively take a short step backwards.

"Please don't do this."

Nico smirks at me then looks over my head to Clinton. "Your little girl fighting your battles?"

"It's okay, Glory," I hear Clinton say. I look back over my

shoulder just as Clinton moves to the left several steps and draws the guys with him away from me. Just as I start to speak again, Nico lunges towards Clinton and swings a fist overhead that Clinton easily dodges. Nico loses his balance and stumbles towards a nearby high-top. He's clearly had too much to drink. He pushes himself upright again and takes another step towards Clinton.

"I wouldn't do that," Clinton says, smiling wide, like the cheshire cat.

I startle as I feel a hand on my shoulder. "Come over here," Red says as she pulls me back behind the bar and suddenly, a large frame shifts to my front. Ellis.

"Leave now and you won't get hurt," Ellis says, his voice low and menacing. "I am only warning you once." Ellis tugs at his collar and takes a few slow steps forward towards Clinton.

Mateus mimics Ellis as he stands and shifts away from Blair to Nico's side. Their other friends stay back a bit but clearly stand ready as backup.

"We are not afraid of two American assholes," Mateus says.

"Three," says a deep, loud voice suddenly as I turn and see Noah lurch forward. He doesn't go to Clinton and Ellis but instead stands within inches of Mateus and Nico. He looks down at them and cocks his head. "I thought he told you to leave."

Nico and Mateus take a step back, but Noah follows them.

"This has nothing to do with you," Nico says then laughs nervously.

"No discussion," Noah says firmly. "I will not ask again."

"Time to leave, boys," I hear an old voice say as Charlie steps from behind Red and noticeably cracks both knuckles at his side. "Or don't," he says then winks.

"Crazy Americans," I hear one of their friend's whisper, and Nico glances quickly over his shoulder at the comment. His backup is now standing at a noticeable distance behind them, clearly intimidated by Noah's stature and Charlie's confidence.

Nico audibly sighs then shrugs. "Whatever," he mutters without looking directly at Noah. "Let's get out of this dump."

We all watch as Nico, Mateus, and his entourage make their way down the path to the parking lot, the dull sound of their defeated grunts disappearing as they turn down the walkway behind a row of palmettos.

Noah turns to Ellis. "I will go make sure they actually leave."

"Text me if there is an issue," Ellis says.

"There won't be," Noah tells him then winks, playfully.

"Thanks buddy," Ellis says. "I really wasn't in the mood."

"Clinton, wait!" I hear Blair shout as she starts after Clinton, who hasn't said a word but has turned and is stomping off angrily.

He stops and jerks towards her. "No, Blair. This is bullshit."

"Clinton, stop," she says and takes a step towards his direction. "I didn't do anything wrong."

Clinton throws his hands in the air in defeat. "Fine, Blair," he shouts over his shoulder. "You didn't do anything wrong."

Blair looks after him for a moment then turns towards us. "I didn't do anything wrong," she repeats. I think she says it more for herself than any of us. Blair looks between us, but no one speaks. The silence is awkward and feels thick with blame.

"Fine," she says into the silence then turns and storms off.

"Blair," Red says after her and starts out from behind the bar. She turns back towards us but continues, walking backward. "I better go talk to her."

I look back to the bar and notice that Aki has come out from the back kitchen. He must have heard all the commotion. Charlie walks back and whispers something in Aki's ear. Aki nods and seems to accept that all is handled. Charlie begins tending to the few remaining customers while Aki grabs a load of dishes to carry back to the kitchen.

'Glory," Ellis says and my attention snaps towards where he is leaning up against the bar. "Are you okay?"

I nod. "I think so. Everything just happened so fast. I think I just want to go back to the house."

"Can I walk you back?"

I don't answer immediately, not sure exactly what to say. On one hand, I welcome the escort back to the house, but on the other, I'm not in a good place with Ellis. Walking up on him talking about me to Dave and Amber has made me self-conscious and not sure about where I stand with him.

"You said that I'm ridiculous. You acted like something was…wrong with me."

Ellis steps forward and turns towards the water. He shakes his head as if frustrated then faces me again. "*You* are not ridiculous, Glory."

"But you said—"

"It's the situation," he says. "Not you. *Never* you." He steps forward and takes my hand. "I wouldn't say something to hurt you, Glory."

I rub my hands across my face as a memory races into my mind. It's Nick. He is telling me to put down the phone. He's mad about something, about someone I've called. I am not sure what.

"You with me?" I hear Ellis ask, and I open my eyes. His crystal blue eyes are locked with mine, and for a moment—the briefest of moments—I feel like I haven't seen him in years.

"Take me home," I say. The words escape from my mouth, an automatic response to a perceived absence that I can't explain.

"What?" he asks, head cocked.

"Back to the apartment."

He shakes free from an invisible hold. "Oh, yeah. Of course."

Ellis takes my hand then pulls me close to his side. Though the walk back to the patio behind the house is short, Ellis doesn't ease his grasp, even slightly. He holds on to me as if afraid I might escape. It's an odd feeling from someone that I've only known a short time, something that should feel premature, but then again, our connection has never felt its age.

At the patio, he stops abruptly. "The way you stepped in front of Clinton and that guy tonight scared me."

I look up to him in a confused kind of way, my brows pulled tightly. "Why?"

"I just…couldn't imagine something happening to you again. I don't think I could take it." He stops speaking and shakes his head. "I'm sorry."

I take his hand in mine. "I am okay, Ellis."

"I know." He responds as he leans in and wraps his arms around me, pulling me close. I let him and turn my head, resting it against the top of his hard abdomen. I close my eyes and inhale the scent of fabric softener and some brand of male deodorant.

"You are so very brave, Cora."

Cora.

I pull back instantly and look up to him. He immediately knows he has made a mistake and purses his lips, shaking his head once in frustration. "Sorry. Old habit."

I squeeze his hands then pull away slightly. "It's okay," I say.

I am not upset with Ellis for accidentally calling me Cora, but an overwhelming sense of sadness bubbles up within me. It's a sadness for Cora, a sadness for Ellis, and a sadness for a strong connection that is developing between Ellis and myself that can't happen. Though we have an undeniable spark, Ellis is clearly not in a place for a new relationship, and if I am being honest with myself, neither am I.

"Look, I better get back and make sure all is okay at the Hut," Ellis says awkwardly then releases my hand from his. He takes a step back. "I'll see you in the morning though, okay?"

I force a smile as he takes another few steps towards the back path. "Okay. Thanks for walking me back."

He doesn't respond but instead raises a hand and smiles as he disappears back towards the resort.

I exhale slowly then turn towards the house. I just make it to the porch when my phone dings.

I pull it up and am instantly relieved when I see a voicemail from a number that I recognize, the University of Tennessee.

"Hi Glory. My name is Barbara Eaton with the University of Tennessee's counseling office. We got your message and are bit confused. We actually do not have a counselor here named Cora. I am sorry, but perhaps you got her confused with another department."

I close my eyes and take a steadying breath. I had a feeling she didn't exist. But what does that say about me? Did I make her up? Is she a spirit or ghost? I listen as the voicemail continues.

"As to your question regarding withdrawal, unfortunately, we cannot seem to locate anyone by the name of Glory Dawson in the student records system. If you would please give us a call at your convenience, we will be happy to—"

I end the voicemail abruptly. I don't understand. What does she mean she can't find me in the records? I have almost graduated. It can't be. I don't have any other name.

"My name is Glory Dawson," I say aloud as I reach up and brush a stray clump of hair from my cheek. My mind races to solve for the mystery.

"Was it a misspelling?" I say to myself just as a crippling vertigo sets in.

I reach for something to steady me, but my hands fall forward into a sudden darkness.

CHAPTER 28

THE LIGHT IS blinding as it bounces from the ripples of the water. I am sitting on the seawall, my feet dangling over its side. And I am not alone.

"This is bullshit, Glory."

I turn to my right and a beautiful blonde is sitting on the wall a few feet away. She has her hair pulled back by a bright orange headband.

"Cora," I say into a sudden burst of salty breeze.

"As soon as I left, you swooped in, didn't you?"

"What do you mean?" I say.

"He likes you, you know?" she says. Her words trail off at the end into a tired sigh. She rubs her face with her free hand, the other still steadying her. "It's not fair. This is not my fault."

"What is not your fault?"

She turns my way and smiles. "It's not your fault, Glory."

"Glory!"

I turn and stand instinctively at the sight of Nick. But I am no longer at Dave's. The crystal blue water is gone, replaced by the cold façade of a dilapidated apartment building. I take a step back, away from him. My heart is pounding in my chest, and I can feel hot beads of sweat roll down my face.

"I called him," I hear myself say defiantly. "You will go to jail."

Nick steps forward again but this time, I step towards him.

He laughs as he approaches, his limbs freely hanging to his side and face turned sideways, smiling devilishly.

"You are never going—"

He closes the distance so fast that I don't have time to think. My eyes close as I fall back, and hands reach around my head instinctively. The pain comes to my cheek first, then resonates around my body as it tumbles down the steps.

I bolt upright and grapple at my body as a crisp white sheet falls to my lap. I am in a bed. It was a dream.

It is dark outside, but the light from a small orange lamp glows from across the room, illuminating a warm brown recliner where I see a familiar long frame lie asleep.

It is Ellis, and I am in his bed.

I clinch my eyes tightly as a dull pain rolls behind my eyes. I pull a hand to the side of my head and wince slightly as it meets a small round lump.

I fell. The memories of the phone call and evening all race back, but I will myself to not focus on the harsh revelations the voicemail has just thrown into my life.

I open my eyes and look back towards Ellis. He looks so peaceful curled up on his chair. He must have found me and carried me to his room. A jolt of emotion bubbles from my chest, perhaps gratitude. Perhaps something more that I refuse to acknowledge. I look around his room and though I feel strangely at ease there, the odd nightmare has made me feel like I am doing something wrong. I think back to the look of disappointment from Cora that accompanied her accusations that I had intentionally "swooped in" to steal Ellis from her.

I need to leave.

The noise of a dull fan provides me cover as I slowly pull the sheet off me and stand. I look down and notice that I am wearing a Florida Gators tee and a pair of grey sweats. Neither are mine. A blush creeps into my cheeks as I tug at the loose fabric of the shirt.

I make my way to the door at the far end of his apartment then look over my shoulder to Ellis once more before stepping out into the tiny entryway that leads to both the kitchen and rooftop. I start towards the kitchen but stop as I think about the swing above. I turn and walk softly to the door to the garden. As I push the door forward, a cool breeze rushes into my face, carrying with it the familiar scent of citrus and blooms.

After closing the door and making sure it isn't sticking, I walk up the stairs and into the rooftop garden.

As the garden comes into view, I take a deep, steadying breath, which is accompanied by a sense of peace that I hadn't realized I had missed.

"I love this place," I say softly as I make my way forward to the swing. Just before I get there, I look to the left and notice that one of the potted flowers is wilting. It's an oddity to me to see something in the garden not doing well, and the disappointment catches me by surprise. I walk over to the plant and reach down to feel the soil. It is bone dry.

"Poor little guy," I say then pull my hand back and look around until I spot a small watering can. I walk over and grab it, then look around for a spigot. With all these plants up here, there must be a water source.

"If I were a hose, where would I be?" I look around then spot a bit of hose just visible from underneath a long wooden bench.

I lose track of time as I make my way around the garden with the watering can, making sure all the plants have been watered. As I do, I also pinch off dead blooms and collect them in a small bucket next to the swing. After I feel like the plants are in pretty good shape, I grab a small wooden broom and proceed to sweep dirt, leaves, and fallen petals into a yellow dustpan that I also empty into the bucket. When I'm done, I gather the hose and place it back under the bench, then stand proudly to admire my work.

"Very nice," I hear a deep voice. I turn to see Ellis shift forward from the steps. I look around as I dust a bit of dirt from my shorts.

"Thanks," I reply. "It was actually kind of fun."

"Fun?" he asks then cocks his head. "Not too many people would call it fun."

"Do you enjoy it?"

He looks around at the garden. "I do." He steps forward and walks to my side. "But I don't do it for me."

I look over to him knowingly. Of course, he does it for Jane. Suddenly, my head starts to throb, so I reach up and rub my temple.

"Want to sit down for a minute?"

I nod. "Good idea." I walk back to the swing and sit. Ellis follows and sits to my left.

"Thanks for taking care of me," I say after a moment. "And for the clothes." I pull at the sweats.

"No problem. I'm just grateful I decided to make sure you got home okay. I should have walked you upstairs, and this might not have—"

"This wasn't because of you," I say, cutting him off. "I just got overwhelmed." His eyes dart around for a moment then he looks back towards me.

"Are you hurt?" he asks as his stare lands on my hairline.

"I don't think so. It's a small bump."

He reaches forward, and I don't pull away as his hand gently rubs the side of my head. After locating the small bump, he pulls his hand back. "You must have broken your fall before you passed out."

"Yeah," I say in agreement as I turn towards the horizon.

"What happened?"

I hesitate for a moment but when I do finally look towards him, our eyes lock and his stare is one of deep concern. He knows something is wrong. People don't just pass out without a reason. I can't tell him the truth, that I feel like I'm losing my mind. I can't tell him that I'm not sure that I even exist. I can't tell him I am haunted. He would think that I am nuts.

"I'm tired of being afraid," I say instead, not giving him details.

After a moment, he holds his hand out towards me, and I don't hesitate to grasp it. His warm grip is instantly comforting, giving me a sense of protection and understanding.

"Me too," he says after a moment, and I am caught off guard by his words. Now it is his turn to gaze out across the horizon.

We sit there for a while in silence, holding hands and staring at the bright crescent moon as it illuminates the distant surf, like a spotlight across the water.

"Sometimes I feel like she is still here and that something as simple as a flick of the switch would bring her back to me. And then other times, I am reminded that she's never coming back." He rubs his face with his free hand. "It's exhausting to feel like I am losing her over and over again."

I exhale sharply as his words resonate within me. I had never thought about his loss being one that he would have to relive repeatedly. "So, is that why you are doing dangerous things, to escape?"

He turns back towards me and his face is laced with shame. He releases my hand then starts to put it behind my shoulders. He hesitates for a moment but continues as I scooch closer to his side. As I do, he wraps his long arm around me and pulls me close. "I'm not always trying to escape. Not anymore."

I rest my cheek along his warm chest and hear the dull, steady thump of his heart.

"What were you afraid of tonight?" he asks after a few minutes of sitting in silence.

I close my eyes, not sure where to start. Though I would love to tell him the truth, how could I? What am I supposed to say, "Oh yeah, I met the ghost of your deceased girlfriend last month," or "By the way, I'm not even sure that I exist." I cringe internally at the thought of his reaction. Instead, I lean on another truth.

"Nick. He has gone silent, and I'm not sure what to expect."

"Maybe he has given up and is not going to bother you anymore."

"I don't think so."

"Staying away would be in his best interest." Ellis's words are laced with threat.

"I'm just scared," I say simply after a moment. "And I'm tired."

"Are you not sleeping well?" Ellis asks, looking down at me.

"Not really, but I do feel better now, actually."

"You slept hard after I got you to the bed."

"Thanks again for carrying me upstairs. I know that was a haul."

Ellis looks at me sideways. "I didn't carry you."

I sit up more fully as he continues.

"When I found you, you were sitting on the ground. I asked if you needed to go to the hospital and you said no."

"I did?"

Ellis sits up straighter and leans forward, looking at me as if looking for something. "You said you just wanted to go get in the bed. You walked straight up to my apartment and asked me for some clothes."

I must be more tired than I realized. And that fall must have really sent a jolt through my system. I don't remember any of it.

"I'm sorry. I just don't remember any of that."

"Then you crawled in the bed and got mad at me."

"I did? I must have been sleepwalking or something. What did I get mad at you about?" I look over and see Ellis blushing.

"You were mad that I was going to sleep in the chair. You wanted me to get in the bed. The last thing I remember was that you were looking around the room for something to cuddle with. Like a pillow or—"

"A stuffed animal?" I say, casually interrupting him.

I look back to Ellis as he nods, his face a blank expression. "Yeah."

I exhale loudly and shake my head. "I can't believe I did that, Ellis. I am so embarrassed."

"It's okay," he says, forcing a laugh. "You are always welcome to hijack my bed." He suddenly smiles wide, then pulls me back close to his side. "I'm just glad you feel better."

"Well, however I got there, I feel like I have slept for hours. That bed of yours is pretty fantastic."

"Thanks," he says then reaches up and stretches an arm high above his head. "I actually feel pretty well rested myself."

"You did look pretty comfortable in that chair."

Ellis laughs. "I was."

"Do you sleep in it often?"

"Never have. But I don't think that's why I was sleeping so well."

I pick my head up and look up towards him. "Why, then?"

Ellis shrugs then looks down, "You want the truth?"

I nod.

"It just felt good having you in the room with me."

My heart skips a beat, and I turn my head back against his abs. "Oh," I say.

I ponder his words for a moment. How can I be comforting? It's not like I am protective. Hell, I even stole his bed.

"I miss the companionship," he says as if reading my mind. "I'm just so tired of being alone."

I hope Ellis doesn't notice as a breath catches in my chest. His honesty is devastating, and I'm not sure how to respond. Instead,

I reach up and take his free hand in mine then rub my thumb along his palm. As I do, I feel him relax into me. It is a relief to know that I can return the comfort that he is providing me.

"Would you want to sleep with me?" I hear him ask flatly. My eyes grow wide as I lift my head and look up at him again. As I do, he blinks as if realizing what he said then shakes his head frantically and shifts in his seat. "No. No. Not that. I mean. Um. Sorry."

I raise up fully, and a laugh escapes as he scrambles to explain his words.

"I mean, would you like to sleep in my apartment at night," he blurts out.

I stare blankly for a moment then speak. "In your bed? With you?"

"No, no," he says waving nervously. "I will sleep in the chair."

"Oh," I say simply then turn and stare out towards the water, pondering my response. Though I am surprised by his question, I am not turned off by the idea at all. Actually, I love the idea. As much for me as I do for him. I look back curiously at him, his face reddening under the lights of the garden. He wiggles nervously.

"Never mind, it's a stupid and—"

"Yes," I say before he can take back the offer.

His head twists towards me suddenly. "Really?"

I nod. "Yeah. I think that would be nice." I pull a leg up under me and twist towards him.

"You would be comfortable with that?"

I nod, and he looks away as if embarrassed or in shock. I don't think he expected to ask me to sleep in his room, but he seems even more surprised by my reply.

"On the condition that we share the bed." I can't make him sleep in a chair each night. I mean, he has a queen-sized bed, and I trust him completely.

"Really?" he repeats, unblinking. "You're kidding right?"

"I'm serious. You can't sleep in that chair."

"Okay. Now I must be dreaming."

I laugh then reach out and rub his leg. "I trust you, Ellis. We can make this work. As friends."

Ellis turns towards me and nods in agreement. "Okay. As friends."

Ellis and I sit in silence for a few more minutes but both of us seem to be nervous with anticipation. Neither of us wants to suggest what the other is thinking. Neither wants to suggest that we go to bed, together. In the end it is me that takes the leap.

"So, should we go to bed?" I say, then look up as Ellis's eyes shift nervously.

"Okay. Sure. Let's, uh, go to bed."

I stand then reach my hand down towards him, and he takes it in his. He stands slowly then we head to bed.

Before bed, Ellis and I take turns going to the bathroom. I go second and can still smell the minty toothpaste as I grab a washcloth and wash my face. I then brush my teeth, maybe taking a bit longer than usual, then feel at the bump on my head that has shrunken a bit.

When I get back to the room, Ellis has changed the sheets and neatly made the bed. I bite my bottom lip as I watch him pile a long row of square couch cushions in the center of the bed. He looks back at me proudly as he lays the last on.

"Just put a little wall up. I don't want you trying to have your way with me in the middle of the night."

A burst of laughter erupts from me first then he joins in. We laugh uncontrollably as we both take a side of the bed and slide in under the crisp, fresh linens. I start to turn to face the side table but stop and look over to where Ellis is. He is still sitting partially up, waiting for me, watching.

"Just making sure you have everything you need," he says then nods.

"I'm good."

He starts to lean forward a bit as if looking for a hug but instead extends his hand forward. "High-five."

I roll my eyes and bolt across the pillow wall, hugging him tightly. "High-five."

<h1 style="text-align:center">CHAPTER 29</h1>

Ellis and I wake up at the exact same time thanks to his old brown square alarm that goes off at 6:30 AM.

"You awake, Glory?" I hear him whisper towards my back after slapping the alarm off.

"Do I have to?" I reply as I pull Ellis's warm quilt around my shoulders.

I hear him laugh then feel the bed shift under his weight as he sits on its side. I lift my head and look over my shoulder.

"Oh, hello," I say as I come face to face with his shirtless back. His tan skin and defined muscles remind me of one of those white marble sculptures. "Got hot, did we?" I ask, as I squeeze my eyes tightly to force away the longing I have to reach out and touch him.

Ellis looks over at me sheepishly then squints. "Sorry. I am kind of hot natured."

"Well, what about down there." I nod downward as I waggle my brows.

Ellis laughs as he stands, revealing a pair of cut off sweats, hiding his firm backside. "You wish."

I grab a pillow and throw it, but he dodges it easily. I pull myself up on my elbows then shift to the left, tossing my legs over the side of the bed. I then yawn silently and look back towards him. "Want some coffee?"

Ellis finishes pulling on a bright orange tee shirt then turns around to face me. "Absolutely. Want me to make us some?"

"Why don't I take a stab at it and give you first dibs on the bathroom?"

"Are you sure you aren't just going to go back to sleep?"

I lift my finger and point in his direction. "I wish. But duty calls." I stand then stretch as I yawn into one hand. I turn and face Ellis who is watching me silently.

"How did you sleep?" he asks as he takes one step towards me.

"Pretty amazing actually," I say then laugh. "You?"

"Same."

I start to walk by him, and he tugs my shirt as I do. "Thanks."

I stop and face him. "For what?"

"For agreeing to this. For agreeing to stay with me."

I don't respond but instead nod slightly. I'm the one who should be thanking him.

By the time I return to his apartment with two coffees, he is back and pulling on a pair of board shorts. As he does, I just get sight of his bare backside. "Oh dang, sorry," I say as I turn with both hands holding full cups.

I hear him laugh from behind me. He walks forward and takes a cup from my hand as I spin towards him. "You know you liked it," he teases before putting the coffee to his lips. He nods afterwards. "Good cup of Joe, Glory."

"Thanks," I say, eyes narrow.

He walks over to his chair but just before he sits down, he pulls his pants down, so the crack of his ass shows. He looks over his shoulder and winks. "How's this?"

I roll my eyes and turn to walk away. "I think I will go get dressed."

"I will just be here waiting for you, and definitely not spying on you while you get dressed, like you spied on me."

I gasp at his playful accusation as I head to my apartment.

Back at my place, I throw on some shorts and a neon yellow Dave's Resort tee-shirt that Red had given me shortly after I had arrived. After I brush my teeth, use the restroom, and pull my hair back, I walk back over to Ellis's apartment.

"Ready," I say as I peak my head back in through the door.

With a swift motion, he flips the Lazy-Z-Boy back to a seated position and pops up from the chair.

"Let's do it."

I follow Ellis down the stairs and to the back porch. He pulls the door open, then steps to the side. "After you."

I wink at him then walk forward. Everyone is already in their typical spots. Red is asleep on Noah, Blair is in the corner with her nose in a book, and Clinton and JJ are playing a video game of some sort.

"Well look what the cat dragged in," Clinton says as we walk inside and proceed to the swing.

"*Good* morning, Glory," I hear Red mumble as she lifts her head and looks towards Ellis and me. "Did you both just come down together?" She narrows her eyes as she looks at Ellis.

Ellis ignores her and leans over to watch Clinton and JJ, so her eyes dart towards me. I don't respond but instead take a noisy sip of coffee.

Red doesn't ask any other questions, and except for Noah threatening to throw JJ in the water if he doesn't keep his voice down, and Blair's pointed glares every so often towards Clinton, the morning is pretty uneventful.

By the time we get to the dive shop, I am well caffeinated and ready to start the day. Dave walks in just after 7:10 am, and Red hands him the clipboard. He thumbs through it for a moment then splits us into two groups, boys and girls. Surprisingly, JJ doesn't complain when his name is again skipped. Instead, he just quietly leaves the office out the back door. Dave ignores him and shuffles back into his office.

Red holds up her hand to Blair. "It's basically all healed now, you know. Maybe we give him another chance."

"Nah," Blair says as she throws a bookmark in her book and tosses it under the counter. "He needs to suffer some more. Right, Clinton?" Blair turns to Clinton, but Clinton ignores her. It seems to surprise her when he doesn't take the bait. He is clearly still pissed off about last night. She starts to speak again, but Clinton abruptly stands and walks out the back door before she can. Ellis winks in my direction before following behind him.

"He will come around," Red says.

Blair shrugs. "Maybe it is best that he doesn't."

"You don't mean that," Red says looking down over her reading glasses.

Blair ignores her then looks pointedly towards me. "Okay, spill it."

I hold my hands up. "Me?"

Blair walks to my side. "Sweet little innocent Glory. I know you slept in Ellis's apartment last night."

I inhale sharply. "How did you—"

"Noah checks on him every night," Red says before grinning ear to ear. "We aren't judging at all."

Blair leans in. "We aren't judging, but I will need some details. I've heard, literally, that Ellis is a good fu—"

I shake both hands in front of me. "It's not like that."

"Blair, shut it," Red chastises.

"It's just that we both needed to—"

"Get some booty," Blair interrupts nonchalantly.

"No! We just sleep more peacefully when we are in the same room."

"Okay, that's cool," Red says.

"Peacefully?" Blair steps back and waves her hands as if in surrender. "What kind of sex is that?"

"No sex. Just sleep."

Blair looks at me as if stunned by my admission. Red steps to Blair's side and pats her shoulder. "Just because they sleep in the same bed together, doesn't mean they have to have sex."

Blair stares between us, mouth agape, then shakes her head in disbelief. "I just can't with you two right now. Sometimes I wonder if I am the only girl in the world that likes to get it on."

Red looks over to me. "She's just wondering why we all aren't hoes, like her."

Blair playfully smacks Red's side. "I am not a hoe."

Red's head tilts. "Really?"

Blair stares silently for a moment then shrugs. "Maybe a bit of a hoe."

We break out in a fit of laughs then head out the back door to the docks to wait on our tour group.

The tour group arrives a bit late, which gives us plenty of time to prep the Seahorse I. I learn that this is, in fact, not a snorkeling trip but a smaller scuba trip. The scuba trips require more gear and supervision, so Dave purposefully sets these to a limit of eight guests.

After we get everyone on board and comfortable, I listen as Blair provides a short review of the basics. The guests seem very well versed with the dangers and process of scuba diving and almost everyone has even brought their own equipment. They pull masks, fins, BC vests, and various instruments from neon mesh bags and black cases.

The boat ride out to our dive location is only about thirty minutes, probably just five or six miles off the coastline.

"Has anyone ever been on Molasses Reef before?" Blair asks just as I hear an anchor line drop into the water.

"Just the swim-through," an older man answers. He appears incredibly confident in the way he holds himself, so I realize he and his wife must be avid divers. "We did it about ten years ago."

"Perfect," Blair says. "So, you know how amazing this is about to be."

I listen as the couple describe the large reef structures, going into greater detail about the large hole in the reef that creates a swim-through between two high coral walls.

"I can't wait," a younger lady says to the two friends she is traveling with before they all lean together for a selfie. I love how the water brings everyone closer through mutual experience, and I suddenly find myself wishing I had had more lessons from Ellis. I think back to the pool and him telling me how well I did. The basics didn't seem too complicated, so maybe I will be able to see the swim-through this summer.

Red comes down the ladder to the main deck then walks over to me. "I'm still a no-go for a couple weeks because of this hand—all the bacteria and stuff—but you could get in."

My head darts towards her, as the opportunity to enjoy Molasses Reef appears before me unexpectedly.

Red smiles then laughs as she reaches out and pats my back. "No worries though if you prefer to take it slowly. Ellis just mentioned that you were amazing in the water."

"He did?"

"Yeah."

I look back to the group of semi-professional divers and a bubble of doubt rises in my chest. "I just don't think I can do that yet."

Red winks. "You don't have to do *that*." I look back towards her. "You could just snorkel. It is deeper than the sand bars, but you don't have to go down the entire way. Just float along the surface."

I feel my brows lower as I ponder what she is saying. Of course, I could snorkel. I just assumed I would need to dive. look back towards the water, which is remarkably peaceful.

"The currents do seem calm."

"Oh, they are," Red agrees. "This is a good time to get your feet wet, literally."

Blair steps towards us. "We are all set to go."

"Glory is thinking about snorkeling."

Blair looks at her and nods approvingly. "You should. You will totally enjoy it. I'll be diving, but I will be around and can keep an eye on you. Watch out for the sharks," Blair jokes, and Red smacks her back.

"She's kidding," Red clarifies, turning towards me while reaching sideways and pinching Blair's side.

"I'm kidding, damn," Blair says, rubbing her side before turning towards me and adding, "I'm kidding. Promise."

"Okay," I say forcing a toothy smile. Though I did hear her tell the guests on the way out that we might see some smaller nurse sharks, I'm not worried about those. I remember something from somewhere about those not being aggressive unless you messed with them, and I didn't plan on pulling any tails.

I look around the deck as my mind settles on the idea that I might go snorkeling on Molasses Reef. I think back to the suit I have on, and that I did remember to wear plenty of sunscreen. I see all the empty gear bags and quickly turn back towards Red. "I don't have any snorkeling stuff, and I don't think we loaded anything extra, since these guests had their own gear."

Red and Blair exchange a knowing look, then Blair turns and walks to the side of the boat and proceeds to dig into her bag. After a moment, she stands and turns back towards Red and me. As she does, she holds out a bright purple and green snorkel and mask set.

"This will work."

I take a step forward and instinctively reach out my hand. "I love these colors. Is this from the dive shop?"

Blair walks forward and puts it in my hand. "Nah. This was a special order."

I lift my head up just as I see Blair winking towards Red.

"Thanks, Blair." I say. "I promise to take good care of these."

Blair waves her hands dismissively. "Oh, they aren't mine."

Red leans in. "Ellis asked that we give these to you today. He bought them for you."

"Really?" I find myself asking in disbelief as I finger what I imagine to be a very expensive mask set.

"They came in yesterday," Blair adds.

"I wonder why he didn't give them to me this morning," I ask.

"I don't think he wanted you to feel pressured to use them until you were ready."

"Oh," I say, nodding. "That is so…thoughtful."

I pull the mask and snorkel closer to my body, as if hugging it. Ellis's generosity lands squarely in my chest, and I feel my eyes water.

"Ma'am, can we go ahead and get in?" I hear a guest ask and Blair's attention snaps to the line of standing divers a few feet away.

She says something to them, but my focus is not on her words as I look back down to my gift, *my* first diving equipment. A burst of pride swells in my chest.

"He also wanted me to give you this," Red says as she reaches out and hands me a small square of paper, folded in half.

I reach out, take it, unfold it, and look down.

-I hope this gives you the peace, love, and healing that it has given me. Until the tide, Ellis

"Until the tide," I say softly to myself. It's an oddly familiar phrase, but I'm not sure what it means.

A warm spray of moist wind catches my hair, and I close my eyes. I breathe slowly as his words infuse in my core, bringing an eerie sense of calm and peace. I feel strums of butterflies in my stomach and shocks of chilling excitement race along my skin. Though these are feelings that I haven't experienced in a very long time, they are unmistakable.

I open my eyes as I fold the paper then hold it out to Red. "Would you mind keeping this someplace safe for me?"

Red takes the note as she nods knowingly. I can tell immediately that she senses the sudden shift in my emotions, a shift only noticeable by someone who is your closest friend, someone you have shared years of life experiences with. We stand there facing each other in silence for a moment before she speaks. "You got this girl."

I nod once with confidence then turn and walk silently over to the open seat on the bench. By the time I strip down to my suit and pull the mask over my head, the other guests are already in the water. I walk to the side of the boat and look outward, immediately spotting Blair twenty or so yards away, bobbing on the surface. When she spots me, I hear her shout with enthusiasm, cheering me on. But at this point, I need no encouragement. I am remarkably calm, driven by an unknown instinct that whispers confidence in my ear, and the prospect of new love upon my return.

CHAPTER 30

"Until the tide," I say softly to myself as I towel dry next to the guests. What does that even mean, and why am I obsessing over those three simple words?

"So how was it?" Red asks as she steps towards me causing me to lose my train of thought.

My eyes instantly light up. "How could I have gone my entire life and not yet done that? It is incredible. Everything was so peaceful and colorful."

"Well, you looked great out there. I think I even saw you fix your mask at one point, which comes with the territory."

"Yeah, I accidentally hit it when I saw that Goliath Grouper. I was lucky it was still down there after I fixed the mask."

"No sharks?" Blair asks as she pulls up to my side. She is shaking her head to one side as if she has water in her ear.

"No sharks, but that Eagle Ray was nuts. I didn't know they got that big. I was playing with this lobster trap, and it just popped up from the sand."

"Yeah, he was a big boy," Blair says as she looks back to Red. "Scared the shit out of the lady over there," she adds as she throws a thumb over her shoulder. We look to an older woman who is sitting at the center of a larger group. "It swam right underneath her," we hear her say, as if telling an old ghost story.

We stand there for a few minutes more, and Red and Blair

listen as I continue to share some of the incredible things I saw. Though I didn't manage to swim through the tunnel, I saw where it was. As we talk, I fidget with the new snorkel and mask and my thoughts drift back to Ellis. I am suddenly so excited to see him and tell him about the incredible experience. And I am excited to thank him, not just for the mask set, but for his commitment to teaching me and giving me the confidence I needed to get in the water at the reef.

As a drip of water rolls along my neck, I reach up with my hand and that's when I notice it. My necklace. It's gone.

Though my heart drops, I pretend not to notice. I don't want the experience to be ruined for Red and Blair, and I don't want anyone trying to find it. I know exactly where it is. The necklace my dad gave me, my most prized possession, is lost forever at the bottom of Molasses Reef.

"Okay, y'all," Red says, "let's wrap it up and get back to land."

"10-4," Blair says as she salutes Red. I force a smile then follow Blair to help with the remaining prep.

As I fold up the ladder and pull in the dive flag, I fight back the urge to scream. Though a few tears escape, I pretend to wipe my face dry with my t-shirt, so no one notices.

I take a calming breath and close my eyes. There is really no use in losing control. The necklace is gone.

"How can you be so stupid?" I say softly then cringe as the words remind me of those Nick had used so many times before. I shake my head in disappointment and push back the urge to chastise myself further. It was a mistake, a painful mistake, but what am I supposed to do? There is nothing I can do, and I need to do my best to accept that.

I stand from putting away the dive flag then stare peacefully toward the reef. The warm sun flickers from behind the clouds and shadows dance along the surface of the cobalt blue water. I take a calming breath.

"At least I know where it is," I say softly, then walk over to sit beside an older man leaning forward, talking to the others about parrotfish. I smile as I watch their excitement, happy for the distraction.

The trip back goes by in a flash, and after all the guests have departed, I work with Red and Blair to get the boat and equipment back in order in record time. Just as I close the last of the dive tanks in the storage cabinet, Red turns towards me.

"Any chance you would want to work with me at the Hut tonight? Blair has a date."

"I am allowed to work there?" I ask as I point to myself. I never had considered working at the Hut, not realizing it is an option.

"Absolutely, silly!" Red says. "It is a great way to make some extra cash." She then stops and waves her hands frantically. "But you don't have to. I know it is short notice, and the shift starts in about an hour. I just thought—"

"I would love to," I blurt out, smiling. "I appreciate the opportunity and could use the extra funds."

"Awesome! The tips are fantastic, and the time flies by. You won't have to make any drinks or anything, just take orders and help behind the bar with dishes and stuff."

"Works for me," I say.

Red turns back towards Blair, who is walking down the dock back towards us, carrying a small bag of trash. "She can do it!"

Blair mouths the words "thank you," as she holds a thumb up high in the air.

I start to say something but stop short as I feel a vibration in my pocket.

I slap my hand to my pocket then force a smile. "Let me grab this real fast. Meet you back at the house?"

Red nods curiously as her eyes dart to my pocket. "Sounds good."

I turn and walk back along the sea wall, away from the dock and pull the phone from my pocket. As I look down at the screen, I am relieved to see the word *Mom* across its screen. I hit answer.

"Hey, Mom." I intentionally try to sound upbeat.

"Glory dear, why haven't you called? I have been worried about you."

"Well, I am fine. I've just been busy with the new job."

"Oh, Glory. Please tell me you aren't down there at that fishing place still. You need to focus on yourself and not chasing some boy."

I roll my eyes even though she can't see me. "Mom, I am not chasing some boy."

"Glory, Nick has stuck by your side all this time and has been there for you. He wants to build a life with you."

"Mom, I know you like him, but we broke up. It is over."

"I just wish you were more appreciative, Glory. He's the one that was there after—"

"No, Mom," I say firmly. "He is not what you think. Please drop it and quit listening to what he says."

I hear her sigh into the phone. "You know, Glory, I am not the bad guy here. I would have been there sooner if you needed me."

"I don't need you, Mom," I say then bite my lip as the words come out harsher than intended. Though my mom has always been focused on herself, I don't hate her. "Look, I am sorry. I do need you, but I am an adult now, and I need you to respect my decisions."

"Fine, Glory," she says after an awkward pause. "Just please don't go get wrapped up with some beach bum. You deserve better."

What the hell does she think I am doing? I close my eyes in frustration. "I won't, Mom. But please, don't tell Nick where I am. If he finds out for sure that I am in Florida, he will—"

"Glory, he knows where you are. How could he not?"

"What do you mean?"

"Well, of course you are down there in Florida."

"But I didn't tell him that, Mom."

"He's not stupid, Glory. Nick is very intelligent."

I sigh as I resign myself to the fact that my mom is easily manipulated. At least I haven't told her exactly where I am. Florida is a big place.

"Okay, Mom. Look, please just don't engage with him anymore. Okay?"

"Geez, Glory. Fine. He has done so much for this family, but you expect me to just forget all that and ignore him."

"Mom, please."

"Fine, Glory, but…only if you promise me that you won't go run off and get married to some loser."

I force a smile. It's an easy promise to make. "Okay, Mom. I promise. That will never happen."

She doesn't respond, but I hear her trademark sigh into the phone. In the brief silence, a thought races to mind. Wouldn't my mom know if I were a student at the University of Tennessee?

"There is one other thing, Mom." I pause and think how best to craft my question without alarming her. "When was the last time you visited me while I was at the University of Tennessee?"

"What are you talking about, dear?"

"Well, did you ever come visit?"

"Of course we did, Glory. Not as much because you had Nick, and he was a lifesaver for us. We always knew he was watching over you."

Mom's fairytale version of Nick is frustrating for me, but I am in no position to confront the reality with her. One day, I will sit down with her and tell her about the pain and trauma, but even as I think about it now, the memories come in flashes and are incomplete. They are also mixed in with memories of my time volunteering at the urgent care.

"You never invited me to any football games or anything," she continues. "I would have liked that, but we never had time. We always had to deal with business. It would have been nice while you were in school there."

I bite my lower lip as I get the confirmation that I'm looking for. I did go to the University of Tennessee. I was a student there. But if that is true, why could they not find my records? Did they make a mistake? Is there something that I am missing?

"Okay, well, I need to go," she says, interrupting my train of thought. "Your dad and I are headed to the club with friends."

"Okay," I say simply as I fight back the urge to tell her that Cliff's not my dad.

"Let's talk again soon, dear, and please be sure to make sure you are taking care of yourself. Going to the doctor, and everything else you need to be doing. Okay?"

"Okay," I parrot back, still staring blankly and lost in a frenzy of thought. I start to say goodbye but stop when I hear a click signaling that she has ended the call. I hold the phone down then shake my head as I look back towards the docks. Red and Blair are gone, and the dock is quiet, except the nearby squawking of a pelican.

I walk silently towards the back of the dive shop then grab my bag from the top of the storage box. I pull it over my shoulder then walk back along the path towards the house. I breathe heavily as I step, an unintentional rhythmic pattern that oddly calms my nerves.

As my eyes look out across the blue water, I try to think back to the blur of my college experience, attending parties, Greek life, classes…all of it. Though the memories are fragments of experience, what college memories are crystal clear? No, I definitely went to college. But even if I did, that doesn't explain Cora. I still had a real conversation with a ghost.

As I turn the corner through a line of palmettos, I reach my hand up and grab for my necklace, sighing heavily when I remember it's gone.

Chapter 31

I welcome the shower back at the apartment. Water, even from a pipe, calms me and takes my mind—although briefly—away from the chaos.

By the time I shower, get dressed, and choke down a granola bar, it is time to head down to the Hut. As I exit the house, I pause for a moment by the back door when I hear arguing coming from the porch. No one is screaming, but Blair's elevated voice carries and easily drowns out the dull pleading that I figure must be coming from Clinton. After a moment, I force myself to walk away, not wanting to eavesdrop on their personal conversation.

"Poor guy," I say softly to myself as I tiptoe along the path furthest away from where the porch overlooks the water, not wanting them to spot me.

As I round the corner and approach the Hut, I immediately notice there is already a crowd. Given it is only early evening, it is no wonder why Red is concerned about covering Blair's shift. The Hut is going to be swamped tonight. I've learned that Thursday nights tend to be the busiest resort days, especially since the locals flock into the resort for the start of an early weekend.

"Hey girl," Red greets me as she walks from the back room and sees me approaching. "You ready to make some money?"

"Absolutely," I say as I catch an apron she tosses my way.

Over the next half hour, Red gives me a run down about my

duties for the evening. It's mostly self-explanatory and doesn't require much training. Specifically, I am to keep the glasses stocked, run food, take orders when things get backed up, and make sure the garnishes don't run empty.

Just as I finish with Red, I notice Ellis walk up next to the far end of the bar. He sits on a stool then swivels towards someone approaching slowly from the distance. He clearly doesn't notice me, so I start to walk towards him, wanting to thank him for the mask set he had ordered me. As I do, the object of his attention emerges from a crowd of people standing around a grouping of high-tops, and I freeze. Ellis raises his hand and stands as a beautiful lady who appears to be in her early thirties with bright blonde hair and curves for days approaches Ellis, smiling wide. Though I can't see his face or hear what he says to her, I can only imagine as I see her smile and lean forward, extending her hands around his waist.

Heat builds in my cheeks, and I turn suddenly, not wanting to see anymore. Ellis is clearly meeting someone at the Hut tonight, maybe a date, and he must not realize I am there. Hell, maybe he doesn't care if I see. And why would he? I try to remind myself that Ellis and I are not a couple, and that he owes me no allegiance. But as my mind tries to pursue reason, I find myself biting hard at my bottom lip. I am not interested in being reasonable.

I walk back towards Red, who is busy with a group of college-aged girls sitting quietly together, clearly on a girls' night out.

Over the next couple of hours, I do my best to keep my head down and focused on the work at hand. Though it is easier said than done, and I do find myself staring over to Ellis from time to time, I am able to distract myself mostly from the sudden jealously that has bubbled up.

"Glory, you are amazing," Red says just as we clear the first big rush of the night. "You put Blair to shame, and JJ is not even close to being in your league. If you aren't careful, I might be dragging you here to work with me more often than not."

"Thanks, Red," I say as I empty a jar of cherries into a small plastic container and kneel to put it back in the lower cooler. As I stand, I see Red has darted back to the end of the bar to an older man in a bright orange polo.

"Excuse me," I suddenly here a soft voice come from my left and I turn and see the lady Ellis was speaking to looking directly at me. My eyes dart around, but Ellis is nowhere to be found. I look back to the lady who is in a pair of tight jeans and tank top, her blonde hair is now pulled high in a messy bun.

I force a smile. "How can I help you?"

She pulls out a stool and sits before turning back to me. "Could I get a water, please?" She places a half-empty fruity drink in front of her then pulls out her phone and sits it on the counter.

"Here you go," I say then start to turn away, stopping when I hear her intentionally clear her throat. "Was there something else?"

"No, no. I am good. Just here visiting a friend."

I assume she means Ellis.

"That's...nice," I say. Part of any bar job is small talk, but it's not my strong suit.

"How long have you been here?" the woman asks. "I don't recognize you from before."

"Oh, I am new. This is my first time behind the bar, but I've been here almost a month." My eyes widen at the realization. Has it already been a month?

She extends her hand. "I'm Shelly."

I reach out and shake her hand. "I'm Glory."

"Beautiful name."

"Thanks."

"Is it a family name?"

The question catches me by surprise, and flashes of memories of my dad rush forward. One specifically seems to replay on a loop. It's of him and I sitting outside, talking about castles and princesses or something. I'm young and he's working. My dad was always doing something with his hands.

"Glory, all good?" I hear Red ask from behind, and I snap out of the daydream and look over my shoulder towards her.

"Yeah," I say smiling before looking back towards Shelly. "Sorry. Brain freeze."

"No worries," Shelly says. She then sips her drink and spins towards the other side of the bar. I follow her gaze as it lands squarely on Ellis, who has reemerged and is speaking to Dave. I see her in my periphery turn back towards me, so my eyes snap forward.

"How long have you known Ellis?" I ask, but then cringe internally, realizing the question might make me come across a bit jealous. Clearly, I am.

Shelly shrugs. "Maybe a couple of years. Dave and I go way back though. They are good people."

I nod as I think back to how Dave had willingly taken me in and offered me a job even though he had never met me. "He just seems like he cares so much about everyone here. He must be an incredible friend."

"You have no idea," Shelly says as she sits her drink down then reaches forward, lifting up one of our menus.

"Would you like anything to eat?" I ask.

"No, thanks, I've eaten already. I mainly came to meet up with someone. I will probably just have one more drink." She holds up her glass. "You think Red would just top this off and save a glass?" She pushes her empty glass my way.

"Sure," I say forcing a smile before walking over and passing the glass to Red, who quickly spins a few bottles around and tops off Shelly's drink. She hands it back to me, then leans down towards my ear.

"She's harmless," she says then pulls back and turns towards an older man who has his hand up at the end of the bar. Red seems to have picked up on my unease. My prior encounter with one of Ellis's love interest, Trish, had not resulted in giggles and smiles. I think back to Trish and her sorority sisters and cringe. They were basically evil.

I walk back towards Shelly, whose eyes light up as they meet mine. She is not Trish and certainly not evil. Suddenly, a weight lifts from my spirit, and I feel my shoulders relax as I walk back towards her. I place the drink in front of her and lean against the bar. She takes a sip and closes her eyes as her head rocks to the beat of a Jimmy Buffett song playing overhead.

Shelly's eyes open after a moment, and she sits her drink down. "I'm a parrot head, Glory."

"I'm definitely a fan too. This place has the best music."

"It does."

"So, you said you've been here a month, huh?"

"Yeah. It has gone by fast."

"What brought you to Dave's?" she asks.

I think back to Cora, and though I have no idea how I met someone who died two years ago, she is the reason I am here. An unintentional sigh escapes. "Well, I met someone who told me about this place and suggested that I come down and check it out. She and her friends used to come here."

"Oh, okay. Word of mouth is the main reason this place has been so successful. Dave has never been into marketing, but he is all about the customer experience." Shelly looks around and lifts her hand. "As you can tell."

"I know," I say smiling. "This place is like a paradise. I love the flowers."

Shelly nods in agreement. "They are amazing. They placed them in all the right spots." I glance at three large, green-glazed planters behind Shelly, filled to the brim. "Some of the plants need to be cut back though."

Shelly looks over her shoulder then back at me. She tilts her head and smiles. "Like the Plumeria?"

"Exactly," I say as I grab a loose rag from the bar and fold it. I look back towards her and shrug.

"Ellis has done a good job with it, but the person who previously worked here was the one who really knew her way around plants and took this place to another level. She was amazing with plants."

Cora Jane.

I instinctively look over towards Ellis, who I catch staring at Shelly and me. I smile towards him, and he stares back at me, blankly, as if in a stupor. He seems uneasy in how he watches us, as if tense. I imagine he must think it awkward for me to be having a conversation with Shelly, who he was flirting with a short while ago. The thought sends a jolt of irritation through me that catches me by surprise, so I turn back towards Shelly.

"You didn't know Jane, did you?"

My eyes widen unconsciously at the unexpected question. I feel my hand clench at the bar in front of me. I'm not sure what to say, but it doesn't matter as words just pour out haphazardly. "Well, just when she told me about Dave's and—"

I stop as I realize what I am saying. Shelly is looking back at me, her brows low as if in deep concentration. "So, you met her?"

I shake my head. "Yeah. I mean no. I have never met her. Sorry, I got confused by your question."

"No problem," she says then lifts her drink up and takes a long sip as she pulls the last of the sweet liquid from the glass through the light blue straw. She sits it down and exhales an exaggerated breath as she does.

"Can I get you another?" I ask.

"Oh, no. I better not." She stands and pushes in her stool

before turning her body towards Ellis. "I am just going to say goodbye to a few people around here then head out. I have a hot date. This was just to loosen me up."

"Okay," I say, but a scream bubbles up inside as I think of her 'date.' Though she is a kind person, the feelings that are developing between Ellis and me are making it difficult for me to ignore her intentions.

"Nice to see you, Glory," she says as she lays a crisp twenty-dollar bill on the counter.

"You too," I say then turn back towards the bar and keep my head down as I busy myself with my duties. By the time I look back up, she and Ellis are gone. My stomach starts to sour as I think about their date, but I do my best to ignore my wicked imagination as it spins off disturbing image after image.

The rest of my shift flies by and before it ends, I feel like I could "barback" in my sleep. The job comes natural to me.

"You were amazing, Glory," Red says as she walks over to where I stand next to one of the high-tops. She turns back towards the bar and offers Charlie a warm goodbye. He lifts his hand and nods approvingly in our direction.

"Does he generally close things up?"

Red nods as she looks at him. "He's a bit of a control freak, but I also think he does it because he doesn't want us closing up on our own."

"He's protective, isn't he?"

"You think?" she says then breaks out in a fit of giggles as she hugs my side. "Okay, Glory. I think we are going to need a shower."

I pull out my stained shirt and wrinkle my nose. "Absolutely."

"So, I spoke to Noah and the boys, and we are thinking since tomorrow is our day off, that we would do a movie night."

I look towards her. "Tonight?"

"Yeah."

I think about the night and what I would do. Ellis and I had planned to stay at his place each night, but we hadn't discussed the details, like what to do when he had a date. I had planned to just stay in my apartment, avoiding the garden and the thin walls of the top floor, as long as I could.

"That would be great."

Back at the house, I head straight to the bathroom. When I enter, a cloud of steam hits me in the face. It smells of men's deodorant and fresh soap. I frown as I lock the door to the hall then leave open my apartment door, so the smell of his date prep doesn't linger.

After, I pull on some pajama shorts and head back down to the girls' apartment. When I knock, Red answers the door. She is also freshly showered, her hair pulled high in a white towel.

"Come on in!"

I walk in, and as I do, I see Clinton emerge from their bathroom. "Hey, Glory," he says, his eyes tired.

"Hey," I say as I walk forward and past him, rubbing my arm as I do. I see the tension in his face, clearly a result of Blair being out on a date with another guy. I can relate more than he knows.

As I walk further in, I see that Noah is already positioned on one couch. Clinton steps around me and lays on the rug with a bright green blanket and two pillows, his head propped up on an end table.

"Let's take that one," I hear from behind me and turn to see Ellis smiling down.

I shake my head as my mouth opens in shock. The look of confusion must catch him off-guard because the wide smile on his face morphs to a look of concern. "What is it?" he says as he reaches out and takes my hand gently into his, leading me to the couch, *our* couch, where we sit.

"I just thought you went out," I whisper in his ear.

"Went out?" He cocks his head to the side.

"You know, with Shelly. On a date."

He jolts as I say her name and leans closer to me. "You thought I was going on a date with Shelly?"

I shrug, suddenly embarrassed. I clearly read the situation wrong. I feel blood rush to my face. "I just—"

"Glory," Ellis says then pulls me closer. "I am not doing that anymore. I thought you knew."

I instinctively pull my free hand to my chest, and as I do, I feel the wild thump of my heart. "Really?"

"Yes, silly." He reaches forward and brushes the hair from my face.

"I just thought that—"

He pulls me fully into his chest before I can finish then rests his head on mine.

As he does, I reach up to rub away a tear that has escaped down my cheek.

I take a steadying breath then lean fully into Ellis as I stretch out my legs. Just as my head hits his abdomen, my eyes tighten as a flash of memory rushes forward that makes me jolt—images of a white room and a deafening screeching sound. The memory is so vivid that I pull my hands to my ears and squeeze my eyes closed. As soon as I do, the terror vanishes.

"Glory?" I hear Ellis say.

I don't answer for a moment, so he speaks again.

"Are you okay?"

I pull back from him, nodding. "Yes, sorry. I just bit my cheek."

The lie flows out effortlessly, but when I look up, I see he isn't buying it.

"I'm going to go to the bathroom real fast. Be right back."

I don't wait for him to respond but instead force a wide smile then shift off his tall body.

When I enter, I lock the door then go to the sink and look down. I take several steadying breaths. "You are okay, Glory."

After a moment, I look up and stare forward into an old mirror with a dull bronze frame. As I do, I jump back. I pause and breathe as I lean in and look carefully at the reflection. Everything about me is exactly as I would expect, dull brown hair, soft white skin, thin lips—everything about the reflection is me, except two small details.

"What the hell," I say as the outline of a pair of bright cobalt blue eyes fades slowly away, leaving in their place, my normal dull blue.

CHAPTER 32

I WAKE UP to the movement of Ellis's large arm tightening around my waist. After the movie, *Happy Gilmore*, Ellis and I had gone upstairs, retreating quickly to bed. Before bed, while Ellis ran to the bathroom, I took the opportunity to turn back the bed and toss the pillows from the middle. I was comfortable with Ellis, and we didn't need some feather barrier between us.

I reach over and take his hand then shift my body backwards until it presses into him. Big mistake. Very big, in fact. My face begins to burn—not embarrassment, but longing. I take a deep breath then start to shift away from him, stopping only when he grumbles something inaudible then proceeds to pull me in closer.

Just as I settle into position, moving past the initial embarrassment of his morning firmness, a loud knock jolts his front door.

"Ellis!" It's Blair's voice.

Ellis instantly shifts and raises his head. "One minute!"

He then leans forward just as my head begins to rise. "Morning," he says as he plants a warm kiss on my cheek. He then stands and spins his body, so he is sitting on the bed, facing away from me. He looks down and sighs, then turns a bit in my direction. "Umm, were you awake?"

I sit up and smile. "Kinda."

He nods down to his crotch. "Sorry about that."

"No big deal," I say.

"Well, it is a pretty *big* deal." He smiles wide then leans down and grabs his jeans, pulling them up with a little jump. As he walks over to the door, I shift to the side of the bed and stand quietly.

"What's up?" I hear him ask.

"Do you know where Clinton is?" The voice is Blair's. I stand and walk over to the door, peaking out behind Ellis. Blair's eyes connect with mine and she forces a little smile.

"I am not sure where Clinton is," Ellis answers.

"What happened?" I ask.

Blair reaches up and rubs her eyes. They appear swollen and red under the soft glow of the hall light. "He walked in on me."

"Walked in how?" Ellis asks then looks over to me.

I hear steps down the hall and see Red shift to Blair's side. "She means he *walked* in on her."

Ellis cocks his head to the side, then his mouth drops open and he pales. "Please tell me you were not with some other guy, Blair," Ellis says after a moment.

She throws her hands up. "Well, not with him, with him, but he was in my bedroom. I came home late and didn't see Clinton on the couch. Me and…my date, went to my room to you know, continued our date."

"Why would you do that, Blair?" Ellis asks, his tone laced with dismay. "You know he loves you."

"Well, I didn't intend to do anything. Well, I did at first," she corrects. "But once we were in the room, I couldn't follow through. I told him he could stay and watch a movie but then would need to leave."

"So, Clinton saw him when he left?" I ask.

"Not really," Red says.

"Well, we kind of fell asleep."

"What!" Ellis says.

"And he walked in on us about an hour ago."

"Oh, shit."

"But we weren't in the bed," Blair explains. "Well, I was. But Jeff fell asleep in the chair."

"Oh shit," Ellis repeats then rubs his hands across his face.

"They didn't do anything," Red echoes, but Ellis doesn't respond and instead shakes his head in disappointment.

Blair pulls a hand across her cheek to wipe away a tear. "When he saw us, he just stood there, just silent. He stared at me and took shallow breaths like he couldn't breathe. It was the worst feeling to sit there and watch him suffer, because of me, because of something I had done. I could feel his heart breaking."

"I am surprised he didn't kill your date," Ellis says flatly.

"He didn't even look at Jeff. He completely ignored him."

"Where did he go?" Ellis asks.

"We can't find him," Red chimes in. "His phone is off. We hoped he was up here with you." Red nods towards Glory. "But now we are at a loss."

"His car's gone," I hear Noah say from behind Red as he steps forward.

"Damn," Red mutters.

"Where could he be? I have to find him. He doesn't know that we didn't do anything. For all he knows, I slept with that fucking distraction." Blair is suddenly pissed, not at Clinton, but herself. "Fucking shit, Blair!" she screams.

"Calm down," Red says, patting her back. "We will find him."

"Okay, let's think," Ellis says calmly. "It's his day off. Does he need a haircut?"

"Nope, he just did that last week," Blair says. "All he has been doing is studying."

"For what?" Noah asks.

"I dunno, just some test I guess, or—"

"I got it!" I shout suddenly.

Everyone looks towards me. "What?"

"What was he wearing?" I ask.

Blair thinks for a moment then her eyes grow wide. "He was dressed up."

"He's at an interview."

"An interview for what?" Red asks.

"It's an interview for admission to the University of Miami Law School. He is planning to go there this Fall. He's turned down everywhere else."

Suddenly Blair starts crying into her hands. "Here I am acting like a total bitch to push him away and that ass is doing everything he can to make this relationship work. I don't deserve him." Blair turns and buries her head into Red's side. "And now I have upset him on the day of his interview. I should have been there, supporting him."

"Well, let's go!" I shout. "It's not too late to show up for him." Everyone turns towards me, Ellis's eyes wide in surprise by my passionate plea. Even Blair looks up from Red and smiles through tears at my off-brand remark.

"Well, you heard the lady!" Ellis says after a moment. "Let's go get him." He looks towards me and winks.

"Let's go," Red echoes.

"Meet in the driveway in five." Ellis says, then he turns abruptly and rushes back into his apartment.

We all follow his lead and quickly get dressed and ready to go. In less than five minutes, Ellis and I are downstairs in the Mercedes.

"You were amazing back there," Ellis says as he reaches over and rests his hand on my leg.

"Thanks," I answer as I cover his hand with mine. "I hope they figure it out."

"Love can make you do crazy things," Ellis adds. "I just hope Blair can keep her crazy in check. I don't want Clinton to lose the love of his life. I don't wish that on anyone." He stares forward in silence for a moment then looks back towards me, a longing in his eyes. Having witnessed the pain Ellis has felt since Jane's death, I understand his sentiment. Just then, a warm morning ray shifts across my face, and I fight back the urge to smile. It's an awkward moment. There's the sadness I feel as a friend of Blair's and Clinton's as they navigate the uncertainty of their relationship. Then, there's the hope I feel for my future and the budding friendship—relationship—between Ellis and me.

"You didn't lose me, Ellis," I say softly into the sun.

"What?" I hear him ask a moment later, and my eyes flash open.

"Sorry," I say instantly as I shake my head and pull back my hand. "I shouldn't have said that. I don't know what I was thinking." I turn away from him in embarrassment. Clearly, he is talking about Jane, not me. I'm just so fixated on our potential, that I am being insensitive to what they had. I need to be more careful.

A moment later, I feel his hand on my face, urging me to look towards him.

I turn my head slightly then pull my hand up to rub at my cheek.

"It's okay," he says.

"I'm just a mess of feelings, Ellis. There is so much in here." I motion to my head. With Nick, the abuse, Dave's, Ellis, and everything else, I am feeling overwhelmed, and it is all bleeding together.

"Me too, Glory. Me too." He leans over, and in the moment our lips touch, I feel something I have only heard about in movies, books. As he kisses me, an electric jolt runs between us that is oddly familiar yet strangely unique.

"Did you feel that?" I say as he pulls away, and I open my eyes.

He starts to speak but stops as Noah, Red, and Blair round the corner.

"Let's move!" Blair shouts as they all hop in.

"Yes, Ma'am" Ellis says as he looks over to me and winks. "We are going to continue this conversation later," he whispers, and I nod in agreement.

The hour and a half flies by with not much said, except for Blair's occasional whimpers. As we pull up and park, Blair is the first to hop out and start running.

"Stop, Blair!" Red shouts. "We don't want to mess up his interview."

Blair stops and turns as she lifts her hands to her head in frustration. The rest of us get out then walk with Blair around the back of the building. It is directly on the water and lined with palms.

"This place is incredible," Blair says as she stands hand in hand with Red.

"See, Blair," Ellis says. "He can stay here and also be near you."

Blair doesn't respond but instead shouts suddenly to the back of the building as a large figure emerges from its central doorway.

"Clinton!"

Think of a movie you've seen where lost loves are finally reunited, then multiply that by ten.

Clinton stops and looks around as if confused. He doesn't see us at first, but after a moment, his eyes lock on Blair. It is hard to ignore a beautiful blonde running towards you screaming at the tops of her lungs.

"What the fuck?" I hear Clinton say just as Blair hits him like a ton of bricks. They both topple to the ground as Blair wraps her hands around his neck. I can't hear what she is saying in his ear, but just as we catch up to her, she hops off him. Clinton stays on the ground for a moment, his hands extended then leans forward and pushes himself up.

"Dang, Blair," he says as he brushes his pants off, pausing at his knee to rub at a grass stain.

"Sorry," she says then steps back and covers her mouth. Though she is excited to have found him, I think she also realizes that she has to face the consequences of her actions.

"What are you doing here?" Clinton says as he looks at her then around to us.

Ellis steps forward and starts to speak but Blair blurts out instead: "They came with me to find you." She tosses her hands helplessly into the air then lets them slap her sides. "I couldn't find you."

"You could have just called me." He reaches down and pats his pocket then closes his eyes when he realizes his phone isn't there. "Except, I left it in the car so it wouldn't go off during the interview."

"Why didn't you tell me about your interview?" Blair asks.

"Because you would have gotten pissed off."

"I wouldn't have—"

"You would have, Blair," Clinton interrupts. "Don't deny it."

She pinches her lips together stubbornly then after a moment nods. "You are right."

"You have to stop this, Blair," Clinton adds. "I mean, look at this place." He spins and holds out his hands. "It is fucking beautiful. It is a top tier school, and it is close to you. It has everything."

"But what about the Ivy—"

Clinton steps forward and for the first time since my arrival, I see him lose his cool. "I. Don't. Want. That. Can't you fucking understand that, Blair? I want this. I want them." He points towards all of us. "I want you, Goddammit!"

Clinton stands, breathing heavily, waiting for her to respond, but she is stunned silent, and instead of speaking, she wipes at her eyes.

"And you aren't going to fuck the love we have away," he

continues, and I gasp softly and step closer into Ellis. Damn, he is pissed.

Blair shakes her head. "I didn't. I promise. I would never do that, Clinton."

"No shit," Clinton says as he smiles angrily and shakes his head at the ground. "I know you wouldn't. And I know you didn't. I mean, fuck. I stayed up all night with my ear to the damn crack at the bottom of your door. It is no wonder I even made it to this interview today."

"You did that?" Blair says.

"Are you kidding, Blair? Do you really think I would let the woman I love go out with a random dude and not keep my eye on her? I stalked you all night on the Find-My-Phone app then when you got home, I moved to the floor."

"I can't believe you did that."

He steps forward and this time speaks through gritted teeth. "Believe this, Blair. If I had seen his shoes get within two feet of you in that bedroom, he would have..." Clinton closes his eyes and shakes his head as if pushing back the image playing in his mind.

"I'm sorry, Clinton," Blair says. "I am just so sorry."

"Are you, Blair?" he says as his eyes open. They are laced with hurt and anger.

"I am."

"Well, then stop this shit and let me love you!" Clinton raises his voice again.

Blair stands motionless except the nodding of her head.

He pauses and takes a deep breath, regaining his composure. "Come here," he says firmly, extending his hands. Without hesitation, Blair steps forward submissively and wraps her arms around him. He exhales deeply and lets his arms fall around her.

"No more," she says into his chest. "I promise."

After a moment, he steps back and looks down, still holding

her hands. "I am going to go to law school here," Clinton says. "And you and I are going to stay together, and as far as I am concerned, I never want to be apart from you again. Okay?"

"Okay," she says sniffling. She then looks around. "But what about the interview? Did I mess that up?"

He shakes his head. "No, dingdong. This was a formality. I am in. I start in August."

Blair doesn't respond but instead jumps back towards him and holds him tightly as she sobs into his chest.

"Hush," he says into her hair.

At this point, Red takes a quiet step away. "I think we should give them some space, y'all. Clinton can bring her home."

"Good idea," Ellis says softly then raises his hand towards Clinton, a silent wave that after a moment, Clinton notices and mimics back.

As Ellis shifts back towards Red, he turns and reaches back to take my hand. It's a small gesture that doesn't go unnoticed by Red, who winks over her trademark toothy grin.

After only a few steps, I feel my phone vibrate in my pocket. I keep smiling as I walk forward, but just as I get to the car, the weight of uncertainty gets to me, and I pull it out and swipe up.

Looking back at me are two simple words below an image of my truck:

Nick: Bingo!

CHAPTER 33

THE RIDE BACK to Dave's flashes by in what feels like an instant as memories of trauma flood my mind. Images of my bed and the sterile white walls of Nick's apartment are coupled with the memories of his soft-spoken threats and of his throwing pillows and food. During the flashbacks, I must have fallen asleep because the next thing I hear is Ellis's voice.

"Okay, sleepyhead," he says. "We are back."

I don't open my eyes immediately, but when I do, Ellis knows something is wrong. I avoid eye contact with him and instead look towards Noah and Red, who have already headed inside.

I silently exit the car and walk around its front towards the house, stopping as Ellis walks to my side and turns towards me as if waiting.

I take one steadying breath then speak. "He's here."

Ellis tilts his head. "Who's here?"

"*He* is. Nick."

Nick's name hits Ellis like a jolt of lightning, and he instantly responds. "At Dave's?" he says as he darts forward and looks around me as if gearing up to fight. "Are you sure?"

I don't respond but instead pull up the text from my phone and pass it to him.

He glances down at it then calmly nods as he takes a steadying breath. He then looks back towards me just as tears begin to stream from my face. He steps forward and takes my hand in his. "I got you, Glory. I got you."

"He's going to kill me."

"He's not going to kill you, Glory. That guy is a coward."

"What am I going to do?"

"Glory. We are going to handle this."

"How?"

Ellis pulls out his phone and speaks into his phone. "Code red. Send."

I wipe at my eyes, which dart side to side. "What are you doing?"

Ellis puts his phone in his pocket then steps towards me and wraps his loose hand around my back. "Glory, do you really think I won't protect you? I knew that bastard would show up eventually, and we have planned for it."

I haven't said anything about Nick to anyone else at Dave's, so his comment throws me off. Did he tell the others about my bruises and the abuse? Do they know about Nick?

"What do the others know about Nick?" I ask directly.

Ellis takes a deep breath then lets his hand fall from me. He steps away then looks at me from the side, as if debating what to say next. He clearly realizes what my question implies: Ellis broke his promise to me.

"Glory, I know what you are thinking."

"Do they know that he hit me?"

He shakes his head. "No. I didn't tell them that." He bites his lip as he watches for my reaction. A flash of anger highlights his face. I know Nick's abuse makes him uncomfortable.

I exhale in relief. "Okay. Thank you for not telling them. I step forward and brush my hand on his arm. "What do they know?"

Ellis rolls his head. "Well, I just asked everyone to be on the lookout for him. That he was your…*ex*…and having a hard time moving on."

"That's okay," I say, "I guess."

But as I give him my assurance, a wave of guilt crashes into me. I had never wanted anyone at Dave's to be dragged into my drama, especially Ellis. But now, even though they don't know the details, everyone is involved. I need to take control of the situation, so no one gets hurt.

"Please call off the *code red*. I'll handle it, Ellis. I don't want you—"

"What?" he interrupts as he steps towards me.

"Just please don't worry about Nick. I don't want you all to have to deal with my drama. It's not fair. I will—"

"No," Ellis says firmly, and I'm caught off-guard by his rebuttal. "You might not realize this, but I would risk everything for you."

"You can't."

"You do not have to do this alone anymore."

"I know but—"

"I should have already taken care of it. I have wanted to deal with this guy…" he pauses as if choosing his words wisely, "since I found out what he did to you. Since I saw you covered in all those damn bruises." He lifts a fist to his mouth and bites it harshly. He starts swaying with his head down as if not knowing his next move, his fury bubbling over, but then he pauses and looks up. I recoil at the sight of his eyes, moistened by emotion. "I promise you that I am going to take care of Nick."

What does he mean *take care of Nick*? I step forward and take his hands in mine, trying to calm him. As I do, he looks away. "Stop. You can't do anything that might impact your future. I can't let you do that. Please don't—"

"You," he says as he turns his head back towards me. "You, Glory."

"Me?"

"You are my future."

I shake my head instantly. No. I can't be his future. "Why? You didn't even know me a couple months ago, and now—"

Ellis leans in and looks so deeply into my eyes that I can see little flecks of brilliant white along the edges of stormy gray irises. "You don't have to hide anymore. Not from him. Not from yourself. I'm here now." He leans forward and rests his forehead on mine. "You are brave. You are fierce. I see you now, even if you can't see yourself."

I start to object but a booming shout comes from the back of the house.

"Ellis!"

I look over and see Dave marching over, Noah in tow. "What's the situation?"

Ellis steps back. "Nick is here. He texted her a picture of her car, in *our* parking lot. He's a sneaky rat, so we all need to be on high alert."

Dave stops by Ellis. "Amber just called Graham. He has put out an alert for his BMW. She is also circulating a picture."

"How do you know what kind of car he drives?" I ask Ellis.

He winks towards me then nods to Noah. "Big guy, can you move the truck for her?"

"Done," Noah says as he steps forward. "Glory, I will go get the keys and check your place, just to be safe."

"Okay," I say. "They are on the counter." I look back towards Ellis. "Do you think he is in the house?"

Ellis shakes his head. "No."

Dave looks my way, his face etched with sympathy. "He might be a twisted dude, Glory," Dave says, "but he doesn't appear to be stupid."

I nod in agreement even though I cringe internally knowing Nick's obsession with me knows no boundary.

Just then, Dave's phone rings. He picks it up and walks a few feet away, where he proceeds to speak in a hushed tone. Ellis and

I watch for a minute in silence. As we do, he reaches around me and rubs my back gently. I lean into his touch.

"Got 'em," Noah says a moment later as I see him turn the corner towards the driveway. "I will park it along the back of the storage shed. No one will ever know it is there."

"Thanks, Noah," I say.

"No problem. Your place is clear too."

"I hope that fucker shows up while you are moving it," Ellis says through gritted teeth as he stares forward blankly.

"Me too, brother," Noah replies as he walks over and pats Ellis's back then turns towards the resort.

Ellis watches Noah jog away then looks over towards me. He bites his lip then shakes his head apologetically. "Sorry. I shouldn't talk like that. I don't want to scare you."

"It's okay," I say, but the truth is, I am scared. I'm scared that he will show up, hit me, or maybe worse. But even more so, I am scared for Ellis, and Noah, and for everyone at Dave's. I don't think I could live with myself if something were to happen to one of them. What if they get in a fight and get hurt, or what if they hurt Nick and get arrested and are put in jail for years? I reach up and squeeze my temples as the anxiety bubbles up. I need to do something about this before someone gets hurt.

"It's alright, Glory. I won't let—"

"Clinton is back," Dave unintentionally interrupts as he drops the phone from his ear and puts it back in his pocket.

I lower my hands and look over just as Clinton's truck comes to a stop in the driveway. The slow gate closing behind him makes a gentle hum against the silence.

He and Blair get out of the car and walk towards us. "What's up? Did he show up?"

"Yeah," Ellis says, flatly.

"What a twat," Blair says. "I can't wait to beat the shit out of this guy."

Clinton looks towards Blair. "Easy, killer."

"He sent Glory a text of her truck in the parking lot."

"Motherfucker," Blair says as she walks over and squeezes my side. "Hang in there girl."

"Thanks," I say as I watch Clinton and Ellis walk towards Noah. Ellis looks over and forces a smile then they walk towards the front gate. I don't know what they are discussing, but it can't be good.

"Red!" I hear Blair shout, and my head darts back towards the back of the house.

"Hey, babe," Red says then steps towards us. "I brought backup."

I start to ask what she means but then see the backup. Charlie appears at the path leading to the resort. He walks as if on a mission with his typical brown shirt tucked into a pair of camo pants. But as he comes closer, my eyes widen. On his back is a large rifle. I stare at it for a solid minute with mixed emotions. Everything from shame to pride to happiness flash as I watch Charlie show up to protect me. My attention is only drawn away when JJ shows up.

"I'll take this bitch!" JJ shouts as he walks in smugly. "Let's go! Where is he?"

Dave looks over his shoulder and rolls his eyes.

"Over here, man," Ellis says as he motions for JJ to join in on the boys' hushed conversation. Even Blair is surprised by the invitation.

"I guess they will enlist any ol' dumbass," she says as she turns towards me.

"Enlist for what?" I ask.

Red shrugs. "I guess they are planning to comb the place and set up lookouts."

I shake my head. "They can't do that. They have guests and stuff to do. They have lives."

Red reaches over and touches my side. "I know you think this is extreme, and I get it. But if you want my honest opinion, I think you should just let him do this."

"Yeah, he's needed to do this," Blair adds, then bites her lip. "I just pray this guy gets the fuck out of town before it's too late. This ain't Tennessee. Those boys know everyone, and he's going to be eaten alive if he hangs around here."

"True," Red says as she shrugs in agreement.

"We need to go eat something," Blair says. "I am starved, and we can't just stand around on the damn driveway all day. Let's tell the boys we are going to the bar. Charlie can escort us with his big ass gun."

Red nods then looks towards me. "Hungry?"

Though my nerves have killed my appetite, I nod as an opportunity presents itself, an opportunity for me to *fix* the mess I have got everyone into.

"Sure," I say, careful not to sound too upbeat. "But I am going to run to the bathroom first."

"Okay, Red says. "We will sort out the details with the crew."

"Okay, thanks," I say then turn and walk back towards the house. As I do, Ellis, on high alert, jolts to the side and looks towards me. He holds up his hand and makes an okay gesture. I return the hand sign then point to the house and mouth the word bathroom. He nods, so I continue inside. Getting away from everyone is going to be tricky, but the first thing I need to do is call Nick.

I waste no time as I turn the corner around the back of the house.

"Well, well, well," Nick says when he picks up my call. "I thought you might be calling me today. I guess I was right again."

I take a calming breath as I step inside the back of the house.

"I am not coming back, Nick. I told you. It is over."

"It is over, *Glory*, when I say it is over."

I pause as his words sink in. Is he even willing to let me go? Maybe if it is on his terms and not mine, he will leave me alone. Maybe his ego just can't take that I was the one who broke up with him, and not the other way around. I might be able to play that angle.

I close my eyes and take a brave leap of faith. "Meet me somewhere. Let's talk about it."

"Meet you?"

"Yeah."

"How about I just come there and pick you up. Maybe that new man of yours would like that."

"I don't have a new man, Nick," I say, but he laughs in response.

"Yeah right. That bum is just trying to get into your panties."

"Where do you want to meet?" I ask defiantly, ignoring him.

"Well, you are the one who knows this place. Where should we meet?"

"Nick, I have been here for a month. Just pick a place."

"Interesting," Nick says then exhales. "Well, what about my place. I have a hotel in the area. Maybe we can work something out. Maybe you can give me that sweet ass that I've been after. You have been playing hard to get long enough, don't you think?"

"*Nick*. Come on," I say. "I am trying to figure this out."

"Fine, Glory," Nick says, laughing. "What about Betty's Coffee Shop about ten minutes from you?"

"Fine," I say. "When?"

"You tell me, princess. You are the one who called me. This is *your* date."

I cringe at the word *date*. "I will be there in thirty minutes."

I start to hang up then he speaks again. "I know you might think you are someone else now, someone brave, but you better think again before you try to play me."

"What do you mean?"

"Oh, you know what I mean. Don't play dumb with me."

"I'm not, Nick."

"And you don't want to fuck this opportunity up by inviting your friends. That won't make me happy."

Though it hadn't crossed my mind to invite Ellis or any of the others, I can see why he might be concerned that this is a trap.

"I won't, Nick."

"If any of those losers show their face, you will regret it."

"It will just be me, Nick."

"It better be," he says, then after a moment, the line goes dead as he exercises control over the conversation.

My heart thumps frantically in my chest, and I lay a hand flat there to still the adrenaline flowing through my veins. I had forgotten how exhausting it was to have a conversation with him. I drop the phone into my pocket then reach out for something to hold onto, wobbling slightly as my hand only meets air.

"You got this, Glory," I say as I take a few deep breaths. This is the right decision. I can't risk Ellis or any of the others thinking that something is up.

I turn the corner and keep my head down as I walk towards the girls.

"Okay. I'm ready."

"Awesome," Red says then she and Blair turn and follow as I lead them over to the boys. When we approach, they quit speaking.

"What's up?"

"We are going to grab a bite at the bar," Red says.

Ellis starts to object but stops as Blair holds up her hand. "We thought maybe Charlie could go with us. Ellis pauses then looks over his shoulder towards Charlie, who has heard his name and is looking curiously our way.

"What we got?" Charlie says as he walks to Blair's side.

"Would you mind taking the girls to grab a bite at the Hut? I don't want them going alone."

"10-4. I am on it." He steps around Ellis and nods towards Red and me. "I've got you covered, ladies. I'll back you up. Just lead the way."

"Thanks, Charlie," Red says as she takes my hand, and we walk back towards the resort.

Just as I turn around the landmark palmettos lining the back path, I look towards Ellis. He is watching intently as if looking for someone.

Chapter 34

It turns out sneaking off isn't as hard physically as I had imagined. But emotionally, as I open the bathroom door just off the back of the Hut and look cautiously to the right towards where Blair and Red are sitting, I hesitate. I don't want to worry them, though I know that there isn't much I can do or say to alleviate their worry. They would never let me go meet Nick without alerting the boys, and even if there is a chance of fixing this without involving any of my friends any further, I need to try. Plus, I will be in a public place. Nick won't try anything around other people.

By the time I hop into the truck, which Noah had carefully parked behind the shed, and drive to Betty's, I arrive with ten minutes to spare. Nick's BMW is already in the parking lot, so I know he is there waiting for me impatiently.

I reach into my pocket and power down my phone. I need my wits about me and can't afford to be distracted by texts or calls that I know will come once the boys find out I have skipped out.

I step out of the truck and take a steadying breath. "Be brave," I hear someone say then realize after a moment they are my own words.

The door chimes as I walk into Betty's, and I see him immediately, sitting with his back to the door. Nick is hard to miss with his jet-black hair slicked back perfectly into a side part. I hesitate again but my legs seem to walk forward on their own.

Be brave.

The voice echoes in my mind as I slide into the booth directly across from him and look up. He is staring down into a cup of black coffee, stirring the spoon methodically, back and forth, back and forth. "Took you long enough," he says without looking up.

I glance over to an old wall clock, a Coca-Cola bottle at its center. "I'm five minutes early."

He looks up and forces a smile. "Cute. Mouthy, but cute."

The server walks over, pen and pad in hand. She has a bright blue diner dress on and even has one of those white head-wraps like you would see at a fifty's diner. She's an older lady and clearly lacks patience. My mind thinks back to the lady at the front desk back at UT who had similar glasses. "Pancakes?" she asks me, putting one brow up.

"She'll have a water," Nick says before I can answer, and the lady looks over to him coldly before forcing a smile. As she walks back to the kitchen, I see her look sideways towards me in her periphery. I imagine what she wonders about our situation. I imagine that she would see me as a dumb, weak girlfriend without a mind of her own.

"Well look at you, Glory, or are you even going by that name anymore?"

"What are you talking about?" I ask.

"Well, you just look like a different person. Next thing I know, you will be bleaching your hair blonde and wearing floral dresses."

"Come on, Nick, I would—"

His finger snaps up in front of me as he leans forward, one side of his mouth turned up menacingly. "I have spent a lot of time on you. I have invested in your ass and deserve the reward."

"I am not some reward."

He ignores me as he continues. "You would have rotted up there without me. That dumbass mom of yours wanted nothing to do with you, always up Cliff's ass. She was so quick to pawn you off on me. All I had to do was smile and say, 'Yes, Ma'am.'"

I close my eyes trying to recall those moments, and as flashes of memory flicker against my closed lashes, I find it difficult. I know there are times when Nick had been kind, such as bringing me food to work, helping me move, or sitting outside with me on the bench at the park. But those memories are fragmented and few and far between. The most vivid memories are those where he threatened to hurt me if I didn't keep my mouth shut, or if I didn't do or say exactly what he wanted. Then there's the push. He was so mad about…something. It's funny how trauma clouds your memory.

"What will it take for you to leave me alone?" I say suddenly without thinking as I sit up straighter and lean forward over the table. The outburst of bravery catches me off-guard, and a moment later, I find myself shrinking back into my seat.

"What do you mean leave you alone? You told me that you would tell."

I sit up and my head tilts to the side. "What? I never told you I would tell on you."

"What the fuck, Glory?"

"I wouldn't tell on you. I just don't want to be with you, Nick. I'm sorry. I just never—"

"After all I did for you, you decide to threaten me? You brought this on yourself."

"What are you talking about?" I say. "How would I threaten you?"

He shakes his head, ignoring me. "Then you leave a note for me and skip town."

"I don't want to be with you, Nick," I say, ignoring his comments. "It didn't work out."

"They all said you were a nut job now and—" He pauses midsentence and cocks his head. He leans in then after a moment begins to laugh. It's a hysterical laugh that is so out of place, that it draws the attention of the server who looks over curiously. "Wait a minute." He holds up a finger then snickers loudly.

"Nick, *please*. Please keep it down."

He shakes his head and holds up a hand. "Okay, okay. Sorry. This is just too funny."

"What is funny about this?"

He throws a hand my way. "You are fucking crazy."

"I'm crazy?"

He shakes his head and takes a sip of coffee then looks around as if anticipating being jumped. "You just don't get it, do you?"

"Just leave, Nick. I won't say anything about the stairs."

"The stairs?"

"Yes. I won't tell anyone," I pause and look around before finishing in a hushed tone, "that you pushed me down those stairs."

He begins laughing again. "You think that I care about stairs? You think that I would come all the way down here because of that?"

I am silent for a moment then nod. "I'm not going to tell."

"I don't care if anyone finds out you fell down some stairs, dumbass."

I start to object then bite back my instinct to argue.

"You think they are going to listen to some nut?"

"Then why are you here? And don't tell me it is because of love. You don't beat someone you love." I spit out the words and start to stand, a mysterious fury burning inside.

Nick flinches as I say the word beat, and he shakes his head and tenses as if he is about to pounce across the table. But I don't back down. Suddenly, I feel empowered to stand my ground, like someone is giving me strength. Someone much stronger than me.

Be strong.

The words are not my own, but someone else's. They are Cora's. Her spirit is here. A cold chill races across my skin.

His eyes dart around, remembering that he is in a public setting, then he looks back towards me as he lowers himself in his seat. Only then, I lean back, even though a rush of adrenaline courses through my veins. I eye the knife sitting in front of me, which Nick notices. His strong-guy image falters for a moment, which further empowers me.

I lower my voice and do something that reminds me oddly of Blair. I smile. "I don't love you, Nick. I never wanted anything to do with you. You are an abusive creep, and if you ever come at me again, I will cut off your balls."

"You wouldn't do—"

"And you might not care about me going to the police for the stairs, but," I stop and feel my face twist and pointedly wink in his direction. It is so out of character for me that I smile as I continue. "We will all hunt you down, and they will never find your body. The sharks will love your fatty ass."

Nick's face turns red and for a moment, I expect him to reach forward and strike me, but as I wait, nothing happens. Instead, the coward shrinks back into his seat and bites his lip as he looks around. By this time, the others in Betty's have noticed us, and the tension is palpable.

He shakes his head then leans forward and takes a noisy sip of coffee before looking back up. As he does, he exhales and shakes his head as if in defeat. "Maybe you don't. And maybe I don't love you either. I've never been fond of whores." He forces a laugh to himself then continues. "But I have spent a lot of time dealing with you. Ever since I saw you at that party. Hell, I wouldn't have even been in this situation had I not—" he pauses as if catching himself.

Could it really be this easy? Will Nick just agree to leave? Did it just take me standing up to him? And who was that person? I am suddenly so proud of my bravery that I must be beaming. Maybe now that he sees that I am not leaving and that I won't tell anyone about the abuse, and that I am willing to fight back, he believes cutting his losses is his best bet.

"Let's just agree to part ways and pretend this never happened," I say.

"Never happened?" he asks then cocks his head. "Really?"

"Really."

"You can do that?"

"Yes."

He sits for a moment then sighs. "You know, Glory, you could have had a good life with me. I would have taken care of you. I will have so much money one day."

I don't respond but just let him say his piece, hopeful that by letting him do so, he will accept our fate.

"Fuck. You are like talking to a brick wall."

"Please, Nick." I think about his ego and lean in for the kill, true mind-fuckery. "I am at your mercy."

Hi eyes light up, and he sits forward. "I know you are."

"Please, Nick," I say again.

"That's the sound I want to hear," he says as he closes his eyes and nods, smiling.

I sit quietly for a moment then he opens his eyes and nods. "Okay, Glory."

I don't want to be over enthusiastic, so I just nod politely, even though my mind is screaming in celebration.

"Okay, Glory," he echoes. "But remember that it was me who ended it. Not you. *Me*. Do you understand?" He leans in and places both hands on the table.

"I will, Nick. I promise that I will."

Nick looks at me for a moment, and I look away submissively before looking back. As I do, he stands.

"I'm out of here." He starts to turn towards the door then stops and reaches into his pocket. He fumbles in it for a moment then pulls out a crumbled up red flower. He gently places it in front of me on the table.

The flower is so symbolic of our relationship. "Hibiscus rosa-sinensis," I say then reach out and touch it gently.

After a moment, I look up just as the door swings closed behind Nick. And with that, he disappears completely from my life.

Chapter 35

As soon as I pull into the parking lot at Dave's, he spots me. We stare at each other for a moment, and I watch him as he yells over his shoulder towards someone off to his right behind a line of trees. He looks back at me, then bends down with his hands on his knees and leans forward, like he's catching his breath after a marathon.

I step out of the truck then walk to its front, where I stand and watch him approach me slowly. He is upset, his face a dull red and eyes pulled low at sharp angles.

"I'm sorry. I just needed to—"

"What the hell happened to you?" His voice is laced with disappointment. "You just disappeared."

"I'm sorry. I had to."

"I thought maybe you went back to Tennessee with him, or that…that you were dead." He reaches up and rubs at his eyes with the back of his hand.

"I'm sorry."

"We had everyone out looking for you."

"I know."

"You just left."

"I know," I repeat.

"You know? Why did you leave? I mean, you just left." I start to speak but he continues. "You didn't think about how that would affect us, affect me?" He points harshly into his chest. "I thought I lost you."

I step forward and reach out towards him, but he pulls away. "I'm sorry. I just couldn't let you get dragged into my mess with Nick."

"Mess?" he says then steps towards me. "What do you mean your mess?"

"You and the others barely know me, Ellis, so how could I just let you all get pulled into a potentially dangerous situation with my ex? It wouldn't be fair. What if something happened to you?"

"To me?" he says incredulously. "What about *you?*"

"I needed to go take care of it, so you all wouldn't worry. I didn't want it to disrupt your…life." I swallow a lump in my throat and fight back tears that are growing heavy beneath my lids.

He takes a deep breath and rubs both hands across his face. "I can't do this. I can't keep pretending."

"Pretending what?" I say then step towards him, but he recoils, holding both hands high. I've hurt Ellis, probably every-one at Dave's, and even though I feel it was the right thing to do, I must face the consequences of my sneaking off.

Ellis takes a few steadying breaths then looks up and shakes his head. "What did you think you would be able to do? That guy is fucking crazy, Glory."

I straighten and my brows lift high. "I met him."

"You did what?" Ellis says as he lets his mouth fall open.

"I texted him and met him at Betty's up the road. I met him to tell him to leave me alone and that I wouldn't be getting back together with him."

"Are you serious?" Ellis says as his face grows pale. "Please tell me you didn't actually see him."

"I had to, Ellis. It was—"

"No. You didn't need to meet him. It was dangerous."

"But it worked out," I say quickly before he continues.

He looks at me as if dumbfounded, shaking his head in disbelief. "Worked out how?"

"Well, we met, and I told him that we weren't getting back together, and I stood up to him."

"You stood up to him how?"

"I don't really know how. I was sitting there listening to him talk and something just came over me. I became brave, like a different person."

"Like a different person?"

"Yeah. I was…brave. And he was caught off-guard, and I think I scared him."

"Scared how?"

"I just told him I would cut his balls off."

Ellis coughs a bit then composes himself. He starts to smile but stops before he does, clearly remembering that he is angry with me.

"He said he was leaving Florida."

"And you believe him, Glory? Seriously?" He says it as if I am naïve, and it makes me feel like a child. I suddenly fold my arms across my midsection and take a step back.

"I do, Ellis. I'm not an idiot."

"I didn't say you—"

"Why can't you be happy for me?"

He shakes his head and holds up his hands. "I just can't right now with you."

"I don't need you to save me, Ellis," I bark back.

"I just want to—"

"Glory!" I hear someone scream, looking over to the noise to see Red running towards us. "Oh, girl, we thought something happened to you."

Red comes over to me and hugs me tightly. No judgement, just pure joy that I am okay.

"I'm fine," I say as I stare daggers over her shoulder at Ellis, whose eyes look back, narrow and cold.

"She worked it out," Ellis says flatly, without breaking his gaze.

Red steps back and looks between us. "Worked out what?" Red asks, searching for an explanation.

"Why don't you ask her?" Ellis replies coldly then turns and walks slowly away. As he gets to the tree line, Blair emerges and walks our way. She stops briefly as Ellis says something to her then turns back towards us, her eyebrows high, an indicator of his mood.

"Dang, girl," Blair says, as she approaches. "And I thought I was in trouble with Clinton. Ellis is super pissed."

"Blair, stop," Red says then turns back towards me. "He was just worried."

"I know," I say as I look down and fidget with my hands. "I'm sorry that I scared him. I'm sorry that I scared all of you."

"It's okay," Red says, reaching out and rubbing my back.

"I just had to go." I shrug in surrender. "I had no choice."

"So, where did you go exactly?" Red asks.

"I went to meet Nick, my ex-boyfriend."

The girls' eyes widen, and Blair opens her mouth, but she finds no words.

"I know," I say. "I wanted to work out the situation, so you all didn't have to deal with it." A tear glides down my cheek, so I quickly turn and wipe it away.

"Glory, you don't have to protect us," Red says.

"We want to help you," Blair adds. "Ellis told us that this guy might show up, so we have been ready to—"

"I know," I blurt out, "but this guy is…dangerous."

The girls exchange a look of concern, speaking between each

other silently as they do. Blair turns back towards me, her face suddenly void of humor. "What do you mean dangerous?"

I'm not sure if it is because I have had no one other than Ellis to talk to about Nick and the abuse, or if it is because I feel so close to Blair and Red, but as I begin describing Nick, the words flow effortlessly.

"I remember him bringing me meals to the apartment and checking in on me. I didn't have many friends, except for some of the nurses that I worked with at the urgent care. I did have some girlfriends once, but I think Nick must have driven them away."

I look up and see Blair biting her lower lip. She steps towards me and extends a hand to both Red and me. We each take one as I continue.

"I don't remember when it all started, but I do remember a slap. Maybe it was when we were moving. I don't remember. But he would yell at me or call me names. He seemed to get angrier and angrier with each passing day."

"Did you tell anyone?" Red asks.

"Who would I have told? My mom wasn't around, and I didn't want to get my coworkers involved. I kept telling myself that I would finish school then get away from him."

"Is that why you are here?" Blair asks. "Were you trying to escape from him?"

I don't respond but look up and nod.

"I'm so sorry you were so alone," Red says. "I just wish…"

"I was. Until I got here. Ellis was…difficult at first, but then the boat happened."

"The boat?" Red asks, and she and Blair exchange a look of confusion.

"I was playing with a dolphin, and Ellis saw." I pause and take a steadying breath. "Ellis saw the bruises."

"The bruises?" Blair says and Red moves to sit by my side. "What do you mean *bruises?*"

I look up and tears roll down my cheeks as I continue. "The night before I left, he got so mad. I don't even remember what it was about. I just remember we were arguing about something. I think maybe I was standing up to him. But something set him off, and he pushed me down a flight of stairs at the apartment."

"Oh my God," Red says.

I look over to Blair who is biting her bottom lip so hard, I can see it brighten red along the edge, a red that matches her sudden crimson color.

"That son-of-a-bitch," she says as she walks back and forth.

"Calm down, Blair," Red says, "She doesn't need us to get worked up."

"Calm down my ass," she replies. "I hope to God he—"

"Please," Red urges, and Blair just holds up her hands in surrender. She stops pacing and takes a deep breath. "Sorry. Go on, Glory."

"I don't think I fully passed out after the fall. But I do remember going in and out of consciousness, and the pain. My entire body hurt."

"What happened to Nick?"

"I remember him bringing me to the couch, our couch, I think. Then, when I woke up, I gathered everything of mine I could find and left. I was lucky my truck was there."

"Thank the Lord for your truck, Glory," Blair says. "A woman needs to be independent and have her own transportation. This is a perfect example why."

"Then I went to withdraw from school and once I did, I headed down here."

Red and Blair exchange a knowing look. "And we are so happy you did," Red says.

"So, what happened with Nick?" Blair asks, and I genuinely smile as I remember that he is gone from my life.

"He's gone back to Tennessee. I met him and told him that

I would never get back with him." A small laugh escapes as I continue. "I actually stood up to him."

Red nods and forces a smile, "Good for you, Glory."

"I'm proud of you, girl," Blair adds.

"And you feel pretty sure that he's gone?" Red asks, and I nod back in response.

"I do. I really do." I laugh again as happiness radiates through me. "I just want to—"

I stop speaking suddenly and stand as my head darts to the side. Red and Blair suddenly stiffen and become alert as I move silently around them and stare towards one of those beautiful iron lanterns just off to our left.

"What is it, Glory?" Blair says as her head mirrors Red's, searching for what startled me.

After a moment, I turn back towards them and force a smile. "It was nothing. I'm just a little jumpy tonight."

Red nods but her eyes flicker towards the area a few more times before finally settling on me.

"Well, it's been an eventful day," Red says finally. "What if we go back to our apartment, put on a movie, and take a nap on the couch?"

"Works for me," Blair says, "but Clinton and I do have a hot date tonight. I plan on getting some of that pre-law di—"

"No, Blair," Red interrupts, and Blair shrugs as she flutters her eyelashes dramatically. "What about you, Glory?"

"Sounds good," I say. I don't want to go back to my place too early, and I feel like I need to give Ellis his space.

"Well then, let's kick it ladies," Blair says.

As I stand, a surge of vertigo catches me by surprise, and I reach out and lay my hand on the back of the bench. No one seems to notice, which I am thankful for. I have already caused them enough distress today, and I don't want them to be concerned about a dizzy spell.

Red extends a hand towards me, and I reach forward and use the opportunity to steady myself without causing much notice. After a few steps forward, the vertigo subsides and is replaced by a dull throbbing in my head.

As we walk together, my hand in Red's, I can't help but feel different, like something has shifted between Red, Blair, and me. Perhaps the tension that I have held since being here has lessened with Nick no longer in the picture, or perhaps it is because I have opened up to them about the abuse. But whatever it is, I feel changed, more confident…more myself.

There is just one problem. Something is still very wrong with me. I have tried over the past weeks to explain away Cora and that no one seems to know my name at the University of Tennessee. I have even put it so far in the back of my mind that it's often not even on my mind at all. But that's the problem. Though I don't want to think about it, someone else is not having it.

Just before I turn down the path beyond the tree line, I look back towards the lantern once more. And though I can no longer see the face of Jane staring back at me, a residual cobalt blue light still reflects across the swaying palmettos.

CHAPTER 36

THE NEXT FEW days fly by as I put my head down and focus on work. It's a welcome distraction from everything. I didn't go to Ellis's after the movie night with the girls, and every night since, I have stayed at my place. It was a simple decision because Ellis is missing. He's not missing in the sense that people are concerned. Actually, the next morning, Dave announced to all of us that Ellis would be gone for a few days. I'm not sure where he went, but I know all this has taken an emotional toll on him, and I don't blame him for wanting to get away from this, from me. Between his feelings for me, his grieving the loss of Jane, and now, my disappearing to confront Nick, I imagine Ellis has a lot to work through.

Each passing day, I feel more and more relaxed and comfortable in my position, and others are noticing. Noah and Red joked with me one morning about being the Captain for the day on Seahorse I, and even JJ has asked me questions about various things, such as equipment care or navigation. He even asked me for his opinion on which flowers to send to his long-distance girlfriend, wanting something non-traditional and perfect for a "gamer girl."

I don't see the spirit of Jane again, and though I am still trying to figure out how all the pieces fit together, I push that to the back of my mind and just enjoy the peace of not having

Nick in my life. There's also a confidence that comes back to me surprisingly fast, as if Nick was somehow preventing me from moving forward…from healing.

Ellis returns on the fourth day, a Monday, but I don't see him at first. I just know he has returned when I walk into the bathroom that morning and a rush of steam, scented with his deodorant, collides into my face. At first, my heart pumps wildly in my chest at the thought of him holding me in his arms once more, but that quickly subsides as I remember why he left in the first place.

I skip the porch that morning. Maybe it is for fear that I will see him, or maybe because I don't want to have a conversation with the others about his return, but when I walk into the office and learn he has already left with Clinton to lead an early morning check-out dive, I find myself wildly disappointed.

"Okay, girls," Red says, "It's us today for the afternoon dive."

We spend the morning going through inventory and helping Amber with the condos. They are trying to update the curtains, so Blair and I offered to pitch in with hanging them.

I keep myself busy with my work, as I had done the prior days, but when the afternoon guests arrive, and Ellis and Clinton have not returned, I find myself disappointed again.

The afternoon dive is uneventful and flies by. I don't get into water, instead choosing to man the helm. It's a welcome opportunity for me to go through charts and read through a study manual Clinton had given me 'just in case' I wanted to get licensed to Captain the ship sometime in the future.

When we return, Blair is excited for her date with Clinton. Over the past few days, they have been inseparable, and for the first time since my arrival, the tension between them has vanished, and they have both leaned into Clinton attending the University of Miami.

"Where are y'all going tonight?" Red asks as she closes the lid of one of the storage cabinets behind the office.

"He was invited to dinner with one of his professors, a criminal law professor, I think."

"Well, look at you," Red says, "and here you are, a criminal who has stolen his heart."

Blair shakes her head, a look of disgust on her face. "Please do not ever say that again."

I laugh. "How can that be worse than the *burning loins* in those romance books?"

"Not you too," Blair says then turns and begins jogging away. "I'm off to get ready, ladies. Enjoy work, Red!"

"You are covering?"

"Yeah, Ellis and I are at the bar tonight."

"Fun," I say then fidget with a knot in one of our mesh bags.

Red stands and I see her lean towards me in her periphery. "Don't worry."

My eyes dart towards her. "I don't know what you could be talking about."

"Oh, Glory, Glory."

"What?"

"It will be okay. He's just having a moment."

I nod without responding, so she continues.

"I don't want to get involved, but I need you to know something."

"What?"

"You know, the night after the movie when you thought he was mad at you for sneaking off to meet Nick?"

"Yeah."

"Well, he was mad at you."

I tilt my head forward and roll my eyes. "Yeah, I know."

"Well, did you also know where he slept that night?"

I stand straighter, then cock my head to the side. "His place?"

She reaches out and lays a hand on my shoulder. "He slept in the hallway outside your door, Glory."

"What?"

"Noah almost tripped over him when he went up that night to check on him."

My mouth opens softly and a shiver races along my back and up my neck. "Are you serious?"

She steps forward and as the rays of sun dance along her freckled face, she whispers, "I won't say he loves you, because that is for him to say, but his actions scream that to everyone else in the world and always have."

I look down suddenly, and I am speechless. I'm ashamed for even questioning how he feels about me. I think back to the subtle moments. The stares of longing, the moments of concern. I think back to the lessons in the pool to make sure I knew how to be safe and the moment on the boat where he fell asleep on my lap, as if it was the only thing that could give him peace. And then I think back to the moment I met him. In that moment, I saw first a flash of anger as he thought that I was there to take Jane's place at Dave's, but for a moment, just after I stepped into the light, there was something else, something hard to place. Was it relief?

"It can't be," I say towards her.

"I know your heart is damaged, Glory. But I also know that you are healing. I want to believe that you will heal completely." She steps forward then and pulls me into a tight hug. "You got this girl," she says before stepping back.

I respond with a simple nod of gratitude. Her words resonate with me, and after we part ways on the docks, she heads straight over to the Hut.

After that conversation, I have one thing on my mind. I need to make this right. An idea forms in my mind, and though it might be a bit unusual for me, I am oddly comfortable with the necessary maneuver.

I head straight to Blair and Red's. I knock on the door, and Blair answers wrapped in a towel.

"I need something sexy," I say flatly.

A sly smile lifts the corner of her mouth, and she waves me in. "I thought you'd never ask."

So, it turns out, Blair has a superpower. She can identify what outfit to deploy to make anyone look the most appealing. Though I had raided her closet before, I hadn't really appreciated the extent of her gift until now.

As I step into the mirror's reflection wearing a tight yellow mini dress with a side slit, I'm shocked by how much I like it. Staring back at me is a reflection that I don't recognize. Instead, I see a confident, beautiful, smart, woman that wears the dress so naturally, I second guess that the reflection is my own. Blair steps to my side, donning an equally appealing dress that also has a slit, but it's a couple inches longer.

"Damn, girl!" she says. "If I were a lesbian."

I wink towards her and turn this way and that to get all the angles.

"Now this is the real you."

"You think?"

"Absolutely. You are hot and need to show that body off!"

"Thank you, Blair. I needed this."

"Well, I think I know what you are up to tonight, and if I am right, *he needs* it too." We both laugh as I nod slowly in agreement. She definitely knows what I'm up to, and fingers crossed, it works.

After leaving Blair's, I head back to my apartment to relax on the couch and play on my phone. I don't want to show up too early to the Hut and risk his being overly distracted, or worse, not interested at all. I need to get there at just the right time.

When he isn't too busy, maybe 9 or so, so I can pull him to the side and tell him how I really feel. I need to be honest about my feelings. I have been inexplicably drawn towards Ellis from the very beginning and have resisted the instalove that I felt between us. But I can't deny it any longer. And if I am right—if all of us are right—he feels the same way.

I debate stretching out on the couch but then decide the best thing to do is lay on the bed, so my dress doesn't wrinkle. I walk to my room, flip off my heels, and take a spot on my bed just as I had done so many times before. I pull out my phone and set an alarm, just in case I don't wake up, then close my eyes. The soft hum of the AC unit purrs and blows a soft breeze throughout my room. The cool, citrus scent of Dave's relaxes me to my core and within moments, I am fast asleep.

I know it's a dream immediately.

I am on a boat watching a young girl play.

"Cora Jane, my dudette, let's make sure that life vest is tight enough."

The little girl rolls her eyes then walks over to a man with tie dye board shorts and dark brown hair pulled back into a messy bun. I don't recognize him at first but as he turns towards me, I see the man is a younger version of someone I know, Dave.

"Oh, we got that fixed, my man," says a larger guy as he walks forward into view. He's a round man with a bright blue shirt on that must be a size triple XL. I look closer to the shirt, but I can't read the words.

"Well, good thing I checked, Aki my man!"

"Aki," I say out loud, but no one can see me.

"Dad!" I hear a young man shout then turn to see a boy, a bit taller than the girl, run to the side of the boat and stare down into the water. "Is it my turn yet?"

I walk to the side of the boat and look towards the water,

where a man with a short crew cut is looking back up towards his son.

"Jump on in, Ellis. I've got you."

I look up surprised as I watch the young Ellis crawl up the side of the rail then stand briefly on the edge of the boat's side before leaping in.

"Woohoo!" he cries, and I see a splash of water jet upward ten feet.

I start to speak but feel someone tap on my shoulder. I turn and am face to face with my dad. I pause and stare at him as he smiles back towards me. He looks radiant, like he's glowing, and much younger than when he died.

"Dad!" I cry and jump into his arms. I feel his embrace encircle me, and I stand there and soak in his love and an over-whelming sense of safety.

"Glory, my girl!" he says as I pull away. "Aren't you going to jump in?"

I look back over my shoulder to the edge of the boat then onward to a crystal blue water.

"I don't think I can." I look back towards him, but this time, he is older.

"Well of course you can, baby. You've done it many times before."

I shake my head. "No. I don't think that I have."

I look back towards the water, and suddenly it is rough, and in the distance, a bolt of lightning cracks.

"They need to get back on the boat," I say then look back towards my dad, but he's gone. I turn around frantically, "Dad!" I run to the side of the boat and look into the water, and in the distance, I see a younger Ellis swimming to the side of the boat, trying to escape the crashing waves.

"Ellis! Swim!" As I call out, a large wave forms behind him and pushes higher into the air. "Hurry! Ellis!"

A cold rain hits my face, and I pull myself onto the side of the boat ready to leap. I pull both legs over the rail, stand high, then jump into the water towards Ellis. As I do, cold water hits my face.

"Time to get up," I hear someone whisper, and I bolt upright in the bed. The room is dark, but in the corner, illuminated by the orange light of the lamp, Nick stands watching over me.

"I told you that one day you would wake up and I would be here."

Chapter 37

"Nick," I say, my eyes darting around for an escape, but there is no way out.

"I wouldn't scream," Nick says as he reaches into his pocket and pulls out a knife that he flicks open. "Unless you want someone to get hurt."

My hands start to shake, and I slide to the edge of the bed. "You said that you were leaving. You said that you were—"

"You are an idiot, Glory. You know that I can't just let you go to the authorities. My parents will kill me, and my future will be over."

"I told you, Nick, that I wouldn't say anything."

"Yeah right. Maybe I would have believed it but come on. Who knows the scientific name of a plant?"

"What are you talking about?"

"At first you had me convinced. I thought for sure that fall had taken care of you for good, but nah, that was just bullshit, wasn't it?"

"What do you mean?"

He steps forward and grabs my hair, pulling me upright. A jolt of pain radiates across my scalp, and I can feel a trickle of warm liquid along my left ear. "Get your ass in here," he says as he steers me up and through my door to the small table in the living room. He throws me toward the couch and my snack bowl crashes to the floor. "Sit."

I move slowly and take a seat at the edge of the couch. I need to be ready to bolt or move without notice if he lunges for me again. I look around the room for anything that I can use as a weapon but only see a small pill bottle sitting on the table in front of me. It wasn't there before.

"Hibiscus rosa-sinensis," he says.

"What?"

"At first, I thought you were a goner. I was surprised when I saw you, and you looked like you would pull through. But then, you got better and better. Then *she* showed up."

"Who showed up?"

"It didn't happen all at once, but when it did, I knew it was too late. She is way too mouthy to deal with."

"Nick, please. I don't know who you mean. I think there is something wrong with you. I think you need to see a doctor." I know the words are a mistake as they leave my mouth, but there is something seriously wrong with Nick, psychological.

"Jane."

"What?"

"Jane showed her ugly face."

"Wait," I say as I hold up a hand and my eyes widen in terror. He is seeing her too? The unexpected confirmation that I am being haunted by the ghost of Ellis's ex-girlfriend sends a fresh wave of chills across my body. "You see her too?"

Nick leans next to a wall and laughs softly as he shakes his head, as if disappointed. "Okay, I get it. You are *haunted* by her."

I nod silently, stunned by the revelation.

He steps forward then leans down and picks up the pill bottle. He opens it then pulls out two capsules. "This should do it," he says then closes the lid back.

"What are those for?" I ask as I watch him stand back up

then look down at me, his face twitching in the soft glow of the nightlight.

"For you," he says then he holds them out to me. I hesitate at first then he steps forward and grasps my hand, forcefully putting them into my palm.

"I don't need these," I say as tears stream down my cheek.

"I didn't know how to do it at first, but a little bit of research can go a long way. Apparently, this type of drug, taken even in low doses, is lethal."

"Why would you *kill* me?" I say as the realization hits me like a freight train. My voice is shaking in terror.

"Consider it a gift, so you don't have to deal with Cora Jane for the rest of your life."

"But I don't want to die, Nick. Please."

"I have no choice," he says shaking his head, a hint of glee in his eye. "You know too much, and if Cora ever shows up and complicates things, I could be in a real mess."

"No one will believe a ghost, Nick. Please!"

Nick laughs again then stops, nodding down to the pills. "You are right about that one. Now put them in your mouth. They dissolve."

Fight!

The voice comes from somewhere, but I'm not sure where. My eyes dart around the room then land on the front door to my right.

"I don't think so," he says then shifts to the right a few steps, so I no longer have direct access to the door.

Run!

The voice is louder now, and I tighten my eyes.

"Take the fucking pills, bitch," Nick shouts and my eyes bolt open, tears streaming down my face. He shifts forward so his knife is closer to me, more threatening.

Run!

This time the voice is clearer, and for a moment, it seems to be coming from me. My shaking subsides, and as I take a deep breath, a bolt of blue light flickers from the hallway, radiating from the bathroom.

You know what to do.

As my mind shifts to a new escape plan, my eyes stay fixated on my hand.

"Now!" he shouts and starts towards me, a threat of force radiates from his demeanor, his fist raised high in the air.

I might be able to escape, but he needs to let his guard down. He won't do that until he sees me take these pills. There is no other way. I take a deep breath, tighten my fist loosely around the pills as it rests on my lap, then toss my hand towards my mouth in one swift motion.

Get ready.

"Finally," he says then lowers his knife, pockets the pill bottle, and turns slightly towards the window, putting his hands on his hips. He thinks he's won the game. Just as he closes his eyes again, I bolt upright and with all the force I have, I push forward into him and knock us both into the floor.

I don't give him a moment to respond or fight back, but instead stand and bolt towards the hallway and the bathroom door. As I do, I hear him start to stand, but his response is slowed by a false sense of security. He believes I am trapped in the bathroom.

But I'm not trapped. I'm free.

As I bolt through the bathroom, I reach the door to the hallway and pull it open just as Nick appears at the opposite side. I look back just long enough to see his eyes widen in terror.

"Glory, you bitch!" he shouts from behind me as I turn to the right and rush down the stairs. I feel him close behind me as I descend, his frantic panting a moment away. I'm so close to escape. I am almost there.

But I'm not fast enough, and just before I get to the second flight that leads to my freedom, my feet are pulled out from under me, and my face smacks directly into the wooden floor.

The blood pouring from my nose is unmistakable now. I instinctively turn over and kick my legs as I scream as loud as I imagine that any person can.

"Get the fuck up, bitch," Nick shouts and effortlessly twists my arm around my back, pulling me up and pushing me forward to the edge of the stairs. My eyes dart frantically, and I twist wildly trying to bite him. I won't let him take me. A moment later, I hear a crack and realize Nick has brought the blunt end of his knife on my head.

"I said shut the fuck up."

My body goes limp for a moment, but then I twitch back to life as he forces me down the first couple of steps to the second level. But then abruptly, he stops.

"You are going to die tonight," I hear someone say, but it isn't Nick. It's the voice of my salvation. It's the voice of Ellis.

"You thought you had it figured it out, didn't you?" Nick says towards Ellis, who I now know is at the bottom of the steps. "You thought you had tracked me down and run me out of town, didn't you?"

"I knew you wouldn't leave so easily."

"You best let her go," I hear another voice from behind me, and I glance to the side and see Noah stalk forward from the girls' apartment, positioning himself behind us, blocking the stairway back to the top floor. He is flanked by someone much smaller, with fiery red hair.

"You are fucked!" a different feminine voice shouts from behind Ellis, and I know Blair is now there. A burst of pride swells inside for a moment as I realize everyone has shown up to protect me.

I watch as Ellis turns to the side and holds his hands out

behind him. "Everyone stay calm," he says then looks back up towards me and shouts. "Noah! Just wait!" Nick's head turns back and forth between them.

"You heard him, fucker," he says, then laughs nervously in my ear.

A moment later, Nick shifts his hand, and I hear the flick of his blade open. As he does, I see Ellis jump a step forward then hesitate as the metal brushes my throat.

"You don't need to do this," another voice says below me, and I immediately recognize Dave's calm tone. He steps into view next to Ellis. "Just let her go, and we will let you leave."

"Yeah right! Do you think I am stupid, old man?"

"Don't make it worse."

"You can't do anything to—"

"You aren't in Tennessee anymore, kid," Dave says, and his tone shifts to something more threatening. "This is my town. And if you hurt her anymore, there will be no trial for you."

Nick starts to respond, but I jerk, and he stops and pulls me tighter into his control.

Control. It has always been about his control. Controlling who I talked to. Controlling what I ate and controlling what I said. He was always so worried about what I would say to others. My head begins to throb as the memories churn inside. The trauma, the abuse, the—"

"The accident," I say softly, and Nick's eyes spin towards me.

"What did you say?"

I don't speak at first as fragmented memories begin to flicker through my mind. Trees, darkness, flashing headlights, rain… and a scream. Then silence. Darkness and silence.

"What the fuck did you say?" Nick says again, and my eyes snap open.

When they do, it is as if a switch has been flicked on. A rush of memories floods my mind and though I can't decipher them all, one specific memory stands out.

"It was you," I say with a shaky voice as my eyes shift towards him. "I see it now."

A slow smirk crosses his face.

"It was you who ran me off the road."

"What?" Ellis says from below us, and I see him look over to Dave.

"I was driving. I was driving to see him." I look pointedly towards Ellis, who stares back with sad eyes. He nods slowly, confirming that what I am remembering is real.

"You were, baby," Ellis says.

I look back to Nick. "But you didn't want me to be with him." Another memory flashes in my mind. I am at a party…a sorority party. I squeeze my eyes shut and as I do, I see Nick approach me. He was in my class. He is smiling, and he gives me a…drink."

"Nick drugged me," I say, but my eyes stay fixed on Ellis. As the words leave my mouth, Ellis furrows his brow then a twitch of rage builds, and his fury shifts to Nick.

"You drugged her," Ellis says to Nick.

"And then when I found out," I continue, "I had to make sure you knew that I didn't cheat on you."

Ellis's eyes shift back towards me. "But I wouldn't pick up the phone."

"It's not your fault, Ellis," I say as firmly as I can muster. I then turn towards Nick.

"You," I say as anger courses through my blood, and the strength of Cora Jane radiates from me. "You ran me off the road." I don't look back towards Ellis but see him shift wildly at the bottom of the stairs as my eyes stay fixated on Nick. "Then during my recovery, you hung around, scared I would remember and turn you in. When my memory started to come back, and I remembered who I was, I confronted you about it."

"Yeah, and so what?" Nick says before laughing nervously.

"And you pushed me down those fucking steps." I spit the words at him and twitch in his grasp, despite the damned pain.

"Once they released you from that place, I knew you had regained some of your memories, but hoped you forgot…certain ones."

"But I remembered. I remembered that you drugged me and ran me off that road. So, you pushed me down those fucking steps in hope that I would forget again, or worse, that I would die."

Nick's sinister laugh makes my skin crawl. "Well, it kind of worked, at least for a while."

"You son of a bitch," Ellis says, and I see his fists tighten with rage.

Nick shakes his head without speaking, realizing that he has been caught. He mumbles inaudibly to himself as if in a debate, and for a moment, I think he is going to let me go when he drops my hand, releasing it from behind my back. But instead, he keeps the knife tight against my neck. He then reaches into his pocket with his free hand. Ellis bolts up a few steps, but Nick twitches the knife higher. A sliver of pain makes me twitch unintentionally.

"I wouldn't do that," Nick says. He then digs around in his pocket and pulls out the small bottle of pills. "Too late anyway," he adds.

"What do you mean?" Ellis says as his eyes widen in terror looking at the bottle.

Nick ignores him and pops open its cap, tossing the remaining contents into his mouth. He chews frantically then stares forward. "You can't have her. None of you can have her."

"What are those?" Ellis asks, and he bolts up another two stairs. Nick's hand jerks and a drip of warm blood leaks down my neck.

"Just something that I forced this dumb bitch to take a few moments ago. She should be dropping dead any second now. I guess you couldn't save her after all."

"No!" Ellis shouts.

"That's right, loser. I might die, but so will she." As he finishes his sentence, his eyes flutter and his body starts to wobble as the effects of the large dose of pills take root. I feel the knife loosen on my neck, and with it, an opportunity to escape emerges. My eyes lock onto Ellis, and instantly, he knows what I'm about to do. He starts to object but stops as I look away. Just as I feel Nick shift once more, I move.

Everything happens so fast. I duck, pulling from his grasp, and as I do, the knife twists, nipping me in the chin.

"Noah!" I hear Ellis shout, then an instant later, I feel the force from Nick's foot slam into my back launching me forward.

Time seems to stop as I fall forward down the steps. A burst of pain courses through my spine, and I close my eyes and surrender to the impact from the wooden stairs.

But I never hit the stairs, and I don't tumble downward. Instead, I feel the warm hands of Ellis take me from the air, catching me and pulling me close to his body.

As he holds me softly, I hesitate to move, not wanting to feel the pain, but my eyes eventually open, and as they do, a flash of blue light flickers around me, and I remember who I am.

"I'm Cora Jane," I say softly.

He gently turns my body towards him, and I see him nodding.

"You are baby."

"And I love you."

He nods. "I know. I love you too."

"I never meant to hurt you."

"You didn't do anything wrong, baby."

"You didn't do anything wrong either." I reach up and touch his face, wiping away a steady stream of tears.

"Don't leave me. Please don't leave me. Not again."

Though pain radiates through my body, I feel the corners of my mouth turn upward in a smile. "I didn't take the pills. I tricked him."

A laugh escapes my lungs just as I pass out.

CHAPTER 38

Ellis
About two years ago...

"Do you mind if I sit?"

I stand facing her, but she looks at me and nods as if I'm a stranger. I start to cringe at the sight of her swollen eye and bruising, but I force back my wanting to hold her, care for her.

"Sure," she says then turns back to face forward. I am a stranger to her now.

"It's a nice day," I say to make small talk. "Good that the rain has held off."

"I haven't been outside in a while and thought it would be nice to get some fresh air." She looks all around at the landscaping. Jane had always loved plants, so I imagine the well-manicured surroundings bring her some degree of peace.

"This is a nice place."

"Yeah," she says, "but I'm not exactly sure what I am doing here."

"Are you a patient?" I ask then bite my lip intentionally. I shouldn't be so direct with her. She has suffered a massive head injury, and I need to be careful what I say.

"I am. I guess. I was in an accident, I think, but I don't remember what happened." She turns and nods back towards the seven-story memory care facility. "This is my apartment. I moved here from…Florida, I think."

"Oh okay," I say. "Well, this is a very nice place."

She nods then stares forward for a moment before turning back towards me. "What about you?"

"I don't live here. I'm just visiting."

"Oh, okay. Well, that is nice. I think having visitors must be nice."

"Don't you get visitors?"

"I think my mom has come a few times."

"Oh yeah?"

"My boyfriend comes by every couple of days to check on me, but I don't think he likes it."

I cringe internally. I'm sure she is referring to Nick, the guy she cheated on me with.

"Why is that?"

She doesn't respond but instead looks towards me and shrugs.

I don't press, but I have a feeling that there is something about him that is bothering her.

"Do you have any other friends?"

She looks back at me and frowns. "Maybe."

I simply nod then sit quietly with her in silence as I enjoy the final moments that I have with the love of my life. Her mother had initially not wanted me to visit, believing that I might trigger a memory for her that is hard to rationalize with what she still recalls. But before I walked away, I had to see for myself that Jane was gone forever. She couldn't keep me away.

I've scoured the internet for everything to know about Severe Retrograde Amnesia, her diagnosis. It can be brought on by an accident, as it was with her case, and there is typically little hope for recovery. Given the severity of her injuries, the doctors had told her mom that recovery was not possible. Her mom was quick to point that out to me.

I take one deep breath after another, not wanting to rise from my seat. Though I didn't want to admit it to myself, I now can see that the time I had with Jane is lost to her injury, and the love we share, or shared, would never return. I look left as a tear rolls down my cheek.

"Glory, dear," I hear a voice call from behind us and turn to see her mother walk up.

Jane turns towards her voice and forces a nervous smile. "Hi, Mom." She clearly knows who her mom is, but there is hesitation, uncertainty that saddens me. I can't imagine how alone Jane must feel at this moment. Unsure who everyone is and not able to remember all the love that so many people have for her.

Her mom steps around the bench then pointedly nods in my direction, a sign that it is time for me to leave. Her mom had never liked that she had dated me and spent so much time in the Keys. She wanted Jane to be married to some wealthy doctor or lawyer. She had no patience for anything else.

Jane leans over and reaches out her hand. "I'm Glory by the way. Nice to meet you."

I force a smile and take her hand in mine one last time. "I'm Ellis."

CHAPTER 39

I HEAR STEADY beeps as I open my eyes. am confused at first by my surroundings, but my pulse slows as I see Ellis sleeping in the hospital chair next to me. I pull myself up gently but quickly regret the movement as bolts of pain run along my side.

I don't wake Ellis but instead sit quietly and watch him sleep while I comb through my memories.

"I am Cora Jane." I repeat the words softly a few times then replay them over and over in my mind. I keep expecting the name to sound odd to me, but it doesn't. It's my name.

I think back to the last several weeks, months, and as I do, bits and pieces of the story, my story, begin to come together. But one memory stands out. It's a key moment in time when my two personalities collided, one lost to the darkness of injury, and one clinging on to a false reality.

Cora had seemed so real. Her blonde hair and blue eyes were envious, and I now realize they were my own, even though my subconscious didn't allow me to recognize my own reflection, instead showing me the hollow shell of my once vibrant self. I tug at the short brown hair that covers my head, and an instant urge overcomes me to go to the local drugstore and remedy the situation. I've always loved my hair blonde, but Glory didn't know that. Hell, how could she? But Cora Jane is my true personality. She is who I really am. And I know that she has been trying to protect me, that I have been trying to protect myself, whispering in my ear and smiling from the darkness of the palmettos, disguised as a helpful spirit.

"That also makes sense," I say softly to myself as I think about the University of Tennessee Registrar not being able to find my record. My name isn't Glory, well, not my legal name. It's Cora Jane Dawson. I had gone by Glory as a child. It was the nickname my dad had given me long ago. "My glorious little Cora Jane," he would say. But as I grew older, I started going by the name Cora Jane, then just Jane, even though those closest to me called me Glory. I smile at the clarity of the memory.

But the other memories are still fragmented, and the timelines are fuzzy at best. For instance, I know my dad has something to do with Dave's, but I'm not sure what the connection is. Not yet. And, I also know Nick abused me, but I now remember that I never lived with Nick but rather, he showed up after the accident to make sure I didn't remember that he had drugged me... raped me. Anger courses through my veins at the reminder of his heinous defiling of my body, and I squeeze my fist so tightly my knuckles crack.

"Hey," I hear Ellis say, and I look over to see that he is watching me. "Are you okay?"

I force a smile. I am happy to see him and to know who he is, but I dare not lie to him. "No. But I will be."

He nods as he stands upright then walks to the bedside. He leans over and kisses my forehead then sits softly on my bed. "You will."

"Is he...dead?" I ask.

Ellis doesn't respond but instead nods his head forward. I turn away from him then look out towards the window. The sharp contrast between the brilliant blue sky of the Keys and the bland white hospital walls is a welcomed distraction as I experience mixed emotions about Nick's death.

Ellis doesn't force me into conversation, but instead just sits quietly on the bed. But as he does, I can tell something important is on his mind. He looks up after a moment as if sensing my stare. He starts to speak but then hesitates before biting his lower lip gently. I have a feeling I know what he is going to ask. It's what I would ask if I were in his shoes.

"It's okay," I say. "You can ask me."

He nods then rubs my leg. "Do you still remember us?" he says, voice shaky. I hear him inhale and hold his breath as he waits for my answer.

For a moment, I think about lying to him, telling him that I remember every detail. But that's not the truth, and though I might recover those precious lost memories, I can't guarantee it.

"I don't remember everything," I say as I reach down and cover my hand over his. "But I do remember us."

His eyes light up as my words register and he exhales. "You do?"

"I do. I remember that I love you fiercely."

"And I love you, baby."

"And I know you will help me remember the rest."

We sit there for a moment in silence just staring at each other, bathing in the awareness of our love. Then he sits straighter and cocks his head.

"Do you remember calling me a day or so before you arrived here?" Ellis asks, breaking the silence.

I shake my head as I search for the recollection. "I don't know. Maybe."

"You didn't say anything, but I heard you breathing into the phone. It was a conversation of only silence, but one I had dreamed of for so very long. I had dreamed of an opportunity to say that I'm sorry. But when I had it, I couldn't form the words." He hangs his head low. "I'm so sorry. For how I spoke to you after I learned about Nick."

Though I don't remember the exact details of the conversation, that is one memory I can access, one littered by anger and pain. I had thought I had made a mistake and slept with Nick, so when I told Ellis, he lost control. The crushing weight of that revelation must have been unimaginable.

"It's okay, Ellis," I say. "You were in pain."

He shakes his head and stands. "No. There was no excuse for how I acted. I should have listened to you. I should have kept my cool. If I had, all this might not have happened."

"What do you mean, Ellis?"

"Before the accident, if I had picked up that fucking phone when you tried calling me and given you the opportunity to explain that you had been…raped, I would have come to you, and you wouldn't have been on the road at night. I would have come to you and saved you from that miserable fuck."

"No, Ellis."

He turns towards the window and looks upwards as if asking the Lord for forgiveness, wiping at his face with the back of one hand. "And you would have never crashed, and never been taken from me, and you never would have been pushed down those—"

"Come here," I interrupt, not wanting him to go down that road of regret. A road we must all fight to avoid. "Come sit with me."

He doesn't move at first but then after a moment, he turns and walks towards my bed. I scoot gently to the side then rub the open area. "Lay down with me."

He starts to object but then nods as I pat the bed with a firmer hand. He slips off his shoes then slowly crawls into the bed and lays by my side, facing towards my back. He wraps his arms around me and snuggles so close, I can feel the ripples of his abdomen.

I close my eyes and take a slow, steady breath, soaking in the comfort of his embrace. After a while, his breathing slows, and he calms down.

As I lay there, my mind floods with old memories, rushing forward as if another door in my mind has been unlocked. The familiarity of it all comforts me, but one memory is odd. It's a memory of him singing to me. I am not sure where I am.

"Can I ask you something?" I say softly, not sure if he has fallen asleep.

"Sure," he says after a moment.

"I remember something, but it's fuzzy. A song."

"A song?"

"Yeah. You sang it to me."

I feel him shift behind me. "I did?"

I close my eyes and focus harder, and after a moment, I realize the steady beep that I hear is not the one from my hospital room, but from my memory."

"You sang it to me after the accident. While I was at the hospital."

"But there's no way. You were in a coma."

I squeeze his hand. "I remember it."

"I can't believe you remember that."

"But I don't remember what it means or where it came from."

"Let me help you," he says as he rubs my back. "Close your eyes"

I nod then follow his direction and close my eyes. As I do, he sings softly to me.

I'll love you through the ebb and flow.
Come back to you when tides are low.
Then once again, as it does rise
I'll love you through the lows and highs
Then once again just like a clock
On and on the sea we rock.
Until the wind has not a gust

Until the sun burns trees to dust
Until my soul from there departs
But even then, you're in my heart
For water there shall not subside.
My love for you, until the tide.

"Dad," I say, and a tear runs down my cheek. "My dad wrote that."

"He did."

"And he used to sing it to me when I was a child."

"He did. And when we saw you, broken and battered from the accident, we didn't know what to do. So, we just sang it to you, over and over, hopeful that the song from your childhood would bring you back to us."

"We?"

"Your dad had been sick for years, and when you got into the accident, he was living at the resort with us. We were all taking care of him. He was very close to Dave, and my dad too, actually."

"He was?"

Ellis nods. "They were in the military together."

"Is that how we met? Through my dad?"

Ellis nods. "He and I immediately rushed to the hospital. Your mom wouldn't have let me in to see you, but she couldn't count on your dad showing up. He had been so sick, and no one expected him to travel.

I shift and turn on my back, so that I can see him. I let out a shaky breath then rub a hand along my forehead. "But my dad died. I remember it. I was with Nick and…"

Realization hits me as the memories of conversations with my dad during my time at the memory care facility move into focus. I stare off into the distance as it all starts to make sense. I remember Dad calling me, speaking to me. He never visited me at Nick's, I mean the care facility, but he called. I spoke to him lots of times. But Nick never liked us speaking. He was always worried it would help me recover my memory.

"I remember when he died. I got a call from his roommate. He died in his sleep."

"That was Dave who you spoke to."

"Was he in pain?" I say as I begin sobbing. He leans in and pulls me closer to him.

"No, baby. He was not in pain. And he died loving you. Until the tide."

CHAPTER 40

I STAY IN the ICU for three more days, and Ellis is with me the entire time. Only once do I manage to force him to go home and take a shower, threatening to kick him out of my bed if he didn't.

Over those few days, he and I spend most of our time going through memories. He does all he can to answer any questions I have, and since he knows me so well, he does a great job at being my care buddy, as the doctor calls it.

My mom also shows up and of course, immediately makes it out like she is the victim. I have to remind her several times that I was the one injured. That said, I do love her, so I don't let her blame herself for trusting Nick, the couple of times she comes close to realizing her role in all this.

If I had a dollar for every time she said, "I'm just trying to help, Glory."

She also begins to warm up to Ellis. I finally understand now why she was so cold to him before, given my dad's connectivity to Dave's, but her seeing him care for me overcomes any opposition she has to our relationship. In fact, by the time she leaves town, I think she actually likes him. Of course, he's a charmer and does lay it on thick.

I also get introduced to Shelly again. It turns out she is a Neurologist and one of Dave's closest friends. He and Ellis had asked Shelly to check in on me in secret. Thinking back to the conversation Shelly and I had, it all makes sense. It turns out that she suspected that my memories were returning, confirming what Ellis also suspected, but didn't want to accept. "I didn't want to lose you again," he later told me.

The days fly by, and before long, I have checked out of the hospital, and I'm on my way back to Dave's…home.

"Okay, buddy," Ellis says as he leans into the passenger side door and kisses my bruised nose. "Try not to get too excited about having a live-in servant for the next several weeks."

"I am fine, Ellis."

"No. No. Shelly said that you are to stay in bed for at least—"

"No way, Ellis. I need fresh air, and plants, lots of plants, and a boat." He shrugs then walks around the front of the truck, stopping in front of the hood to stick his tongue out at me. When he enters the driver's seat of my old truck, I turn towards him so fast it makes him jump. "Can you please take me out on the boat? Please, please, please."

He shakes his head playfully. "I don't know. All those bumpy waves."

"Ellis!" I say shrieking then lean over and smack the tight blue denim covering his thick leg.

He doesn't respond but looks towards me and winks.

When we pull into Dave's, something is off. He doesn't pull into the house's driveway but instead the roundabout, and it is lined with cars.

"Dang, this place is crowded today," I say. "Should we just park at the house?"

"Nah," he says as Ellis pulls forward to the spot closest to the resort and double-parks. "Let's go say hello to everyone first."

I nod then furrow my brows. "Dave might like me, Ellis, but you are seriously going to get me towed. You are blocking everyone in."

"Yeah, yeah."

"Just drop me and the bags off and I'll wait while you park the car."

He ignores me as he pulls the key from the ignition then hops out.

I wait as he walks around to my side and opens the door.

"Right this way," he says.

I roll my eyes then step out as he grabs my bag from the bed of the truck. As I look to the right, my head shifts so my ear faces the unexpected sound of loud music coming from the path leading to the Hut.

"Well, someone is having a good time," I say as Ellis leans down and picks up my bag then extends his hand towards me. I take it and walk alongside him. As I do, a memory returns that makes me stop and turn towards him. "How long have we known each other?"

Ellis laughs. "I thought you would never ask. What do you think?"

I look out towards the direction of the water, as a picture of a little blonde-haired boy running down the pier materializes in my memory. It's Ellis.

"You were an annoying little boy."

Ellis laughs loud then sets the bag down and pulls me into a loose embrace. He is still so cautious of my injuries.

"What?" I ask as I push away from him playfully.

"I'm just happy."

I reach up and rub a hand along his cheek. He hasn't shaved in days, so I tug it a bit before removing my hand. "You were, you know?"

He winks towards me. "I know."

As we walk together towards the Tiki bar, the sounds grow louder and louder until finally, we turn into the Hut. It is covered in balloons and there are at least a hundred people standing around in sun dresses, Hawaiian shirts, and even bathing suits—people of all ages.

I start to ask what is going on, but just as I open my mouth, Red, Blair, Noah, Dave, Amber, and Clinton emerge from the crowd and step forward.

"Welcome home!" everyone shouts at once and the crowd breaks out in shouts, whistles and clapping.

"Are you serious?" I say as I step forward from Ellis, in a state of shock.

"Come here girl," Red says, leaning in to give me a hug, followed by Blair.

"That's my tough bitch!" Blair says and Red punches her.

Clinton and Noah are both next in line. Poor Noah looks a bit awkward as he leans down two feet and tries to position himself under my arms.

"Thanks, big guy," I say as I squeeze him tightly.

"Jane," Amber says, and she and Dave step towards me.

"Thank you for all of this, Amber," I say. "I know you had a lot to do with this."

"No big deal at all, sweetie. We are just stoked you are okay and back home."

"Home," I repeat softly.

"You got that right, Glory," says Dave who steps forward.

"Thank you for all this, Dave."

"Oh, don't thank me. I couldn't plan my way out of a paper bag. That guy over there was a big help though." He points over my shoulder. I turn and see Ellis cutting up with Clinton and JJ. After a moment, he looks back towards me and our eyes lock.

The party is not just a party, but a homecoming. Ellis, Dave, Red, and the others take turns parading me throughout the crowds, introducing and reintroducing me to more people than I can count. I remember some of them, and others I don't, but everyone is so kind and they treat me not as a broken shell of my former self, but as an old friend.

"That was amazing, Ellis," I say as we start to walk hand in hand back to the house a couple of hours later. "Thank you."

Though I know the party will continue into the night, we met no resistance when we decided to leave early and head back to the house. Though I am out of the hospital, where I slept a lot, my body is still drained and craving the warm space next to Ellis in his bed.

Just beyond the dive shop, he stops and turns towards me.

"I almost forgot." His eyes are wide as he reaches into his pocket and fumbles around.

"What?" I say, suddenly excited by his infectious energy.

"They said you must have dropped it on the way in."

"What?" I say as I cock my head to the side.

"I got it when you were being discharged. They said an older guy had found it outside your room."

His eyes light up as he removes his hand and lets a small gold chain fall from the weight of a golden infinity charm.

"Impossible," I say softly, but he doesn't register my words.

"I know how much you love this. Your dad had one just like it."

I don't take it from him right away but instead stare at it as it sways in the ocean breeze, spinning and capturing the last bits of the day's golden sunlight.

"Someone must be looking after you, baby," Ellis says. "I know you would be devastated if you lost this." He spins a finger in the air. "Turn around."

I turn and stand still as he gently pulls back my hair and closes the clasp before letting it fall onto my chest.

I spin back towards him, then reach down and clench the charm as I stare up into Ellis's joyful eyes.

"I love you, my glorious Cora Jane Dawson."

The meaning of the necklace hits me like a bolt, and as I look into the eyes of my future and trace the sideways figure eight over and over, three simple words fall from my mouth.

"Until the tide."

Thank you for reading Until the Tide and for supporting independent authors!

Enjoyed the story?

- **Leave a review.** Reviews help other readers discover the book and are one of the most valuable ways you can support an independent author.
- **Tell a friend.** Word of mouth remains one of the best ways independent authors find new readers.
- **Join THE NEXT WAVE CLUB** for future ARCs, pre-release content, bonus chapters, exclusive cover reveals, character graphics, behind-the-scenes content, and more.

www.authorchristopherkent.com

Happy reading!

Christopher Kent